I0653101

ABOUT THIS BOOK

Three novellas (books 10-12) in the Legends of Havenwood Falls historical fantasy series, sharing the legacies of our town's supernatural residents.

Kiss the Ashes by Desiree Lafawn

Mocked, ridiculed, and sentenced to death, seven-year-old River is saved from the noose when the Sisters McNee find her. They take her to their home in Havenwood Falls, a place for people like her to live safely, without fear of persecution. But what if the threat to their safety is River herself? Her fire-maiden origins are a mystery. One a child has no hope of explaining. Then one futuristic vision from a well-respected member of the community seals her fate.

Hidden Truths by Colleen Nye

For her more than five hundred years, kitsune Kaori Ishida has never strayed from her beloved homeland of Japan or her family. But when she falls for an American and sees hope of a normal life, she embarks on a journey to the United States. She leaves everything she knows behind, including her familiar appearance, to follow love. Only, what she finds in the strange little town in Colorado isn't what she expects.

Wrath and Retribution by Belinda Boring

Sequel to *Blood and Damnation*—Marcus St. James has been searching for Catriona for over a year, leaving Victorian England and landing in Havenwood Falls, but it seems he and his trusted assistant Knox have arrived at a dead end. Cursed to exist as a blood-drinker, Marcus is no stranger to gossip and speculation, so when dead bodies start appearing, he is immediately under suspicion. Then a new discovery threatens to shatter his world, forcing Marcus to make his most devastating choice yet.

LEGENDS OF HAVENWOOD FALLS VOLUME FOUR

A LEGENDS OF HAVENWOOD FALLS COLLECTION

BELINDA BORING   DESIREE LAFAWN   COLLEEN

Copyright © 2019 *Kiss the Ashes* by Desiree Lafawn, *Hidden Truths* by Colleen Nye, *Wrath and Retribution* by Belinda Boring, Ang'dora Productions, LLC

All rights reserved.

Published by

Ang'dora Productions, LLC

5621 Strand Blvd, Ste 210

Naples, FL 34110

Havenwood Falls and Ang'dora Productions and their associated logos are trademarks and/or registered trademarks of Ang'dora Productions, LLC.

Cover design by Regina Wamba at MaeIDesign.com

Except as permitted under the U.S. Copyright Act of 1976, no part of this publication may be reproduced, stored in a retrieval system, or transmitted in any form or by any means, electronic, mechanical, photocopying, recording, or otherwise, without written permission of the owner of this book.

Please do not participate in or encourage piracy of copyrighted materials in violation of the author's rights. Purchase only authorized editions.

This book is a work of fiction. Names, characters, and events are either products of the author's imagination or are used fictitiously, and any resemblance to actual persons, living or dead, is entirely coincidental.

Also try the signature New Adult/Adult series, Havenwood Falls, and the YA series, Havenwood Falls High

Stay up to date at www.HavenwoodFalls.com

KISS THE ASHES

DESIREE LAFAWN

~ A Legends of Havenwood Falls Novella ~

HAVENWOOD FALLS LEGENDS

KISS THE ASHES

DESIREE LAFAWN

ALSO BY DESIREE LAFAWN

CONTEMPORARY ROMANCE

The Permanence of Pain

Beck the Halls – A Gallery B Christmas

GLASS CITY HEARTS

Gabe (Book One)

Dino (Book Two)

Jesse (Book Three)

PARANORMAL ROMANCE

Havenwood Falls Short Story Anthology 2018

Kiss the Ashes (A Legends of Havenwood Falls Novella)

Coming March 2019

Shiny Dancer: Mountain Mermaids (Sapphire Lake)

A sincere thank you to every reader that loses yourself in these pages. I hope you enjoy this glimpse into the past of Havenwood Falls, and it leaves you curious for the future. This book, and every book I write, is for you.

Fear not for the future, weep not for the past.
—Percy Bysshe Shelley

CHAPTER 1

RIVER

SUMMER 1908, CARLISLE, PENNSYLVANIA

I would never get used to hard-soled shoes even as an adult, but as a girl of seven I hated them. I'd much rather have gone barefoot, but the teachers in Carlisle were adamant the children properly dress themselves at all times. Dressed according to their standards, anyway. Our parents stood opposed even as the soldiers dragged us from the reservation.

"Who are you to take our children?" they cried out, unable to do more than shake their fists and stomp their feet; our once proud nation reduced to servants of a government foreign to us. A government so hell-bent on erasing our existence they uprooted the native children and forced them into boarding schools to learn the English way. Eliminate the savages and teach the children to be productive members of society.

Kill the Indian. Save the man.

Even now, many years later and grown, I have trouble wrapping my mind around the thought process that led to the exodus of the children—the reeducation process. But that had happened. And the history books will more than likely gloss it over

9

the more time marches on, but I will never forget being five years old and plucked from the small plot of land I considered my home.

Parents wept.

But not my parents. They died of the great sickness a year before. I had no parents to hold me in their arms as the soldiers came and separated us. No one fought for me, so when the time came to leave—aside from dragging my heels in the dirt—nothing stopped the soldiers from putting me on the wagon, squeezing me up against the rows of other crying, terrified children.

But I was different. If they knew how different, would they have placed me with the other children? Would they have taken me? There was no way to know, and I wouldn't explain because I had learned long ago that *my* kind of different was best kept hidden. Even from my own people.

So to the Carlisle Indian Industrial School I went, sandwiched in with many other children from mixed tribes, all learning to speak English and change everything about themselves. The administration beat the students who cried, and the angry, rebellious ones received a harsher punishment. One so severe, we feared talking about it amongst ourselves—because those students left without warning and didn't come back. But I didn't cry, and I didn't rebel. I obeyed, because I knew no other way. And there I lived for two years, suffering at the hands of my oppressors under the guise of spiritual cleansing until the summer of my seventh year.

I made a mistake.

It was playtime in the yard. That short time of day between morning chores and evening chores when there was a small sliver of space to remember that we were just children. It was my favorite time, and every chance I thought I could get away with it, I'd chuck my shoes under the shade of a white oak tree and curl my toes in the grass. Not running, not moving, just standing in place, anchored to the earth. Eyes closed, I stood under the tree with my arms raised out to the sides, feeling the wind above and below me.

The Great Thunder is near, I thought to myself, smelling the rain on the wind. *I wonder what mischief the Thunder Boys will be up to tonight.* The Great Thunder and his sons were a myth, and I dared not speak of it out loud, not when the teachers could hear. Speaking the stories of my people was forbidden and the punishment severe. But since no one controlled what went on in my head, I would think as I pleased.

"Come back here, Thomas," a voice shouted angrily, interrupting my peaceful moment. "You've stolen the bread; we know you have. Come receive your punishment."

A small brown blur came running across the packed dirt yard, and children of various ages stopped mid-play to see the boy running with the bit of bread locked in his fist. He came to a screeching halt about fifteen feet from where I stood, under my oak tree, and facing off like a boxer, he scowled at his aggressor.

I recognized the boy from my old village. I remembered when his mother had clung to him and the soldiers yanked him, only a year younger than myself, from her grieving arms. They'd given him a new name when he'd come to this school, just as they'd done me, but I knew his real name was Wesa. I knew because his mother had screamed it to the sky as they had taken away the children.

Wesa. Two years he'd been here, knowing the rules. And still he stole the bread.

Oh, Wesa, what will happen to you now?

Thomas now, no longer Wesa, stood in front of the man who'd been so aggressively calling his name. His cotton button-down shirt had come untucked from his plain brown breeches while chasing the boy, and he stood, panting, mouth drawn down in a formidable frown.

"Thomas. You've stolen food. Accept the punishment." The man's expression was stern, his eyes hard and unfeeling.

Wesa fidgeted before opening his hand to show the small bit of bread clutched in his fist. "But I'm so hungry, Mr. Crane." He looked at the food, his eyes wet and his lower lip trembling. "Please, I didn't want to steal, but I'm so hungry."

Sorrow gripped my heart for him. My stomach often felt hollow from the slim allotment of rations we were each given per day. And he was so young. *Poor Wesa.* Mr. Crane's features relaxed, and I breathed an inaudible sigh of relief. Mr. Crane was not a very nice man by nature, but I'd never *seen* him hurt any of the students. The same couldn't be said for other teachers. Several of them seemed to only be working at the boarding school because they loved tormenting children, seeking reasons to dole out discipline.

Mr. Crane just always had a sour look on his face, and even though he always smelled like whiskey, I'd never seen him raise his hand in anger.

"Bring it, Thomas." Mr. Crane raised his hand and beckoned Thomas closer. Two tears snaked down the small boy's cheeks, but the will of the older man won, and the younger of the two made slow shuffling steps across the packed dirt of the yard, head hanging low in defeat. Eyes so downcast he didn't see the blow coming and didn't even get to react. My seven-year-old self could do nothing but watch openmouthed at the violence that unfolded.

The cuff on the side of his six-year-old head lifted him straight off the ground and onto his back where he lay, a sad pile of arms and legs in the dirt.

"Thieves are beaten, Thomas," Mr. Crane said calmly, standing over the small boy on the ground too stunned to even react as the older man plucked the bread from his now slack grip. He grimaced and crumbled the small loaf with one hand until it was nothing but crumbs drifting to the ground. I mourned the loss of the food myself, hand drifting to my empty stomach. Now no one would get to eat it.

"If we let you do it, then everyone would think it entitled them to more than we give them, boy. You aren't special. None of you are. But if you're so hungry, you can eat your bread in the mud like an animal. Are you an animal, Thomas?" Mr.

Crane's face twisted into something monstrous, and he stepped on the small pile of bread crumbs with his dusty brown shoe. "Go on, Thomas; eat it if you're hungry. This is good enough for you."

The small boy looked up from his place on the ground, afraid to move. More tears fell down his face, his little shoulders shaking with fear—or pain—maybe both. He made no move toward the pile in the dirt and crumbs, and still I stood in place, caught inside the vision with no way out. Mr. Crane sneered at him, his eyes a window to the depths of an ugly soul. Without warning, Mr. Crane's leg shot out, and his dirty brown shoe connected with the small boy's legs, lifting him up a few inches and sending him spinning farther in the dirt. Wesa—or Thomas, as they called him —lay on his back, clutching his side and crying. He made no move to get to his feet.

The air no longer smelled of rain. Instead, the wind carried the scent of burning. Similar to that of the blaze we gathered around when we had our own land, where the warriors told the tales of the hunt and the women sang their songs and cooked the meat. It was the smell of the fatwood just sparking, smoky and warm but not yet blistering. It was a small fire, but with enough tending it would become a great blaze, hot enough to sear anything placed before it. The breeze tickled my skin and moved the stray hairs that stuck out of my braids around my face. I didn't know where the wind had come from, but it did nothing to cool the aching itch marching up and down my skin, nor the anger that was bubbling just below the surface.

Mr. Crane was hurting Wesa—and no one was doing a thing to stop it.

He was a small boy, not so different from myself, who was just hungry. We all were, and that was a fact, but he was only six and didn't have as much of a grasp of self-control, even after two years in their Anglo prison. But Mr. Crane would make an example out of him regardless. The older man bore down on the child, his face as red as his facial hair, a grim smile plastered on his face.

He's happy. My inner thoughts echoed the stark reality. Even as a young child, I still understood. *He wants to hurt Wesa.*

But Wesa was so small, he couldn't take much more. Still no one in the yard moved. All those small faces looked on with fear in their eyes. No one would stand up for Wesa; no one could. Everyone knew what the punishment for rebellion was. I had seen the stone markings before—set up in the woods a short bit away from the school. That's where rebellion led you—to your very own stone marking in the dirt.

But even so, watching Mr. Crane as he reached the spot where he had kicked the young boy and hauled him back to his feet by his close-cropped hair had me gritting my teeth, the taste of bile and ash in my throat. He cocked back his fist and hit Wesa once; the impact split the skin on his chin and blood spurted out. Wesa cried. The smoke in the air stung my eyes, and my voice was that of a stranger croaking out of a throat lined with rocks and silt.

"No."

I wasn't loud enough. Mr. Crane didn't hear me, or at least pretended he didn't as he shook the boy until his feet left the ground, and he hung there in his master's hands, limp as an animal removed from a trap. "Come, Thomas, to punishment with you."

To punishment. As if the six-year-old hadn't been through enough. There was nowhere that Mr. Crane would take him that could be any improvement, and I doubted Wesa could even walk by himself. Blood poured from that angry cut on his face, and the crimson trail dripping from his tiny chin matched the hue of my blistering rage.

I found my voice.

"No." The heated breeze carried the word farther this time. This time Mr. Crane heard me, and his head snapped up, his eyes zeroing in on me from where he stood a short distance away. His mouth dropped open, but he didn't release his hold on the small boy.

"Mary, what are you doing?" *Mary.* That was my new name. I wasn't supposed to think of myself as River anymore, but sometimes I forgot. Times like now, when the atrocity I had just witnessed placed me somewhere outside of myself—outside of my safety nets and away from right and wrong.

I was just so *angry*.

Uncertainty graced Mr. Crane's face, and he took a small step back. I didn't want him to take a step back. I wanted him to let go of Wesa.

"No. You let him go. You hurt him—you're a bad man." The air snapped and crackled around me, and my braids rose and fell in this new heated breeze before unraveling completely. My long tresses danced in the angry wind.

"What are you doing?" the older man whispered, his eyes no longer narrow and cruel, but wide and fearful. "What are you—? Stay back. Stay away—"

But I didn't stay away. I couldn't, because Mr. Crane still had his meaty hand fisted in Wesa's short dark hair and was dragging him backward across the ground. Rage burned in my belly. He was a bad man. He hurt Wesa. He needed to be punished.

The ground I stood on cracked beneath my feet, the air so hot, the dirt released what little moisture it had and hardened like wood. The small bit of grass I'd curled my toes in earlier incinerated as if it had never been. I barely noticed. The heat. The smell. The acidic swell burning and churning deep in my belly— all were secondary to my rage as I looked at the man who had beaten a small boy to near unconsciousness.

"Drop him." The words blasted out of my mouth with ferocity, and Mr. Crane complied without thinking. Wesa just lay there, crumpled where he fell. The only movement in the entire yard was the myriad of small heads swiveling to look from Mr. Crane to me. The same look of horror that had been focused on Mr. Crane now moved to me. I didn't care.

I couldn't see any of them anymore. All I could see was the form of the man in front of me, the one who had such blackness in his soul, he could beat a child with a smile on his face. I only had eyes for him. Two other teachers had come into the yard by now—Mr. Weisman and Mrs. Crane. They had come out to see what was going on, I was sure, but I couldn't count on either of them to help in this situation. No, I'd witnessed their punishments before. No help would come from any of the adults in this building. I'd need to take care of them myself.

"What on earth is going on out here? Oh—" Mrs. Crane's sentence ended in a bloodcurdling shriek. "Mary! It's witchcraft! Savage witchcraft!"

I ignored her. I was far too focused on the backward steps of Mr. Crane as he tried to put as much space between the two of us as possible. Mr. Weisman had no such sense of self-preservation, and he marched to where I stood, circumventing Wesa on the ground as if he was nothing more than a puddle of dirty water. He almost made it in time to stop me. Almost.

I felt the graze of his fingers on my arm before I opened my mouth to scream. Dry, cracked lips pulled back as far as I was able, but no sound escaped. I spoke no words because I had none to give. But I had something else. That which I had been hiding for as long as I could remember. That twisting ache in my guts I had spent years learning to ignore, or at least keep hidden from everyone around me. My parents had taught me that, if not much else. Hide it away or bad things would happen.

Well, I'd hidden it all this time, and bad things still happened. There was no need to hide it anymore, so I let the mangled ropes of burning fury snake their way out of the depths of my body and erupt from my mouth in a single blast of heat and flame. I might not have any words to exorcise my rage, but I did have my fire.

CHAPTER 2

RIVER

*A*s a child I'd never thought of killing anyone before. I'd seen dead people, but I'd never inflicted damage on another human soul intending to end their life. But with Mr. Crane lying in a pile on the charred ground in front of me, I was having trouble dredging up any regret about what I had done.

Especially when I could still see the little ball of crying boy on the ground just a little farther away.

Mr. Crane was a bad man.

He also wasn't dead. The fire had spewed forth from my belly angry and hot, but it had done little damage besides heating the air and charring his hair and clothes. He threw himself on the ground in what was probably a mixture of self-preservation and fear, and had smothered the flames most likely without even thinking about it.

I'd acted without thinking, as most children do, but my actions still had the desired effect. Mr. Crane had stopped hurting Wesa. I'd not thought a single second past that goal, and I wasn't prepared to defend myself as the hands of the other adults in the yard descended on my seven-year-old self, slinging me over a meaty shoulder by my legs as my hair hung down over my face, obscuring my vision.

"Get her out of here, Hank," Mrs. Crane squawked as Mr. Weisman carted me out of the yard at a run. "I don't know what dirty little trick she pulled, but she won't get another chance. Lock her away until we decide on her punishment. Get up, Yancy," she leveled at Mr. Crane where he still lay on the ground. "You've been had by the tricks of a child. You're an embarrassment to everyone."

She may have had more to say, but Mr. Weisman carried me too far to hear, and I couldn't see through the hair that hung down over my face. He carried me far enough that the blood rushing to my head obliterated any sound at all, and I had trouble getting my bearings as I was suddenly righted and sat down on an upside-down crate in a dark room I'd never been in before.

With my hair now out of my face and the blood that had been thundering in my head receding, I could see the face of Mr. Weisman as he towered above me.

"I'm afraid you've stepped in something you can't step out of, Mary girl." He sighed and scrubbed his hands over his face. I didn't want to think about what he meant, but I couldn't help but notice I was in an old storeroom out back, away from other people, and not back in the dormitory to await a normal punishment like I had thought I would be. "I know you thought you were helping Thomas, but it will only be worse for you now, you know? Not sure what they'll do with you, but it can't be good from the look of things. You attacked a teacher. They'll nip that right away, I'm sure."

I said nothing, just looked up at Mr. Weisman, trying not to let the fear I felt show on my face. I'd learned long ago to hide the things that were strange about me. To swallow it down and not let it out. It wasn't just strangers and those at the school who would persecute me if they knew. My own people were not immune to fear either. My parents had taught me long ago that the world was a dangerous place, and I knew the cost of letting my power show.

But my parents died, and I'd revealed my secret.

Not a single soul in this world would help me now.

"Hold out your hands, then, Mary," Mr. Weisman said as he

18

pulled a heavy cord from a hook on the wall. Willing my arms not to shake, I did as he asked. "Now Michelle thinks you pulled some trick on Yancy to get him to leave Thomas alone, but I was there. I know what I saw. Even now I see—your eyes are straight black, all the way through. Just a little bit of the white showing on the outside now, when there was none earlier. That's not normal, girl." He continued to speak as he wound the corded rope around my wrists, binding my hands together in front of me. I didn't know what to say to him. I'd only used my fire once before, and only in front of my parents, so I didn't know my eyes changed colors at all.

"I know you're something different. I've met others like you before. Well, not exactly like you. I don't know what you are," he said as he cut off the trailing ends of rope and patted my knee where I sat. "Once met a man who could tell things would happen before they did. Knew a lady that could tell what you were thinking when the words hadn't even left your mouth yet. You're someone like them, I suppose, although that was a pitiful display back there." Stepping away from me and walking toward the door, he paused, his back to me. "I hope it was worth it, Mary. You might have gotten the eyes off young Thomas, but now they're all on you. Lord knows what they're going to do with you now. That Michelle—she doesn't have a compassionate bone in her body. It's a damn shame, it is, but you called her attention on you now."

So he was one of *those* kind, then. I'd met people like Hank Weisman before. People who didn't like the hard-hearted things they saw going on around them, but did nothing to fix them. It wasn't that he wanted to tie me up—he didn't want anything bad to happen to me. He just didn't care enough to help me, even though he knew it would be bad. I hoped that when I died, as I was going to, I could come back to the earth in another time period, when the world wasn't full of so many evil people and cowards.

If everyone was just a little bit braver, we could change the world.

Taking my silence as acceptance, Mr. Weisman opened the

door to leave, letting a tiny sliver of sunlight in through the open door, illuminating the rest of the room I was being held in. It was a storage room—mostly extra wood and tools—as well as drums of oil for lamps stacked in a corner.

"You'll need to sit tight for a while, Miss Mary, until she comes for you. I wouldn't try any of your fancy smoke effects either—I doubt even you would survive the explosion if you breathe hot in here." And with that, he shut me in, locking the door behind him and eliminating the only light in the entire room.

I didn't know if I would survive or not. I didn't know a single thing about my power to produce fire besides the fact that I could do it at all. It wasn't something that had passed from my parents, that was for sure. No one knew what I was, or what I was capable of; we only knew to suppress it so no one would find out. And this was why. I may have saved Wesa temporarily, but I had doomed myself instead. It terrified my seven-year-old self, and I cried in the dark, knowing there would be no one to let me out even if I made enough noise to be heard.

AFTER AN UNDETERMINED AMOUNT of time sitting on the edge of the crate with my bound hands in my lap, my back cramping and complaining, I slid to the floor and rested my back against the wood. I must have rested my eyes as well, because they popped open with a start when the storage room door opened. No daylight streamed in through the doorway this time, so I guessed they had confined me for half a day at least, as it was full night. The soft light of an oil lantern flickered in the doorway for an instant, and then I saw nothing but blackness as a heavy sack was pulled tight over my head and they lifted me to my feet.

I thought I'd been afraid when the soldiers had come and rounded up the children to go to that school in the first place. I knew nothing then. Crying in the solitude of the darkened storage shed, with my hands bound in front of me and my legs shaking with dread, I'd been woefully unprepared. For no other experience in my life compared to the absolute terror of having my eyes covered and my body slung over the shoulder of a man who wasn't Mr. Weisman this time.

The smell of whiskey filled my nose, and it wasn't until they dumped me into the back of a wagon and the horse moved that I understood who had taken me.

"You're drunk, Yancy. Can you even see to steer the horse? Move aside. Give me the reins." That was the voice of Mrs. Crane for sure. I didn't know where we were going, but I could tell by the way my little body bumped and rolled around in the cart it was uneven ground, and by the length of time we traveled, I imagined we were quite a way from the school.

It's a terrifying thing for any adult—that moment of realization when they know *without a shred of doubt* they are living their last moments. But for me, as a child who'd only known the fear of hiding my entire life, it was a different feeling. The rough fibers of fraying rope digging into the sensitive skin over my collarbone and the dark canvas bag that had been slapped over my head just seemed like the obvious ending to my short, pitiful story.

This wasn't punishment. This was death. I deserved this end, and I didn't belong here.

They never took the bag off my head, not even for a moment. Not when they slid me feet first off the wagon and made me walk behind them, my hands still bound in front of me and someone, probably Mr. Crane, leading by the rope already tied around my neck. I stumbled once, and the rope pulled tight, cutting my airway closed. Was this what it would be like to die? I didn't want it. Panic bloomed in my chest, and I cried, my sobs fighting to be free from my already restricted throat.

"It's too late for that, you little witch," Mrs. Crane hissed in my ear. "Every opportunity we've given you to become a good Christian, and you resort to filthy heathen ways."

"Attacked me, she did," Mr. Crane hiccupped from somewhere

in front of me. "Burned the whiskers right off my chin. Can't let that go. One bad apple, you know, Michelle?"

"Yes, Yancy, I know. You have to cull the herd to keep the sheep in line. We won't suffer troublemakers, Mary."

I wanted to yell and scream. I wanted to tell them my name wasn't Mary, but I couldn't say a word. That rope cutting the air from my lungs, even just briefly, froze my entire body. Any amount of energy I had left was focusing on moving one foot in front of the other in a straight line, so I didn't stumble again.

Then we stopped walking, and no one spoke again for quite some time. The silence was just as unnerving as when they were talking. There were the light sounds of people at work, like the Cranes were setting up whatever they would do, and I was left to stand by a tree with my hands still tied in front of me and the rough bark scraping against my back. It was difficult to breathe inside the sack on my head, but after that tiny taste of suffocation, any breaths were a luxury.

I thought I'd imagined it—a shuffling behind the tree I was standing against, a quiet whispering through the tall grass that tickled my shins. But it continued, and as I strained my ears to catch the sounds that the Cranes were too busy to notice, a small voice carried through the air next to my head, as if coming from my mind itself.

"Little girl," it whispered. "Don't make a sound, but if you can hear me, tap your foot two times." I was sure I was crazy. A disembodied voice in the woods. Talking to me. And only I could hear it? Maybe I was going insane before they put me to death. I was too young to know any better.

"Sister, you have to be more specific. Maybe she doesn't understand what you mean?" A different yet similar voice to the first floated by my other ear.

"Will you be quiet and let me work? I'm trying not to scare her, and you're jabbering away."

"Sister, just tell her we'll help her. If she knows, she'll be able to handle the after parts."

"You're right, sister," the first voice replied. "We will help you, dear. If you understand that, can you tap your left foot two times? It doesn't have to be a big tap; we'll be able to see it."

I tapped my left foot two times softly in the grass. I could hear the Cranes moving around in the near distance, somehow missing the entire exchange. I did not understand what was going on, but the strange voices whispering were the friendliest I'd heard in ages, so I listened.

"Okay now, dear, just do what they want you to do and don't be afraid anymore. It will get loud . . ."

"It's going to sound like the hounds of hell are coming for their souls, if we play our cards right," the other voice interrupted, still barely a thought on the breeze, "but it should get their britches in a twist enough for us to steal you away."

"Yes, thank you, sister," the first voice chided. "We'll be stealing you away, is that all right?" For what purpose they would be stealing me for I didn't know, but it couldn't be as bad as dying at the end of a dirty rope, so I nodded my head slightly, and the voice continued. "It will be loud, dear, and I'm sorry ahead of time for that, but you can't move, okay? Act like you don't hear it at all."

And then the voices disappeared, and I felt the slack on the rope tighten as the Cranes finished whatever prep work had kept them busy for the last few minutes. I wasn't sure what would happen, but hope swelled in my small chest as I gave myself over to the possibility I might just get saved.

CHAPTER 3

RIVER

*E*ven with advance notice, I wasn't prepared for the horrifying sound. It started with footsteps, running through the grass on all sides of me; one going from right to left, and one going from left to right. That canvas bag was still over my head, but my covered eyes just made my ears that much sharper, and I could just about hear the grass blades bending as they circled our little patch.

"What in the hell is that?" Mr. Crane bellowed.

"Who's out there?" Mrs. Crane whimpered, letting me know the two voices had moved but still could not be seen.

"It's probably just animals, badger maybe, or raccoons."

"Yancy, I don't think raccoons move that fast, do they?"

"How the hell should I know, woman?" Mr. Crane mumbled irritably. "Just get her strung up, kick the stool, and let's go."

So that was how it was to be then? They would prop me up, tie my rope off and then let me swing until I was dead? Those heartless people. A little less afraid now I knew someone was in my corner, I could only find sadness in my heart for how hateful they were.

And then the wailing started.

A ghastly moaning started low, rising in pitch until it hit a full crescendo of keening sobs. Cries. Phantom noises seemed to come from everywhere, and still nowhere. The shivers started in my toes and ran up, marching like insects from the soles of my feet up and out through the top of my head, but I willed my body not to move. I acted like I didn't hear a thing.

Mrs. Crane screamed. So did Mr. Crane, and the noises sounded shockingly similar to each other.

Still, I didn't move.

The wailing continued. If anything, it grew louder and more concentrated, closer even, until it sounded like the source was two inches in front of my face even though I couldn't see through the bag on my head.

"It's fairies!" shrieked a terrified Mrs. Crane. "She's called fairies, and they will steal us away."

"Shut up, Michelle," Mr. Crane bellowed, and I felt slack in the rope hanging around my neck. "Get on the buggy, and let's get out of here."

"But the girl—"

"Let the fairies take her then. Are you so ignorant you want to hang around and go with them?"

And the wailing continued. On and on it went for an undetermined amount of time while I heard a whip crack and answering neighs as the horse thundered off at a fast clip. My ears picked up the sound of wagon wheels bouncing on the dirt and then . . . nothing.

The noise halted as if a door shut on it, and even the normal night noises ceased to exist in the wake of that performance. And yet still I didn't move. I acted like I heard nothing and knew nothing, just as the two voices had instructed me to. I remained as still as a stone until someone whipped the bag off my head, and I stumbled against the tree I'd been standing against with a shriek.

Two gray heads popped into my field of vision. The faces on those heads were smiling kindly—the kind of smiles that reached their eyes—and their faces were lined with time and experience.

"Hullo," said one of the gray-haired ladies.

"Hullo," chimed in the other.

I stood there, still trussed with a rope hanging around my neck, its tail end lying in the dirt.

"Are you really fairies?" I whispered. I didn't know what *fairies* were, but these old women weren't so scary.

"Pfft," one of the gray-haired ladies sputtered, and the other smiled wide, showing a row of white, even teeth.

"Your version of fairies and ours are two different things, is what I think. You're probably thinking of sprites anyway. They're the wee buzzy ones with wings."

"Sister is right, and anyway, we're banshees. Didn't you hear the wailin'? No fairies I know can make a racket like that. Not that I've heard, anyway."

So they weren't fairies, but they had met some before? I didn't know what a fairy was; I'd only just heard the word from Mrs. Crane's screaming, so it was all news to me.

"I'm Meri," one woman said, laying her hand on the ropes that bound my hands. There was a gentle warmth, and the bindings fell away from me as if cut with an unseen knife. "That's my sister Alice."

As I turned my head to acknowledge the woman standing next to me, Meri placed her hands on my neck. After another brief warmth, the rope fell to the ground with a little plop in the dirt.

My little hands shook as I touched the raw marks where the rope had abraded my tender flesh. I'd felt death's breath on my skin, and these two had swooped in and saved me. I knew nothing more than that, but if they were here to spirit me away, I would go with them. These two kindly older women had given me more smiles and care in the last five minutes than I had been given in the last two years. I would follow them even if they didn't want me; that's how smitten I was in that moment.

"How did you know I was here?"

Alice looked at me shrewdly, assessing how much information she could give me, how much I could process in that moment, before she smiled again and nodded. "I had a dream about you,

you see. Crying in the dark. Scared. You needed us, and we need you."

"You need me?" My voice was but a whisper. No one had needed me before. "But I'm not very good. I don't try to be bad, but . . ."

"Hush now," and before I knew it, Meri gathered me in the softest, warmest hug I had ever experienced. "You're not a bad girl, heavens no. You're just a wee bit different is all."

"You aren't a bad girl," Alice said from over my shoulder. "I dreamed of you. You're our girl, and if you're willing, we'll take you home with us."

"You want to take me with you?" I sniffed and peeked over Meri's shoulder at Alice, who winked at me and nodded.

"It's quite a journey from here, though," she said. "It'll probably take time. But when we get to where we're going, you'll finally have a safe place. There are lots of different people there. Like us, like yourself. Not exactly the same, but we're all special in our own ways. It's a safe place, girl."

I smiled at the thought. My life had been so dirty and ugly; a safe place seemed almost unimaginable.

Meri grumbled as I pulled out of her embrace during Alice's conversation. "What is your name? We can't just be on about calling you girl all the time. We've said ours—what are you called?"

"Wait!" Alice interrupted. "I dreamed it. I know. It's on the tip of my tongue and has something to do with water . . . its Stream isn't it?"

I giggled at her obviously wrong answer. Maybe her dreams weren't as clear as she thought.

"Raindrop," guessed Meri.

"Muddy Puddle!"

I dissolved in a fit of laughter at the last one when I figured out they were playing with me, and I realized it had been so long since I had laughed that I didn't even recognize the sound of my own.

"River, we've a long way to go before we're home," Alice said gently, taking one of my hands in hers as Meri took the other. "Are you ready to leave this all behind?"

I turned to look at the circle of forest for the first time since they had removed the bag. There were deep cuts in the earth where the wagon had sunk in and hoof prints all around. I looked up at the tree I had been destined to hang from, and down at the ground where my ropes lay like dead discarded snakes. Was I ready to leave this all behind?

I couldn't get away fast enough.

With the wide-eyed wonder of a child, I thought back to what the sisters had said about the wee fairies with wings.

"Are we going to fly to where we're going?" I asked in awe.

Meri regarded me thoughtfully. "That might require calling in a few favors I don't know we've earned as yet." She scratched her chin, and her eyes twinkled brightly. "I was thinking we'd take the train."

CHAPTER 4

JONAS

JUNE 1924, HAVENWOOD FALLS, COLORADO

There were a lot of things to look forward to in life: birthdays, anniversaries, the weekend, and holidays. The thing I most looked forward to, however, was that daily noon bell. The four long blasts coming from the quarry rippled through the air like a punch, announcing to those of us working it was time to stop and eat.

Lunch break.

Not something to celebrate, at least not to the extent that I did, but it wasn't just the food I was looking forward to—it was the company. There were a lot of things I loved about Havenwood Falls after coming here as a lad of just sixteen, but my favorite by far was a certain someone that didn't even live within the town limits. I had to be content with those tiny stolen bits of company I was graced with, every day at noon.

The midday sun burned across my neck and back, through the work shirt to the white skin below. While I preferred the cool and dark inside the mine, I spent a lot of my time laboring in the sun. Being a mine worker was a hard job, but per my lineage, I was good at it. As cool as a Colorado mountain summer could be, even at seventy-one degrees my skin was flustered, prickly, and covered in a fine layer of grit.

It was to be expected, considering my line of work, but for a meeting with the most beautiful girl I had ever laid eyes on in all of my years on this earth, it wouldn't do. I picked the fabric of my shirt and pulled it away from my body, attempting to shake the dust and grime off as I walked up the steep hill to the place where the dirt and rock smoothed out into a wide grassy slope.

"It doesn't matter how you primp, she'll avoid you today just like she has every other day." The cheerful voice of Ian, my friend and fellow mine worker, sounded off behind me. "Is today the day you'll push past her defense? Or will you chicken out?"

"I don't chicken out," I said, as I shoved him in the arm. I didn't strike him hard at all, but I still felt a sense of satisfaction when he stumbled to the side a few feet before righting himself, grinning like a loon.

"I know you watch your strength around us tiny mortals," Ian mused, "but I think you might have maybe wanted to knock me down with that one."

"If I'd wanted you down, you'd be at the bottom of the mine by now." I returned his grin. He and I both knew I would never hurt him on purpose, just as we both knew no one in Havenwood Falls had ever seen my *real* strength. And that was all right. I was who I was and I wouldn't change that, but by nature, stone men weren't the most handsome of creatures, so I was very selective of those I showed my second self to. The girl I was trying to get to be mine was not on the short list.

"I will not chicken out, Ian." I smiled as we both crested the hill, stepped into the line where the dusty quarry rock met the grass, and scraped our dirty boots on the soft green carpet. "Today, I've a plan."

Ian's dark eyebrows rose in surprise, and his green eyes twinkled with mirth. "Oh, a plan, you have? Please share it with the rest of the class."

"I'm not telling you anything; now go have lunch with your fan club—I have a lady to woo."

Ian sputtered and coughed as he looked over his shoulder in the general direction I had been pointing. There was already a line of young ladies there, holding boxed lunches and drinks, presumably brought for their fathers and brothers, but I knew the truth. Their matchmaking mamas had sent them. Ian was an eligible young bachelor, and there was more than one way to net a husband.

"*My* fan club, you say?" Ian hissed under his breath. But I barely heard him, as I was already looking ahead, at the dark-haired young beauty who was bringing her motorcycle to a stop alongside the grassy area where we all gathered. A line was already forming in front of her, other men like me who ordered packed lunches from her cart every day. That was okay. I didn't need to be first in line—I needed to be last.

River McNee was the twenty-three-year-old adopted niece of the Sisters McNee, and she took orders for packed lunches and cold drinks from the laborers in town. Every day like a clock, she would bring those lunches in, collect our money, then ride that little motorbike with the side cart back out of town, and out of my life. I didn't like her for the lunches, although they were good enough in their own right. Sandwiches made with soft homemade bread piled high with—depending on the day—roast beef, salt ham, or thick slices of turkey meat. There was a crisp cold vegetable of some sort, and always, but always, a thick slice of pie. Whether River or the sisters was in charge of that pie, it was like magic in every bite. Peach, berry cobblers, apple—even when the fruit wasn't in season—the pie tasted like someone had plucked the fruit straight from the tree itself. That was the power of the pie.

But it still wasn't the reason I ordered lunch from that side cart every workday, without fail.

I watched as she chatted with everyone in line until it was my turn to address the young woman with the beautiful doe eyes and strangely colored hair. She kept it tied back in braids most often, but she couldn't hide the streaks of rust and flame that wove in and out no matter how tightly she bound it. Today she wore a short-sleeved dress the color of the bluebells that peppered the mountainside. It was plain, and the skirt hung damn near down to her ankles, but she still looked lovely to me. She tried to dress as modestly as she could, but there wasn't any amount of clothing aside from a winter parka that would hide the generous curve of those assets. Even now, as she smiled at me in greeting, the seams of her dress pulled tight in the front, and one little white button looked in dire need of saving. I imagined if she filled her lungs too deeply, it would come screaming off, pinging into the grass.

I wonder if I can get her to yell, I thought before giving myself a mental knock upside the head.

Don't disrespect her like that, you bastard, I told myself. *You're on a mission; remember your purpose.*

"What's the matter, Jonas? Is everything all right?"

It was that soft melodious voice, nothing more than a murmur really, that shook me from my perverse thoughts. I'd been inside my own head, and who knew how long I'd been standing in front of her, staring at her chest like a deviant without saying a word?

"W-what?" I hated that I stumbled over the word, but I wasn't sure if I had even heard her correctly. She was holding my sack lunch out, a bemused half smile on her face and her dark eyes laughing.

"You look so angry, what with your eyebrows all drawn together. I would have thought you didn't like your food, but you haven't even taken it from me yet." Then there was a flash of white as she smiled, a true smile that lit up her face, the grassy lawn we were standing in, and hell, half the town of Havenwood Falls. "And if it's cheering up you need, there's something in that bag that will surely do the trick." She leaned in close, and I willed my hands not to shake as I took the paper bag from her hands. "There's peach pie in there. But only if you eat your vegetables, right? You're still a growing boy." And with that obvious joke at my expense, given my six foot three frame and shoulders as wide as you'd think they would be, River McNee dissolved into peals of the most musical laughter I had ever heard.

"Hilarious, River." I tried to look miffed, but it was hard to feign hurt feelings when she was gifting me with that smile. "Since it's Friday, I would like to put my order in for next week," I said, grabbing the money out of my billfold to pay for the next week's lunches, the same as I did every Friday. It saved us all time that way, paying for the week ahead of time.

"You know, not that I want to turn down the money that earns me a living, but you'd save a lot if you packed your own lunches, you know?" River folded the bills without counting them and slipped them into the brown leather satchel she wore over one shoulder.

"I can't cook worth a damn, and even if I could, I wouldn't. If I packed my own lunches, I wouldn't get to see your sweet smile every day, River, and you can't put a price on that." I don't know where those accidentally smooth words came from, but I was both proud of myself and terrified at the same time. It was a blatant come on, and who knew how she would respond? I always got a few kind words from River when she brought lunches. She was always so pleasant and kind to everyone, but every time I tried to get more than a few sentences out of her, she rushed away like her skirt was on fire.

But she didn't move from her spot.

She froze, eyes downcast, looking at some mark I couldn't see, but seemed like it occupied one hundred percent of her attention. I wondered if she'd even heard me, until I saw the blush staining her cheeks. A flush of scarlet on her tanned skinned ran down her neck and disappeared under the neckline of that straining blue fabric.

How far down does that blush go? I was dying to find out.

I knew one thing—not only had she heard me, but she thought enough about my words to become flustered.

Pressing on, I pushed my luck a little further. "River, it's Friday. What are you doing this weekend?"

Surprised, she looked away from whatever interesting thing she had found on the ground and replied without thinking. "Helping the sisters with the washing, and then I don't know what else. I'm busy during the week; I plan little else on those days."

"So would you say you have free time?" I said, leaning my elbow on the side cart and wincing at the creaking noise as it gave a little under my considerable weight. I straightened immediately. The scarlet blood had not faded from her cheeks, and she was looking everywhere but at my face as she stammered out a reply.

She was embarrassed? This was fun. It was one thing if she wouldn't give me the time of day, but I was getting all kinds of fun reactions out of Miss River McNee today. She took a deep breath and met my eyes again. I dragged them up from her dancing button at just the right second so she didn't see me staring at her chest again. There's teasing a lady and then there's being a right ass. I wouldn't mind the first, but refused to be the second.

"Well, I don't really have much planned besides chores," she hemmed. Her eyes darted nervously over my shoulder and then back to me. She backed away from me and made as if to get back on her motorcycle. I didn't know what had her so spooked, but I wasn't letting her get away from me until I said what I had to say.

"It was nice to see you, Jonas." River tried to beat a hasty exit, but I grabbed her hand as she tried to slip away. It was strange how she kept looking around me, but not at me. Everything was fine until I asked her about the weekend. When I grabbed her hand, she froze, eyes wide and fearful, and her full pink lips parted in a little *o* shape.

"Woman, would you stop running?" My voice was louder than I meant it to be, but damn if I didn't need her to pay attention. I'd been trying for a month to ask her on a proper date, and this was as close as I'd come in that time. "You've been avoiding me for several weeks now, and I'd like more of a conversation than the time it takes for a good afternoon and exchange of a few coins."

Now I was a big guy, and I could intimidate without trying. With that in mind, I had been prepared for a few different reactions. There could have been outright refusal; after all, she was such a gentle lady, and I was a pretty clumsy oaf on my best day. I wasn't as smooth or handsome as Ian. I didn't have women fawning all over me all the time, so it took courage to even get the words out to River.

She could have laughed, thinking it was a joke. I knew women could react that way, as well. She could have reacted a dozen different ways, but I wasn't prepared for the sting in my arm as she pinched me as hard as she could, and with a scowl that completely changed the features of her face, hissed, "What is wrong with you, Jonas? Are you trying to get me killed?"

Say what now? She wasn't waiting for me to answer her question; she plowed right ahead, pulling one long braid over her shoulder in frustration.

"Do you not know where we are and *must you shout?*"

I still wasn't following, but she was mad enough to spit nails, so I tried to come up with an answer that would make her not be mad at me anymore.

"This is the only time I see you, River. I'd like to see more of you, but the only way to do that is to ask you, right? Did I do it wrong? Are you that opposed to spending time with me?" She must not have realized that I was still holding her hand as she had made no move to yank it back, so I released her and stepped back. "I can respect if you don't want to, but I'm not sorry I asked. If you want an apology because I kissed you in front of Callie's Trinkets, I didn't mean to embarrass you. But I won't say I'm sorry for being interested. We were on a date, River. First you acted like you wanted to be seen with me, and everything was going fine, and the next thing I know, you are pulling away and treating me like a regular customer. I won't understand if you don't tell me. Are you not interested in me anymore? Are you interested in someone else?"

Was she dating someone else now? Unthinkable. The thought of it made me sick, and I had to rein in the anger to keep my arms from turning to granite right in front of her. River's face was beet red now, and she raised her eyes to the sky and mumbled words that sounded suspiciously like a prayer for patience before she bit her lip and sighed.

"The first rule of the Jonas Pederson fan club is that Jonas Pederson belongs to everyone and no one."

"Come again?"

With a deep sigh, River threw her hands in the air and closed the gap between us. She placed one small hand on my forearm, and I gasped at the heat. Was I craving her closeness so much that my body burned at the touch? I wouldn't doubt it. I'd been thinking of her since the day I met her.

"Turn around and see what I mean."

I turned my head to oblige her, but all I saw behind me was Ian and his row of followers. They were all staring at us, though, and a few of the women had disgruntled looks on their faces. One blond girl on the end of the row was clutching a basket in her hands until her knuckles were white, and she narrowed her eyes, glaring daggers in our direction.

"Is that woman angry with me? If looks could kill, I'd have a spade through my forehead right now."

"Oh she's irate for sure, but not at you." River sighed again. "Jonas, could it be that you *are* that oblivious? You don't see all those women looking at you?"

I turned my head again. Of course I could see them; any fool with eyes could see them. I didn't know why they would be mad at me, though. "Who are we talking about? Ian's ladies?"

"Ian's . . . what?" River paused, her doe-brown eyes as wide as saucers before she laughed, a full rich laugh that rang like church bells. The sound was so beautiful to my ears, I would make a complete ass out of myself as many times as she liked if I could just hear her laughter again. She laughed until tears collected in the corners of her eyes and she had to fill her lungs with air again, the movement causing that poor overworked button on her dress to pull the sides of the fabric near to tearing.

"Jonas," River tried to speak, but her laughter caused the

words to come out in gasps. "Those aren't Ian's women. That is a throng of hopeful ladies wishing you would turn your face to them. They come every day to get a glimpse of you. Look at them, all dressed up like it's Sunday, and you not even sparing a glance." River clutched her sides and bent over, her full laughter dying down to hysterical giggles. "You are prime bachelor real estate, Jonas, and you just broke no less than ten or twelve hearts by asking me on a date right here in front of them. I know if I lived in town, every one of their mamas would try to snuff me out in my sleep."

What? I turned to look again, and this time Ian was laughing, and the blond girl who was staring angrily now had tears in her eyes. When she saw me looking, she pivoted and with her back to me, walked away from the grassy lunch area. Within a second or two, the others followed, leaving only Ian standing off to the side, a stupid grin on his face and his cheeks puffed out with whatever food he'd swiped.

I still didn't understand, but the shrill whistle blow that filled the air around the yard told me one thing—lunch was over, and with it, my time with River. I hadn't even gotten an answer to my question yet, and I wasn't about to leave without getting it—even if she was trying to pack her cart and go while I turned my back. I flustered her, that much I knew, and until she gave me a solid no, I would take it as a maybe.

"Oh no, you don't." I put my hand on the side cart of the little motorbike, pinning it down as River swung her skirted leg over the seat and tried to start the bike. She couldn't figure out why it wouldn't go. Little did she know it was just a tiny bit of my strength that had that cart pinned in place.

"Oh, I don't what? You've wasted your whole lunch time chatting with me, and now you don't even have time to eat. Don't you need to get back to work?" River gave up trying to start the bike and crossed her arms over her ample chest with a huff. She looked angry, but the corners of her mouth quirked up regardless, and I saw it.

"They'll get their sweat off my back later for sure," I replied, confidence making my smile wide and lazy. The cart creaked under the light pressure of my hand, but it was going nowhere. "I can eat later, after I've gotten an answer to the question I've yet to ask properly. Miss River McNee, would you do the honor of being my date this Saturday afternoon and possibly into the evening a bit as well?" Were her eyes always this dark? So deep brown they appeared to be black, and the pupils two dark pools so wide they almost touched the whites. She mumbled something under her breath, and I paused. "Is that a yes or a no?"

Taking a deep breath, she squared her shoulders. "Will you protect me from the likes of Ginny Mickelson and the other girls who've hearts you squashed just now when they try to tear me limb from limb?"

The words mocked, but her eyes were serious. It seemed like a joke, but she needed reassurance, so I would give it to her.

"River, I'll not let anything happen to you when you're with me. Never. My body is your shield." It might have been a little overkill, but when had I ever been anything less than direct? Besides, this was the first time I'd got this far with River since she had become skittish on our last date, and I needed to use every opening I could get. I picked her hand up in mine and brought it to my lips for a quick, chaste kiss, once again marveling at the heat of her skin when we touched. It was a good sign, surely.

Sighing again, she pulled her hand from my grasp, and this time couldn't hide the smile from my eyes. "All right, but you'd better make it worth my while. I don't think you know what you've done today, Jonas Pederson, but you'll find out soon enough, I suppose. I'd be happy to spend Saturday afternoon with you, and some of the evening as well. Pick me up at four and be prepared to deal with the sisters when you do."

I felt Ian walk up behind me more than I heard him as I took my hand off the cart and River finally got the engine to turn over. I grinned and waved at her as she drove away, back out of town to the small home she shared with the Sisters McNee. My mood considerably lifted, my body feeling lightened after my conversation with River. I could move mountains today, if I wanted.

"Can you come back to work now, before we all get our hides chewed, loverboy?"

I laughed and slapped Ian on the shoulder, laughing even harder as he stumbled heavily under my light shove.

"I'll work circles around everyone else, and they know it. Let someone say otherwise." I wouldn't get into trouble for being late back from lunch, but I quickened my pace, just in case. "Can I ask you something, though? Aren't all those women always lined up to see you at lunch time? River made it sound like I destroyed some sacred lady trust when I asked her out on a date, but that can't be right."

Ian looked as if he'd swallowed a peach pit, his face screwed up so tight, and then he burst into laughter at my innocent question.

"Sometimes I like you, Jonas, and sometimes I want to knock you upside your giant skull. I'm so jealous of you, you thick son of a bitch." Ian turned to walk the short distance back to work but then paused, sniffed the air, then walked back and sniffed the space close to me. He looked around, didn't find what he was looking for, and threw his hands in the air before asking, "Why do you smell like smoke?"

CHAPTER 5

RIVER

I'd made it out of town and was mostly down the rough dirt road that led to the house I shared with the sisters before I realized I'd melted the grips on the handlebars of my bike. The acrid smell of burning rubber and foam reached my nose seconds before I saw the tiny tendrils of smoke wafting in front of my eyes. *Dammit.* What was it about Jonas Pederson that made me lose control?

I hated my fire and everything that had ever come from it, but just thinking about that giant of a man had me unable to stop the heat from rising to my skin. I may have hated my fire, but I did not hate Jonas Pederson.

And he had asked me for a second date.

In front of his entourage.

It was laughable, that he had plucked the words right out of a dream and told me he wanted to spend time with me, only me. What a pity he had to do it in front of half of the women in town of marriageable age. Women who'd had their eyes fixed on him for a while. Of all the rotten luck.

And he was right. I had been giving him the cold shoulder for the last few weeks. But it wasn't because he tried to kiss me in front of Callie's when we were walking through town. Rather, it was because I almost lit his hair on fire, I was so worked up over him paying attention to me. Remembering how I had barely caught myself in time sent shudders through my whole body. Sometimes I really hated myself. My hormones were a lit match looking for something to burn.

I pulled the motorbike into the side yard of the small white two-story house I shared with Alice and Meri. The house we'd inhabited for the last sixteen years—ever since the sisters had gotten frustrated with the Court and moved us out of the town proper. That was a long time ago, but the sisters were holding an uncharacteristically long grudge. I was free to do what I wanted to do, but Alice and Meri wouldn't move back inside Havenwood Falls until "that Bishop boy knocks on the door and begs." But we all knew that would not happen. No matter which Bishop "boy" was in question, we would never see a single one of those tall, dark, and handsomes banging on our door and begging forgiveness. The sisters didn't care. They felt I had been wrongfully evaluated as a child, and no matter how I felt about the subject, they would never be assuaged.

I opened the front door and tossed my apron and money satchel over the coat rack by the door. I didn't count the money, and I didn't worry about someone taking it. We lived comfortably enough out here in the woods, and no stranger was likely to come waltzing through our front door with nefarious intentions. The sisters' natural glamour made sure of that. People only found our home if the sisters willed it; otherwise, they could search forever and only find trees, tall grass, and wildlife. It was laughable really, considering I could see the Havenwood Falls sign next to the road from my front yard. It was the sisters' way of thumbing their noses at the Court of the Sun and the Moon all those years ago. I knew that as long as we weren't causing trouble, the Court wouldn't spare us a thought, and moving out of town didn't make them feel one way or another, but the sisters felt differently.

I didn't have the same aggravation or negative feelings. I loved Havenwood Falls, and I loved the sisters. They had blessed my life

for the best from the moment I met the Sisters McNee—
everything that had happened since then had been gravy.

Until Jonas Pederson, that is.

"River, what's the matter?" I passed through the house at top
speed and out through the rear kitchen door to find Meri in the
front part of the garden, a wide-brimmed hat pulled low over her
eyes and her steel gray braid trailing down behind it. "You're all in
a tizz. What's got you so worked up you're throwing sparks?"

"I'm not throwing sparks, Aunt Meri," I said, looking down at
my hands just to make sure, considering I had ruined the handles
of my bike. And who knew when I could get replacements?
Motorcycles weren't common in these parts, and women riders
even less so.

"Maybe not now," she said, straightening from the herbs she'd
been stooping over and sliding her mini shears into her apron
pocket. "But I smelled smoke on the wind, River—and Alice had a
dream . . ."

Alice's dreams were nothing to laugh at, even if they were a
little vague. After all, I also was once a dream Alice had.

"Oh." I stood next to Meri—we were the same height now—
and took the basket full of herbs out of her arms as we both
headed back through the kitchen door. "And what kind of dream
would that be?"

We didn't quite make it all the way through the door before I
heard a voice, huffing and puffing with exertion behind me. "We'll
be getting a visitor tomorrow then, won't we? A handsome one,
I'm thinking."

I didn't have to turn around to know Alice was smiling, but I
did anyway. She was pushing a wheelbarrow filled to the brim with
fruit—apples and pears, figs and peaches, all perfectly ripe for
eating. The sisters used their Celtic nature magic to keep the small
orchard at optimal conditions for growing at all times. Even in
winter, we could tend the fruit trees. People had long since
stopped trying to figure out how we could make our pies with
fruit out of season, and we didn't volunteer the information. Of

course she'd be out of breath from pushing that load. Handing Meri her basket through the kitchen door, I made my way back out into the yard.

"Barring your correct assumption, Aunt Alice, I told you to let me do these things. I'm stronger than I look, you know." I manned the wheelbarrow while she stood there chuckling, and Meri came back out the door with a couple of empty baskets. Among the three of us, we made quick work of emptying the wheelbarrow, sorting the fruit, bringing it all back into the large kitchen, and stacking it in the pantry shelves that were laid empty for just such a purpose.

"Care to tell me why such a large harvest today?" Normally we picked only what was needed for orders, and not so many different fruits at a time. Usually such a large harvest was for some catering function, like a wedding or a party, or for canning, but that wouldn't be until later in the fall.

"What kind of pie does Jonas Pederson like, River?" Meri asked, as she pulled the sugar and flour out of the cabinets and tied an apron around her waist.

"Yes, River, and I picked the figs and pears for you to take to Napoli's tomorrow. I'm guessing they will need them right about now, so please take them while you're out." Alice busied herself with pulling her rolling pins and dough cutter from the wooden drawers we kept them in and acted for all the world like there was nothing strange about her request.

"Did Napoli's place an order?"

"No, but I have a feeling."

"And what makes you think I know what kind of pie Jonas Pederson likes, hmm?" I murmured the question, but I already knew the answer, and it was just a farce even acting like it surprised me.

"I dreamed our young River would get a gentleman caller, and there is only one gentleman you would say yes to. You've only had eyes for him since you were just a teenager. Although the real mystery is why it would take so long for you two to get together.

He's a man of thirty now, for goodness sake. And you are a woman in your own right."

"There are other ladies in town, you know," I admonished the older woman as I automatically washed the peaches that Meri pulled out of the pantry and handed to me. "Just because I've had a crush on him since creation doesn't mean he has any obligation to pick me out of the masses."

"But he did, River. He picked you. And he's coming tomorrow, and he's taking you to Napoli's or I'll bet double the money in that satchel by the door. Bet me." By the stubborn tilt to her chin, I knew I was better off not taking the bet. Besides, money didn't mean a whole lot to the sisters. They lived simply, and money was a means to get by, not something to be coveted. All extra funds went into savings I personally took to the bank in town. It had been like that since as long as I could remember, and probably since before then.

"You two are awfully well informed for rarely having been in town for sixteen years and not owning a telephone," I grumbled half-heartedly.

"We aren't hermits, River. We still get visitors, and we still talk to people." Meri cut a small x on the bottom of a peach and slid it into a pot of just boiling water.

"Yeah, we just get to be a lot choosier about the people we talk to." Alice hooted, her laughter catching on until all three of us were giggling in the kitchen like children. I knew the ladies moved out of town for me, but it made me happy to know the decision had not been such a burden to them. I would stay with them as long as they would have me—they were my family now.

And apparently, my family knew peach pie was Jonas Pederson's favorite.

CHAPTER 6

RIVER

*B*eing as young as I was and having such a limited view of the world, I didn't always have a keen grasp of my surroundings, but fear was a universal feeling. Everyone knew how to recognize that, and as I stared, wide-eyed, at the solemn faces of the people seated in front of me, I was cloaked in the inky black blanket of terror.

I was seven years old again—I hated this dream.

To the left of me, sitting at a table away from where I was placed, sat the sisters, who had saved my life and proclaimed themselves my protectors. They stared at the row of faces in front of us, their features tight and pinched, their eyes mirroring the same sternness.

"This isn't a hearing. It's a meeting." Meri slapped her hand on the polished wood table in front of her, silver curls bobbing against her ears. "So do you mind telling me then, why you're all lined up like ducklings?"

"Wrong metaphor, sister." Alice patted her sister's hand and clucked her tongue against her teeth. "Ducklings are sweet little creatures. The Court of the Sun and the Moon looks like it is ready to hand out a death sentence. I'll have you explain what's going on right now, if you would." Alice's voice was hard, a complete directional change from the soft even tone she had been using since I met her. "You all knew we were bringing her home with us; we brought her here as a formality. You are treating her like a convict. She's a little girl, not a thief or a murderer."

My little legs shook with fear, and I put my hands in my lap to keep my knees from knocking together. Not a murderer. No, I wasn't, but I could have been. It wasn't lack of effort on my part that had kept me from ending that teacher at school. I hadn't been trying to kill him exactly, but I hadn't been thinking about *not* killing him either.

I'd only been with the sisters for a short time, essentially the time it took for us to travel from Carlisle, Pennsylvania, where they found me, to Havenwood Falls—all the way across the country and into the Colorado mountains. But in that short time, they'd shown me more kindness than I had found in the two years I'd been at the Carlisle school. They had not only saved my life, but they'd shown me that there were other people in the world like me. Maybe not exactly like me, but people with powers. They told me they would welcome me in Havenwood Falls.

But they met us with this.

"What is your name?" The tall, dark-haired man stood in front of me and spoke for the first time. Unlike the others in the room, he was the only one standing, and he regarded me with his unsmiling face, waiting for my answer. "Are you a mute? Your elder has asked you a question. What is your name? Surely you know it." His expression was as black as his slicked-back hair, and his eyes brooked no argument.

"River," I replied softly, not knowing what else to say.

"Is that all? No last name?" he prompted, looking both bored and irritated all at the same time. But I had no other information to give him.

"Rodavan, you're being obtuse," Meri admonished. I stole a nervous glance over my shoulder, and Alice winked at me. People yelled all the time. It couldn't be all bad if Alice was winking at me, could it?

46

"I'm just asking questions, Miss McNee. I don't intend to frighten, merely to learn all I can. With power comes responsibility, and it is the Court's responsibility to keep the residents of Havenwood Falls safe. Especially considering our town's tragic . . . history." The man called Rodavan let his gaze drift around the room. A terribly intimidating man, he oozed authority. Dream me tried to recall the faces of everyone who sat across from me, but no matter how many times I tried, or how many times I had this same dream, I couldn't remember them. Even though I'd since seen them all many times over the last sixteen years, in this dream, when I was only seven again, everyone's face was a blur. Everyone but the Sisters McNee, Rodavan Bishop, and one other.

"What can you tell us, little girl? About yourself? About where you came from? Leave nothing out, because if you do, I'll know. I have no patience for liars." The voice behind Rodavan belonged to a striking man. So tall and slender, sitting straight up in his chair he was almost as tall as a normal man standing. Long silvery hair flowed just past his shoulders, and I would have thought it was the most interesting feature about him but for his eyes—so pale and frosty, they could freeze the breath in your lungs. And his voice. That wasn't the voice of a fragile man. He commanded just as much attention as Rodavan, if not more. I knew, when talking to this man, I dared not tell an untruth. Finding the small amount of courage afforded by Meri and Alice in the courtroom, I addressed the Court as bravely as I knew how.

"My name is River. At least that's what the translation is, I'm told. I've forgotten how my parents pronounced it, it's been so long. They died of a great sickness years ago. Long before the people from the government came and took the children from our native lands. They took us to a boarding school to teach us English and to leave behind our heathen ways. Kill the Indian, save the man." I said all these things without heat. I probably should have had hate in my heart for what had happened, but it was all I knew. And even now, it seemed a million years away. It wasn't happy or sad. It was just something that happened. It was my truth. "So when I tell you my name is River, I mean just that. I don't have the thing you refer to as a surname. If I did, I've long forgotten it. The people at the Carlisle school called me Mary Smith, but I don't recognize that name."

I focused on Rodavan when I was speaking, because even with his serious and stern face, it was still easier to look at him than at the older man behind him. There was something scary about him I couldn't place. Like he could see right into my mind.

"Something like that, River," the older man said, as if he could read my mind indeed.

"If you're done, Elsmed, may I continue my quest for answers?" Rodavan murmured, but not soft enough that the sisters didn't hear him.

"More like an inquisition," Alice grumbled. "I'd like to know what good comes from terrifying a child. You knew about me before we even left Havenwood Falls to get her. We sat in this very room while Meri told you my dream. You already know the circumstances, so why are we doing this right now?"

"Because you aren't the only one in this town who has premonitions." He didn't yell, but Elsmed's voice cut through the noise of the room regardless. "And Rodavan did some searching after you left. The results were . . . inconclusive."

"Inconclusive to you; I know what I saw." Rodavan was talking to Elsmed like I wasn't even in the room anymore, and what they were discussing was much more supernatural than just a girl who could spit fire from her mouth. I didn't know it at the time, being new to Havenwood Falls, but had learned since that Elsmed was fae, and Rodavan was a mage. One could read minds and the other could wreak havoc on them. They didn't just look scary—they *were*.

"Well then, stop beating around the bush and ask her what you want to know," Alice slapped her hand on the wooden desk again to show her displeasure. "Stop the bully session and let's get on with it. River, they want to know about your fire. That's all. Tell them what you told us."

With Alice's prodding, the words came out in a hurried rush. I spoke quickly, afraid that at any moment they would tear me away from the two women I thought of as my saviors. I told them everything. About my power. About how my parents taught me at an early age to hide it, to bury it and never use it, lest someone find out. How they had died, and how it had terrified me when all the children were taken away. How I had lived at the school, trying to blend in, until the incident with Wesa—I choked up then, and the tears fell. Not only for Wesa, but for what had happened after I had used my fire on Mr. Crane. I'd done something bad, and they had almost put me to death for it. That's what they wanted to know, really. If I would do something like that again.

"I'm not a bad girl." I ended my story on a breathless sob. "I'm not bad. I don't want to hurt people. I won't use it again, I won't." It was my fire I referred to. And I wasn't making an empty promise. I wouldn't use it again. It scared the hell out of me. And what good was a power that hurt people anyway?

"She speaks the truth as she knows it," Elsmed said, not looking at me but at Rodavan, who needed the most convincing. There were feminine murmurs from the rest of the Court, but they were just white noise at this point. There may have been more conversation than what I remembered, but this was my dream, and as far as dreams went, it focused solely on what was important —Rodavan's words.

"She may speak *her* truth."

Rodavan turned to address the rest of the Court, turning so the only thing I could see was the back of his tailored waistcoat. "But trust me, I know what I saw. I can't see her future. All I see is flames. All-encompassing flames." He turned around and faced me again, his dark stare oddly enthralling, and even though I didn't want to look at him, I couldn't look away. "Someday, you will burn. The question is, can we afford to have you in Havenwood Falls when you combust?"

. . .

I AWOKE THEN, just like I always did at that part of the dream. I simply opened my eyes; I no longer woke up sweating or breathing heavily. I'd had the dream so many times, I could recite it in my sleep, so to speak. Rodavan had looked into my future and seen calamity. There was no arguing that. He was a powerful mage in his own right; if he saw it, it must be true. No one had argued with him after that, but neither had they come to a decision about what to do with me.

I smiled in my comfortable bed as I stared at the white-painted ceiling of my room, in the house that had been built just for Meri, Alice, and me. The sisters had interrupted the meeting in a flurry of anger and hurt feelings.

"We're not waiting around for you," they'd said almost in unison. "She's ours, and we don't need you to protect her. We can do it on our own."

And that was it. They moved out of Havenwood Falls as soon as they finished their new house. And it was finished quickly, because even though the people of Havenwood Falls didn't know me, a little native girl from halfway across the country, the Sisters McNee were beloved members of the community. No one wanted to see them go, but everyone for sure pitched in to make sure their new home was built quickly and comfortably.

This home. The one I lived in now, with Alice and Meri. The Court gifted us all with amulets that allowed us to come and go through town as we pleased. I didn't delude myself thinking they did it out of the goodness of their hearts. I knew it was because it helped them keep an eye on me. Even though we lived outside of town limits, we were still just barely within the wards, and those wards would ripple at the sign of trouble. Well, I'd been here for sixteen years with nary a burp in the wards, so I didn't have a care. Living *just* inside the wards was tricky, though. If we weren't careful, we would gradually lose our memory of the place, the more time and distance from the wards passed. That didn't stop the sisters from settling down outside the town limits, though. It may have seemed immature, but I think the sisters knew one day I would need Havenwood Falls, even if they didn't. Besides, for all their anger on my behalf, Havenwood Falls was their home, as well. And it was where all their friends lived.

The amulets allowed us all to stay close, and as someone who had been saved quite literally from the noose, I would take what I could get. And what I had was a loving home. I would never do anything to jeopardize that, no matter what Rodavan Bishop said. I no longer worried over anything he may have said when I was a child, considering both he and his brother had since been banished from Havenwood Falls for using dark magic. My suppressed power was the least of anyone's worries these days.

I CHECKED the slim gold watch on my left wrist for probably the twentieth time in a matter of as many minutes. He was going to show up soon, and I still hadn't selected the right outfit. I picked at the pile of clothes on my bed in frustration. It wasn't that I had a lot to choose from, and I never paid much attention to the fashions in the first place, but . . .

My chest.

I had to admit it was a nightmare to choose a nice outfit because of my large chest. Both Alice and Meri told me to stop whining whenever I complained about my ample bosom, but they didn't have to pray for their buttons to hold, or press their forearms across their chests when running up and down the stairs to keep them from bouncing painfully. If I dared say anything, they would just tell me I shouldn't be running up and down the stairs.

The current fashion trends were shorter hemlines and loose cuts. Well, that didn't work for me because I was short of stature, so everything was long until Meri altered it for me. I couldn't sew a stitch. I could, however, get my motorcycle started in subzero winter mountain weather, so I tried not to let myself get too down about my lack of mending skills. And loose cuts? Sure, those worked if you were flat as an ironing board—which I was not.

I settled on a navy blue sleeveless cotton dress with a drop waist and a skirt that fell to just below my knees. I paired it with a peach cardigan that barely managed to stay buttoned if I left the top two undone. I rolled my shoulders after I put it on, just to test the strength of that third button, and it stretched at the hole a bit but held. I topped it off with a pair of nude Mary Janes and gave a twirl in the mirror. Perfectly presentable, if a little boring.

As much as I said I never cared much for fashions, I'd never been on a real date before Jonas, and the last one I went on was a disaster. It was a little embarrassing, but I just hadn't had an interest in any of the other young men in town. Not since I'd first laid eyes on Jonas Pederson when I'd started making regular deliveries six years ago. We'd never even spoken to each other until a year after that. I'd about given up hoping he would make a move other than to order lunch every day, especially with the throng of hopeful ladies all but throwing themselves at him every chance they had. Now not only had he asked me out once, but he was enamored enough he pursued me again, even after I tried so studiously to cut ties with him. After all that effort on his part, I wanted to look nice for him.

At the bottom of the stairs, I met Alice, who waited until I descended all the way before pressing something small and metallic into the palm of my hand. I should have known by the wicked gleam in her eye she was up to something. Turning my hand palm out, I found a shiny new penny.

"What's this for?"

Alice smiled with delight. "It's a good luck charm, River. Special magic for you if you're going to be seeing Jonas on a regular basis."

"Magic?" I'd seen the sisters do some amazing things, but a penny? That was new to me.

"Yes. You simply take the penny and place it between your knees when you're out with a handsome man . . ."

"Then what?" I still didn't understand.

"Nothing—you leave it there. As long as that penny is held up by your knees, there is no way for a handsome devil to make his way between them."

And then she opened her mouth and laughed. Side-splitting laughter spilled from her while I stood on the bottom step, holding a penny in my hand, and realizing that I, River McNee, a girl who had almost lit up like a candle the man who'd given her her first kiss, had just been the butt of a sex joke told by an old lady. Red-faced and shaken, I didn't even have time to think of a suitable response before the knock on the door commanded all of our attention.

CHAPTER 7

JONAS

I'd been given my second chance. I'd braved the sisters, left with my dignity intact, and gotten some precious alone time with River, only to come across another obstacle as soon as we were seated at Napoli's Ristorante Italiano. An obstacle sitting so close behind me, I could feel him staring through the back of my head.

Gabriel Doyle. *Yay.*

I don't know how I missed him when we walked in, but somewhere between the charcuterie board and the Tuscan rabbit stew, I glimpsed him, slightly to the left and behind me at a private table in a dimly lit corner. Watching us.

Not that I didn't care much for Gabriel. He'd helped me out a time or two, and I maybe owed him a few favors, but he took a special interest in River McNee. Now we were occupying the same space at the same time, and there was no way he would leave us alone. That was my fault.

I'd gone to him for help, a little information, against my better judgment after River dropped me like a hot rock. Everyone who's anyone knew better than to get under Gabriel Doyle's thumb, but I was confused and desperate at the time. And no one knew how to get unobtainable information better than Gabriel and the Lilith

Nest, unless you counted Roman Bishop, and I wasn't about to ask that guy for a hand crawling out of hell. There were jackasses, and there were *irredeemable* jackasses.

Gabriel Doyle was just the regular kind.

I hadn't known River's history with the Court when she came to Havenwood Falls, but after meeting with Gabriel, I knew a lot more. Things I shouldn't know unless she told me. Things she would be upset to know I found out from Gabriel Doyle, dammit. All I wanted to do was court my lady, but the back of my neck was crawling with the stare of a bored rich vampire with lots of power and a need to meddle in the affairs of others. There was no way he would leave us alone.

I was right.

Even if I couldn't feel him approach, I could see the fear in River's eyes as he walked up and stopped directly in front of our little table off to the side of the kitchen. Her gaze had gone from friendly to apprehensive to downright terrified as she took in his perfectly tailored suit, his dark slicked-back hair, and sardonically raised brow. It wasn't the way he was dressed that scared her. It was probably the fact he was a vampire, and a powerful one at that. He was also insufferably handsome, and I didn't want him anywhere near my River.

Go away, Gabriel! I hissed in my mind. His mouth quirked at the corner as if he could hear the thoughts running through my mind. That ass knew he was intruding, and he for certain did not care.

"It's rare I see you in town outside of your business hours, Miss McNee," he said smoothly, bending slightly at the waist as a courtesy. River was not impressed, and she tried to keep her face free from expression, but I witnessed the tightening around her eyes.

"I might not live within the town limits, Mr. Doyle," she said, "but I'm sure you're well aware I have leave to come and go as I please."

"Can we help you with something, Gabriel?" I cut in. I didn't know why he was pressing River, but I wouldn't let him harass her, especially in front of me. Gabriel smiled a predatory smile that made his cold blue eyes turn up at the corners. That idiot was having fun.

"I was simply saying hello. I haven't seen River much in the last few years and wanted to inquire about the sisters. Are they in good health? You know we would love for them to come back and live in town again."

"The sisters are fine, but I'll extend your regards. Although I find your concern about them strange. Why do you care?"

I knew River's history and how it pertained to the sisters, having been informed by Gabriel previously, but I wisely kept it from showing on my face. Gabriel was silent for a moment, almost pensive even.

"River, you weren't banned from living in Havenwood Falls, from what I understand," he said, his voice low, so as not to attract attention from other diners.

"No, but I wasn't welcomed either. You weren't there, Gabriel, but you act awfully well informed. The Court thought to label me as a threat."

"But they didn't."

"Only because the sisters decided for everyone. They uprooted their home and left it all behind to start new. For me." The atmosphere was frigid as River ground out the words from between clenched teeth. "They made that decision to protect me, no one else. So please don't make it sound like you have some interest in the affairs of the sisters or me. You are not a member of the Court. Nothing we do should matter to you whatsoever."

Gabriel looked amused by River's candor, but my chest swelled with pride at the steel in her spine. He may have been giving her a hard time, but she damn well was dishing it right back. I didn't think I had ever been more attracted to her than I was in that moment, her gaze fierce and unyielding, her chest heaving with emotion. My eyes flickered down a bit at the thought of the heaving, noticing the button, or as I fondly referred to it, "my button," was pulling at the threads of the fastening on her sweater. Averting my gaze so I wouldn't get in trouble for looking overly long at something I shouldn't, I found I wasn't the only one who found that button fascinating.

Anger, hot and quick, shot like a rifle through my blood, and the change happened so fast, I couldn't stop the thickening of my blood or the roughness of the voice that resembled stone grating against stone as I barked out one quick word.

"Gabriel." *You will not look at her.* I left the second part unsaid, but I infused every part of his name with my intent. *No. Mine. Avert your eyes.*

It was River's startled face that had me regaining my control. I absolutely could not, would not, let my other self burst forth inside Napoli's. Not if I wanted to keep the sheriff from jumping up my ass. Not if I wanted to stay in Havenwood Falls. More importantly, it wasn't the side of me I wanted to show River either.

"I apologize," Gabriel said, and he *almost* looked like he meant it. "I did not intend to foster any hostility; I merely wanted to extend my regards. I'll leave you to yourselves, but please accept my apologies again. I hope to see you around more often, River. I must say, when Jonas came to me *begging* for information about you, the strength of his feelings impressed me."

Always one to get the last word in—that was Gabriel. While River stared at me, open-mouthed at the bomb Gabriel had just dropped, he walked away from the table, straightening his jacket as he went, looking for all the world like he'd gotten exactly what he wanted.

"Don't give me that look, woman." I grabbed hold of the situation right out of the gate while her mouth opened and closed like a fish on dry land. "I told you I went a little crazy when you started avoiding me. I had my reasons, and they were honorable . . . as far as reasons go."

River clapped her mouth shut with a snap. "I wouldn't say going to Gabriel Doyle for information was crazy." She sighed irritably. "I would say it shows questionable judgment, but you aren't crazy." She was embarrassed; the pink tinge of her cheeks told me so.

"Look, River, Gabriel isn't a bad guy; he's just a bit of an ass is all. I've had other dealings with him in the past. He's done me a few favors, to be honest." I didn't tell her that those favors came at a steep price. There were some things a gentle lady didn't need to know. I'd said Gabriel wasn't a bad guy. And he wasn't, at least not to me. He wasn't necessarily a good guy either.

"Gabriel Doyle does what is good for Gabriel Doyle. It so happens, thus far, that it has all been parallel to what you consider acceptable. But I was quite enjoying our evening and our delicious dinner. I don't want to wreck it with more talk about that vampire. But I have to ask—and because it's painful for me, I ask you to be gentle in your judgments of me—what did he tell you?"

Because she was wringing her hands in agitation and for no other reason than I sought to comfort her, I took both of her small delicate fingers in mine. "You'll get no judgments from me, River McNee. I'll tell you everything I know, and if there is an untruth there, you can tell me. I simply wanted to know more about you, and was desperate to find a reason why you pushed me away. There was no other cause for my actions at all, but if I've hurt you by doing so, I'm sorry. I'm serious about you, and I thought we were making a connection. So when you cut me off, I was confused. I just wanted to know why."

It was the truth, and she could take it or leave it, but my heart was thumping in my chest so loudly, I was sure she could hear it. She wasn't looking at me, though, but at the way I held her hands in mine. She made no move to pull away, so I took it as a positive sign.

"Did he tell you what I did? What I am? I wonder how he knows." She whispered the words into the checkered tablecloth.

"You mean, did he tell me how you almost died when you were younger? About that horrible school and the mistreatment you withstood? Yes, he did. Or at least what he learned from his vast network connections." I didn't ask him how he got the information he did. I probably wouldn't like the answer.

"Did he give you that information for free?"

"Nothing is free, River, but he didn't ask for anything I wouldn't have given anyway." Gabriel Doyle never did something for nothing, but it wasn't anything she needed to worry about. "If you're thinking he fed from me, then I can tell you that didn't happen either. I don't make good vampire food." Not that I didn't taste good to vampires; it was that they literally couldn't feed from me. I was a Scandinavian stone man, and no matter how hard they tried, a vampire could not get blood from a stone. It was funny to watch them try, though.

River lifted her head and looked at me then, really looked at me, and maybe it was the candlelight, but her eyes looked blacker than their normal deep brown. She spoke, her lips quivering just slightly as she said, "Are you afraid of me too?"

It floored me. Was I afraid of her? What in the actual hell kind of question was that?

"The only thing I'm afraid of, River, is you telling me you don't feel the same things I do, and that you don't want to see me again. As far as your personality or the things you're capable of, I'll make my own character judgments, thank you. I'm enough of a man to tell my own mind. But just because you seem so worried about it, I'll tell you this—I'm not putting stock in a vision someone had more than sixteen years ago. There's truth in everything, but there is also room for interpretation. It doesn't look like anyone bothered to look too deeply into what Rodavan Bishop or Elsmed Fairchild saw when they tried to look into your future. They didn't see me there, did they? That can't be right, because I plan on being a large part of all of your tomorrows if you'll let me."

Please don't ask how I know all this right now, I pleaded silently. While most of us in Havenwood Falls with supernatural backgrounds generally knew of each other, we didn't run around proclaiming our sordid histories to each other, and unless a person could sense it on their own, we didn't go around announcing our magical heritage either. I'd never run around town yelling "I can shape-shift into a giant rock man," so River wouldn't know that about me. By rights, I shouldn't know a damn thing about her dealings, or her power.

But I couldn't plead my case, not after what I'd just said. That was about as smooth a line as ever had come out of my mouth, and I couldn't think of another word to say after that. It didn't matter, because I felt the squeeze of her fingers in mine, and I knew even if she said nothing in return, she heard me. She heard me just fine.

"I hate my power, Jonas." This time I wasn't imagining the sheen in her eyes, the tears that collected in the corners and threatened to fall. "And just so you know, I didn't push you away because I didn't want to see you again. My feelings for you . . . I . . ." She faltered on the words. "I can't control myself around you, Jonas. My body gets hot when you're close, and my insides go all a mess. The pressure builds up to where I think I will explode with it, and I don't know about you, but me and the word explosion aren't a good omen. While I want to be with you all the time, I think . . . I think I might be allergic to you? Or something like that. I've spent my whole life suppressing those flames and for me to not be able to control them around you— Well, I never want to hurt you. I don't want to hurt anyone, never again, but I wouldn't be able to live with myself if I hurt you."

I sat there dumbfounded while she told me that my nearness caused her to lose control over her body, and I tried very hard not to lose control of my own. Lustful thoughts be damned but she was serious. She thought there was something wrong with her. How innocent was River? I knew the sisters had raised her, but surely she knew something of what went on between a woman and a man? Allergies weren't her problem. Dealing with her desire was.

But I couldn't tell her that. At least, not right this moment. I could only continue holding her warm hands in mine and try to think of something to say to make her feel better.

"You can't be allergic to me, River. It's not possible," I said as I thought about my people and our predisposition to becoming men made of solid rock. "I'm a stone man. I'll not make you sneeze."

I don't know if she thought I was crazy or lying or both, but I was still grateful for the laughter that burst from her throat, and the tears that ran down her cheeks were of mirth, of that much I was certain. She kept laughing while I paid the bill and was still chuckling to herself as I held her sweater over my arm and walked out of the restaurant with her. The night air was warm, at least for those of us used to the mountain summer nights, and the street was deserted. I was feeling good about the evening until we rounded the side of the strip of buildings and took a turn around the back. The lighting was poor on this end of the street, and River stumbled over a loose sidewalk slate.

Fearing she would turn her ankle, I caught her as she fell and propped her up against the bricks behind her, focusing only on keeping her from injury.

I swear to the gods that's what I was thinking.

Until I stumbled myself, and instead of catching my body with the brick wall next to me, I found myself pressed chest to chest with one incredibly soft River McNee, her arms reaching around my back to keep me from knocking her to the ground.

There wasn't self-control on this earth to keep the groan from leaving my body.

I should have released her. I should have. But there was something about the warmth of her soft curves against the hard—and getting harder—planes of my own body that held me immobile. I couldn't let her go. Instead, I threw caution to the wind and buried my head in the crook of her neck, inhaling the scent that was uniquely River. Leaves on the wind, a campfire on a fall day, bliss. I felt her hands tighten against my back, an almost imperceptible grasping of her fingers into my flesh through the layer of my cotton shirt.

"River." I groaned again at the effort my words were costing me. "I want to kiss you right now."

"We shouldn't," she whispered, and I felt the skin of her throat move against my lips as I nuzzled my face even deeper into her hair. She shivered, and the vibration ran through my entire body. I could not move away on my own.

"I'll need you to be more firm, then, because I don't know that I'm strong enough to let you go at the moment. After all, anyone can see us." I didn't give a damn if the whole town was watching.

"There's no one here at all," she mused, her lips curving up into a smile. She wasn't helping matters at all, not with her feet lifting up on her toes so she could press even closer to me, the heat of our bodies becoming a tangible force.

"River, that isn't a no." And this time I couldn't stop myself from tasting her, from laying my lips against the skin of her neck then upwards across her chin. Just little nibbles. Not too much. Surely she would push me away any moment, and I would have to apologize. Beg forgiveness for the liberties I was currently taking.

But she didn't push.

She pulled.

Pulled me in just a little bit closer as she rose on her tiptoes, and as I raised my head again, it was her hot mouth that captured mine. And even if it was my tongue that swept inside her mouth, she opened it all of her own volition. River McNee wanted me, and her desire was scorching hot. Gods help me, I wanted it to burn me up.

One hand crept up to her breast and squeezed, filling with the flesh I had only dreamed about for the last however long. Probably as long as I'd known her, who knew? She moaned into my mouth and wriggled against me, trying to push herself more fully into my grasp. We were both gone, so lost in each other that neither of us heard the spark or smelled the smoke. Neither of us noticed the flames until they traveled from River's arms and arced between us. I felt the heat through my shirt and down to my skin, and it was only then I smelled the acrid scent of burning cloth.

My shirt was on fire. With a startled shriek that pierced the silence of the night, she pushed me away and stood there, horrified as the flames licked her skin, sputtered and went out. As quickly as they had appeared, they were extinguished, and so was our moment. My body mourned the warmth of hers, but she wasn't the only one who'd had an unwanted reaction. One look at my right arm had me swiftly hiding it behind my back lest she see how my body had reacted to the flames.

While she stared at the ground, unable to meet my eyes, I flexed my fingers into a fist, out of sight, and willed my arm to return to normal. I willed the stone to become blood and bone again, to recede from the granite gray to the normal tones of the flesh. I wasn't ready for River to see that side of me yet, and she was already worked up as it was.

"I hurt you. I hurt you. I'm so sorry, Jonas. I swore I'd never . . . and I did. I didn't mean to, but it happened regardless. I don't . . . I can't . . ." She hadn't hurt me, not really. My body naturally reacted to preserve itself, so her flames did nothing more than scorch my shirt—but there would be no telling her that now. She was working herself up into a frenzy of guilt.

"River," I said, trying to choose my words carefully to keep her calm. "It's fine. I'm not hurt—look." And I waved my now normal arms in front of her, thankful that I had stopped the change in time.

"Jonas, you don't understand. I caught you on fire just because you kissed me. I lost myself. I had no control. Can you imagine if something more were to happen between us? You don't understand —this is exactly what Rodavan meant when he saw my future. Flames. Chaos. Destruction. If we continue to see each other, I'll burn you up. I never want do that to you. I'd rather never see you again than hurt you."

I opened my mouth to argue, but the tears running down her cheeks were enough to close it again. She was distraught. Anything I had to say to her then would fall on deaf ears.

"Jonas, please take me home."

And I did. The ride out of town was silent, marked only by the rattling of my Model T truck, the one I had serviced recently but still sounded like it would blow apart at any minute. She didn't say a word as she left the vehicle and went into the white house with the darkened windows. It didn't look like anyone was waiting up for her, but then again, I wouldn't put anything past the Sisters McNee. It was up to River what story she would tell them, but I knew one thing—there had to be a way to fix this thing with River.

It seemed her flames were attached to her emotions. The stronger the emotions she was feeling, the more out of control the flames. I smiled to myself as I maneuvered the truck back onto the road and started the long drive back to town. She was forgetting one thing. Yeah, she had a problem all right, but this was Havenwood Falls. We were all a little different, a little strange. There were many supernatural issues and ways to solve them. If she thought avoiding me was her best option, then River McNee had another think coming.

She wasn't doing this alone. Not anymore. Never again. I'd sell my soul to the devil if it meant keeping River.

CHAPTER 8

RIVER

*U*nbelievable. Not only was no one waiting up for me when Jonas dropped me off at home, for which I should have been grateful, neither of the aunts asked me for any details of the evening when we all got up for breakfast the next morning.

"Can't talk now, the pears are ready for picking today," Meri had cheerfully called as she'd walked out of the kitchen with no other explanation. Alice said nothing, just looked at me sadly and followed her sister out the back door, leaving me to wonder just how much those banshee sisters knew and the extent of their powers. Regardless, they left me alone, with no words of wisdom to lift the cloud of gloom over my head.

And then Monday came, and Jonas wasn't at the mine for lunch either. Not that I wanted to see him. Actually, it was the opposite—I wanted to avoid running into him, but still. It struck me in the heart to not see him lining up like the rest of the men to pick up lunch. I was out of sorts for sure, but I knew I made the right choice. I wish I felt better about it, especially since I could still taste Jonas Pederson on my lips every time I had the misfortune of thinking about it. Which was too often.

"Um . . . River? Can I have my lunch now?"

Two blinks. That's what it took to tear my thoughts away from a certain blond-haired blue-eyed giant who seemed to occupy the air I breathed even when he wasn't around. I came here every day with lunch orders for busy mine workers who either didn't have a knack for cooking to pack their lunches, or those that could but just had a taste for having me do it for them. It was easy money for me. Every day, I packed the orders from the day before and included a thick slice of whatever delicious confection Alice and Meri had ready, filled the side cart of my motorbike, and set off into town. I brought home orders and restaurant orders as well— but hitting the mine at noon bell was by far the most lucrative for me. And right now in front of me, one such hungry miner was standing, hand out in expectation.

"I am so sorry, Ian," I exclaimed, grabbing the brown paper sack with his name on it and handing it off with a sloppy grin. "I'm so distracted today. I don't know what came over me." I slipped the coins from his hand into the leather satchel I kept slung around my shoulder, listening with satisfaction as they clinked against the pile of coins already gathering at the bottom.

"Not too distracted to take my money though, I see," Ian grumbled, his dark facial hair doing nothing to hide the grin playing along the corners of his mouth.

"Well, if I ever get that distracted, Ian, might as well put me in a hole in the ground."

I liked Ian. He was only a little older than me and a normal human. One of many that populated Havenwood Falls, but Ian was a little more aware of the rest of us than most of the people who lived in town. Funny thing was, he never made a stink about it. Ian had been to see the sisters before and took their "otherness" in stride. None of us were any different from anyone else to Ian. I wish I had the luxury of being so blissfully ignorant.

"If you're looking for Jonas, he's not here today. Something came up."

I could imagine that something was me, and his need to avoid me after I set him on fire just a few days prior, but I couldn't say that to Ian.

"I'm not looking for him. I don't know why you would think that," I murmured under my breath. I'd meant it to come out louder, but my lungs froze up on the lie.

"Yeah, okay, River," Ian mumbled, opening the brown bag and tearing the wax paper away before ripping off a bite of roast beef sandwich and chewing. "You two are so weird, you deserve each other. God, this is good." He continued to chew, leaning against the side of my cart without a care in the world. Or apparently a place to be, as he seemed in no hurry to leave me be. "I don't know your story, but that guy has it bad for you. And you run him ragged, making him chase your skirts day after day. You're a real nice girl, River, but if you can't be serious about Jonas, then you need to cut him loose. It isn't right."

Cut him loose? My chest squeezed at the thought. Even though the advice was solid, I deserved it, and it was what I was trying to do, it still hurt to hear it.

"What do you know about Jonas?" I asked Ian, wondering just how much he knew about the man who had just hinted at his otherness before, but never quite come out with the specifics until recently.

"I know enough to tell you that's something you should discuss with him, and not with me." Ian winked before shoving his face full of food again. "What do *you* know about him?"

Thinking back to our conversation from the night before, I spoke. Ian may have been friends with Jonas, but I didn't know how much he knew. Some things were private.

"Well, I know he doesn't have an animal." Doesn't *have* an animal was polite speech for he doesn't *turn into* an animal. You know, because some people did.

"Why do you think that?" Ian had swallowed his food and now regarded me thoughtfully.

"Because he said I couldn't be allergic to him, because he was hypoallergenic." I was only being half serious, but I still didn't expect the belly laugh that exploded out of Ian with a force great enough for him to drop his sandwich on the ground. The laughter cut off as he realized what he'd done, and staring mournfully at the food in the dirt, he sighed.

"River, that was your fault. You made me laugh, and look." He pointed sadly at the ground.

"Here, take this. It was Jonas's anyway."

He smiled as he took the extra bag lunch from me. "Thanks, River, you're an okay girl. Try not to be too hard on Jonas, all right? He's my friend, and a good man. He deserves better than the runaround."

I didn't have time to answer him because he had turned and walked away, across the grassy field, his hand already digging another sandwich out of the brown paper bag. It wouldn't have mattered if he'd stayed; I had no good answer to give him. Ian may have had knowledge of what was going on in this town, but that didn't mean he was equipped to handle my type of baggage.

Ian was it. He was the last in line, and no matter how I strained my eyes and neck looking, Jonas was gone. It was fine. It was better that way, but I would be a liar if I said it didn't hurt. A lot. That was probably the reason that, instead of turning around and going down the long winding road back home, I kept riding my motorcycle toward town. Maybe it was that melancholy ache in my chest, the wanting of things I couldn't have, that had me stopping outside of the elementary school.

There was nothing wrong with it as far as schools go, but since I didn't live in town, I didn't have the option to attend. I missed nothing growing up, because the sisters saw to my education well enough, and even took my reading, writing, and arithmetic skills above and beyond what a young woman like myself might have learned. If I hadn't been so adamant about not using my powers ever again, I might have ended up at the Academy, but there was no reason for me to go if I didn't need to learn. Besides, no one else knew what I was, anyway. Still, I parked my bike outside of the schoolyard and sat there for a little while, caught up in the wistful wonderings of what might have been had I been born a normal child. This was Havenwood Falls.

If I'd been born a normal child, I'd never have even seen this place.

It must have been the same whim that sent me in the school's direction in the first place that caused me to notice the figures leaving the school yard. It was otherwise empty—there was no reason for anyone to be in the place at all, considering it was July, and the primary term ran from September to May. There were neither children nor teachers required to be on property, so what were those two figures doing, wearing formal clothing and walking away from the school as if they had business there?

It didn't concern me. I shouldn't have paid any attention, but there was something about the bowler hat the older man wore that prodded a memory I had kept buried for a long time. And even something about the younger man with him, something about the sun-burnished color of his skin, and his features, which even from far away seemed so similar to mine and so oddly out of place in this hidden town in the Colorado mountains. There were other native people here, but even from a distance, they looked so *familiar*. But how could they? I didn't know them.

But I did. And it wasn't until they came closer to the place where I stood, frozen next to my motorbike, that I realized why I shouldn't have come here. The mustached face. The bowler hat. The mustache had more gray in it than brown anymore, and his once large frame had shrunken considerably, but I knew the name that went with the face I now recognized.

Hank Weisman. The man that lamented my fate as he left me bound in a shed to await my punishment. And the younger man next to him, with skin like mine and the features of a people I'd almost forgotten my connection to, was Wesa. Now he was fully grown into a man with a thin jagged scar on his chin—but still Wesa.

They pulled up short when they reached the spot where I stood. Mr. Weisman reached a hand up to tip his hat in polite greeting, and I almost thought I could get away with a smile without being recognized, but I couldn't be that lucky. His hand froze on the brim of his hat, Wesa's brown eyes widened, and both men gasped their surprise.

"Mary? It isn't you. It can't be you."

Rooted to the spot, my breath froze in my lungs. This wasn't good. They shouldn't be here. They had no reason to be here.

"I'm sorry." I tried to be polite yet distant, all while throwing my leg over my bike seat and cursing myself for wearing such a long skirt that made maneuvering difficult. Trousers would be more practical. "I'm not who you think I am. My name isn't Mary."

"River," Wesa finally spoke. His voice, no longer that of an angry little boy, carried with it the deep timbre of a man. "River, it's you. There's no one in this world with hair like that, and you still wear it in the same braids you did when we were kids. Dark black with ribbons of red and orange flowing through it. It's you— but how? You died. They said you died."

I knew who "they" were. The Cranes. Those nasty evil people who tried to take my life from me.

"I'm sorry. I'm not her. Now, if you'll excuse me, I need to be going."

Keep calm, keep calm. The words ran on a loop in my mind. Nothing good would come from this, I was sure. These people shouldn't be here in Havenwood Falls. Thinking about how close they had come to the sisters made my skin clammy and my stomach heave. They had to have ridden right past my house to even get here. I swung my leg over the side of the bike and had almost got it started before I heard the sobbing behind me.

"It *is* you. Mary. I'm so happy . . . so happy to see you." Mr. Weisman crumpled a little, his shoulders shaking and his gnarled hands reaching for my own. Frozen with shock, I could only let him do it, feeling his bony fingers curl around mine and squeeze. "I've always regretted . . . I mourned you . . . I've regretted every day the part I played. To see you alive again, I'm so joyous, Mary." I didn't know where this breakdown came from, but it was obvious I would not bluff my way out of this one. And there was something so heartbreaking about watching an old man fall over himself to apologize. There was one thing to get straight before we continued with the conversation.

"My name isn't Mary. It never was. My name is River McNee."

$\sim$

IT TURNED out that the reason those two were in Havenwood Falls, and at the school no less, was because Wesa was a teacher and the two of them had traveled to Havenwood Falls in response to a "Colorado call for educators." Apparently, there was a shortage of people who wanted to shape young minds. Who knew?

I couldn't believe it. Little Wesa all grown up and teaching primary school. Shortly after I had "died," things had taken a turn for the dangerous at the Carlisle school. Government regulations were becoming stricter against teachers and their treatment of the native students. There was reform in the works, but even so, it would take more than a few regulations to make Carlisle an upstanding school. At least in my mind.

As we sat in the grass at the edge of the empty schoolyard, Mr. Weisman explained what had happened in the years since I'd been gone, with Wesa filling in the details when Mr. Weisman, whether from old age memory failure or just overwhelming emotion, couldn't continue. Wesa—Mr. Weisman still called him Thomas—explained that both Mr. and Mrs. Crane had met with terrible ends. Mrs. Crane had died in a kitchen accident, and Mr. Crane had shot himself in mourning.

Wesa's voice had gone flat when talking about the Cranes, but I could imagine there was no love lost there. Mr. Crane was the one who had beaten a young Wesa all those years ago, right in front of me. *That scar on his chin is probably from that incident*, I supposed. Thinking of the Cranes made my neck itch; I could still feel the rough fibers of the noose as they tightened it around my neck like a leash. Horrible people. I couldn't scrounge up even a flash of sympathy for them.

Wheezing and coughing interrupted my negative thoughts, and I looked at Mr. Weisman, startled, noticing not for the first time how ancient and worn out he looked. Nothing like the large imposing instructor he'd been when I was a child. *Time changes everything, I suppose.*

"We just stopped by to look at the school today," Wesa murmured as he patted Mr. Weisman on the back, rubbing his hand in soothing circles as the coughing subsided. "I have an interview in two days, and we were just taking a quick look. We weren't prepared to stay outside for long, and I think he might be adjusting poorly to the mountain air."

I didn't doubt he was having difficulty breathing. For people who had spent little time in the mountains, adapting to the thinner air could be difficult. And given his age, and considering a possible compromised immune system, it would be a lot for anyone to adjust to.

"You should probably let him take a rest, Wesa," I mentioned, still feeling oddly detached from both people who had been so closely connected to my past. "Where are you staying?"

Wesa looked over his shoulder in the direction of the town's square. "We're staying at Whisper Falls Inn at the moment. If the teaching position is offered to me, then we'll look for more permanent housing, but for now the inn it is."

I nodded; that made sense. There was no reason for me to stick around either, but Wesa's eyes were speaking to me without words, so I paused before saying goodbye.

"River, you keep calling me Wesa, but you should know I go by Thomas now. I have since I was young."

"I'm sorry. I didn't mean to offend you," I stammered, embarrassed because I assumed that like me, he didn't want to be called by the name that Carlisle had forced on him. I guess it didn't occur to me that after all he went through as a child, he would want to carry anything with him from that place, least of all his identifier.

"No, it's all right," he said as he helped Mr. Weisman to his feet. "I wanted you to know, especially if we will be staying in Havenwood Falls. I kept the name Thomas because it's more professional. People are more apt to hire a teacher named Thomas Weisman than they are a Cherokee man named Wesa."

I flinched inwardly. Living so long near Havenwood Falls had been both a blessing and a curse. I'd almost forgotten about how the rest of the world operated. We didn't have as much of that prejudice around here. After all, Havenwood Falls was where the *really* different folk gathered. Hopefully neither Wesa nor Mr. Weisman would ever find out just how different. It also didn't escape my notice that Wesa, or Thomas as he preferred, now carried Mr. Weisman's last name as well. Just what kind of relationship did they have? Had Mr. Weisman adopted him?

"River, I'd like to see you again, if I could." Thomas caught my attention again with that statement. He'd been glad to see me, sure, but the look in his eyes was like something I'd seen before in how Jonas had looked at me, and I wasn't sure how to respond to it. I recognized that male interest, but I couldn't return it. Not when my heart was still shattered over what I had almost done to Jonas. "There's just so much I want to know about how you came to be here. How have you lived? Who took care of you?"

I couldn't tell him any of those things, especially not the truth. Because no matter the history I had with Thomas and with Mr. Weisman, they could never know how I came to be here. That would require breaking all of the rules I had been bound by. I might not live inside the limits of Havenwood Falls, but the wards still protected me, and the sisters as well. I loved this town, and I didn't want to ruin any part of it by breaking the rules. I would have to tell them something, though. Thomas would need an answer, and I needed time to come up with something suitable.

"I've some time in the morning tomorrow." I hesitated on the words. I wasn't so sure I wanted to talk to the sisters about this yet. They would find out soon enough, but I didn't want them to worry if I told them someone from my Carlisle past had shown up in Havenwood Falls. They might feel compelled to interfere. I didn't want them to have the burden of that kind of worry. I could handle this, I was sure. "I have my deliveries to make in the afternoon, but I can spare some time to meet, if you'd like."

Wesa liked that idea. He offered to meet me at my home, but that was a little too personal for me. The thought of him meeting the sisters made me uncomfortable, so I offered to meet him in town instead. As I watched him help Mr. Weisman into a car and drive in the inn's direction, I could only marvel at how very different both men were from my memories. Was Mr. Weisman really just a doddering old man after all this time? And Thomas? Just what kind of man had he become?

CHAPTER 9

JONAS

t wasn't that I hated owing Gabriel Doyle a favor, although that brought its own complications to the table. I just didn't know he would call it in so soon, and that it would require me to be away from the mine and, in that vein, away from River, just when I needed to be right in her face. Because that was the only way to handle her—catch her attention before she had time to get lost in her own head and overthink.

I had no intention of giving River her space. I had every intention of going to work and showing up last in her lunch line, showing her I would always be there, that she couldn't scare me away. Instead, I was spending the day playing the sidekick for Gabriel because he needed someone to deliver black-market goods. Not what I thought I'd be hauling with my truck when I built the custom covered wagon bed two years ago.

"Does it bother you I asked you to do something outside the law like this?" he asked me after I finished the last run and stopped at his office to confirm the details and deliver the money I'd collected. The question surprised me. Not the question itself, but that Gabriel had thought enough to ask it.

"Not especially," I replied. "There are things you might have asked me to do that I would have refused as reprehensible. To be honest, delivering questionable cargo is probably low on the spectrum of dangerous errands you could have had me running." I rolled my shoulders to get the stiffness of being cramped up in the cab of my truck all day out of my body. "You gave me information, and I owed you a favor. I'm a man of my word."

"As am I," Gabriel said as he counted the money I had given him, along with the list of clients I had visited that day, and wrote everything down in a leather-bound ledger on the desk in front of him. I had no idea what was in the cases and packages I delivered today, and I had zero interest in finding out. The less I knew, the better when it came to the Lilith Nest.

"If we're finished, then I'll take my leave." I'd been gone all day and had already missed River, but that didn't mean I wanted to hang around all evening, too. Conversation with Gabriel was awkward and exhausting.

"Just a moment." Gabriel looked up from his figures, counted out a sum of money, and handed it to me. I took it without thinking, but my surprise must have shown on my face. "The requirement was doing the job for me today. I needed you to do it; I didn't need you to do it for free."

"Are you a good guy in disguise, Gabriel?" I pocketed the money. I had expected that the favor was doing his running for free, but I would not turn down cash I had earned, no matter who offered it.

"I don't labor under those types of notions, Jonas. I'm a businessman, nothing more and nothing less. I also might feel a little guilty about ruining your evening last night. I didn't intend to start a fight, and I get the distinct feeling your Miss McNee doesn't like me."

Well, that was news. "I highly doubt you feel any definition of bad over your behavior last night. And I don't think it's a dislike as much as fear. You're a vampire, Gabriel. That's scary, you know? Plus you know much more about her situation than anyone not on the Court should. She already hates her powers, and finding out that other people know about them is probably disconcerting."

"True," Gabriel admitted. "But I like being scary. Fear is a marvelous motivator. And I find River and her power very interesting indeed. Such a pity she isn't using it to her full potential."

"Why are you so interested in River?" I wasn't afraid of Gabriel, but I didn't want him focusing on my girl, either. Viktor may have been the head of the Lilith nest of vampires, but when he was away, Gabriel was number one, and he had an entire army of vampire underlings at his disposal. They weren't a threat to me. The same couldn't be said of River.

"Flames. Chaos. Destruction. The vision Rodavan had was of River killing herself with her own fire. The entire scene was nothing but River in agony, voices screaming, and the crackling of the all-encompassing flames. Tell me, what isn't fascinating about that? A beautiful woman wielding a terrible power—it's an intoxicating thought."

"You're a pervert, and we aren't talking about River now. We're talking about what happened when she was a child," I admonished.

Gabriel tugged at the sleeves of his perfectly pressed white shirt, the only indication he was becoming irritated with my questioning. Gabriel didn't like being questioned. Gabriel was the type of man used to being obeyed, not challenged. I didn't give a damn.

"From what I can tell, the Court had nothing to do with River being raised outside of town at all; that was all the McNees getting wound up at the way Rodavan treated them when they brought River to Havenwood Falls. Not that I blame them. I can't stand the Bishops. The best the Court could do was allowing the sisters to raise her, not within the town itself, but still within the protection of the wards."

"You mean still within the wards so they could keep an eye on her, right?" I was seeing how things had unfolded. I'd always wondered why the Court would order someone outside of the town but still inside the wards. It didn't seem like something they would do. In Havenwood Falls, either you were in or you were so far out you didn't remember the town existed.

"Who knows what they were thinking?" Gabriel said, as he moved along the office wall and studied the books that lined it on the right side. "But I'm not on the Court, not that I give a damn what they do, and I'm not the one who made those decisions. She doesn't live inside Havenwood Falls, and she has no reason to, unless you plan on giving her one?"

Some feral part of me growled in irritation. Not so much because Gabriel suggested it, more so because it reminded me of how the evening had turned out. "Not likely, at least not anytime soon. Not that it isn't my end game. I had a setback."

I didn't know why I was even discussing this with him. This was the longest exchange of words I'd ever had with the man, and I was sure he had some ulterior motive for even talking to me. There was always an ulterior motive.

"Yes, your smoke show in the alley. What a pitiful display."

He had to be joking. He saw the whole thing? Was he spying on us?

"I didn't know voyeurism was your thing, Gabriel."

"I was observing, Jonas. Trust me, I'm not a Peeping Tom, and even if I was, my interests run more exotic than sneaking around in alleys at night. I'm curious about River's powers and the extent she goes through to repress them. I wasn't aware that you would be groping each other the minute you thought you were alone." Gabriel paused and laughed under his breath—a deep, knowing chuckle that raised the hair on the back of my neck. Repressing the urge to punch him in the face was becoming more and more difficult, but I needed Gabriel, and he knew it. "She lit you on fire, Jonas. I think that's concerning for your future, don't you think?"

"You think this is funny, Gabriel? Because I don't. This is frustrating, and I want to help her, but she keeps pushing me away."

"Well, someone had better help her." Gabriel was all business again. "The vision that the Court had—it still stands."

"And?" I prodded, irritated that he was drawing this out. I also wondered how he had come by this information. The Court was tight-lipped about anything that went on in their proceedings. Gabriel must have been a mind reader to glean that sort of information.

"And it was the same thing. Flames. Chaos. Destruction. River has hated and suppressed her power for so long. She's ignored it, tried to act like it isn't a part of her very being. What happens when you deny yourself, Jonas, your very soul? You poison yourself. She will destroy herself simply because she knows no better. What a waste." Gabriel shook his head as if he couldn't understand the folly of youth.

"How do you know all this? Why do you care?" It made little sense. I didn't like having Gabriel's focus on River. Not for any amount of time.

"Does it matter why I care? The point is she's dangerous. To herself and others. That is an undeniable fact. The Court saw it then, and you can deny it all you want, but you are seeing it too. Hell, even River knows. Why do you think she keeps pushing you away?" Gabriel's tone was heated, his eyes a swirling storm of blue as he gave his passionate dialogue. He was more than likely right, but his timing was suspect. Why talk to me about this? Why now?

"Something will happen soon," he continued. Almost as if he had read my mind. I knew he couldn't, though. That wasn't his bread and butter. Old Man Elsmed was the one who could read thoughts.

"Old Man Elsmed isn't the only one. Some of us hold our cards a little closer to our chest."

That explained a lot, but at the same time, opened the door for a lot more questions.

"That's a nasty little secret to keep hidden, Gabriel." I held my breath and tried to keep my mind as blank as possible. With as many times as I had mentally punched him in the face, I didn't want to think about him knowing I had been imagining it.

He rolled his eyes in an uncharacteristic look of exasperation.

"Relax. It's not something I enjoy. It's a little curse I picked up during a scuffle in New Orleans a while back."

Gabriel was an immortal vampire; a while back could cover a lot of ground.

"A scuffle?" What the hell kind of scuffle ends in a curse?

"Let's just say the reason Viktor is gone right now and I'm here is because my presence in New Orleans would make his negotiations . . . difficult."

"You mean you aren't allowed back there?" I smirked, but he acted like he didn't see it.

"Do you think you have the luxury of time to pick apart my past? I've lived more lifetimes than you could dream of. Perhaps you should switch your focus back to your damsel and her imminent danger. Because she is, you know." Gabriel arched his perfect dark eyebrows and picked at an imaginary piece of lint on his sleeve. "In danger."

My blood turned to ice in my veins. "How do you know?"

"There are two new humans in town. No powers. But one of them . . . he's got a dark soul. Some real nasty thoughts, that one. And there's a connection to River, though they aren't here for her. I think if they run into each other, it could be bad."

"What kind of bad?"

"Flames. Chaos. Destruction."

"Why are you so damn cryptic all the time? Spell it out for me, dammit." One should know better than to cross swords or words with a vampire who had a short temper like Gabriel, and I was probably using up whatever good luck I had, but damn if he wasn't a frustrating man. "And for someone who just told me you don't read thoughts regularly, you are *frightfully* in the know about all kinds of urgent business."

Ignoring me as if my insult was beneath his notice, Gabriel pulled a book off the shelf. The cover was deep hunter green, and the binding was cracked and worn. It looked to be a well-used book, and I didn't believe he had just magically plucked it from its place by accident. He knew damn well what he had been looking for. Just like he enjoyed feeding me important information piece by agonizing piece, everything was a production to Gabriel Doyle. Everything was a dramatic power trip. He'd probably been waiting for this exact moment, to pull his prize out with a flourish. *Bastard.* I didn't even bother trying to hide the thought; I hoped he heard it.

Turns out, the book wasn't a book at all, but a hollowed-out box made to look like one. He opened the lid and paused. "Let me ask you this before I go any further," he said, his voice heavy with warning. "How far are you willing to go to save River McNee?"

I didn't question how he knew what he did. Nor did I think for even a minute he was offering me information out of the goodness of his heart. He was dangling the bait before me, his lips curved into the smile of a man who knew he had the hook embedded deeply enough, he could reel in as slow as he liked; there was no danger of losing the prize. He wanted to know how far I would go for River? He didn't even have to ask. If he read minds, then he already knew the answer.

I looked him dead in the eyes. "I'll go as far as it takes, and then I'll go ten steps farther. What's in the book?"

CHAPTER 10

RIVER

I'd made good on my promise to myself not to breathe a word to the sisters. I'd packed my side cart like I always did, and if I left for town several hours earlier than I normally would, no one thought anything was amiss. They probably thought I would spend more time with Jonas. They didn't know what happened between us. Hell, I didn't know if I could explain it to them if I wanted to. I was what happened between us. Me. I'd broken us before we could even be together. I wasn't fit for him. He deserved someone better. Someone stronger. Someone less *flammable.*

But I couldn't worry about that now. I had to deal with Wesa —*sorry*, Thomas—and Mr. Weisman being in Havenwood Falls. I had to convince them both that there was a normal explanation for how I came to be here. They couldn't know, or even question the normalcy of this town. If I told them about all of the supernatural creatures, or the magic of the falls themselves, that would be a one-way ticket to banishment. Even the Sisters McNee couldn't save me from that.

Per our agreement, I met Thomas in the same place we met the day before, and as I parked the motorbike next to the schoolyard, he came walking around the corner. I had to admit, he cut a fine figure in his brown britches and pale blue cotton shirt, sleeves rolled up to the elbows. He wore no hat, and I saw that he kept his dark hair short, as was the fashion these days. He smiled when he saw me, and it lit up his whole face. The jagged scar on his chin did nothing to take away from the handsomeness of his strong, angular features.

He's handsome, but he looks nothing like my Jonas.

Where that thought came from, I didn't know, but I had no business comparing the two men. It wasn't fair to either of them, and I had no intention of dallying with either. Thinking of him as *my* Jonas was part of how I got in bad shape to begin with. I looked behind Thomas, but didn't see a vehicle.

"Where's your car?" I also wondered where he had left Mr. Weisman.

"Hank has the car today. I don't need it. I walked here from the inn and left him to his own devices today. You can leave your motorcycle here if you like—I thought maybe we could go exploring? I did some walking about here yesterday afternoon and found a mountain path I'd like to check out."

Exploring? He wanted to hike? I hadn't expected that, and here I was, in another one of my long skirts and wearing a pair of soft-soled shoes, similar to slippers. He must have seen the look on my face, and looking to see where my gaze landed, he laughed.

"Still hate wearing hard-soled shoes, River? It's nice to see not everything about you has changed." He laughed again and offered me his arm. "Relax, River, I'm not asking you to forge a road through the thickening forest. I won't let you ruin your dress or your shoes. I want to walk with you, and have a private discussion while doing it. I would imagine the things we'll talk about are probably words you don't want others to overhear?"

He said it lightly, but I didn't miss the implication. He wouldn't be so easy to redirect with talks about two kindly old ladies who stumbled upon me in the forest and adopted me on the spot. Thomas wanted answers. The kind only I could give. He was right; privacy was our best option.

I had to admit the walk was nice, even if the path he found was more like a faded, hardened dirt line barely big enough for two people to walk across. The foliage had already taken over, and I imagined it was an old hunting trail we were treading on, unused for some time, if the state of the grass growing over it was any sign. But the conversation was pleasant, and Thomas was quick to grab my arm and hold me steady on the occasion I snagged my shoe on an errant root.

"I've lived in this area for the last sixteen years, and I've never been up this patch of mountain," I told Thomas, looking around nervously. I would hate for either of us to get lost, especially with him being a visitor, of all things.

"Don't worry, River. I walked this yesterday. There's a hunting cabin not far up ahead. I don't know that anyone's used it in a while, but it's clean enough. We can have our conversation there."

"That's a lot of prep work just for a conversation."

I hadn't meant it to sound like an accusation, but once the words were out, the implication was clear enough. Thomas stopped walking and put his hand on my arm, and I had no choice but to stop walking and face him. His eyes were dark and serious, and I couldn't handle the emotion swimming in their depths, so I focused on his chin instead.

"River. Hank Weisman is a tired old man now, but he wasn't always that way, and I'm not so old myself that I don't remember what happened in the schoolyard all those years ago. I *know* what I saw. And I know that in the years since, Hank told me all about the storeroom he locked you in and the plans the Cranes had for you. He might not have been there for it, but he knew what they would do, and the guilt of it has eaten away at his mind ever since. He also told me some things the Cranes were ranting about when they came back that night. They told everyone you ran away and died in the woods. They used you as a deterrent for any of the rest of us to get out of line. That what happened to you is what would happen to any of the other kids who thought of running away. Hank assumed they killed you. We now know that isn't the case, so I'd like to know what happened, and I imagine you want no one overhearing when you tell me."

He spoke with the authority of a man who was used to getting what he wanted; even though his earlier words had hinted at a depth of persecution I had blessedly been spared. I smiled and walked again. "You've become a man now, haven't you, Thomas?"

"Good of you to notice." He returned my smile, picking up the pace until he was walking ahead of me. "Just a few more moments, and we'll be there. I'll race you, if you think you can catch me."

"I can't and let's not," I said, laughing at his happy face. *Ah, Wesa . . . no matter what name you go by now, it's so good to see your smile.*

"I think I see why no one comes up to this place anymore," I whispered nervously as I took in the ramshackle outbuilding. While the walls seemed sturdy enough, the ground beneath it was another story. Whether from years of washout and erosion, or another reason I hadn't thought about, the ground to the side of the cabin plummeted, revealing a drop of fifty feet at least before angling down into the rocky plains below.

"Thomas, that cabin is two big bad wolf breaths away from being blown right down the side of this mountain."

"Nonsense. I was just in there yesterday. It's perfectly stable." Thomas smiled with a wicked glint in his eyes. "It would take four breaths at least before we slid to our doom."

"I'll stay outside of it, all the same." I couldn't help but smile with him. "We're far enough away from prying ears this far up, I would think, anyway." I found a fallen log, worn over on the ends from time and nature, and sat on it, smoothing my skirt down over my legs. Thomas took a seat on a large flat stone that sat high out of the ground nearby.

"Can you tell me your story, River? We suffered so much when you were gone. How did you get away?"

"Before I tell you, can I ask you how you came to be traveling with Mr. Weisman? It was a shock to see you after all these years . . . and together even. My last memory of him wasn't so pleasant, so I'm not sure of what kind of man he turned out to be that you would still be with him after all this time."

Thomas looked at me and smiled. "You know, it was only a school, not a prison." His head hung low, and his shirt strained against his shoulders as he rested his elbows on his knees. "Everyone got to go home to their parents when their schooling was through, but me? I couldn't do it. I was too different, too changed. I never went back."

I didn't understand. What did he mean, he never went back? I asked him as much.

"I mean, I never went home. The Cranes passed probably seven years after you left, and they brought in new teachers. I had learned everything they would teach me, and it came time to go home to my parents. I couldn't do it. Hank had mentioned taking a teaching position at another school—I don't know, I think the memories were terrible for him too, so he asked me if I wanted to go with him. Maybe he felt guilty for turning his back on all the nasty things the Cranes did to us kids. To me. To you. I don't know. But he adopted me, and I have his last name, and it's been the two of us ever since. Hank is too old and infirm to teach anymore, so our roles are reversed now. I do the teaching and take care of him. He's the one who found the advertisement for the teaching positions in Colorado and brought it to my attention. It's sheer coincidence that one of them happened to be in Havenwood Falls. This place is out in the middle of nowhere. I'm surprised we could find it at all. I would imagine the winters are difficult to navigate."

I would imagine the winter would be impossible for you to navigate, I thought to myself, keeping my face schooled and impassive. Havenwood Falls was secluded by design. The only people that made it to us were the people we wanted here. Even so, the serendipity of our situation still amazed me.

"You know, I was just a small boy when I saw you last, River," Thomas continued, his eyes dark and serious. "But I still remember like it was yesterday. I still see it in my dreams. I remember the air got hot, and the ground beneath me, too. I wanted to get up and run away, but I couldn't. I'm ashamed to say I was afraid. You were so angry, and your hair had pulled out of your braids somehow and was floating around your shoulders all wild and bright. You looked like a devil or a god, I couldn't tell which. Afterwards, they said it'd been a trick you did, something with kerosene, but I know the truth. When you opened your mouth and spit the fire . . . how did you do that?" Our eyes met while I considered how to answer him. Did I tell the truth or a half truth? How much of me would Thomas be able to handle?

"I don't know how I did it," I answered truthfully. "I was just so angry, I couldn't keep it inside anymore." I tugged on the end of my braid like I always did when I was thinking. "That's how it works mostly, anyway," I whispered almost to myself. "I stuff it down, deep inside. I don't think about it until I get emotional about something, and then . . ."

"And then what? Has something else happened?" Wesa's face was a mask of concern. He was so nice, this sweet boy from the past, to be concerned over me after all this time.

"Did you know the only ones of our people that knew about me were my parents? I had to keep it under wraps all this time. Do you think the elders would have been okay with me breathing fire like someone from the stories? No, I would have been put to death."

Wesa nodded. "That was our way."

I couldn't argue with him. That *was* our way. We told the stories of our ancestors, and we worshipped our gods, but people weren't born with power like I had. I would have been seen as a threat. And that wasn't limited to just my people. The men who took us to the Carlisle school and forced their beliefs down our throats? Those same people that called us savages and beseeched us to leave our witching ways, they were the same. It was also their way. And hadn't I the invisible marks around my neck to prove it? They couldn't be seen, but those marks would never fade for me.

"So you showed no one? Never?" Thomas looked like he didn't believe me, and I guess I understood that.

"Not since I showed my mother I could burn pretty pictures into the grass when I was young. The fear in my mother's eyes . . . it was awful. She made me promise never to do it again. I was never to show anyone, because terrible things would happen if I did. Then she and father both died. After that, the soldiers came and took us all away. So I was afraid. And I didn't do it again. Not until—"

"Not until you saw me being beaten in the schoolyard." Thomas finished the sentence for me solemnly.

"We were just children. Hungry children," I cried, tears forming in the corners of my eyes as I recalled the memory. "And he was smiling, Wesa. He was smiling as he beat you and your blood was all over his hands." I'd forgotten again to call him Thomas, but he didn't correct me.

"And you haven't used it since then?"

"Not on purpose." I didn't know any other way to answer that question. I'd thought I'd buried my flames until Jonas got me all stirred up inside. Emotional. He made me feel . . . things. I couldn't explain that to Thomas. Not something that personal.

"So how did you get away from the Cranes? The story they gave Hank was fantastic, although I would imagine by the time I was old enough to hear it, some minor details may have changed. They said something about an ungodly wailing . . ."

"I don't know what to tell you about that," I said, going the cautious route and telling as simple a tale as I could. "Mr. Crane was drunk, that much I know, and they tied the sloppiest noose in the world. They tied me up high to a rotten branch that broke under my weight almost immediately. They just got spooked by something and didn't bother to check to make sure they had actually killed me. They just assumed they'd done the job." It was a lie, but I wove as much of the truth in there as I could.

"What could have spooked those two so much that they would leave without checking that you were dead? It makes little sense.

How did you get out of the woods then? You were just a child, too." He was asking all of the good questions, but I'd already decided not to tell him anything that would jeopardize the sisters or Havenwood Falls.

Sorry, Thomas, I just can't.

"After I got the rope from around my neck, I ran as fast and as hard as I could in the complete opposite direction. I ran throughout the night until my legs wouldn't move anymore, and then when I thought I was just going to lie on the ground and die, I made it to a road. And passing by on that road were two women, traveling west. They took pity on me, and finding out I had no family, let me stay with them. After all of that traveling, I ended up here in the mountains, where I've been ever since. It's not that exciting a tale, once you get past the attempted murder and danger."

His eyes were as flat as the line of his mouth. "I don't buy that story. It's a little too far-fetched."

"As far-fetched as a girl who can breathe fire and escaped being executed?"

His stare was sharp now, almost a weapon, cutting through my defensive layers and trying to find the truth revealed within. "Mrs. Crane swore it was fairies."

Oh, God, she was pretty damn close.

"Fairies?" I laughed it off. "Now who's got a far-fetched story, Thomas?"

He said nothing in reply, so I continued on, emboldened by my determination to stick to my lie. "That's what happened, and you can take it or leave it. I mean, I don't know why I could use the flames, but it isn't anything I'm proud of. It isn't anything I enjoy. And I have never met anyone else able to do so, either. I'm a freak; even our own people would have thought so. There's no safe place for me if anyone finds out, you know? Look what happened with the Cranes."

"The Cranes were awful people."

I happened to share his sentiment.

"He was an evil drunk, she was a hysterical nutter, and I'm not sorry they're dead. I'm not sorry at all." The words flew out of my mouth in a frenzy. I meant them, even though I would probably be ashamed that I'd said such a thing later. It wasn't ladylike, and Alice and Meri had always taught me not to speak ill of the dead lest you bring their sorrows upon yourself. It had sounded like suspicious nonsense at the time, but one never could be too careful.

Thomas smiled then, a slow curving of his lips that spread up his face but just didn't quite seem to reach his eyes. The breeze blew down through the trees on our side of the mountain, and the wooden walls of the tiny cabin creaked on the unsteady foundation.

"I'm so happy to hear it, River. I'm so glad you feel that way." Thomas stood and walked toward me, stopping when our knees were almost touching, and he grabbed both of my hands in his. "I'm overjoyed right now. I'm so happy, I think I want to tell you my secret. Since you know. Since you hated them, too. They hurt you so much, just like me." Then he laughed, and it wasn't a nice laugh. It was high pitched and nasal, like it traveled through his nose instead of his throat. The jagged scar on his chin shone white against his burnished skin, and his lips stretched too wide when he grinned. "It makes me so glad I killed them."

CHAPTER 11

JONAS

*S*he wasn't there.

It wasn't like River to not show up to the mine for lunch—especially when there were orders to fill. In the last few years since she'd been catering to laborers, she had never not shown up. I could count on one hand the amount of times she'd been sick with a cold or some other ailment, and had one of the sisters' friends in town take over for the day, but that was it. Today she was a complete no-show.

The hungry men who'd climbed the grassy hill like they did every day stood in line, questioning looks on their faces. Where in the hell was River?

"I don't understand," Ian mumbled next to me. "She was here yesterday. Everything seemed fine; she even let me eat your lunch."

"Did she say anything?"

"What, you mean about you? She didn't have to. She looked like someone had kicked her puppy right in front of her. Not sure what happened between you guys, Jonas, but I told her to stop jerking you around."

He said what now?

"That's not your place," I growled low in my throat, letting the threat simmer close to the surface.

"It wasn't like that, idiot. We didn't have that type of conversation. Besides, she looked sad that you weren't in her line, even though you said she'd be trying to avoid you."

"Even not knowing I wouldn't be here, she showed up yesterday, so why wouldn't she be here today?" I didn't have the answer, but after the discussion Gabriel and I had the day before, a sick feeling began in the pit of my stomach. This could be nothing, but since it was River, it was probably something.

"Man, I'm so hungry," Ian grumbled next to me.

"I have to go."

"What do you mean, you have to go? It's the middle of the work day. Are you going to find food somewhere? I doubt you have time for a sit-down meal right now."

"No. I mean I have to go. Right now." I didn't have time to explain to him. The feeling in my stomach was growing stronger, and I had the horrible urge to run in five directions at once. My skin itched, and I felt my transformation hovering close to the surface. I needed to find River. Now.

"Do you know what you're doing? This is your job, man."

"No, Ian," I threw over my shoulder as I jogged back down the hill toward the dirt lot where I parked my truck that morning. "It's *just* a job. She's my priority."

Two new humans in town with a connection to River, and now she didn't show up for deliveries when you could set a clock to her?

No way could I sit on that, no way.

I BURST into Gabriel's study so hard, the heavy wooden doors slammed back against the wall. Heedless to the snapping and growling of the vampires who knew they couldn't even dent my skin, I blew past them so fast their hair wafted in the breeze. I had no time for politeness or pleasantries. I might have been less hasty if the master had been home, but since Viktor wasn't around and I had business with Gabriel, I allowed myself the bravery of throwing myself into the Lilith Nest.

He was expecting me. Of course he was.

Or at least it looked to be so. He was sitting with his jacket over the back of the chair and his elbows resting on the desk in front of him. In one hand he held a strange looking amulet, a black stone swinging lightly from a chain. It had no shine, no luster, but more of a flat matte finish. In his right hand was an ornate pen, which he used to write in a ledger in front of him. He was taking notes, but I couldn't be bothered to find out why. I recognized the amulet from the day before. It was the same one he'd pulled out of the book on the shelf that was not a book, but a safe to hide objects in plain sight. He'd stolen it from a voodoo woman and added it to his already long list of reasons he shouldn't return to New Orleans. I didn't care about the origins; I only cared about how it would help River.

"Something's happened to her." The words came out low and raspy. My change was close, and it was a testament to my desperation that I was having such a hard time controlling such a simple bodily function.

"No it hasn't. Not yet, anyway" was all he said in reply as he scribbled a few more notes down in his book. His indifference was infuriating, considering recent events. I slammed my hand down on the desk, the weight of my fist cracking the highly polished wood and sending his notebook and obnoxiously expensive-looking pen skittering sideways. I was a stone man, and a big one at that. Had I wanted to use my full power, I could have split that solid wood desk in half, and quite possibly the body sitting behind it, as well. But I didn't want to hurt him. I wanted his attention.

"That desk cost more than your wages can keep up with," Gabriel murmured, but the threat lacked heat.

"We can wax poetic about your prissy obsession with overpriced furniture another time," I growled. "But River didn't show up to the mine today. She's not late, and she didn't send a substitute—she's just not there. I already checked her house; the sisters said she left early this morning. Where is she, Gabriel?"

I don't know why I thought he would know, maybe because he was always so cocksure and *seemed* to know something about everything under the sun. I'd lost precious time already, running out of town to the sisters, but it seemed the obvious first place to check. I regretted upsetting them, but I had to check every option, and when I'd left, they had begged me to find their girl. To banshees, there is nothing more important than their family. Once a banshee claims you as her own, it's a most powerful bond.

"I don't know why you think I know so much about what's going on." The bastard had the nerve to smile while he said it.

"I'll have you swallow your next flippant comment, I swear it. Where is she? What do we do?"

"What is this *we* you speak of?" Gabriel asked, one finely shaped brow arched high on his aristocratic forehead. "I supply you with information, Jonas. The rest is based purely on the amount of effort you will exert for this female. Are you sure she's worth it?"

The only response I could give was a low grinding sound. My stone form would explode through my skin if he didn't change his tone.

"Gabriel," I ground out. "Where. Is. River." It wasn't even a question this time, but pure demand. Polite Jonas was about to disappear, and my feral side was not in the mood to mince words.

Gabriel sighed, like dealing with someone too thick to appreciate his prose was exhausting, and closing his fingers around the black amulet, he held it out to me. "Here, take this. You know well the cost of it, though. I'll have what I want out of this deal. I don't know exactly where she is, but I have a guess."

"You have a guess?"

"It's an educated guess," he replied. "Take the damn amulet before I change my mind and let you figure this little debacle out on your own."

I took the amulet from him and willed myself to stay

composed and not punch him in the face until my fist came out the other side. My regular self was pretty nonviolent but my wild self was . . . something different.

To distract myself, I studied the small amulet in my hands. It looked plain, plainer than I would have thought coming from Gabriel, and upon closer inspection, I saw that the surface of the stone was rife with uneven pock marks.

"This is lava rock, isn't it?" I'd seen one once before from a visiting merchant. Lava rock was stone created from cooled magma that had erupted from volcanos.

"Fitting, isn't it?" Gabriel said, his composure restored and his usual mocking smile in place. "That stone can take high heat without breaking down, and with the wicked nasty juju it's infused with, this little amulet should work for our needs."

Our needs. I mustn't forget our discussion and the real reason Gabriel was helping me right now. There was always a catch. Gabriel Doyle was a shrewd businessman, after all, and this was another transaction. I'd take this deal, though, to save River, and may she not forever hate me for it.

I said I'd do whatever it takes.

Gabriel walked toward the door, swinging his jacket from the chair and around his shoulders as he went. It was much too warm for such an article of clothing on a warm summer day, even high in the mountains, but it was a fashion. And Gabriel was at all times nattily dressed.

"Are you coming?" Gabriel peered over his shoulder, as if I was the one holding up the show. "You drive; I'll tell you where to go."

"YOUR TRUCK IS A TRAVESTY, PEDERSON," Gabriel grumbled as his head hit the roof of the cab when I went over a deep groove in the road.

"I bought this truck brand new in 1921, and it's only three years old. She's perfect; she just needs some tweaking now and again." He'd better not insult my baby. I'd saved my coins like a miser to afford this truck, and I custom built the back end for cargo. Not everyone had a vehicle in Havenwood Falls, but I did.

"Tweaking?" Gabriel looked at me, incredulous. His normally put-together persona wore a mask of disbelief.

"It's practical," I shot back, as I careened too quickly around the corner toward Havenwood Falls Elementary School.

"It's barbaric is what it is." His grumble turned into a pained yelp as I slammed the brakes and his knees hit the dash. "You're crazy, Pederson!"

I didn't answer him. I was too busy staring at what had caused me to hit the brakes in the first place—River's motorbike. It was right there in front of the school. Leaving Gabriel to follow, I swung the truck door open and leapt from the vehicle.

She was here. I didn't know how he knew it, but she was here.

But she wasn't any longer. The side cart was still stocked with all of the brown-bagged lunches that never got delivered to the miners, and there was no sign of her at all. "How did you know she'd be inside the school?"

"She isn't," Gabriel said from behind me.

"Okay, where is she then?" I didn't have time for the word games he seemed to love so much.

"Shut up." Surprised, I looked at Gabriel. He had his eyes closed and his mouth drawn down in concentration. He mumbled something too low for me to hear, but he wasn't talking to me, anyway. Moving his right arm in an arc in front of him and his left in the opposite direction he stood stock still for a moment. It was if he commanded even the birds and the insects to be silent so he could hear even the faintest of sounds. Then his eyes snapped open, the irises blazing blue and focused on something only he could see. "There," he said, making an about face and pointing up the mountain side. "She's up there."

"Hell. That's going to be a hike on foot," I said, staring at the dense forest that started in the near distance and crept up in a wall of green. I wouldn't be doing it in this form, that was for sure.

Gabriel seemed to read what I was thinking. "I'll need you to at least wait until you are hidden by the tree line before you do anything drastic, Pederson. I can get away with a lot of things in this town, but I think a giant rock man charging up the mountainside at breakneck speed would be difficult to hide from the Court."

"You think that's bad? My body transforms, but my clothes do not." *Let that sink in for a moment.*

"That sounds like a personal problem." Gabriel smirked. "It must be difficult to operate under such . . . limitations."

"Do you want a fireman carry, or a princess carry?" I asked with a grin, already moving toward the cool dark of the tree line.

"Don't flatter yourself, stone man," Gabriel said as he jogged past me, a genuine grin on his face for the first time I had ever witnessed. "I'll get up this mountainside on my own. I don't need your primitive methods. Worry about yourself."

I would worry about myself. And I would worry about River. If she was in trouble, and that was most likely the case, I'd smash through anything that kept her from me. No humans from her past or River's raging flames would keep me from her side, even if I had to expose my true nature in the process.

CHAPTER 12

RIVER

*T*he odd look on Thomas's face distracted me. That was why I surely had not heard him correctly. There was no way he had said what I thought he'd said. It didn't fit.

"I'm sorry, what did you say? I think I misheard." I smiled in embarrassment.

He squeezed my hands again, this time harder than normal. "I killed the Cranes—both of them. I knew you of all people would understand. Oh, River," he sighed as he pulled me to my feet and embraced me. "I'm so happy to have found you here. It's like a gift from the gods. Surely I'm on the right path." He nuzzled his face in my neck and inhaled deeply while I stood frozen in shock.

This wasn't right. My brain couldn't keep up with the complete one-eighty turn of events, and Thomas was definitely taking physical liberties with me. Jonas had held me the same way not two days ago, but it had felt completely different.

"I don't understand." I pushed against his chest, and he stepped back, still smiling that creepy smile that didn't reach his eyes.

"You poor thing." His misplaced sympathy combined with the sudden strength of his grip on me rang warning bells throughout my entire body. What was he talking about?

"You poor, poor girl," he repeated, his hands rubbing my arms as if to comfort me. It had the opposite effect. "After all this time, you still live in fear when you hold the key to making those people all pay for what they did."

"Making who pay? For what? And what about the Cranes? Thomas, I don't understand." For lack of any better idea, and because I wanted to pull out of his weird hypnotic embrace, I sat back down on the log, while Thomas remained standing in front of me.

He smiled proudly. "They all thought she slipped in the kitchen and fell. The impact of her head hitting the iron cook stove killed her instantly, and she bled out on the floor." Thomas tilted his head like he was imparting a great secret. "While the blow killed her, she didn't slip. It was my hand that knocked her down. It wasn't an accident she hit the stove. Although if I had known it would kill her so quickly, I would have thought of something else. She ought to have suffered."

My breath caught in my throat, but no sound escaped.

"And he wasn't much better. Moping around after she died. I'd expected more sport with him, but he was so drunk all the time, it wasn't even fun, waiting until he was asleep and then propping him just right with his shotgun. That was much messier than I had expected. I had to burn my clothes." Thomas shuddered at the memory, and I didn't know what disturbed me more—that he had killed the Cranes, or that he was only disturbed by how the whole affair had damaged his clothing.

Thomas was *not* okay.

My head was spinning, and I couldn't get a grasp of the situation. "But you travel with Mr. Weisman. How could he not know?"

"I only kept that old fool alive because he was useful," Thomas sneered. His polite mask was gone, and now in its place was something twisted and ugly. "He was so riddled with guilt, he'd believe anything I said. He got me out of that school and away from that place. He'll spend the rest of his life trying to make up for turning his back on things, and even though he's about ready to keel over now, there's still use in him yet. And now that we found you—it can only get better."

The way he said those words made bile rise in my throat.

"River, aren't you angry? Don't you want to hurt the ones that hurt you?"

The ones that hurt me?

"Is that why you killed the Cranes?" I whispered. Not because I was trying to stay quiet, but because that's all the strength I had to speak. This Thomas was terrifying.

"They were nasty people, and they deserved to die. I'm glad they're dead. You said the same thing. But what about the other wrongs? The soldiers that stole us from our families—the ones that raped our lands and killed our people—shouldn't they pay, River? They should. They should all pay." Thomas nodded even though I hadn't given him a reply. He was living in a fantasy of his own making; he didn't need a response from me. In his mind, *of course* I agreed with him. There was no need to confirm this.

"With your flames, we could destroy armies, River."

"No." Just one word, but I made it firm.

"Hmm?" He wasn't even listening.

"No, I won't do that. I won't hurt anyone. I think you're sick, Thomas, and my heart hurts for the things that have happened to you, but I won't use my power to hurt anyone. Ever." There were a few seconds of silence as my words sunk in, and then the world tipped upside down.

"Why not?" The words erupted from his mouth in the first real anger he had shown, and the slap across my face came so hard and so fast, it knocked me clean off the stump I sat on. I flew backward into the dirt, my head hitting the hard packed-dirt ground and my skirts getting tangled in my legs.

You've got to get away from him.

"River," Thomas said as he stood over me, one leg on each side of my body caging me in. "I don't want to force you. I mean I will, and I'm going to." He laughed as he grabbed the front of my blouse and flung me to my feet, catching me in his cruel grasp. "I wish you could see things from my eyes. We could have everything."

"Your eyes are clouded, Wesa," I said, saying his true name with a gasp as one of his hands wound its way through one thick braid and yanked. I gritted my teeth and pressed on. "What would your parents think?"

"My parents? What about them? They let the soldiers take me away. They never even tried to come get me. Why would I care about them? I wonder if they're dead now," he mused, never letting go of me.

"Let me go," I pleaded. I needed to think of a plan, but in the meantime I also needed to keep him talking. "I don't want to use my power to hurt people, and you can't make me."

This time I saw the blow coming, but I still couldn't block it, and the force of his fist on the side of my head took my vision and my breath all at the same time. Pain exploded through my body, and the urge to vomit was severe. He threw me to the ground with a thud, and I lacked the strength to right myself. A thin stream of blood ran from my nose, down my lip, and plopped into the dirt.

"I can make you do anything, River. It's a matter of finding the right motivation." Thomas laughed again, and this time I gave in to the urge, retching into the dirt until my stomach was empty. Wiping my nose and mouth on my sleeve, I glared up at him. My vision was still blurry from the blow to my head, and he wavered in front of me like a mirage.

"I won't give you my fire."

"You don't have to give me anything. I'll take what I want, like I always have."

"Not likely, you criminal." I was hurting and having problems seeing straight. He probably thought he could beat me into doing what he wanted, and if that was the case, he would be disappointed. It wasn't *my* pain I was afraid of. It never had been.

"I think I have you figured out now, and you're so easy, it's laughable. You care too much about others, River. That's your weakness, and it's what I will use to make you my tool." He grinned again, all tan skin and white teeth, the scar on his chin a macabre reminder of the violence he'd endured to become this way.

"I'm a schoolteacher, River. How many kids' mysterious deaths would it take for you to come to heel? One? Two? An entire classroom? Let me know, and I can get started. Or you can just give me what I want, and we both leave Havenwood Falls exactly like we found it." He crouched down in front of me so that our eyes were level, and it took everything in me not to cower away from him in fear. "Say the word, and I'll get started. I'm amenable to whatever."

God, he was sick. I'd been so stupid.

"You're crazy, you know that?" I spit in his face, and he laughed.

The boot to my shoulder knocked me on my back, and I didn't even try to get up.

"You're the one who went walking deep in the woods with a complete stranger, little girl," he said in a singsong voice, as he walked a tight circle around where I lay in the dirt, my whole body racked with the pain of his earlier blows. My head still wasn't right. There was a rhythmic thumping noise coming from the ground under me. Like a pack of wild horses was thundering up the mountainside, hurrying to get to the top. I was addled, there were no horses, and I was surely imagining the ground moving underneath me.

"This town isn't what you think it is," I said, not even bothering to open my eyes, considering I couldn't see straight, anyway. "You won't get away with anything like what you're planning so easily. Whatever you do, it'll be found out. And your punishment will be severe." I was dead serious. The Court of the Sun and the Moon did not mess around with outsiders who sought to wreak havoc in their refuge.

"Oh, I won't do anything to *you*, River. I need you." Thomas stepped away from me and looked off in the distance, over the space where the tree line ended and the unseen town stretched out below. "But those two ladies who adopted you. What about them? It shouldn't take too much digging to figure out who they are, and then I can have fun. What was it you mentioned about your flames going out of control? Emotional stimuli? I can make you bathe in their blood, River. Would that encourage you to lend me your flames?"

My aunties?

The change took over so fast, I was on my feet before my eyes were even open, the familiar sizzle in the air zipping through my skin and out through my fingertips and the soles of my feet. The feeling was rage. I was angry.

"You'll never come close to them," I shouted, and with my words came a stream of heat. I flung my arms in the air without thinking, and the force of my rage emerged from my fingertips in a stream of flame, right into the ramshackle cabin perched on the edge of the eroded cliff. The old and rotted wood absorbed the blast like a sponge absorbed water, and the flames ate away at the walls until the entire structure was nothing but a sea of red and orange.

"No." Horror at what I'd done froze me in place, but Thomas just laughed wildly, clapping his hands together with glee.

"See? You can do it if you put your mind to it, River. Doesn't it feel good? Doesn't it feel amazing to destroy? Come with me, and let's punish them all. Everyone who took from us. Everyone who hurt us. Let's burn it all to the ground."

I didn't want this. I didn't mean to. The more agitated and scared I got, the more the flames licked the ground in front of me. The surrounding air both crackled and spit in defiance, and I couldn't pull it back inside me if I tried. My arms and legs were awash with that burning energy, and if I tried to shake it away, I would paint the scenery in a savage inferno. Forget Thomas. I was the most dangerous being on this mountain. And he wanted to use me as a weapon.

"You won't get what you want."

"But I already have, River. I already have you, and I'll destroy everything and everyone you love to keep you." Thomas's face was a distortion, a twisted mask of cruelty. I didn't recognize this man, but I knew one thing. I had helped create him. I set everything in motion that day sixteen years ago; this was my fault.

All I ever did was hurt people. Wesa . . . Jonas . . . and now the sisters and countless residents of Havenwood Falls would be in danger, just because he wanted me.

Me.

I was the common denominator.

I was the answer and the formula for the equation. To fix this, to make sure that no one else suffered because of me, I needed to remove myself from the picture.

They would mourn, but it was the only way to make sure I never used my power to hurt anyone again. And I was so tired of fighting myself. Of suppressing the power that manifested at the most inconvenient moments.

The air shook with a boom, and something inside the burning shack exploded, probably a leftover can of kerosene or an oil lamp. Taking advantage of the distraction, I looked around as the heat of my body caused the ground to blister in front of me. I took a step toward the slope, where the foundation of dirt crumbled into a sheer drop. Twenty feet to the edge and then fifty feet down.

The sisters had taught me you should never take life lightly. They would be sad when I was gone, I knew. Tears trickled from my eyes and evaporated instantly, the heat of my skin causing them to disappear in a puff of vaporous smoke. Wesa observed the burning cabin absently, and I took five more steps toward the edge of the cliff, willing myself not to lose heart. My clothes were burning now; I wondered how long they would last. It didn't matter anymore.

It was a coward's way out, and I was about to take it, but I didn't know what else to do. If I died, no more flames would come from my body, and Wesa would have no weapon to wield. The sisters would wail. I knew they would be heard all the way into town and up the surrounding mountains.

"I'm sorry," I whispered into the wind. To the sisters and to Jonas, the man I felt so much for. But my feelings were a curse, just like my flames, and I would take them both over the side of this cliff with me.

"What do you think you're doing?" Wesa, his attention no longer occupied by the burning cabin, now stared at me with growing alarm. "Get away from there, River. I won't let you do whatever silly thing it is you're thinking." He walked toward me, and I was awash with a new emotion. Disgust.

Wesa was a bad man.

Taking a deep breath, I reached out to the flames, sucking them away from the burning foliage, away from the rickety cabin that was almost razed to the ground. I filled my lungs and my body with every bit of fire that had been expunged, and I held it inside me. It filled my veins and my organs, burning inside, twisting and turning and begging for release.

I didn't know I could do that, but then again, I'd never tried.

But the flames didn't want to stay inside me. They wanted release. They'd had a brief taste of freedom, and I was too distraught to keep them contained. They would come out of me, one way or another. That was okay, though. They would come out in a place where they couldn't hurt anyone ever again.

Wesa picked up the pace as I inched closer to the edge. I wasn't afraid now. It was he who showed his fear as the toy he'd wanted was about to disappear forever out of his reach. I would wait a couple seconds for him to come closer. I'd already realized I would never be successful at suppressing this terrible power. Hadn't I proved it by losing control and creating a circle of destruction right in front of me? *Again?* I wasn't a scared little girl anymore, tearfully promising a panel of Court members I would be good. That I wouldn't use my power again. That I would never hurt anyone. It was only a matter of time before our actions on the mountainside alerted the Luna Coven, and then the Court, of exactly what was happening. There would be no saving me from them. I'd broken my promise, and not even the sisters could step in on my behalf this time.

But I could do one last thing to make it right. To keep this damaged man in front of me from ever harming another soul ever again. I could do this *one thing right*.

"River, stop."

I wanted to say "Make me," but I couldn't. I couldn't open my mouth because the flames I'd sucked back into my body beat against my teeth and tongue, demanding release. I just needed him to get a little closer. My vision swam with the effort it cost to wrestle the demons inside me—the ones burning at my insides and fighting to be free. Through the haze of smoke, I saw a figure, large and imposing, break through the tree line and come charging into the clearing with a roar.

"River, no." I don't how I understood the words, garbled and deep. Maybe it was just a testament to how much of my mind I had lost in this battle that I was imagining it was Jonas wishing me a final farewell. I wanted to call his name, but again, to let it slip past my lips would invite disaster, and I was having a hard enough time keeping it at bay. Wesa was almost to me, and I reached out to grab his arm, flinging myself back. The weight of my body would send us both plummeting over the edge and wipe us both from this existence.

But that was not to be.

Wesa was snatched backward out of my grasp, and he went hurtling through the air, a boneless rag doll with arms and legs flailing. I didn't see where he landed, because my body was also yanked forward, away from the ledge, and I was crushed up against a wall of solid rock. Wider than I was and taller, with two massive arms of stone circled around me, the wall closed in. The roar of the flames pounded in my ears, and at last I had reached my physical limit. As two massive hands, gentle despite being made of solid stone, caressed my back, I lost the battle with my self-control.

And weeping for all of the things I would lose, I opened my mouth.

CHAPTER 13

JONAS

$\mathcal{W}$e would not make it. I saw the smoke rising above the trees and heard the explosion a scant second later. Stripping my shirt and my pants as I ran, I let the change take me as skin and bone swelled and hardened into solid stone. My footsteps, once light and soundless, now thundered as I heaved my massive bulk up the overgrown pass, feet leaving large craters in the dirt.

"Wait a second," Gabriel drawled from behind me, keeping pace with me and not looking the least bit winded. "Take this too, you thick-headed fool." I saw the lava rock amulet dangling in his fist.

I'd almost forgotten the key.

"Are you sure you don't want me to carry you?" The words came out in a booming groan. Speaking was hard when your face was solid rock.

"There's no sense in me wasting the effort on running if you are. You'll get there faster, and you don't need me." Gabriel straightened his jacket, which had been flapping around him while we had run for the tree line. Well, I had run. I didn't see Gabriel moving. He appeared where I was when I had the thought to look for him. Vampires had many tricks up their sleeves.

He was right. He wasn't involved in this any more than a simple business transaction. It was up to me to take care of what needed done.

"Then hold these. I'll need them later," I said, and tossed my shirt and pants over my shoulder.

"Rude." Gabriel could complain all he wanted, but I couldn't wait any longer, and I took off as fast as my massive stone legs could take me. Speed wasn't a strong point in this form, but my size tripled as a stone man, and my longer stride ate up the distance between me and the place up the mountain that Gabriel had pointed to earlier. The place that was now marked with a thin plume of rising smoke.

I had to get there.

Stealth was not a skill I owned as a stone man, and the ground shook under my feet as I thundered up the path, snapping branches and sometimes even whole trees. Normally I took more care when in this form, but now time was not my friend. I couldn't count on the element of surprise, and I didn't know what I would find when I got to where I was going. I didn't even know where that was. I followed the smoke.

When I got to the source of the smoke, I almost couldn't believe my eyes. It looked to be the scene of a devastating fire, but there were no flames anywhere, even though I could smell fresh ash in the air. River stood on the edge of a steep drop, her hair a tangled mess pulled free from her braids, and her eyes were wild. They were solid black—no white showing at all—and the entire side of her face was red and purple, her lip and nose swollen and bleeding. Just steps in front of her stood a man I'd never seen before, but here he was approaching River with his arms outstretched. Her eyes stared ahead at him, seeing nothing but his face.

In a split second, I understood what she was trying to do—and I was having none of it.

"River, no!" I roared the words, but I'm sure it sounded like nothing more than the booming of thunder, and she didn't even acknowledge she heard me. She grasped the wrist of the man in front of her and reared back, shuffling her feet backward to launch them both over the sheer drop below.

Like hell.

I plucked the man right out of her grasp with one hand and tossed him over my shoulder. I didn't check to see where he landed, and I didn't care. I could deal with him later. I would rip his arms clean from his body for daring to lay a hand on River. My main target was in front of me, about to throw her life and our love away as she hurtled to her death for some self-sacrificing notion. Whatever her reasoning, it wasn't good enough, but I would let her tell me all about it later, when I knew she was safe and the black madness had bled from her eyes.

I reached her as her foot met the space where the eroded ground gave way to empty air, and instead of falling backward down the drop-off, I yanked her forward and spun her around, putting my large, immovable form between her and certain death. She couldn't go. I wouldn't let her. Even if it meant scaring her with my ugly form, I would hold her still and not let her go. I curled around her as best as I could, stroking her back as gently as was possible with my giant hands carved from stone. She turned her face up, her eyes still black and unseeing—and then she opened her mouth.

If I were a smaller man, and not a fifteen-foot-tall rock monster, I might have been bowled over by the blast. Instead, I took it full in the face, letting the heat of her rage surround me until I was nothing more than a glowing ball of flame, holding a smaller, hotter ball of flame. A human kiln, she baked me, firing my entire being until the surrounding grass burned to nothing and the soil dried out and cracked under our bodies. And still she burned. And still I held her tighter.

I could feel the heat, but it was nothing more than the heat of opening an oven and pulling out the dishes inside. I was a man of stone, and fire could not hurt me.

And still she burned.

But then, when I thought we might burn forever and would remain that way until the end of time, I felt something else—something different. The amulet I still had clasped in the cage of my fingers burned as well, but instead of disappearing into the flames, it called to them, coaxing the light into its matte mottled darkness.

And if that wasn't a strange enough sight to behold, the flames flowed into the amulet. Just like Gabriel had said they would. Soundlessly, they streamed from River's mouth, over our bodies, and into the amulet. On a current of their own, they traveled continuously into the depths of a stone that had no bottom. I don't know how long I knelt there, waiting for the flames to cease —forever or maybe just a moment. It was impossible to tell. There was no lessening of power, no gradual decrease of fire. It was there, and then it was gone, leaving River hanging limply in my arms, her eyes and mouth now closed, her chest heaving from her efforts. I was so close to the edge of the cliff my heels hung over the side where I knelt. One false move, and I would plummet to the bottom.

But the amulet had worked. River lived.

I had no way of knowing if there would be a second outburst. Gabriel had told me before that the spell that had been placed on the amulet was strong, and that if used correctly should suck in not only her flames, but the source of her power, leaving her with nothing left.

But had it worked?

I couldn't take the chance and release my stone form. It was the only defense I had against River's flames. I also didn't want to scare her, looking as I did, but holding her still was all I could think to do. So I knelt there, on the crumbling earth at the edge of a precipice, holding her until she returned to herself. Until she returned to me.

"Jonas?" Her voice quivered after what seemed like an eternity of silence.

"Don't be afraid." I said the words as quietly and as gently as I could, but the sound still reverberated off the surrounding trees.

As she lifted her head, I could see the black had bled away, and there were her big beautiful brown eyes staring at me—the eyes I loved—although one had a bluish tinge growing underneath it that sparked rage in my soul, and the glassy sheen of unshed tears slid across the surface.

"So this is the part you've kept hidden?" Her question was muffled as she dipped her head again, not meeting my eyes.

"Please don't be afraid," I repeated in the same growling voice.

"I could never be afraid of you, Jonas. Never. Where's Wesa?"

I lifted her chin with one massive finger until she met my eyes. "Is he the man that struck you? If so, he's in a pile behind you, and if he moves, I'll stomp him until he becomes one with the dirt he's lying on." That man was the least of her problems. There was something else she hadn't noticed yet, something that had happened while we had been sitting there, huddled together in the dirt. It would be an issue when she did.

I let go of her chin, and her eyes traveled up my body, taking in my mountainous form. The fingers of her right hand reached up to trace the hardness of my jaw. I barely felt her touch, soft as a butterfly's wings on the side of my face.

"Can I touch you?" she asked in wonder.

"Love, you're touching me now." And I smiled. It was grotesque, a stone ogre's grin, but I couldn't stop the expression. She gave me such joy by wanting to put her hands, even the smallest bit, on me in this formidable body.

Slowly, her gaze traveled down from my face to the wide expanse of my chest, lower still to my abdomen, and then even lower. I heard the gasp as she saw the entirety of me laid bare. When I took my stone form, my size tripled. That included *every* part.

"Jonas," River shrieked, the sound cutting through the stillness of the forest. "You're naked!"

"But River, so are you."

Her arms shot out in embarrassment, and she pushed me away, her hands splaying over the breasts she hadn't known until that moment were bare. And I watched her face go from embarrassment to horror as I slid backwards, over the edge of the cliff and down the side, cutting through the air like a lead weight as the ground rushed up to meet me with all the subtlety of a sledgehammer.

She'd pushed me off the cliff.

CHAPTER 14

RIVER

I'd pushed him off a cliff.

Jonas Pederson, a stone man in full glory, had bounded up the side of the mountain and saved me from certain death. And I returned that favor by getting embarrassed and pushing him off a cliff.

I thought I'd killed him.

But, as I knelt on the ledge barely far enough away to be safe, my head in my hands and weeping over the loss, I felt something settling over my shoulders. Startled out of my mourning, I lifted my head to see Gabriel Doyle calmly placing what looked to be one of Jonas's button-down shirts around my shoulders. I clutched the ends together over my naked body and sniffed. Yes, it was Jonas's. It smelled just like him, a mixture of woodsy outdoors, sawdust, and soap. None of those things by themselves were anything special, but together they were uniquely him. My tears began anew.

Gabriel took no notice of my naked form other than to cover it, and ambling over to the edge of the drop off, he looked over and whistled.

"That's a bit of a fall," he said to me, before turning and yelling over the side. "Pederson, we had a deal."

I don't know if he was waiting for some response, but a few seconds passed before he shook his head and grimaced.

"Oh, all right," he mumbled to himself, and I watched in silent stupor as he walked past me, retrieved a pair of pants from the grass, and walking back over to the edge, pitched them down the cliff side.

I'd fainted and was a prisoner of some sort of madness. That was the only explanation that made sense.

Gabriel stood there for a minute, staring down at what had to be Jonas's mangled body before something came hurtling through the air from down below. Gabriel caught it in his right hand, snatching it right out of the sky. I didn't know what it was, but it was attached to a slim silver chain—I saw the end of it dangling from his fist.

"Thanks, partner," he said and turned his head once more to look at whatever mess had been left on the forest floor below. "Are you coming, then?"

He wasn't talking to me.

There was no way Jonas was all right, was there?

Throwing his hands in the air in the perfect representation of complete exasperation, he sighed.

"Turn around," he said, his face serious.

"What?" I wasn't following.

"Turn. Around." He raised one finger in the air and gave it a twirling motion. "The last time you got a look at him without clothes on, you pushed him down a cliff. Your knight in stone armor isn't coming back until you turn around." Gabriel made a shooing motion with his hands, like he was ushering a naughty child out of the kitchen. "And you might want to close those buttons while you're at it, not that I'm opposed to the view." And then the heathen had the gall to wink at me.

With a gasp, I realized my state of undress, although to my credit, I had just had a traumatizing experience. I put my back to Gabriel Doyle as I fumbled with the buttons on the borrowed shirt. It was four sizes too large and covered me from my neck to my knees.

There was a lot of grunting and the sound of rocks and dirt sliding around, and I was just about to turn around when Gabriel stopped me. "No, not yet. I'll tell you when it's okay." A few more agonizing minutes later, he said, "All right now, River, you can turn around."

I turned to find a very bored-looking Gabriel standing next to a very sheepish-looking Jonas, who was wearing nothing but a pair of pants and a blush across his pale cheeks. His hair looked even more blond with his skin flushed red up to the roots, deepening in color the longer I looked. Fully clothed Jonas was a large handsome man. Half-dressed he was sinful perfection, and I forgot Gabriel was even standing there as I took in the sight of Jonas, not dead at the bottom of the cliff, but alive and in front of me.

I took three seconds to cross the distance between us and throw myself into his arms.

"You scared me today," he said, and his voice was normal and smooth again, not the deep rasp of his stone self.

"I was terrified, too," I whispered, while I rained kisses across his forehead, cheeks, and finally his lips, a light peppering of thanks for coming to my rescue. And for not perishing when I pushed him into a fifty-foot drop.

"I wasn't scared at all, if anyone cares," Gabriel drawled from next to us, reminding us we weren't alone.

"Where is Wesa?" I couldn't believe I had forgotten about him. Had he run off? Was he still hell-bent on terrorizing the people of the town if I didn't bend to his will?

"Oh, he's fine where he is." Gabriel walked over to Wesa's still form in the grass. He lay in a crumpled pile, where I assumed he'd landed when Jonas tossed him through the air.

"He's a bad man."

"He's just a human," Gabriel said, nudging Wesa's backside with the toe of his expensive shoe. "But his heart was filled with enough malice to cause irreparable damage, that's for sure. His mind was a grotesque thing, and I know the real bogeyman." Gabriel was unaffected by everything that had gone down, and as I studied him, I noticed the chain still dangling from his hand. He saw me looking and opened his fist to show me a large black stone in the center of his palm. Well, it looked black at first glance, but inside the light danced and played as if inside an ember burned.

"Sorry, my dear, no take-backs."

"I don't understand," I said, for what seemed like the hundredth time. I looked over at Jonas for clarification.

"I've done something, River," Jonas told me. "I was desperate, and you'll be angry, but I don't regret it, and it can't be undone, so even if you never want to see me again, I'd do it again in a heartbeat." He looked at me defiantly, but when I said nothing to challenge him, he continued. "River, your power is gone. I took it. We took it from you."

What? That couldn't be true. I reached down deep and tried to pull a flame—nothing. Not that I had much practice calling the fire on purpose, but still, that place that had always been bubbling inside me, just waiting for a chance to escape? That was gone. Inside me was just a quiet peaceful serenity. A calm.

"Also, just so you know, there was a bit of a wager made, and to the victor go the spoils," Gabriel interrupted, swinging the chain in his hand like a pendulum. "But in this instance, even though you are the victor, the spoils go to me."

"Gabriel, you're being obtuse," Jonas warned.

"No, I'm being honest. Your power is gone, River. I hold it here in this stone, and the stone belongs to me. Your power is now mine."

"Dammit, Gabriel . . ."

"You mean it?" The words came out on a shallow joyous breath.

"What?" the two men said in unison.

"You mean it's gone? Forever? As in no more spontaneous eruptions? No chance of me hurting anyone by accident or choice?

No emotional outburst will cause me to light someone on fire?" I side-eyed Jonas as I asked the last question.

"Not a chance, my dear. You are an empty tank, so to speak, forever more."

"Oh, thank the gods," I cried, and as the tears rained down, I threw myself into Jonas's arms once again. "Let's test it. Kiss me, Jonas."

And so he did.

For so long and with so much enthusiasm that when I next came up for air, the sun had sunk low behind the trees. There was no sign of Gabriel Doyle anymore, nor was there any sign of Wesa. I had a hard time believing the dapperly dressed vampire of the Lilith Nest had dragged that sorry human down the mountainside by the shoe, but with that vampire, anything was possible.

"Jonas," I asked, turning to face him once again and caressing the side of his face. No longer was I afraid to touch him lest I singe off something important. "What do I do now?"

"I think you should continue to do the same things you have always done," he said as he grabbed my hand and we picked our way back down the path. It was much wider than I remembered on the way up, and there were downed trees all along the path, like a huge storm had whipped right up the mountain. "After all, that's the River I fell in love with."

My blush burned hot, and I could only hope I was saved from him seeing it by the dimming of the evening light. He would not let me turn away, though, and he pulled my hand until I stumbled into him. And as he pressed my small soft body against his larger, harder frame, he whispered in my ear.

"I just ask that whatever you decide to do, it's by my side, River. No more running."

I wholeheartedly agreed. "No more running."

EPILOGUE

RIVER

I don't know why Jonas ever hid his other form from me. He had said it was because he was so grotesque he didn't want to scare me, but he looked no different to me when he changed. Just much bigger . . . and harder.

To say there was a large mess to clean up would be an understatement. I knew the Court of the Sun and the Moon had a lot to do with what went on in town, but this would have been a cover-up of massive proportions. There was no way to hide what had happened, and I would have to deal with the consequences of my actions.

And I had ample time, considering I was dragged in front of the Court again, much like I had been as a child. They looked, tested, and read my mind until it satisfied them, but there was not even a minute trace of the flames left inside my body. They were well and truly gone.

And so was Wesa.

I don't mean he left town; I mean he was gone. Like he never existed. There wasn't even a whisper of a new teacher that had come into town. It was as if he had never been there in the first place. I couldn't get any information from Elsmed or any of the other members of the Court. And I would not ask Roman Bishop, who'd taken over the Court seat in his father's place. That entire family scared the hell out of me.

I'd gotten over my fear of Gabriel Doyle. Well, mostly. He was a lot easier to deal with now he'd gotten something he wanted from me, and at the very least, I was more comfortable peppering him with questions about what happened to Wesa than anyone else. After all, Gabriel could read minds, so surely he could glean that tiny bit of information.

But all I'd gotten out of Gabriel was something about sirens and the name Alverson. I didn't know what a siren was, but even Gabriel had looked uncomfortable talking about it. I might not have known a lot about the histories of other supernaturals, but I still knew enough not to pry into something that made even a vampire nervous. Wesa was gone—that was a fact. And with him went the hate, the trauma, and the violence he brought with him.

Jonas told me that Hank Weisman's memory was wiped before he left town. I didn't ask what story they gave him to replace his memory of having been in Havenwood Falls. I didn't care. It was best I let that memory leave in peace. Hopefully, the court had done a small kindness and wiped away his memory of me as well, but I couldn't ask such things.

It seemed Jonas had made a deal with Gabriel to drain my power, and as possession was nine-tenths of the law, it belonged to Gabriel now. I should have been angry, but I wasn't. I could only feel sharp relief and gratitude. It was one of those situations where the ends justified the means, even if Meri and Alice harrumphed about it. They claimed he would do something nefarious with the amulet and were shocked that the Court let him keep it. I wasn't shocked, because I was pretty sure he worked something out with Roman Bishop, since those two spoke the same language of greed. I guessed he'd just hold on to it until he could sell it to the highest bidder. Maybe Roman would be involved in that, too. Regardless, it was better off in his hands than my body, of that I was sure. I couldn't find it in me to be upset about it at all.

And now, a solid year later, summer was in full swing again. I still worked with the sisters occasionally, but I did things differently. I made the lunches and catering orders out of the home I shared with Jonas since we were married in the spring. We bought our fruits from the sisters, whose only labor now was to tend their orchards lovingly, and Jonas made me promise to drive his truck instead of my motorbike from now on.

"It isn't good for the baby," he said.

I think I'll let him have his way this once.

Want to read about Jonas and River's descendent? Get *Chase the Flames* (Havenwood Falls Sin & Silk).

ABOUT THE AUTHOR

Desiree lives in Northwest Ohio with her husband, children, and two rowdy cats. She is a multi-genre author who writes contemporary romance and romantic suspense as well as paranormal romance. She's a craft-addicted amateur foodie who loves wine and snacks. Mostly snacks. In her free time, Desiree enjoys living in suburbia and being a typical soccer mom—a soccer mom who makes up amazing stories and watches a lot of anime.

Desiree can be found at her website https://desireelafawn.com/
Or on social media:
Twitter https://twitter.com/DesireeLafawn
Facebook https://www.facebook.com/DesireeLafawnAuthor/
Instagram https://www.instagram.com/desireelafawn/

ACKNOWLEDGMENTS

There are so many people to thank I don't even know where to begin. Kristie Cook and all of the collaborating authors of Havenwood Falls, thank you for letting in this little contemporary author. I'm rough around the edges and oftentimes a misfit. Thank you for opening the wards and letting me in.

E.J. Fechenda, Randi Cooley Wilson, and Victoria Flynn, thank you for sharing your characters with me. Victoria, our early morning and late night messages helped me in ways words can't describe. This book was different than anything I've written before, and you helped alleviate my fears and general curling up in a corner in the fetal position.

Thank you to the editing team for not chopping my fingers off for inappropriate comma use. I would love to promise you that I will do better in the future, but we all know better, don't we?

Regina Wamba, I am so blessed to have your designs grace my cover. I'm a lucky little author to be participating in something so huge, so amazing, so *bright*.

And readers, especially those of you who have been with this group since the very beginning, thank you for your support. You are the reason we write the words. I look forward to my future with you and the rest of Havenwood Falls.

HIDDEN TRUTHS

COLLEEN NYE

~ A Legends of Havenwood Falls Novella ~

HAVENWOOD FALLS

LEGENDS

HIDDEN TRUTHS

COLLEEN NYE

ALSO BY COLLEEN NYE

The Unattainable Series:

When in Maui

When in Doubt

When in Love

Letters To Cora

The Long Summer

Immersion

The Manifest Experience Series:

The Pull

To all my tabletop, pen & paper, RPG, and virtual gaming friends. Without you, my knowledge of the supernatural worlds and beings would be FAR less.

CHAPTER 1

"This is foolish, Kaori. I simply do not understand." An elderly woman in a kimono held a cup of tea, the lines on her face deep with worry.

"You do not have to understand, *Okaasan*. I'm just grateful for all you've done for me—teaching me more English, helping me get my new clothes, and arranging my passage to the Americas. Not to mention always being home for me in a world I have never felt at home in." Kaori bowed slightly before embracing her mother.

Pulling back and looking over her daughter's expression, Kaori's mother sighed. "It is foolish to travel around the world for a *kareshi*."

"He's more than a boyfriend, *Okaasan*. I plan to marry him. To make him my *shujin*."

Her mother set her tea down and gripped Kaori's hands. "*Watashi no musume*. You are *nobody's* property. Never let anyone be your master."

Kaori chuckled. "I simply meant husband. Even in today's world, in the modern times of the 1920s, we women still want husbands. And he wants me as his wife. I know it. Besides, you know that no matter how much I love our family, I have never felt like I belong."

The older woman nodded slowly. "I know. And I did hear his proposal. But any man who would leave his love to go to the other side of the world, saying goodbye and leaving all that matters behind for money alone, is not honorable."

Kaori's brows furrowed. "*Okaasan*, these are different times than we come from. When will you see this?"

Her mother dropped her hands almost as fast as her expression. "Honor should not have an expiration date in society, *shin'ainaru-kun e*."

Kaori lifted her hands again. "It's not a matter of honor as much as it is a matter of necessity and laws. Laws of many have changed our world, *Okaasan*. I am not allowed in the States as is. The recent immigration acts prohibit all Asians from entering American soil. Many of our people over there are in camps right now, simply for being of Asian descent. He could not take me with him when his employer wrote for his return because of the risks."

"Then how can you go now?"

"I shall assume a different face and body. We are kitsune. We have this power." Kaori smiled proudly.

"Why didn't you just do this and go with him then? Why wait and travel alone?" Her mother pulled away and lifted the tea once more.

Kaori put a hand on her mother's shoulder. "He does not know what we are. Not yet. But he will, once I explain. I feel it in my soul, *Okaasan*. I need to go."

"Do what you must, but know that I will not rest well without hearing from you. So visit my dreams often. *Kudasai*." The elder hugged her daughter. "It's been over five hundred years since your birth, and we have never been more than a village away from one another."

"*Okaasan*, you can feel me wherever I am. You can hear the world."

Her mother kissed her forehead. "But I will want to *see* you. Not just spy."

Kaori's eyes filled with tears. "*Watashi wa, anata o aishiteimasu.*"

"I love you, too, Kaori."

Picking up her bags, Kaori gave her mother one last hug, made her way down to the harbor, and boarded the ship to America an Asian woman.

CHAPTER 2

*K*aori stepped onto American soil in the state of California with the appearance of a slender, attractive, brunette Englishwoman. Her dress was a bit more formal, with the new style slip dress topped with a jacket instead of the commonly seen shawl or stole. She figured, with the exhaustion and stress of the journey, she would need the extra layers to help hide her tails, which liked to slip out when she wasn't keeping them hidden.

Stepping down onto the dock, she pulled out documents from her shoulder bag and presented them as she took in the scenery. Thanks to her contacts in Japan, her paperwork was flawless. However, she worked to say as little as possible, considering that she hadn't had much practice with her accent. As much as she looked of European descent, she wasn't ready to chance anyone's reaction to her having a fluent Japanese accent, despite having just sailed from there.

Refraining from her engrained ritual of bowing when greeting someone, she simply gave a sweet smile. "Hello, sir."

After a brief moment as he looked over her documents, she was granted entrance. "Everything looks good, Miss Ipsley." He handed her back the documents. "Welcome home."

She folded the pages and put them back in her bag. "Katherine or Kay is fine." She tried on her new name.

He tipped his hat. "Have a wonderful day, Miss Ipsley."

"Thank you. You as well." She smiled.

American dollars in hand, Kaori paid a young man on the dock to help her with her trunk and find her a car to a local hotel. It didn't take her even twenty-four hours to plan a route, pay for tickets, and be on her way to Colorado. As eager as she was, she didn't want to waste any time. She boarded a train as early as she could and was on her way to Warren.

"HAVENWOOD FALLS, PLEASE." Kaori rested her hands on the sill of the ticket window at the train station in Grand Junction, Colorado. "The station in California said they only had tickets for trains to here and to ask once I arrived about getting closer."

The man behind the counter quirked an eyebrow. "I'm sorry, ma'am. Where did you say?"

She cleared her throat and repeated herself. "Havenwood Falls, please."

His brows furrowed at her question. "I'm sorry, miss. I'm not sure we have a train to that town. Is it in Colorado or another state?" He was flipping through a small stack of papers that listed all of the towns the trains went to. "Is it newly established?"

Kaori's heart thudded as her mind raced. She wasn't sure if she'd gotten the name of the town wrong or if she'd purposefully been given the wrong name. Either way, all she knew was that she was standing in a train station in the middle of a foreign country, completely unsure of where to go. Panic rose in her throat, and she fought to keep the guise of her appearance and not to turn into her true fox form and run out of there and all the way back to Japan.

Before she could speak, a tall, dark-haired man stepped up. He loomed over her with his stature, not just in height but build as well. "No trains go up there, but I am going that way, ma'am. You're welcome to ride along." He nodded to the older man behind the counter. "Hello, Fred."

She looked the man over before glancing back at the employee behind the booth, who had moved on to other tasks after nodding in return to being greeted. She was well aware that a human woman should be intimidated or even frightened about going off with some random stranger, especially one his size. It was dangerous even for her. But Kaori wasn't human, and she often had to remind herself of proper reactions to keep up appearances. So she put on a slight show of hesitation. "Alone? Are you um . . ."

He put a hand on her shoulder. "You are safe with me." Dropping his hand, he pulled his coat on. "My name is Theodore Brooks. Or Theo for short. I run a lumber company. I was just dropping my sister off. She was heading home after visiting for holiday."

Adjusting her shoulder bag, she reached a hand out. "Kaor— Katherine. Katherine Ipsley or Kay. Sorry. Either is fine."

He took her hand, much more gently than she expected. "Miss Ipsley, do you have luggage I can assist with?"

Giving up the façade, seeing he wasn't looking for her to be the damsel in distress just so he could pretend to be her knight in shining armor, Kaori motioned to her trunk as she lifted her handbag. "Just this. Thank you."

He gripped the handle and waved his hand for her to go ahead of him. "I'm parked just outside."

The pair stepped out into the brisk Colorado air. Theo opened the passenger door for her before pulling the trunk onto the rear of his truck and securing it with a rope. The entire vehicle jostled as he climbed in behind the wheel, reminding her of his size. But when he gave her a shy smile as he started the engine, she returned the smile and smoothed out her skirts.

After a few twists and turns on the mountain roads and many miles, Theo broke the silence. "Meeting someone?"

"Yes, I am," she replied, staring out over the landscape, still attempting to hide her lack of fluency in the American accent.

"Figures. Nobody comes to Havenwood Falls without a reason." The truck growled as he downshifted. "I won't pry."

She snapped her full attention to him. "I'm so sorry. I didn't mean to be rude."

"You're not being rude at all. It is none of my business." Theo pulled the wheel to steer them around a sharp corner.

Kaori took a breath and sat up straight, figuring this was as good a time as any to practice not only speaking but her story as well. "I've been away, and I picked up a bit of an accent, so I am shy about speaking still. Especially with the laws in effect."

"Your accent is barely noticeable." His eyes didn't leave the road.

"Thank you." Her gaze returned to the mountainside. "The gentleman I was planning to marry was called back here sooner than expected, and I am just coming to join him."

He nodded as she spoke. "Oh? In Havenwood Falls? Really? What is his name?"

"Mr. Warren Bennet." She blushed. "He's a bookkeeper."

Sitting upright at Warren's name, Theo's posture became a bit more rigid. He appeared thankful that she was distracted by the view so he could regain his composure. "Ah, yes. Warren. Would you like me to deliver you and your luggage to his home or to your lodgings?"

"You know him?" She turned back, surprised.

"Everyone knows everyone in Havenwood Falls, miss." He turned them around another sharp curve and pulled onto County Road 13.

"Ah yes. I see." She bit her lip. "Since I don't have a room settled as of yet, if you know where he lives, I would love to surprise him. He's not expecting me."

"Oh. No doubt he isn't." Theo chuckled.

"Should I be privy to some information you know that I do

not, Mr. Brooks?" Kaori searched his expression, unsettled by his reaction.

He shook his head. "No, ma'am. As I said, this is none of my business. I am just offering you transportation since I was going this way. What you're doing is truly romantic. Such an adventure for a woman."

As much as she wanted to take offense at the comment, he wasn't wrong. The world had made great strides, including the United States allowing women to vote five years prior, but women did not often travel alone, let alone long distances. And women were not likely to do the romantic gesture for a man, especially not one as grand as traveling as far as she had.

Kaori fussed with her hair, repinning a few locks that had fallen astray. "I suppose I'm not a typical woman, Mr. Brooks."

"No, Miss Ipsley. I can see that you are not." She thought she could see a smirk form on his lips for a moment, but it was gone before she could be sure.

"Katherine or Kay, please. We have crossed miles together unchaperoned. I believe we can address each other by our first names." Her words came out more formal than she'd intended.

He matched her tone. "All right. Kay it is, then."

"Thank you." She fought a smile.

Turning the wheel again, Theo drove them through a narrow portion of a side road for a few minutes before turning into a driveway. "Here's Warren's home. Are you sure this is where you want me to leave you? If he's not home, or you decide not to stay, you won't find a car passing by to take you the rest of the way into town."

She peered up the dirt path, thinking for a moment. "No. I'll be fine. He should be home, and he will be overjoyed to see me. I'm sure."

"Well then, Kay, I'll help you unload your trunk. The ground is dry, so you should have no problem wheeling it up to the house. Uninvited and such, I very much doubt Warren would take kindly to seeing you escorted by another man." Theo stopped the vehicle, came around, and held a hand out to her to help her out of the car.

"Thank you." She gave him a slight bow. Quickly, she recovered and attempted to make it a more English bow than Japanese, hoping she didn't look too awkward.

He chuckled. "You know, just because the government doesn't allow Asians in, I'm pretty sure they'll not throw you on a boat, considering you come from here. Besides, how will they see how beautiful a culture it is if they're not exposed to it?"

She moved her hand slowly out of his and looked up at him, slightly surprised. "Have you been there? Asia?"

He nodded. "Yes, ma'am. I did a couple of trips with a shipping line. Not hard for a man like myself to get a job doing grunt work."

She fluffed her skirts out as he unloaded her luggage. "You sound far more educated than what your muscles probably imply for you."

A corner of his mouth turned up into a smirk. "Are you implying that I appear uneducated? A ruffian?"

Her eyes went wide. "Oh no! I didn't mean to insult you, sir. I just—"

He stopped her. "I am teasing you, Kay. I understand that my stature lends a certain pre-established sense of who I must be versus who I am. I am older than I look, and I'm far more traveled than most."

She let the tension drop out of her shoulders. "I can relate, Mr. Brooks. Very much so."

He took her hand and kissed the back of it gently. "Theo, please."

"Theo." She smiled and bowed her head.

He returned the gesture. "Good luck, Kay. If you run into any issues with finding accommodations or ever need any lumber while you're here, you know where to find me."

"Yes, I do." She gripped her trunk. "Thank you very much for the escort, Theo. You are very sweet. I hope to see you around town."

"I am sure you will." He climbed back into the vehicle and backed out of the driveway, waving as he pulled out onto the narrow dirt road and out of sight.

Kaori tugged the trunk and started for the house. Her shoulders back, a smile on her face, and her heart racing slightly, she peered through the windows and across the yard to see if she could catch sight of him. But as she closed in on the front porch, she realized that everything was still . . . a bit too still.

Her heart's fluttering turned to pounding as the hairs on the back of her neck stood. Letting her luggage rest on the bottom step, she ascended the rest and stood in front of the door, hand raised to knock but unable to bring herself to do so. Instead, she clasped her hands in front of her, closed her eyes, and breathed.

Waves of her consciousness fanned out, feeling for signs of life. A raccoon, a few mice, and a number of spiders were all inside. A doe and her two offspring were just inside the woods to the east, lapping up water from the creek that ran into the nearby river. And a bear was lazily eating something to the north, a ways into the woods.

There was no sign of a human.

She took a breath and concentrated again, this time searching for less conventional beings. As a kitsune, Kaori had several abilities and heightened senses. And being as old as she was, she had become aware of them. However, she had spent the majority of her life with her family—her mother, father, six brothers, an aunt and uncle, and their eleven kids. Her grandparents had only passed away a little over a hundred years prior. Or, as her kind would see it, they ascended to another level of being, as kitsune do at a thousand years old.

Overall, they were all close-knit and lived in villages together or neighboring villages, moving to new areas when enough time had passed for their extremely decelerated aging to become an issue. Sometimes they joined up with more extended family or even others of their kind. But overall, they strived to fit in and live fairly normal lives. Sure, Kaori and her family were more than aware of their powers and explored them enough to be able to know the basics of what they could do, but they didn't hone them or study them.

So standing there, searching for anyone or anything at Warren's home, she had to work harder at concentrating and focusing on that ability. And when she found nothing, she questioned if she was even doing it right when a voice echoed in her mind. "Remember, Kaori, you will only feel what you're familiar with. Energies you've felt before, whether species or, even stronger, specific beings."

An extremely light sensation of someone she knew mixed with the brief moment of joy she felt, hearing her mother's voice in her head and knowing she was watching over her, was interrupted with a hand on her shoulder. "Kay?"

She spun around, tripping over her own feet, which sent her stumbling into the front door of the house. She let out a small scream caused both by being startled and the fear that she was going to hit the porch. Having to choose between the two, she opted for falling over, keeping her concentration on staying in human form.

She closed her eyes just before feeling a hand grab hers and an arm around her waist. "Woah there. Steady now." He helped her gain her footing. "I didn't mean to frighten you."

A moment later, with her guise in place and breathing controlled, she opened her eyes. "I apologize. I don't normally scare so easily. I hadn't heard you approach."

"Yeah, I left my vehicle by the road in case all was set up here, but I felt bad for leaving you without knowing for sure." Theo took off his bowler hat and dusted it. "If nobody is here, it's quite a distance into town on foot. Not to say you couldn't do it, but I certainly wouldn't want to myself. What kind of gentleman would I be if I allowed a lady such torture?"

Kaori took a step back and pushed away several strands of hair from her face. "You're too kind." She glanced over at the door. "It seems there's nobody here after all. At least not at this time. Maybe it's best if I come into town and find accommodations first. Thank you."

He turned and waved an arm toward the driveway. "Well, then. By all means. Ladies first."

She did a slight bow and walked past him, reaching for her trunk as she stepped down onto the ground.

He walked up next to her and slipped his hand around the handle before she could. "I have this." When she quirked an eyebrow at him, he chuckled. "Again—gentleman."

Together, they made their way to the car and down the road. Once past the almost oppressive woods, they emerged into town. She watched as they passed by houses, buildings, shops, parks, and the occasional person or two walking along the finely manicured sidewalks. A trinket shop, a sign for a restaurant named Napoli's Ristorante Italiano, and City Hall all stood along the sidewalks as proud, American architecture that made the corners of Kaori's mouth curve up as she wondered at the passing scene.

Her eyes opened even wider as they passed Town Square Park. The ornate gazebo adorned the area along with trees, foliage, and pathways. But it was the fountain that caught her eye. As the sun peeked through the clouds, it seemed to almost shimmer in the sunlight in gold tones embedded into the paint. Something about it drew Kaori in, making her follow it with her eyes as they drove on.

"You seem taken with something. I take it Warren is on your mind." Theo stopped at a cross street to let a young couple make their way across.

She blinked. "Warren? Oh. No. I was just taking in our surroundings. I wasn't expecting this."

"This?" he asked.

She had returned her gaze out the window. "Yes. Havenwood Falls is so much more beautiful and progressive than I expected. I think I would like to experience that Italian restaurant soon. It looks very nice." She sounded almost surprised.

He let out a humored scoff. "Did you take us for backwoods and uncivilized?"

Her eyes grew big and cheeks red as she looked over at him. "Oh no, Theo. I didn't mean that. I just . . . I just thought it was a small town in the middle of this huge land. I expected it to be more like one of the many small towns I passed through on my way here. But even you, a lumber company owner, are far from what one would consider a lumberjack. Even your attire is more dapper. And for your size and such, one wouldn't take you for such pleasantries and manners at first sight, I would think. Even your car. A Rolls-Royce Phantom? Not exactly what I would think to see the local lumber yard owners tooling around in. But I'm from Japan—or rather have been there for so long," she tried to correct herself, "that I could be very mistaken."

He patiently listened as she babbled before allowing a grin to form on his lips. "Thank you . . . I think."

Her shoulders dropped. "I'm sorry. I'm coming off all wrong."

Theo steered the car onto the side of the road in front of what looked like a diner. "You know cars?"

She laughed. "Out of all of that, *that* is what you took away from my ramblings?"

He nodded and propped an arm over the back of the seat. "Yes."

She returned the nod. "Yes, I do. I do not know why, but they have fascinated me. Maybe because I always longed to travel more than I have ever been allowed to. A car represents freedom to do so. Beautiful cars like this one"—she ran her hands over the dash —"let you do it in both style and comfort. But—" She paused and studied it for a moment. "This is not the version that the British built. This one was made here in America, no?"

"What makes you say that? The cost of shipping a vehicle like a Rolls-Royce across the ocean?" His eyes searched her face.

She chewed her lip. "No. I believe that wouldn't have been a problem for you. I more say it because of the metals used." She stopped, a bit surprised at her mention of something she shouldn't know about just by looking at the car. "The fuel gauge. It is on the dash. I do not believe that they install those in Britain."

"You are correct." Theo got out and rounded the car, opening her door. "Hungry?"

She eyed him a moment, wondering if he heard her comment about the materials of the car or was ignoring it. "Yes, actually."

Opting to follow his lead on the matter, Kaori gave another slight bow, mentally scolding herself for the gesture.

They took a booth that overlooked the street. She, once again, found herself enraptured by her surroundings. It was so different than her homelands. But there was something even more unusual about Havenwood Falls that seemed to pull her in and fascinate her. It wasn't just the different foods, the difference in the area's vegetation, or even the look of the people and styles of clothing. There was something in the air of the small town that seemed to pull her in.

Her attention was snapped back when the waitress approached the table. "And for you, doll?"

"Excuse me?" She looked up, confused.

The waitress was wearing a bright red shade of lipstick that had left a few specks on her teeth. That would have seemed rather out of place if it wasn't for the woman's obvious preference for too much blush and eyeshadow as well. She sighed. "New to town, I take it?" Before Kaori could reply, she spoke again. "Drink or food? What would you like?"

"Oh!" Kaori glanced at Theo, who was sitting patiently. "Water and soup, please."

"One tall glass of orange juice and the full breakfast for the gentleman and a water and soup for the lady." The server repeated their orders, using a slightly disgusted tone for Kaori's portion.

"I believe you have some teriyaki in the back and maybe some rice? Could you have the cook whip something together with those as well, please?" Theo left his eyes on the woman an extra beat after he spoke.

She didn't reply right away. She just looked at him. Finally, as if she'd stopped breathing for that moment, she took in a sharp breath and smiled. "Sure thing, Mr. Brooks." And she scurried off.

"Meeting you was not accidental, was it?" Kaori sat up straight as she directed her question to Theo.

Taken a bit by surprise, he had to clear his throat before speaking. "Accident?"

Smiling at the waitress as the beverages were set down, Kaori waited until she walked away again before responding. "You being at that train station. There wasn't a sister, and you didn't just happen upon me. It wasn't an accident. You were waiting for *me*, no?"

He opened his mouth to retort, but she continued. "But what I can't figure out is why you came back for me."

Kaori lifted her glass of water, inspected it, then took a long drink, looking over the rim of the glass at him as she did. He hadn't replied. He just sat there, one eyebrow raised and lips slightly pursed. His fingers drummed on the table as she slowly lowered her glass and set it down. "You're smart. And gifted."

"Am I in trouble?"

"Not as much as you probably were."

"Are you in trouble now? And what do you mean by probably?"

The server sat their plates down in front of them, asked if anything else was needed, and left the table again. He leaned back and crossed his arms. "No."

"Ah. There it is." She lifted the first spoonful of soup to her lips and sipped, letting the warmth coat her insides.

He tilted his head. "There what is? And why aren't you trying to run?"

She sipped in another spoonful and dabbed her lips. "Run?" She laughed. "Where would I go? You brought me here down a long, windy road full of dangers. How would I get anywhere?

Besides, you came back for me. I'm guessing you know something, and you were delivering me to someone or something, but you changed your mind."

He groaned. "I knew nothing more than I was clearing a debt by picking you up and dropping you off. Nothing more."

"But you had a bad feeling . . . just as I did. Isn't that right, Mr. Brooks?" She set her spoon down.

He sat up. "We're back to last names, Miss Ipsley?"

"You tell me. Should I be fearing for our safety?" She paused. "Theo."

"I don't know."

"No?"

He shook his head. "We will find out soon enough."

"And what about the knowledge of who I am?"

"You mean what you are," he corrected her.

"Tsk tsk." She wagged her finger. "Manners, Theo. I'm a lady, not a beast."

The corner of his mouth turned up. "Consider me corrected. My blunder, my lady."

Her head bowed slightly. "You are forgiven. But yes, you know. Do you not?"

He shook his head. "I know nothing other than I was sent to pick you up. But yes, I can sense something about you."

She studied him for a few moments, taking another sip of her soup without saying anything while trying to work out the situation.

Finally deciding to take a bite of his breakfast, he chewed as she looked at him. "And you? What do you know?"

"I know that I left my country and family to follow my heart. Not just for a man but for my soul. Something pulled me here, and I'm not a foolish, young girl who blindly follows love without something more to it. There was something out at that house I didn't recognize. I also know that you do not vibrate like a mortal. But what I don't know is why I'm here, what you are, and where my Warren is." Worry veiled her expression once again.

148

After swallowing another bite, Theo sipped his beverage and leaned on the table. "I am going to find out what I can. Like you, I follow my gut when it's yelling at me. And mine told me to come back for you. If I knew anything more, I would tell you."

"Thank you."

"Don't thank me until I make sure I didn't just make matters worse." He noticed she was eyeing the plate of teriyaki chicken. "That is for you. You need to eat. Then we will find you a room at Whisper Falls Inn. I know Mihail and Irina. They own it."

She glanced out the window and back to him, giggling softly. "In a town this size, I'm sure everybody knows everybody."

His teeth gritted together slightly as his hand started rubbing his left wrist. "Speaking of everybody knowing everybody, we will have to make a stop on the way to the inn."

Taking a chunk of the chicken and rice, she nodded toward his arm. "What kind of stop?"

"You have to register." His nostrils flared.

Her eyebrow quirked up. "Register?"

His gazed moved from her to outside the diner. "Yes. They ask that everyone register so they know who all is here and if they're moving in or in town temporarily."

"And if they don't?"

He turned back to her. "Let's just say everyone registers."

"I see." She folded her hands on the table in front of her. "When do I need to do this? On our way to this inn you were telling me about?"

"Yes. Might as well get it done so you can stay long enough to look for Warren." He flagged down the waitress. "Check please."

Kaori worked on the chicken more. "Anything else I should know about this town?"

He chuckled. "So much more."

CHAPTER 3

Standing in the back of City Hall, Kaori glanced between Theo and the plain, utilitarian-looking door. "I'm supposed to trust you enough to go into the back door of a building in some strange town with you?"

He lifted a shoulder as he opened the door. "You got into a vehicle at a strange train station and went to this town with me with less hesitation."

Kaori huffed. "Valid point, Theo."

He reached around her and gripped the handle, pulling it open. She shivered. As she peered into the space inside, her feet refused to move for a moment. She closed her eyes and allowed herself to feel the energies around her. Of course, she felt Theo standing close by, patiently waiting for her to make a move. She also picked up several humans and other beings throughout the building. As far as the level they were entering, it felt mostly empty. That is, until someone appeared inside suddenly, boldly, swiftly moving toward the door. The movements jolted Kaori so much that she stumbled backward.

"Hello," a woman greeted them.

Once again, before she landed on the ground, Theo reached out and steadied her. "Hello, Saundra."

"Good day, Mr. Brooks. Do we have a visitor?" The woman gave a Kaori a smile before looking back at Theo. "She yours?"

"What?" Kaori gasped. "No! I'm spoken for."

"Oh, pardon me." She waved her hand dismissively. "Come in. We will get this over with quickly. I sadly can't visit with you, as I have urgent duties waiting."

Kaori followed as the woman walked back inside. She glanced back to Theo and raised an eyebrow. "What do I need? My documents that I came to this continent with?"

"No." He motioned for her to keep walking. "Your real name, species, and plans while here. They will also ask if you're—"

Saundra interrupted as she sat behind a desk. "Take a seat." Both of them did as instructed. "Name, species, and why you're here. I'll also need to take a blood sample as well as one last thing once we're done . . . if you're granted permission to stay."

"What is that?" Kaori looked back and forth between them.

"Start with your name, species, and why you're here while I take your blood." Saundra stood and rounded the oak desk with the necessary items to take the sample. "Wait. Is there anything I should know about your blood or your skin that would make this difficult or even dangerous?"

Confused, Kaori's eyes went wide as her brows pulled in. "No? I mean, not that I know of."

"Okay, then proceed." Saundra readied the needle.

"Okay?" Still confused, she watched the woman carefully. "My name is Katherine Ipsley."

"Good. Now your real name." Saundra spoke pointedly.

Kaori cleared her throat. "Kaori Ishida."

"Species and reason for coming to Havenwood Falls?" the woman asked.

"I'm a kitsune. And I'm here because I believe the man I was supposed to marry was called back to the States for work, and I've come to be with him." Kaori spoke around the lump in her throat.

Saundra stopped and looked at Kaori. "Kitsune?"

She nodded proudly. "Yes, ma'am."

"Japanese?" Saundra eyed her.

Kaori bowed her head slowly. "Yes."

Theo sat forward, raising a hand. "Kay . . . I mean, Kaori is . . ."

She waved him off. "I am not concerned with the mortal laws. If it was up to most humans, we would all be killed off or sent away. I am curious about her being kitsune. Curious." Saundra looked into Kaori's eyes as if she was studying her. "I believe you are our first."

Kaori attempted a smile. "I hope that my stay is a positive one."

Saundra returned her smile. "I'm sure it will be, as long as we have no troubles. Now, give me a moment. I'll return."

Saundra left with the vial of blood in hand. Kaori inspected the spot where the draw had been taken from, rubbing the bandage that had been taped over it. "What now?"

"We wait," Theo replied.

"For what?"

He sighed. "Approval."

"Then?" She picked at the bandage.

"Your tattoo." Saundra reentered the room with a new set of items in hand.

"Tattoo?" Kaori stood. "I never agreed to a tattoo!"

Saundra stopped and just looked at the woman.

Kaori vigorously shook her head. "No. Is it not illegal?"

"No." Saundra started laying out the items on her desk. "In fact, it's the only way you may legally stay in our town."

Theo leaned up and looked Kaori in the face. "It's okay. In order for you to stay to look for him, you have to register. The tattooing is part of it. But don't worry. It disappears when you leave here. So if you're worried about having it if you return to your family, you can rest assured that won't be an issue."

"It disappears?" she asked.

Saundra nodded. "Yes, it does. Now, I have something to get back to. How about we get this over with?"

After a moment of hesitation, Kaori looked at Theo one more time for reassurance. After he nodded, she held out her arm. "Yes. I need to stay and find Warren."

The needle hit Kaori's arm, and she flinched. Taking a breath, she centered herself as Saundra worked the needle expertly. It didn't take long before it was complete. With a clean cloth, Saundra wiped her skin and put a layer of ointment over it. "There. That will seal it. Just as Theo said, if you leave, this will disappear. Also, if you choose to stay permanently, you *must* come back and register as permanent."

Kaori touched the fresh ink and hissed as it stung. "I will."

Standing, Theo moved toward the door. "Now, the inn. Shall we?"

Seeing he didn't want to stay any longer than necessary, she looked at Saundra. "Are we all set?"

"Yes." She cleaned up and tucked everything away. "Goodbye."

Then she was gone.

Kaori looked around them, confused. "Where did she go?"

Theo shrugged. "I could not tell you. She does that, though."

Her finger traced a circle around her new adornment as the two of them went back out the door and to the car. As he pulled out onto the road, Kaori sighed.

"When I left my village, I thought that with coming to America, I would be the strangest one and would have to hide who I am. But despite being used to living with an entire family of kitsune—my family—I'm encountering even more strange people and things here."

Theo laughed. "You just got here, Kay. Give it time."

"Things get less weird?" she asked.

He shook his head. "No. They get more bizarre."

Another sigh escaped her lungs. "I see."

They drove the rest of the way in silence. Kaori, deep in thought, sat quietly. Obviously struggling with her thoughts, she continued to stay poised in her seat. Just as Theo held his posture as he steered the car in front of the inn.

"Allow me." He got out and rounded the car to open her door. She exited, giving a slight bow. "Thank you."

After shutting the door, he went back and started to lift the trunk out of the back end of the vehicle, when Kaori screamed.

❧

THEO DROPPED THE TRUNK. "KAY?"

He ran around, scanning the area.

She was gone, only her attire left in a heap on the ground.

Theo, obviously completely baffled, called out, "Kay? Kay!"

He crossed the front yard of the inn in a few strides, peering around trees, looking for any sign of her. But there was nobody, only a dog that was on a tie near the side of a nearby home. It barked, and Theo realized he'd not registered its bark before that, being used to random neighborhood dogs. Disregarding the dog, he kept looking for anyone. But there was no sign of another person anywhere. And there was no sign of Kaori.

He picked up her gown, shoes, and other garments, laying them in the back seat of his car before setting the jewelry in his pocket, afraid someone might take them. Once everything was secure, he walked in the direction he wouldn't have seen from where he had been standing, continuing to call her name out. "Kay!"

After walking several blocks and crossing the threshold into the woods, he still bellowed for her. His deep voice resonated through the landscape. Pulling back branches and lifting sides of small bushes, Theo sniffed everything, trying to pick up a trail or even a general direction she could have gone. Frustrated, he stopped in a clearing and slowly turned in a circle, examining every tree, bush, and pile of leaves for signs of being disturbed.

He lifted his hands and cupped them, palms facing each other, straight out in front of his chest. Light started to spark between them as he opened his mouth to speak. "Nádar . . ."

He stopped, the sparks in his palm dying out, and he looked

down, seeing a fox at his feet. The small creature sat, looking up at him. But when a dog started barking again, the noise echoing into the woods, the fox took off and ran, hiding under a nearby bush.

He walked over and knelt down. "Kay?"

The fox peeked out, sniffing the air.

"The dog?" he asked.

The creature looked him in the eye.

"All right. I'm not sure what to do." He thought for a moment. "I can carry you out and into the car."

She backed up a couple steps.

He chuckled. "Okay. No carrying. I understand. Well? The dog is tied up. If you stay close, I will walk with you and make sure you're in the car before I get in."

She emerged from her hiding spot, trembling softly.

The two made their way back to the vehicle. Theo did just as he said, letting her in first and shutting the door before making his way to his side of the car. The dog was making it well known that it knew they were there. With a hand gripping the handle to his door, Theo gave a low growl and looked back at the animal. The dog, tail between his legs, bowed down to the ground and stopped its noisemaking.

He got in, started the car, and pulled away. Kaori, still in fox form, sat in the passenger seat, curled up in her tail, trembling.

Once around the corner, Theo glanced over at her. "I take it you will need your clothes and a private place to put them on in order to return to human form. There's a limited number of places I can take you, so I will just take you to my home. I have a spare bedroom that my sister uses when she is visiting. Nobody will bother you there."

Theo drove up his driveway and parked, letting Kaori out and leading her inside. He showed her to the spare room and set her garments and jewelry on the bed, closing the door tight behind him.

∽

SEVERAL MINUTES LATER, Kaori emerged into the living room, fastened neatly into her dress, her hair pulled up just as it had been before her transition. Her cheeks were red, and her head was tilted down. "My apologies. I do not do well around dogs."

Theo laughed, doubling over slightly. "That is perfect."

"Perfect?" Kaori was confused.

He gathered himself. "It is my turn to apologize. It's just . . . well? You're a shifter, no?"

"I am kitsune," she replied.

"Kistune?"

She nodded. "Yes, I am fox. But we can transform into humans or even other creatures. The older we are, the more abilities we have and the stronger we are." She shifted her appearance into her Japanese human form. "This is what I am used to looking like as a human . . . you already saw me as a fox." She blushed again.

"Very interested. I would love to learn more," he said.

She bowed. "For helping me, I would love to tell you more. But I'm curious what species you are. I can sense you are not human. And I know it by the registration process and knowledge." She held up her freshly tattooed wrist.

He pushed the sleeve of his right arm up, revealing one of his own. "I am not human. I am . . . complicated."

"Complicated? Do explain." She took a seat.

He pursed his lips, thinking over his words. "To start, I am druid. My mother's family lineage is druid. We believe and practice what many see as magic."

"Not unlike those we call Shinto," she observed.

"Yes," he agreed. "But that is not all. I am also lycan."

She tilted her head.

"My father's lineage is lycan. So, I am a shifter like you. There are shifters and were-kin in the world, yes. Lycan are a bit different, though. I shift into a wolf—larger than normal wolves by far, and I'm forced to shift on the full moon. But I'm capable of shifting other times as well. And I also shift into a bipedal form. I suppose, really, it's simpler to say we have more than one form of wolf, which makes me different than other wolf shifters. But . . ."

She sat up. "This is why you were laughing. You're a dog."

He crossed his arms. "I am lycan. Thus, wolf, not dog. But I am part canine. Yes."

Kaori watched him, her eyes studying him as neither spoke. Occasionally, her eyebrows would pull in, then release. A smile would sneak onto her lips, then disappear. Finally, she let out a sigh and bit her lip. "I do not seem to fear you like I do other dogs."

"Wolf—canine. Not dog," he corrected her.

She shrugged. "Large dog-wolf person with magical powers. I have no room to judge you. I am a fox that is able to appear human and has magical powers as well. We are not unalike in that matter."

He chuckled. "You have a very valid point, Kay." He held his hand out to her. "Allies then?"

She shook his hand. "Yes. That is most appreciated."

"Now, we need to figure out accommodations for you. Then we can sort out this Warren situation." Theo wrung his hands.

"Yes. A place to stay would be very good, but . . ." Kaori glanced off in the direction of the dog. "How many dogs are in town? Are they all tied up or roaming free? How often is that one, out there, able to be out?" She rapid-fired off question after question.

He studied her for a moment. "Your fear is strong, isn't it?"

She brought her gaze back to him. "Yes." She shook her head as if trying to clear it. "Not unlike the legendary strife between vampires and werewolves, kitsune fear dogs. It's almost ingrained in us. Like a child fearing the dark or their bedroom closet at night."

"Or my fear of clowns. I don't know why and can't explain it, but clowns freak me out." Theo chuckled nervously.

She nodded, her eyes not leaving his face. "That's a pretty strange fear, Theo."

"Yes. I suppose it makes far less sense than your fear of dogs." Theo shrugged, shifting his weight between his feet. "I gather staying at the inn is going to be a problem with the dog across the street. Therefore, I propose you stay in my spare bedroom. My sister will not be back in Havenwood Falls for a while, so it will just be sitting empty."

"I wouldn't dream of imposing on you." Kaori clasped her hands.

He stepped to the hallway and pulled a quilt out of the linen closet there. "You would not be a bother. The company would be nice. Plus, then I will be easier to get in touch with should you need someone."

"But—"

"But nothing." He handed her the quilt. "I cannot, in good conscience, allow you to not have a place to stay. Now, bring the quilt, and we can change the dusty bed coverings with clean ones. Then I will retrieve your trunk for you." He saw the worried look on her face. "Unless you truly oppose. I wouldn't want to force you into a situation you were entirely uncomfortable with."

The decision not only weighed on her mind but showed in her features as well. Still wringing her hands, she took a couple breaths before replying. "It is not customary. Some may even say it is inappropriate. However, I cannot bear the idea of going near that mongrel by the inn every day. So if you say there is no other inn, then I must accept your offer. And if you do not mind, I would like to cook dinner if you could just take me to a market to purchase a few supplies."

"I am glad to hear it. I will retrieve your things from the car. There is a private bathroom off your bedroom. Make yourself comfortable. You are welcome to go to the kitchen and see what I have. If you do not find what you need, we can go to the market then."

Kaori bowed. "You are most generous. I am thankful for you."

"It is no problem at all. I will return." He left to get her trunk. Once settled, Kaori surveyed the contents of the kitchen before joining Theo in the living room. He was sitting and reading a book by candlelight, the rocking chair he sat in creaking with the occasional shift of his weight.

She stood in the archway that separated the living room from the kitchen, debating whether to offer to turn on the lamp but figuring his lighting choice was a preference. "Have you not had a woman in this home for a while?"

"A woman?" he asked, puzzled.

"Yes." She giggled. "I believe all I found was meat and potatoes. I did not even find a cellar filled with jars of food."

"It seems my sister's absence has taken a toll on my menu. Then I say we should go into town and pick up something other than meat and potatoes." He smirked.

"Yes, we should," she agreed.

It was a short drive there, just as most things were in such a small town. Granted, to get to the nearest city or anything else, it would take a stretch of time. But within the town itself? Kaori marveled once again as they drove, taking in the shop signs, architecture, and the people. Only this time, it was as if a veil had been taken off her eyes; she finally let her kitsune senses kick in and felt the essence of those around her. It was something she normally blocked. This time, though, she allowed herself to open up. She knew that many, if not most, of those people were not humans. And this made her wonder what species they each were. Her expression conveyed her fascination as her eyes darted around.

"I am surprised at your excitement. You have spent your life in a large family of supernatural beings. Yet you seem in awe of the cluster of them here." Theo turned off the engine in front of the general store.

"Oh!" Kaori spun in her seat. "I am only used to my kind— kitsune. I have come across some others. At my age, I am not entirely sheltered. Yet, never in a setting such as this. So many in one place . . . all living together in harmony, it seems."

"Havenwood Falls is definitely a unique town. But it is not

without some struggle that we achieve this." He opened his door. "I will be right around."

She exited as he opened her door. "Thank you."

Inside, Theo made his way to the counter. "Good day, Laura. How is business?"

A petite woman set a couple of packaged items on a shelf behind the counter and turned around. "Good. It pays to be the only store in a town that carries basic necessities."

He chuckled. "That's very true."

She grinned. "Not unlike being the lumber yard owner, no?"

"Exactly." He glanced over at Kaori, who was gathering items off a list she'd made. "Hey, I was wondering—you see people coming in and out of here all the time. And I suppose many people stop and fill you in on things as they pass through."

"Not unlike being a bartender some days," she agreed.

He leaned against the counter casually, turned slightly away to be able to see Kaori. "You wouldn't happen to know a Warren Bennet, would you? He'd be new to town, if he's here."

She thought for a moment, straightening the stack of packaged cigarettes near her as she did. "No, not that I can think of. But there are people that come through town all the time. That Porter Patterson that lives up on the mountainside always has people in and out of his place, and sometimes they come down here to purchase goods."

"Porter, huh?" He pulled his wallet out as Kaori approached.

"Yes." Laura started pushing buttons on her metal cash register, totaling up the items Kaori had selected and placing them in paper bags. She gave Theo an inquisitive look. "And who is this?"

"My apologies, ladies." He stood up straight. "Laura, this is Kay. She just arrived and is here looking for Warren, her fiancé. Kay, this is Laura. She owns and runs this shop. A mighty fine achievement for a woman, if you ask me."

Laura smirked. "When the previous owner passed, the store was going to close. I saw a need, and I provided it. It is not as if this town is conventional. Thus, I was able to take over the general store without too much strife from the menfolk."

Kaori held a hand out. "It is very nice to meet you. Congratulations on your success."

Laura returned the gesture and finished bagging the several items Theo and Kay had brought to the counter. "Thank you. Two dollars and sixteen cents, please."

Kaori started to open her purse. "Yes. Of course."

But Theo beat her to it. "Here you go. Keep the change. Let me know if you find anything out, if you don't mind?"

Laura took the money from him and slipped it into the drawer. "Will do."

"It was very nice to meet you." Kaori went for the bags.

Again, Theo beat her to it. "See you soon."

With a slight twinkle in her eyes, she replied to him, "I certainly hope so."

Once back in the car, Kaori giggled. "She likes you very much."

"Yes. We are good friends. I have helped her with most of the shelving and a number of other things for her store," he explained.

"No," she argued. "She likes you for more than a handyman."

He blinked. "You think?"

"I know," she replied.

He laughed. "You *know*? One of your gifts?"

She pursed her lips. "Simple observation reveals that, but I do have a couple of other gifts that aided me in this conclusion. Have you considered her in that way?"

He cleared his throat. "No, not that I can think of. She has always just been my friend."

"I see," Kaori said.

The matter was dropped. While they drove back through town, Kaori's enthusiasm was far less as she watched out the window. Her hands were folded in her lap, the corners of her mouth turned down, and her shoulders set and poised. Seeing her change in demeanor, Theo asked, "Would you like to drive by the house one more time and see if there's a car or a buggy?"

She perked up. "As wonderful as that would be, I do not want to inconvenience you any more than I already am."

"Nonsense." He waved a hand. "You are no bother. This town can be downright sleepy at times. And as much as I prefer things that way, I do not mind helping someone in need. I would just be home reading today, otherwise. Instead, I will be getting a home-cooked meal other than meat and potatoes."

She giggled. "Then I shall find something more to do in exchange for your kindness." Her eyes returned to the scenery, a little brighter again. "Thank you."

"You are very welcome."

Taking County Road 13 back out of town, Theo drove into the driveway this time, pulling up to the house. "I'll get out and look around. I'll be right back."

Kaori waited several minutes, but when he didn't come back around the house, she started to climb out, worried.

"Theo?" she called out. "Is everything okay?"

Silence greeted her for only a moment before he came jogging around from behind the house, slightly out of breath. "I checked back in the woods a ways to see if maybe he was gathering firewood or anything. I hope I didn't alarm you."

"I suppose I am on edge, that is all," she replied. "I did not mean to overreact."

He crossed the yard and opened her door for her. "Kaori, I would not have blamed you if you had run across the yard crying. You've been through enough."

"I've been through far worse in my years," she exclaimed once back in the car.

"*That* I do not doubt."

CHAPTER 4

Theo had asked Kaori several times if she would like or need help in the kitchen, but she insisted she was fine. Finally, she asked for several sticks—"thin as twigs but sturdy as branches"—for her to finish cooking the dish she was working on. He retrieved them, then brought in some firewood and went to his chair. He had taken up residence back in his rocking chair, reading a book.

Once dinner was ready, she called him in to the table, where he found a spread of yakitori, rice, and a pot of udon noodle soup. He took his seat, and she dished out a serving as he took a deep breath, smelling the aromas. "This smells delicious."

"Arigatu." She bowed slightly. "I will have to learn more recipes from other cultures. And maybe Laura can procure some foods that I could use for more of my people's dishes, as well."

After waiting for her to sit with a full plate and bowl as well, he took his first bite. "If this is the quality of meals you'll keep cooking while you're here, I will certainly make sure she does, or I will go into the city myself."

A blush washed over Kaori's cheeks. "You are too kind."

He tapped the corners of his mouth with a napkin. "Laura can usually find anything I ask her for. Which reminds me. Since she is privy to a lot of the town's chattering, I asked her if she had seen your Warren."

"You did?" She perked up with a child's enthusiasm. "Has he been in there recently? Does she know where I might find him?"

He shook his head solemnly. "No. I'm so sorry. She has not seen him nor heard of his whereabouts."

"So we're no closer to knowing anything." Kaori looked defeated.

"I'm truly sorry, Kay. But this could be as simple as him having gone into the city for supplies or being at work. You told me he came back for his job."

"He did." She set her napkin on the table. "He would have made it here three weeks ago. The fact that we cannot find him has stirred something in my stomach that's sour."

"Supplies. Like I said, I think he's just gone for supplies." Theo sat up straight, confident in his statement.

"I am sure I am just anxious to see him. You are probably right." She laid her napkin back across her lap and finished her meal in silence.

Theo didn't disturb her, seeing she obviously needed a moment to let her thoughts process. When they were done, he insisted on clearing the table and washing the dishes himself. "You go rest. The journey here surely must have taken a toll on you. Take a nap, read a book, whatever you need to rest. If you need to go outside, though, please let me know. You shouldn't be out there on your own, being new to town. You do not know what is in the woods yet, and they do not know you."

She gave a weak smile. "A book sounds fine just about now." She was crossing the threshold into the living room when she turned around. "Thank you, Theo. Very much."

He tipped his head. "Just rest. You will see him soon enough."

"I hope so." Kaori handed him the last dish off the table and went into the spare room, closing the door behind her.

∼

KAORI EMERGED from the room after falling asleep while reading, not sure how much time had passed. She walked through the common areas of the house to find Theo and let him know she was up, but she did not find him. Thinking he possibly went into his own room for a nap himself, she went out onto the front porch to sit.

A few moments later, the silence was interrupted by the sound of Theo's voice. "No. I need to know if he's even here, or if I'm just participating in some wild goose chase. For that matter, if he even exists at all. That woman is starting to panic."

A woman's voice replied. "As you were told, you know only what you need to know. You were supposed to drop her off and then wash your hands of it."

"I owed Porter one favor. And that favor was to pick her up, pretend to know Warren and where he lived, and bring her to Havenwood Falls. I fulfilled this." His tone was growing more tense as he spoke.

She replied with equal frustration. "You were supposed to leave her at that house for us."

"For what?" His words were pointed.

She didn't pause. "*That* is none of your concern, Theodore."

A wind picked up, making it hard to hear what was said next, but when it died down, she heard him say, "It is my issue when I was the one to bring her here. Now explain to me what is going on."

"I cannot," the woman replied.

"Then she stays with me until she gives up on this Warren or decides to go home. I do not trust Porter or anyone who works for him."

The woman growled. "Yet you agreed to bring her here for him?"

"I made the mistake of getting into debt with him on a job . . . a small debt. A mistake I will never make again. And I fulfilled that. But I could not, in good conscience, leave that lady to lord knows what he had planned for her." The winds picked up for another quick moment.

"That's where you're wrong. Porter wants me to bring her to him. So I will be taking her with me." There was a snarky confidence in the woman's voice.

Kaori heard crunching as if someone's footfalls were heavy. "I would like to see you try to take her. But I must advise against it."

Both the heavy footfalls and another set started coming around the side of the house. Holding her breath, Kaori tucked herself back inside the door and readied herself to transform, if needed. She pressed her back against the wall just inside the door, but only one set of feet came across the snow and up the porch steps.

Slowly, she turned and dared to peek through the sheer curtain that adorned the front window. Theo was standing, facing the direction of the driveway, arms crossed over his chest, shoulders tight. She could see them rise and fall with every slow, deliberate breath he took.

She carefully opened the door and stepped out onto the porch. "I am in some trouble, am I not?"

"Get back inside. It is not safe for you outside right now." He took her by the arm, a bit more gently than she expected, and guided her back inside.

"I am not wrong."

"You overheard?"

She looked down at her clasped hands. "Yes."

He looked at her solemnly. "No. You are not wrong."

She took a deep breath. "Warren . . . is he . . ."

"I do not know." He dropped his hands. "These people cannot be trusted. I do not know who that woman is . . . or *what* she is. But Porter Patterson is not a good man. What he wants with you cannot be a good thing, knowing your abilities."

"But what if they have Warren?" Panic filled her eyes with tears.

"I will do what I can to find out, but this man . . . he lives in a large home in the woods. I'd say he's secluded out there, but he has people coming and going day and night. Trust me, none of it is good dealings. He owns a portion of the railroad, which makes him rich. And he did not attain it, nor his riches, by honorable means." Theo stepped inside, closing the door and bolting it. "I am not sure anyone in town has much to do with him. And those that do are either in trouble from their ties to him or just as bad as he is."

She slumped down onto the window bench, the tears that were filling her eyes moments before now sliding down her cheeks. "I do not want to put you in danger."

"What do you mean?" He knelt down in front of her.

Her eyes were ringed with red. "My being here puts you in danger. Like you said, you do not know who or what that woman was. She could have harmed you." Kaori stood, adjusting her dress. "I cannot put you in any more danger. I will just find this Porter Patterson's house, sneak there in my fox form, and see if I can find Warren myself."

"Kay, that is not safe."

"Neither is me being here. For you . . . for either of us."

"I can handle them."

She paced. "I cannot."

"And I cannot let you walk into danger alone."

They stopped and looked at each other, both standing with postures that betrayed something beyond their stubbornness. Both obviously concerned and unwilling to walk away.

Kaori broke the standoff first. "Why?"

"Why what?" he asked.

She huffed. "Why are you deliberately putting yourself in danger for some strange woman?"

"Why are you so willing to put yourself in unknown danger when someone is willing to help you?"

She crossed her arms. "Do not answer my question with a question."

"Fine." He mirrored her stance. "I do not know."

"You . . . what?" She scrunched her face. "You do not know?"

He relaxed his stance. "No. Could be because I have too big a heart to let someone get hurt when I'm sure that is what will happen. Could be my protective nature. Could be that there is something about you. Could be . . ."

She stormed out of the room.

Left standing in the middle of the living room, Theo growled deep and low. "Could be because I'm a fool."

Kaori did not come out of the spare room the rest of the night.

CHAPTER 5

The aromas of bacon, eggs, flapjacks, and potatoes filled the air. Various shades of reds, yellows, and oranges had invaded the dark blues of the early morning sky, overpowering the twinkling white light of the stars. Theo stood at the stove, flipping a golden brown flapjack while munching on a slice of crisp bacon. His eyelids were drooping as his mouth opened wide in a yawn.

"Good morning." Kaori's voice was soft.

He turned and saw her standing in the archway. "Good morning. I hope you are hungry."

"I have never had an American-style breakfast before." She didn't move from her position.

Tossing the flapjack onto a plate, he shoveled on some of each of the other foods that were prepared and set it on the table. "There's fresh-squeezed orange juice in the icebox. Help yourself."

"I couldn't—" she started.

He whipped around, spatula in hand. "Sit. Eat. Enjoy some orange juice. And relax. For someone from your culture, you are awfully uptight."

"I just don't want to keep putting you out." She made her way to the end of the table and placed her hands on the edge.

He poured more batter into the cast-iron skillet. "You'd be putting me through worse by not letting me help at this point."

She eyed him, studying his posture as much as his words. "I can see that now. My apologies."

He stomped over to the icebox, yanked out the canister of orange juice, and dropped it onto the table next to two juice glasses. "And if you wouldn't mind, please stop apologizing."

"I'm s—" She rolled her lips in between her teeth. "Yes. I will do my best."

"Good." He went back to the stovetop just in time to flip the contents of each of the pans before anything burned.

Together, they ate, neither saying much more than how delicious the food was and what Theo had to do down at the lumberyard that day. He insisted Kaori come with him, since leaving her alone in his home left her vulnerable.

She was reluctant, but seeing he was firm, she gave in. "Maybe I can be of some help to repay you."

"I am sure I can find something for you to do. I can understand the need to feel of some use." He started clearing the dishes.

She took them from him. "You cleaned when I cooked. I will do the same for you before I get ready."

"Deal." He smiled.

She made quick work of cleaning up the kitchen and herself, emerging from the room in a fresh knit dress, her hair pinned up stylishly, with a modest amount of makeup on. "I hope I did not delay you."

"No." He stood from his rocking chair. "This allowed me to get some reading in that I didn't accomplish last night."

"Good." She fought a smile.

"Yes. Good."

The tension between them was thick. And it continued. The drive was silent other than the noise of the car and the sounds of nature around them. Once again, Kaori found herself gazing out the window as they drove the several miles to Brooks Lumber.

Theo held the door open for her and introduced several employees to Kaori, being careful to refer to her as Kay, on their way into the office. They stopped at the front counter, which was situated in front of his office. He waved his hand toward the woman behind the register. "This is Winnifred Rose. She runs our front counter and tends to keep many of the boys in line around here."

"Including you, Mr. Brooks," she added with a giggle.

"Including me at times, yes, Winnie." He chuckled. "This is Kay. She is a friend from out of town . . . and recently out of the country. She will probably be helping me out with some office work here and there while she is in Havenwood Falls."

Winnie looked Kaori up and down before fixing a polite smile on her face. "Nice to meet you."

"Nice to meet you, too," Kaori replied.

But before her words were fully out, Winnie had gone back to her paperwork, glancing up only once more with a not-so-pleased expression on her face.

Once in the office with the door closed, Kaori laughed. "You certainly have a trail of weeping women around here."

He was shuffling through some paperwork. "Excuse me?"

"You cannot possibly pretend to be oblivious that the woman you employ out there is completely taken with you." Kaori sat, crossing her legs and smirking.

He looked up, puzzlement pulling his eyebrows together. "I umm . . . well? I suppose I never thought much about it, let alone took any notice. But you certainly take quite a lot of notice of my love life."

"I just . . . I didn't mean to . . ." She stumbled over her words.

He roared with laughter. "I am teasing you, Kay."

She scrunched her nose. "Funny."

"Yes, I can be from time to time." He continued to laugh as he pulled a box out from under some pages. "Here. I need to go out into the yard and check on my crews. This box is all of the paid invoices that need to be checked against the receipts and totaled by month in the enclosed ledger." He then pointed out other boxes, explaining what needed to be done with those as well.

Kaori took the first box and set it on her lap. "I will do my best."

She looked around at the cluttered and dusty room, filled with haphazard stacks of file boxes, paperwork, samples, and so much more.

He grinned. "I have no doubt."

He looked nervous, hovering a bit longer than needed over the desk.

She stayed sitting as he made his way to the door slowly, her hands over the box he had handed her. "I will stay in here."

"Yes, that will be good. I will try to check on you, but I need to push my guys, get them on task, and get it done with as quickly as possible so we can just leave." He gripped the doorknob. "If you need anything, feel free to ask Winnie. She can get you what you need."

"I doubt she will enjoy waiting on me." A corner of her mouth turned up.

He blinked, a slight blush on his cheeks. "Yeah, well, she can set that aside. I'll be back." He ducked out of the room, shutting the door behind him.

Kaori heard Theo on the other side of the wall instructing Winnie to take care of anything Kaori might need, still being careful to call her Kay instead of her real name. The other side of her mouth turned up, joining the one side and making a full smile. A smile that Kaori quashed once she felt it hit her eyes.

"Work. You are here to work to repay this man for helping. Nothing more." She stalked over to the desk and started in on the invoices.

She was so engrossed in her work that she barely looked up and hadn't noticed he hadn't peeked his head in for a few hours. But when he did, his jaw dropped. "Wow. What did you do?"

She blew at a strand of hair that had come loose and was

hanging in front of her face, tickling her nose. "I'm sorry. Did I do something wrong?"

He cleared his throat. "What did I say about apologizing?"

"To stop."

"Exactly."

"So I did not do something wrong?"

"I am not sure yet." His eyes were wide. "Would you care to explain where all of my paperwork, boxes, and ledgers are?"

"Yes." She stood from the office chair. "I finished all of the invoices, then moved on to sorting the rest of the paperwork, making sure to set them in their appropriate boxes once I found the others in the cabinets. There was a young man that came looking for you, and he knew where you kept a number of empty file boxes, and he retrieved several more for me. I wrote labels out for each, and they are put away by chronological order and organized. I hope it is a system that makes sense for you. And all the samples are in their own bin over by the door for quick access if a customer needs to view them. Everything has its place now." She gasped. "Oh. Except these. I was unsure what to do with these." She handed him a small stack of invoices.

He took them on his way to the wall of cabinets. Looking in, he found all of the boxes labeled, stacked, and neater than he'd ever had his office. The current ledgers were on his desk in a stack. The top of his desk was cleaned and organized. And there were no more piles of anything on the floor. He finally looked at the pages she'd handed him. "Oh wow. Yeah. These are long-unpaid accounts. I might as well give up on them."

She took them back. "We will see about that."

He took them back from her and tossed them onto the desk. "How about we retire for the day. Since you did a year's worth of work today, you can focus on that next time."

She glanced over at the small stack. "Okay."

"Shall we?" He motioned for the door.

"Okay." She followed him, reaching over and straightening the stack on her way past.

He chuckled as he held the door and let her pass.

"Have a good rest of your day, Winnie." He nodded at the woman as they walked by her.

She had caught a glimpse past the door in his office and shot Kaori a glance, ignoring her in her response. "See you soon, Theodore."

The level of obvious flirting was almost as embarrassing as the amount of cleavage she showed. Kaori, diverting her eyes, fought her nose from curling in disgust. Instead, she gathered her composure and gave the woman a sweet smile. "It was *very* nice meeting you. I am sure I will see you around often."

Winnie huffed. "Goodbye."

A snarky grin played on Kaori's lips as she left with Theo.

"You're a lot more feisty than I took you for." Theo closed her car door and went around, getting behind the wheel.

"Oh?" She sat, poised, her hands in her lap.

He scoffed, amused. "It works for you."

Winnie was standing inside, looking out the large picture window on the front of the showroom. The lettering for "Brooks Lumber" curved in gold, almost hiding her face and her failed attempt to appear as if she wasn't looking out at them.

Kaori plastered on a cheesy grin and waved. "She seems nice."

Theo shook his head. "Not looking to make friends, are you?"

Folding her hands in her lap once more, she lifted a shoulder. "Friends? Yes. You are my friend. She would never be a true friend."

"I cannot argue with you on that point. She has few friends." The rocks crunched under the tires as they pulled away from the building.

"Do you?" she asked. "Have friends, that is. Do you have friends?"

"What?" He blinked.

She giggled. "Do you have friends?"

"Is that supposed to be a sincere question or a mocking stab at me?" His eyes stayed on the road.

She shrugged. "You know? I'm not sure. Maybe both?"

They both looked at each other, paused, then began to laugh.

Conversation continued, both of them relating stories of people they'd known with similar temperaments. The whole ride, Kaori continued to tease Theo about Winnie's obvious affections for him. He continued to deny it, which just encouraged her all that much more.

The rest of the day was relatively calm as the two of them cleaned, ate, read, and chatted. Whatever nervousness Kaori was holding onto, as far as staying with Theo went, disappeared with the level of comfort they had with each other. At one point, she brought up her predicament, but she calmed with his confidence as he explained he would start making further inquiries first thing in the morning.

Later that night, when Kaori couldn't sleep, she knew it was far less her accommodations and precisely her concern for Warren and unease about her situation. Her mind was racing. Unable to just continue to lie there, Kaori got up, pulled on a sweater and shoes, and made her way out into the backyard.

There was a slight chill in the air for an early summer night, but the sky was clear, the moon was bright, and Kaori was feeling like her shoulders were not so burdened. She stepped down onto the grass and breathed in deep. Her hands ran across the leaves of a nearby bush as she left the bottom step and ventured out into the yard.

The landscape being so different than her home back in Japan, Kaori marveled at her surroundings. And for the first time, she did it do not through a vehicle window but standing on the ground, still. She was able to feel the breeze tickle her cheeks, the brush of the greenery on her palms, the prick of the twigs on her flesh.

The light from the moon lit up the yard, illuminating the lush foliage where she'd wandered to the edge of the woods that bordered the manicured lawn. Hearing some rustling in front of her, she let her eyes focus and saw a large raccoon and her babies emerging from the pile of leaves beneath the large oak tree she was standing under. She knelt down and reached out, allowing the raccoon to sniff her fingers before the animal scurried away, nudging her babies along with her.

Kaori stood back up and took in her surroundings. Contentment played across her features, and, for the first time in a long time, she felt at peace.

~

THEO WOKE, his arms stretching out over his head as a yawn escaped him. It had been such a long time since he'd had a pleasant night relaxing and conversing with someone. Something about the interaction was calming. So calming that it also seemed to have brought about the first good night's sleep he'd had in even longer.

He flung the comforter off, slipped his feet into his slippers, and pulled on his robe before emerging from his room. Checking the time on the grandfather clock in the living room, he was a little surprised that Kaori wasn't up. Chalking it up to her possibly having an equally good night's sleep, he decided to make breakfast again. After all, his stomach was grumbling and growing louder.

Opting for omelets and toast, he scrambled up the eggs, cut a slab of ham into chunks, and diced the onion and tomato. While everything was cooking, he shredded some cheese and started grilling the bread over the fire. Finally, as he plated everything, he checked the icebox to make sure there was some fresh orange juice left, enough for both of them.

Satisfied, he knocked on the door to the spare room. "Kay, I made breakfast. Care to join me?" He didn't hear a response, so he knocked again. "Kay? Are you feeling unwell?"

A slight rustling sound came from the other side of the door but no reply.

Waiting a moment, a little bit of his excitement for the day washed away as he took a step back from the door. "I hope you slept well. Your plate is on the table if you are hungry."

He waited one more moment before turning away and going back to the kitchen. He sat and ate his breakfast. Eating alone had never been an issue for him before, but something about it that morning was different. Something about it felt a bit empty.

He picked up his plate, took it to the sink, and set it down a little harder than intended. Theo gripped the side of the sink, nostrils flaring as he huffed at his own foolishness. "She is spoken for, you fool. A friend and nothing more."

Gruffly, he washed the morning dishes, putting her still full plate of food in the icebox in case she emerged hungry later on. Not quite feeling settled, he went outside and chopped some wood, took a bath, then straightened the already spotless living room. Still, something was unsettling him.

Realizing he hadn't seen Kaori all morning, he knocked on the door once again. "Kay? I'm a bit concerned about you."

He waited for just a moment before turning the doorknob. "I'm coming in."

Slowly, he pushed the door open. Leaning in, he looked around. "Kay?"

He stepped across the threshold.

Nobody answered, and nobody was in the room. He checked and found her trunk, its contents and several of her belongings still in place. The bed was made. Her handbag was on the stand next to the armoire. All signs pointed to the fact she was there, but he did not see her.

Wondering if they'd simply not crossed paths as he moved about the house, he went back out and searched through the other rooms. Emerging out the back door, finishing with the kitchen last, Theo stood on the back deck and sniffed the air, trying to pick up any scent of her, his nose twitching.

He jumped as footfalls sounded up the side steps to the wood platform. Relieved, he sighed. "Kay. Thank goodness."

She was smiling from ear to ear. "Theo! I have fantastic news!"

His words came with a growl. "Where have you been? You had me worried half to death!"

She batted her eyes. "I'm sorry. I didn't mean to."

"Please stop doing that to me." He relaxed his shoulders. "Now, what is this fantastic news?"

She clapped her hands in front of her. "Warren! He is here! Well, not here, but he is in town! I was able to see him this morning, and he has asked me to join him as he leaves for New York with his company. I am leaving with him, Theodore. Is that not wonderful?"

His eyes narrowed. "You saw Warren, and you are leaving with him?"

"Yes." She stopped bouncing and contained herself, looking him in the eye.

"You saw Warren? Where?" His jaw set.

She pursed her lips, hand waving dismissively. "He heard I was here and came early this morning. I went for a drive with him and just returned."

"And where is he now?" Theo asked.

"He had to go home and pack his necessities." A bit of the enthusiasm dropped out of her tone.

He crossed his arms in front of his chest. He studied her as she moved toward the door. "I *do* have friends, you know."

"Is that a threat?" she hissed, not fully turning back.

He crossed the deck and closed the space between them, his hand going straight for her throat, pinning her against the wood siding of the house. "It is now."

She choked as she attempted to speak, her hands gripping his as she tried to free herself. "Have you lost your mind?"

"Where is she?"

Kay looked at him with pleading eyes. "Please stop, Theodore. You're going to kill me."

"I won't ask again. Where is she?" His grip tightened.

The flesh beneath his hand shifted as the image in front of him changed. The hair came down, cascading over his fingers. The body filled out with a bit more muscle. The facial features became more hardened. While female, the woman he was holding to the wall was no longer Kaori.

She sneered. "Why do you care so much? You barely know her."

"Did you know her at all before you chose to condemn her to whatever fate your boss has for her?" He loosened his fingers but didn't let go.

She coughed beneath his palm, all signs of her amusement gone. "Just let it go, Theodore."

"Let's try this another way." He gripped her hair, finally releasing her neck. "Who are you? Other than Porter's little lackey."

Her knees buckled slightly. Nails dug into his arms as she reached up, gripping his arm to steady herself. "Let's just say, you can just think of me as a ghost."

She transformed into a fox, writhing in his grip. Her teeth sunk into his hand, and he let go, pulling his bleeding palm up to his chest. "You little . . ."

She scrambled off the deck with him running after her, but her tiny frame skittered under places he couldn't. Finally, almost a mile into the woods, after jumping over piles of brush, ducking under branches, and cursing the entire way, Theo stopped.

Sniffing, he worked to pick up the kitsune's scent. He cursed himself for letting his tracking skills go slack with his mundane life. He was just about to give up when he caught her scent and darted in its direction.

CHAPTER 6

*K*aori woke, her head aching worse than the strongest hangover she'd ever experienced. She tried to sit up, but the room spun in such a sickening way that she fell back against the pillow and rolled onto her side, hand covering her mouth.

"It should pass shortly. Sorry to bring you here this way." A man's voice came from somewhere in the room.

She attempted to look for him as the wave of nausea subsided. "What's going on? Who are you? Why am I here?"

The man chuckled. "You're not unlike her. So many questions."

Kaori's head was starting to clear. She sat up and propped herself against the wall. "Are you going to answer any of them?"

"It's no wonder he fell for you." The man took a seat in the chair next to the door, legs crossed and arms folded across his chest. He waited a moment before going on. "My name is Porter Patterson. You're here to help your family."

At that, she leaped up. "My family? Are they in trouble? If something has happened, all you needed to do was tell me. I would go to their aid. I didn't need to be convinced to do so." She was looking around for her shoes and any belongings. "What has happened? And I still would like to know who you are."

A look of amusement washed over him as he watched her. "I like you. We're going to get along great, once you learn your place."

She stopped, leaning over to peer under the bed she woke up on to see if her things were under there. With one hand on the mattress, she slowly lifted up halfway, her eyes fixed on the floor beneath her. "Learn what?"

"Come. Join me in the sitting room. Once Emiko returns, we will explain everything." He started for the door.

Standing up fully, Kaori balled her fists.

"What is going on?" She punctuated each word.

He waved casually, signaling for her to follow. "As I said, once Emiko returns, you will find out. Until then, come have a brandy with me. We might as well get on more friendly terms."

"Friendly terms? You drugged and kidnapped me! You're not going to get hatefully pleasant out of me!" she roared.

Kaori hadn't seen him move. She blinked, and suddenly, he was nose to nose with her. Not touching, but she could feel his warm breath on her face as he spoke. "You'd be wise to cooperate. Once you find out why you're here, you will certainly change your tune. But until then, do not make me teach you what I can do to unruly kitsune."

"You know what I am?" She sucked in a breath. "Are you—"

"No," he spat. "I am *not* one of you cruel beasts. But I know all about your lineage."

He spun and stormed out of the room. Kaori watched. Fear had crawled up from the pit of her stomach and was strangling her throat, threatening to cut off her ability to breathe. She couldn't move. She just stared at the doorway he exited through, unsure if she should, in fact, join him or stay in that room. Unable to think clearly, she just stood there, her thoughts spiraling out of control.

Kaori had no concept of how much time had passed when a

figure entered the doorway. She looked at Kaori with a deep sadness that was plain on her features, pinching what was clearly a beautiful face into one that was weary and deeply hurt. The woman gathered herself, breathing away the expression in exchange for a colder one, then spoke. "Kaori Ishida?"

Kaori looked at her blankly. "Yes?"

"Follow me, please." Her voice was melodic.

"Are you Emiko?" Kaori started to come out of her daze.

The woman didn't look back. She paused. "Follow me," she said, then continued walking.

"Wait!" Kaori ran to catch up. She grabbed the woman's shoulder, tears in her eyes. "If you're Emiko, please tell me what's going on."

"I am Emiko." She swallowed hard, then lifted Kaori's hand off her shoulder, letting it drop, still unable to look at her. Clearing her throat, her words came out slightly choked. "Follow me."

"Why does everyone seem to want me to just blindly follow them?" Kaori bellowed.

Emiko gritted her teeth. "Suit yourself, but you won't want to deal with him if you don't."

Kaori watched as Emiko walked out of the room, turning down the hallway to the right, the same direction Porter had gone. Her feet felt like cement bricks, keeping her in place. Still not wanting to leave the room, she wrapped her arms around herself and took a few deliberately steady breaths.

Her mind becoming slightly less foggy, she peered out the door. Once she was sure nobody was there, she retreated back into the room, transformed into a fox and started sniffing the walls, looking for a way out.

Going the opposite direction from Porter and Emiko, she made her way to the staircase and down. All the windows were closed, and nobody else seemed to be in or around the house. Still, Kaori made sure to make as little noise as possible.

The front entry was massive. Two solid, ornately carved wood doors loomed over her in her fox form as she studied them. Though she wanted so badly to turn back into her human form, burst through the doors, and run outside and away, something made the hairs on her neck stand up.

Turning away from the doors, afraid of making too much noise, she made her way back to the kitchen, sniffing for hints of the various scents of food that might be there. She slowly creeped in, making sure it was devoid of people. Once sure, she went in, passing counters and appliances on her way to the door off the back of the house.

She looked up at the doorknob, readying herself to grip it the moment she transformed. Just as she was about to, a hand gripped her scruff and lifted her up into the air. "Now, now, Miss Ishida. I do believe that I asked you to join me. Your manners seem to have escaped you."

Kaori let herself go limp in his grip, knowing that anything else would risk him lashing out at her physically. As he turned with her in hand, she caught a glimpse of Emiko standing there with Kaori's dress and shoes in hand. Her eyes were cast down.

An unexplained pang of empathy for Emiko shot through Kaori, but before she could figure out why, Porter yanked her down the hall and into the study, tossing her down onto a chair. "I'll turn around while you get dressed . . . as a human." His words were pointed.

Emiko tossed the items onto the floor next to the chair and turned so her back was to Kaori. "Make it quick, please."

Kaori sat in the chair, looking back and forth between her captors. Her gaze falling past them, she calculated a few options of attempting to escape—all of which ended with it not going her way. She let out a snort, her little nose twitching, before she reluctantly phased back into human form, then quickly reached over, grabbed her clothing, and slid into her dress.

Feeling violated, she wrapped her arms around herself before announcing her transformation. "I'm human again. Well, as human as I can be. Can you *please* explain to me what is going on now?"

Turning and taking their seats casually, Porter and Emiko sat, poised, as if conducting a business deal, not addressing someone they'd just kidnapped. Porter's arrogance came through in his movements, while Emiko's attitude reflected a clear reservation and a sorrow.

Porter straightened a pile of papers on his desk. "So Emiko here has been my companion for a number of years."

"Centuries. Three centuries," she corrected him.

"Yes. Three centuries," he agreed, speaking through his teeth. He relaxed his jaw and continued. "And I've agreed to let her go if she were to find a replacement for herself."

"And you think that replacement is going to be me?" Kaori stood. "Absolutely not!"

"But you haven't heard the pay, Miss Ishida." He sat in his office chair, tapping an envelope opener on the desk, amused.

She stayed standing, her hands on her hips. "With how you brought me here, I cannot imagine that you could propose any amount of pay that would entice me to stay and be some sort of companion for you."

"You'd be surprised," Emiko said, almost under her breath.

"Please, sit." He nodded to Kaori.

He waited and let her take a moment to stay there, defiantly, before finally sitting back down. Emiko's lips were pursed as she watched the other woman, an eyebrow quirked. As Kaori sat, she rolled her eyes, then turned and waited for Porter to continue.

He started to explain. "Just over three hundred years ago, I was a young, budding priest. The Christian god infiltrated everything I did and felt. And one year, I was selected to go on a pilgrimage from my home in France all the way to the Orient to spread the word. It was a wonderful trip, since I'd never been there, and it was my first time being selected to go on such a journey. I'll admit, I got a little overzealous. And despite it being illegal and dangerous to practice Christianity in Japan, I wanted to bring enlightenment to the world. So I went.

"I met a girl," he continued. "She was exotic, enticing, and undeniable. At least she was to me. So one night, I took her to my bedchamber. In exchange for showing me carnal pleasures, I told her all about my god and church. But come morning, that bitch had told both the Japanese government as well as my church elders what had happened between us."

He flashed a scathing look at Emiko before setting his jaw. "I took refuge in a cave a few miles outside of town, knowing that the local government would imprison me for my religion, or possibly worse. Then there was the matter of my elders. I was not sure what my church would do to me. So I hid. And who do you think I saw out there in those woods? The very young woman that had me out in that cave. She went by the name Tamao."

"Tamao?" Kaori gasped. "As in . . ."

"Our cousin," Emiko answered her question.

"*Our*? Wait. What do you mean?" Kaori looked back and forth between the two of them, anxious for an explanation.

Porter waved his hand dismissively. "Yes, Tamao was romping around in the forest—naked. She'd transformed from her fox form and was picking berries and flowers, putting them in a basket. I didn't know what was going on at first. At least, not until Emiko here joined Tamao. She approached as a fox and transformed, giggling and helping her cousin with the berries while they laughed about the man Tamao had turned in. They were bragging about the line of men they would seduce and turn in to authorities, ruining their lives and even sentencing some to their deaths."

Kaori's face contorted with fear and anger. "Emiko? You're my cousin, Emiko? The Emiko my family said had run off like so many others?"

Emiko nodded coldly. "Yes. That's what they say when someone disappears, isn't it? If only you knew the truth behind so many of those disappearances. Most are *not* a simple case of wanderlust. That's for sure."

Porter interjected. "Before we get all mushy with the rest of the family reunion between you two, allow me to finish my story."

Emiko folded her hands in her lap as Kaori sat upright. "All right. Finish."

"Thank you." He smiled and nodded. "So I took my cloak and snuck out, draping it over the frolicking women. Emiko, being the spry one of the two, escaped my grasp. Tamao, on the other hand, did not. She *did* try to change back into her fox form, but that just allowed me to wrap her up even more. And once little Emiko here saw that her dear cousin was without hope of escape, she was sweet enough to come back for her. Standing in front of me with every bit of her flesh for me to see, she demanded I let her go."

"I didn't care if you saw me like that. I was trying to save my cousin," Emiko snarled.

"Watch your tongue," Porter scolded her, his eyes changing from poised and pleasant to angry and threatening. He regained his composure quickly, though, and returned to his story. "I told Emiko that I was going to turn in their family—your family—for not only being scandalous sluts, but also for the fact that I'd seen them turn into humans from their fox shapes. Sure, Emiko questioned me as to how, since I was more or less a wanted man. But I kindly explained that this sort of thing would get me off the hook with my elders in the church, and that mattered far more than anything else. I would simply have to explain that Tamao cast a spell upon me, and I had no control over my actions. But more than that, they would most assuredly go after every one of your kind, starting with your family. And we would start by burning Tamao at the stake for witchcraft."

"You're a monster." Kaori felt ill.

"I am a man of survival," he replied smugly. "Now, mind you, the night Tamao and I spent together, she told me tales of beings with a variety of capabilities. She spoke of changing from animals to humans. She spoke of sensing another's presence, changing a person's moods, and far more. When I learned that her tales were true and that she was speaking of her family, it became obvious to me I needed to keep them both and see what they could do for me. One power, in particular, was of great interest to me. She explained that some had the ability to feed a mortal life force to keep them alive. And do you know what she did?"

"Obviously not escape." Kaori's words were full of venom.

"No, she did not." Porter raised an eyebrow. "Tamao bargained with me. She said she would give me some valuable information in exchange for her freedom." He roared with laughter. "And when I agreed, she explained that her very own cousin, Emiko, had that very ability. Emiko didn't deny this, of course. She agreed to provide me with immortality and aid me in some business pursuits in exchange for her cousin's freedom and the survival of your family."

Kaori choked back her churning stomach. "What?"

"To save your ungrateful lives," Emiko growled.

Porter waved his hand, signaling for her to back off. "Once I had Emiko's promise to come with me in exchange for your family's safety, I kept them both, making sure Emiko understood that her cousin's safety was still at risk unless she showed me a few of her tricks."

"You kept them both? But you had an agreement. How could you go back on that?" Kaori was stunned.

He shrugged. "I had a promise but no evidence. I needed to know for sure. And I needed an insurance, so to speak. Tamao wasn't going to get off the hook that easily, even if Emiko was going to take her place."

Kaori grimaced. "How could you help this monster all these years, Emiko? Certainly you could have done something!"

"How could I? *How could I?*" Emiko rose, her fists balled tight. "I did what I had to do to save us!"

"She did what she knew was best," he added.

Kaori went to speak again, but Emiko cut her off, stepping forward while waving a finger at her. "Don't you *dare* judge me.

You and I saw firsthand what people of his church did to nonbelievers. Remember? Remember how we had to watch them drag people out of their homes? There was no way I was going to let them do that—or worse—to our family."

Kaori had to swallow back a swell of emotions. "But why all these years?"

Emiko quickly wiped tears from her eyes before they could fall. "Did you ever second-guess my disappearance? Did you ever try to find me?"

"No?" Kaori replied, confused. "But the elders said that you'd gone off on your own. Was I supposed to track down every family member that decided to go off on their own?"

"That's exactly it!" Emiko raised her voice. "Not a single one of you came after me. Nobody tried to find either Tamao *or* me! And do you know how many others that just 'went their own way' that didn't do it by choice? You haven't even asked where Tamao is, have you? Because she sure didn't come back to the family, did she?"

Kaori's stomach sank. "What happened to Tamao? And what others? What happened to the others?"

Porter approached Kaori and put a hand on her shoulder. "You look a bit overwhelmed. Should we take a break? Maybe get something to eat or drink before you have to take more of all of this in?"

She flung her arm, throwing his hand off of her. "No, I don't want to *take a break*! I want to know what happened to my family! Our elders said people were just going off on their own. I thought people were just living a different life." She looked at Emiko with pleading eyes. "Please. Tell me!"

Emiko looked hardened. The pity and sadness that had shown through her expressions was gone. "Death."

"Death?" Kaori's hand flew to her mouth.

"Wait. Wait. Wait." Porter shook his head. "To be fair, there's a story to each. And each story is linked to Emiko's attempt at escaping or even trying to kill me. It took her well over two hundred years before she figured out that my powers were growing the longer she kept me alive. And by my powers, I mean that she was not only giving me her life force, but in it was the ability to do some things of my own. One of which was being linked to her." He snickered. "Now, of course, I didn't tell her this when I realized it many, many years before she did. And it took her foolish pride quite a long time to clear away and see what was happening. But we've been in a good partnership ever since. Would you say, Emiko?"

He gripped Emiko's shoulder and pinched, causing her knees to buckle slightly. But she held her gaze on Kaori. "Yes. Perfect. Wouldn't wish for a better arrangement."

"That's right." He let her go.

"Tamao? So she's dead?" Kaori's breaths were heavy.

"Tamao?" he repeated. "Oh. No. I forced Emiko to take her to my elders at the church for punishment for attempting to kill me. They are still holding her. Can you imagine? She's been shackled in the basement of their monastery in Italy all these years, being studied and tested by generation after generation of clergymen."

"You let them take her?" Kaori felt her stomach rising once again.

Emiko didn't answer this time. She stood as cold as a stone. Porter, with his ego flaring, explained, "I believe you had a couple of family members disappear together? An uncle and a very young kit, not even able to turn human yet."

The blood drained out of Kaori's cheeks. "You didn't."

"Not for some years." Porter shrugged. "But they were fantastic collateral to get Emiko to take Tamao to the church. But eventually, her antics did cost them their lives . . . and several others. Once I had her ability to sense your kind, it was easy to find others. And with her as bait, they came seeking her."

"And you can be so callous about all of this?" Kaori spat.

He gripped her arm. "I was owed a life that Tamao was so callously willing to take from me."

"You've gotten it many times over with as long as you've lived.

And you've taken a number of other lives that didn't owe you a thing." Kaori struggled to escape his grip in vain.

"But if you look at it another way, maybe *this* was the life I was meant to live, and I'll be damned if I let it slip through my fingers. Obviously I wasn't made to be a priest." He chuckled.

"So what do you want with me? Did Emiko step out of line again, and I'm the tool to put her back in?" Kaori looked back and forth between them.

"No. No. This is actually the interesting part." Porter motioned for Emiko to speak.

She hung her head for a moment before looking back up with an anger in her eyes. "I have saved the family long enough. It's someone else's turn."

"You?" Kaori scoffed. "It doesn't sound like you've saved us. It sounds like you've doomed us to millennium of him picking us off one by one!"

Emiko slapped Kaori hard enough to leave a handprint on her cheek. "I have done the best I could. Without what I've done— what I've sacrificed—you would have all met a far worse fate centuries ago. So don't pretend like I'm the villain here!"

Kaori's hand flew up and held her burning cheek, a little stunned by her cousin's action. "What now? Obviously he isn't going to just let you go and let himself wither away. Am I the collateral for making you stay this time?"

"No." She slumped into a chair. "You're my replacement."

"Me?"

Exhaustion pulled her shoulders down. "I remember, when I was a very young kit, you had fallen in love with a human. A young man you'd met on the docks of Kyoto. A sailor, if I remember correctly. And you refused to let him go. It was a huge scandal that he lived for so long with such a young appearance, never seeming to age. Whispers turned to fact when it came out that you could keep other creatures alive."

"Ryu Saito," Kaori said, solemnly.

"Yes. Ryu," Emiko repeated. "It was known then that you had the gift like mine. So it's your turn, *itoko*."

Kaori took a step toward Emiko. "*Itoko*? How dare you even consider yourself family, let alone my cousin! You are a traitor to our family!"

"A traitor?" Emiko screamed. "I have sacrificed over three hundred years of my life to keep as many of you safe as I could! Sure, I've made mistakes that have cost lives, and I have to live with that. Trust me, it haunts me every single day. But I'm done. I want to live. So I brought you here to take my place." She looked over to Porter. "You have her. Please let me go. I have no desire to spend another moment going over this. You have what you want —my replacement. Now please, let me go."

Kaori's eyes went wide. "Wait. What do you mean you brought me here? You mean earlier, when you drugged me, right? Did you have something to do with Warren's disappearance? Where is he? Is he harmed?"

Porter held a hand out to Emiko, signaling for her to stand down as he waited for Kaori's string of questions to stop. Once she was finished, he turned his hand over, as if presenting Emiko. Kaori's eyes slowly shifted back to her cousin and went wide, her face stark white as Emiko shifted and changed into Warren.

Kaori breathed, "No." Tears started streaming down her cheeks. "How could you?"

Emiko turned back into her American appearance, her head turned down. "I couldn't cost another life."

"Cost another life?" Kaori angrily wiped her cheeks. "You came for *my* life, yet you say you couldn't cost another life? That's a bit backward, isn't it?"

Emiko didn't reply. Porter, on the other hand, nodded to the doorway before putting a hand on Kaori's shoulder once again. "Now, dear, do you really think I would let her go off to Japan to retrieve you without a reason for her to return?"

Reaching up, Kaori pushed Porter's hand off of her with disgust on her face. "What did you do with the others in our family you murdered? Why didn't you just get me here like you did them?"

"Taking members of your family was far easier back when we lived much, much closer. When we moved to America, Emiko attempted to betray me once. I'm sure you remember several of your family members going off on their own about a hundred years ago, outside of Kitsuki—a name I have chuckled at, considering the closeness of your kind's name and the district's name. Is that on purpose?" He tilted is head.

Kaori's nostrils flared. "Are you serious right now?"

"Yes," he stated, plainly.

She just looked at him, completely shocked at his audacity.

Finally, he waved off his inquiry. "Fine. A question for another time. It's not like we don't have plenty of that—time. But back to story time. Since I'd seen your family's migration patterns, it didn't take much to predict where they'd be. And considering that Emiko's little stunt spurred our trip back to Japan to remind her of her place, I slit one neck in front of her and sent five other little kitsune to join Tamao, thanks to a young, eager priest who kept my secret of my long life in exchange for taking the credit for finding them. Oh!" He almost leaped at recalling something as he practically bounded out of the room, calling back, "Don't move, ladies. I nearly forgot your surprise."

Kaori cringed at Porter's sing-song tone in his voice. She looked over at Emiko, her words hissing through her teeth. "What *surprise?*"

Emiko paced. "I don't know."

"Do *not* play stupid, *itoko!*" Kaori shouted.

"I *don't know!*" Emiko's fists were balled. "He takes great joy in his tortures."

"Joy? And this is the life you want to condemn me to?"

"You all left me to this life without any hope of rescue. I may have chosen it in the beginning, but I prayed one of you would come for me."

"Emiko, I thought you were fine. I thought you chose to leave us!"

"You should have known I hadn't." Emiko rubbed her forehead.

"How could I have known that?" Kaori started to close the gap between them.

Stopping and putting her hands out, not letting Kaori get any closer, Emiko swallowed back tears. "We were too close for you not to know. All I ever talked about was the future of our family and how much I loved you all. What could have possibly changed my mind so swiftly?"

"The elders believed you all had been thinking about it for some time and finally took action." Kaori clasped her hands in front of her heart. "The elders said we were not to go looking for anyone and risk the family. And I blindly did as they said."

"The elders are cowards. And you were so willing to follow a man, yet you were not willing to come look for your closest cousin? Your best friend?" Emiko pursed her lips.

Kaori closed her eyes. "I believed them."

"And I will never forgive you for it. You should have known." Emiko stormed across the room and stared out the window.

The two women stood, tense, quiet, Emiko holding her anger back, and Kaori completely lost. Their silence broke with Kaori's gasp as she saw Porter re-enter the room with a man by his side. "Kai?"

Emiko whipped around. "Kai!" She ran across the room and stopped short of the two men. "What is this, Porter? I've done what you want. I brought you my replacement."

Kai stood, his hands bound behind his back, ankles shackled, his mouth gagged. He was covered in bruises and a number of cuts, some still bleeding. His hair was long, shaggy, and dirty, matching his clothes that were torn and covered in filth. It was obvious they had once fit him but just hung on him now.

Emiko fell to her knees. "Please, Porter. No!"

"Can you imagine Kai's excitement when he learned Emiko

was alive, and he could come to where she was? But his disappointment rivaled that excitement when he figured out that he wasn't going to see her." Arrogance laced Porter's words.

Kai struggled under his gag, trying to speak. Porter kicked the back of his knees, causing Kai to fall painfully to the ground. Emiko dove forward, sobbing. "Stop! Please stop!"

"You see, Kaori? Emiko sacrificed a lot. And while I cannot bear to see her go—nor can I risk her being free, knowing my secrets—I figured I'd bring him here as well. Now I have three of you!" He clapped his hands. "We can be one big, happy family!"

Emiko crawled across to Kai, her hand on his cheek. She looked up at Porter. "What do you mean, can't let me go? We had an arrangement! And how did you find Kai? Or even know about him?" Her words were choppy around her sobs.

Porter knelt down next to the two, blocking Emiko from getting to Kai. "It's amazing what you learn about someone over three hundred years with them, connected to their energy. When we went back to Japan that last time, your heart fluttered when you saw him. Sensing his species, thanks to you, Emiko, I knew that he would come in very handy."

She looked up at him in horror. "You've had him this entire time?"

Porter reached out and stroked her hair. "The church has had their little experiments. I wanted the chance to test a few things out on my own, and I needed you for all your errands. So Kai has been helping me with some scientific research, so to speak."

Emiko sprang up and lunged at Porter. Her hands wrapped around his neck as she pushed him back and into the nearby archway frame. His breath left him as he hit, catching him completely off guard. He scrambled, trying to get a grip on her and push her off of him.

Kaori rushed over to Kai, who was pulling at his restraints. She untied his gag and started working on the knots in the rope around his wrists. Every bit of her wanted to see who was winning the scuffle, but she wasn't sure she was safe either way. She kept her attention on the knot as anxiety rose into her throat the closer she was to untying it.

She felt the tension in the knot finally give. Fumbling with the newly slack rope, she started to pull the loosened knot apart. Then everything went black.

CHAPTER 7

$\mathcal{T}$heo chased after the scent for several miles before slowing. He stood, taking in his surroundings, calming, frustrated that he'd lost her. His hands came up to his face, rubbing it as he shook his head.

He pulled his hands back when the cloud of anger cleared. This time, he looked around to determine his exact location before starting off north. The tree branches scraped him as he ran, leaping over large rocks, dodging bushes, and launching off fallen trees. He only stopped when he came to a clearing at the edge of a neatly landscaped plot of land.

He stood, looking over the gardens and house, evaluating the terrain and its inhabitants. Then, hastily, he gathered some twigs, placing them in a circle at the tree line. He left the foliage on the last two small branches, and placed them one crossed over the other in the center of the circle, before going back into the woods and digging for several small rocks, a young pinecone, and other items.

Returning to the circle, he placed them deliberately around it. He pulled out a pen from his pocket. Recalling that Kaori had used it the day before in his office, her energy still resonating within its metal components, he laid it across the center twigs.

Theo knelt and raised his hands, palms down, over the arrangement and closed his eyes. He took in long, deep breaths again, this time searching for energy signals of other beings on the property with a focus on Kaori's in particular. His fury and fear both attempted to cloud his ability to focus, so he had to work harder than he ever had before in order to achieve something he'd been taught as a kid. Finally, he zeroed in past his emotions and let the incantation within him take control.

Kaori's energy washed over him like a strong wind, pushing him back onto the ground. He struggled to keep his grasp on the others' as he leaned up on his elbows. Moving back onto his knees, he put his hands down on the dirt on either side of the circle. Kaori's energy was strong still, but he filtered around her and could tell that, among several humans moving about inside and outside of the house, Kaori herself was in a room with two others with similar energy footprints. Theo could feel that she was there with one man he could tell was Porter Patterson, and he growled.

Brushing the twigs and stones aside so as not to leave it to be found, Theo scanned the yard. Once positive no one was within sight, he ran for the house, tucking himself in behind a line of hedges that ran along the south wall, then began to check each window. If the curtains were pulled open, he peered inside to make sure the room was empty before testing the window, moving on as he found them locked.

Then he froze.

Theo looked inside the large picture window just before the corner to the front of the house. It took everything he had not to crash through it in that moment. There was Kaori, lying on the floor, appearing unconscious. There was a man on the floor close to her who seemed to be tied up. Porter was standing over the man with a gun pointed to his head. He was shouting at a woman who was lifting Kaori up by the shoulders, dragging her to the couch.

Hastily, Theo bent down and placed his hands on the earth, drawing as much extra energy as he could before standing back up and placing those hands on the side of the house. He listened, trying to assess what was going on inside.

Again, his focus faltered. And again, he tried to regroup to get past it. But seeing Kaori like that had him fighting with his savage side. The urge to burst into the room, kill everyone else in it, and carry her out was so overwhelming that he had to take a break, lean his back against the siding, and put a block up—to wall himself in and isolate his mind from the world around him.

∼

KAORI'S HEAD pounded when she came to. Her hand went up, feeling the lump on her scalp where she'd been hit. She sorted through the events that had unfolded before she'd been knocked out, not sure if Emiko or Porter had been the one to do it. So when Emiko stood from the chair across the room, Kaori jumped.

Emiko held her hands up. "Relax. I'm locked in here just like you."

Kaori squinted. "So you weren't the one to render me unconscious?" She flinched as she tried to sit up.

"No," Emiko replied.

"What happened, then?" Kaori asked. She looked around, seeing they were still in the study, but the doors were all closed, and there was no sign of Porter or Kai.

"He took him." Emiko folded her arms across her chest and looked off at the fire in the stone fireplace. "He knocked you out, pulled out a pistol from his waistband that I didn't even know he had on him, and threatened to shoot Kai if I didn't back down." Emiko swallowed hard. "I carried you to that couch, and he locked us in here, taking Kai with him."

Kaori held her head with both hands. "So let me get this straight. You tried to save Tamao's life and everyone in the family by taking Tamao's place in his revenge, but he took you both. She's locked in some dungeon, being tortured while you've been forced to do lord knows what for over three hundred years, keeping him alive through our magic, costing several lives when you'd attempt to kill him or escape, instead of coming and telling the elders so they could take care of it?"

Emiko started to speak, but Kaori cut her off. "And *now*, you thought you were sick of it finally and, instead of killing him or—again—coming to our elders, you track me down and trick me into thinking that you're someone else, making me fall in love with that fictional person and follow a lie to America, only to be lured into this trap. And you *didn't* think he would keep us both? Do I have this right?"

"Close enough." Emiko's tone was full of venom.

"What were you *thinking*?" Kaori shouted, then regretted it right away. Her head started pounding harder. The pulsing of the pain brought her up to her feet, and she paced as she rubbed her forehead.

"I *thought* I was doing the right thing," Emiko shot back. "I was young and scared. I had no clue he was this much of a monster. And I never, in my worst nightmares, thought it would go on for this long."

Kaori pinched the bridge of her nose, the thudding pain slowing a little. "I'm sorry I never went looking for you."

Emiko's jaw set. "It doesn't matter anymore."

"Yes, it does." Kaori stopped, her back to the window. "What you said was right. We *were* close. I should have known you better. I just blindly trusted our elders to not lie. And I still don't understand why that would be their reaction if you'd just disappeared. Why didn't *they* go looking for *any* of you who had disappeared?"

Emiko shook her head, disgusted. "I once heard, when I was little, that the elders would always use that as an explanation for any disappearance. My great-grandmother said it was to protect the family. They felt that looking for people would draw attention to our kind and put us in danger."

"So they'd rather just let people go missing than be a true

family and find them? To help them?" Kaori felt nausea roll up into her stomach.

Emiko looked right at her. "Yes."

"So you knew that this would happen when you agreed to go with Porter?" Kaori covered her mouth.

"Yes," she replied plainly.

"And you hoped I'd know better and would come regardless?" Kaori asked.

"Not at first." Emiko wrung her hands. "At first, I was settled in my decisions and hoped you would stay away . . . to stay safe. But over the years, I grew resentful toward the family . . . the entire family. Even more so toward you, since I thought you'd see through it one day and come help me like you used to help me when we were young. How you used to get me out of jams when whatever little prank I'd pulled backfired and got me into trouble. But when you never came, I grew to hate you for abandoning me."

"I didn't abandon you, Emiko." Kaori ground her teeth. "You should have come to me. You should have let me help you instead of letting him take you. And even if you couldn't have gotten out of that then, you should have come to me this time instead of luring me here like this!"

"Like I said, I grew to hate you. I didn't trust that you would help me. I just wanted my freedom." Emiko's voice went cold again.

"Damn it, Emiko! You've doomed me to the same fate! You cannot expect me to just accept it!" Kaori shouted.

"No, I don't." Emiko turned away.

Kaori threw her hands up. "And yet, you meet me with such disdain and callousness?"

Emiko turned. "What? Should I have buddied up to you right before I was to leave you to that monster? Should I let all those warm family feelings surface so it could kill me even more when I walked away, knowing I was leaving you to suffer what I have for so long?"

"No. But—"

"But what?" Emiko turned away again. "Nobody wins in this scenario. Being closed off is the best for me, no matter what. I tried to do the right thing, but it cost me everything. It's cost people their lives. So excuse me if I seem a bit disconnected and distant, dear cousin. No matter what I do, it's not going to be right."

"You should have come to me!" Kaori clenched her fists.

Emiko ran her hands through her hair. "Do we need to keep reliving this? I didn't, all right? I didn't go to *anyone*! And through him, I'm a con artist, an impersonator, and a murderer. And yet, with as many gifts as we have, I still can't seem to go back in time to change *any* of it."

Kaori turned and looked out the window. Before she could say anything more to Emiko, she jumped back, almost stumbling over the chair nearby, covering her mouth to stifle a scream. She hit the floor with a thud, sending a shooting pain through her hip. "Theo!"

He motioned for her to stay quiet, looking around to make sure he was still not spotted. Scrambling to her feet, Kaori rushed over and tried to unlock the window, but it wouldn't budge. She looked down at him and shook her head, mouthing, "It won't open."

He attempted to move the frame to no avail. He tapped and waved his hand, signaling for her to stay put.

She looked confused.

He mouthed, "Get back," as he pulled his shirt off and wrapped it around his elbow.

Kaori moved several steps away from the window, giving plenty of distance between herself and the glass, calling over to Emiko as quietly as she could, "Stay back!"

He rammed the glass, shattering it. Scraping the frame free of larger shards, he waved them over. "Hurry! Someone *had* to have heard that. Let's get you out of here."

Kaori ran for him. "Come on, Emiko!"

"You trust her?" he asked as he helped her through the opening.

"I'll explain later." She jumped. "Emiko! Come on!"

"I can't." Emiko backed up against the fireplace mantel.

Kaori reached in. "What do you mean, you can't? This is your chance!"

"Don't you see, Kaori? I can't! He'll kill everyone we love, starting with Kai! I need to stay." She looked away.

"We can come back for him. Maybe even bring help. Please, Emiko!" Kaori pleaded with her cousin.

Theo started pulling Kaori with him. "We need to go."

Her brows pulled in with worry. "I can't just leave her here, Theo. I just can't!"

"If we stay any longer, we might not be able to leave." He scanned the yard again.

Emiko ran to the window. "Go! Now! I've had three hundred years of this. I'm used to it. And if me staying saves you and Kai? Then it's worth it as much as it was when I agreed to go with him back then. Now go!"

"Please!" Kaori put her hand on Emiko's.

Emiko shouted, "She's escaping!" Then turned back and spoke low. "Go! Now!" She yanked her hand back and went for the door, banging on it. "Porter! She's escaping!"

Theo lifted a reluctant Kaori over his shoulder and ran for the woods, the branches scraping over them as he ran as fast as he could, not stopping until he reached a clearing by the river. He dropped her onto a fallen tree and started pacing.

"I told you not to go outside by yourself. And that woman," he pointed in the direction they came from, "is *not* someone you can trust. You could have been killed!"

She started sobbing. "But—"

"But nothing! Don't you get it? This isn't a situation that your family can easily help you out of. This entire area is filled with dangerous people, and your friend back there is in deep with one of the worst." He punched a tree. "I might not have been able to save you!"

"I'm sorry, but—"

"Stop." He held a hand out.

She stood, reaching her hands out. "But, truly, Theo. Let me explain."

He ran back over to her, taking her by the arm. "Later. They're coming. We need to go. Now."

CHAPTER 8

*A*fter walking a few miles, Theo lifted Kaori again, carrying her a while longer, across a field and up the side of the mountain ridge. Finally, they came across a clearing which held a small cabin on its edge. The windows were dark, and there were no wheel or hoof marks, which gave the appearance that nobody had visited the tiny log home in quite some time.

Theo set her down on the front porch and unlocked the door. They went inside. He blew dust off the lamp next to the door before striking a match out of the box next to it and lighting the oil wick.

Kaori stepped inside and looked around. "Where are we?"

He took the box of matches and lit a couple more lamps. "I built this cabin for two purposes. For emergencies and for my transformations."

"Transformations?" She tilted her head.

He set the box down and patted out the dust from one of the chairs in the living room. "Yes. Remember, I told you I'm a lycan? And for those times I know a transformation is coming, but I don't trust myself out there, I have a cellar under this cabin, away from town, that I can lock myself away in. It's just a precaution, but it's come in handy a few times."

"You have to do that—lock yourself away? How do you get out?" She took one of the other seats, coughing as the dust bloomed up around her.

"There's no way my hands and fingers in wolf form could ever work a small lock and key. So I hang the key on the wall, and there's a stick on the floor I have to use to get the key once I'm human again. Then I have to unlock it through the bars." He saw her concerned expression. "It's not an infallible setup, but it's worked thus far."

She blinked. "Sorry. I'm just shocked you have to do that. Our fox forms are similar in mentality to us in human form. I can't imagine having to lock myself away to keep myself safe."

"It's not to keep *me* safe," he explained. "It's to keep everybody else safe. I'm not like other wolf shifters, who tend to have more control over themselves in their animal forms. At times, lycan have control like a shifter, but other times, we lose our humanity completely and become . . . predatory."

Her eyes roamed over him. "I see."

"Does that make you afraid of me now?"

"Should I be? Afraid of you, that is," she replied.

"I hope not."

"There are other wolf shifters here, but not like you?"

"There's the Kasun Wolf Pack, and others. Sheriff Kasun's wife is the pack leader. I'm not deeply involved with the pack itself, but I respect their position in town and her authority over our kind. However, my druid blood doesn't allow the tattoo to control my shifting the way it can theirs. Thus, this place." Hoping to put the conversation behind them, Theo grabbed a wooden box from under the chair he was sitting in and went for the door. "I will have to retrieve a change of clothes for you later. But until I can safely, there are supplies in the bathroom you can use to wash up if you would like. I need to secure the property."

"I can help." She touched his arm. "I know it may look like I was helpless back there, but that's just because I didn't expect everything I learned. But I've got my wits about me more now. I'm not helpless."

"I know you're not." He pushed a lock of hair out from in front of her face. "Go. Refresh and relax. I won't be long."

She watched as he exited, pulling on a fresh shirt on his way, and looked around, feeling far more lost than she wanted him to see. In the kitchen, she took a glass out and filled it with water, refilling it two more times before finally feeling like she wasn't parched. She set the glass in the sink and attempted to spot Theo outside as she passed windows on her way to the bathroom, but there was no sign of him. And not seeing him left a pit in her stomach she didn't like.

Kaori shut and locked the door to the bathroom, pulling out the soap and a small towel. She washed quickly, stopping only when she saw the bruise on her cheek from Emiko's slap. A dam broke inside her, and the flood of emotions came rushing over her. She crumpled to the floor, curling around herself. Hot tears ran down her cheeks, soaking the front of her dress.

The door crashed open, wood splintering. Theo came rushing in, dropping to the floor next to her, gripping her by the shoulders. "Kaori! What happened? Are you all right?"

She was shaking, the tears refusing to cease. "I . . . I . . . It was all a lie."

"A lie?" He grabbed the towel and wiped her face. "What was a lie?"

Her sobs broke apart her words as she tried to speak. "All my family members we thought had just gone to find a life away from the rest, many of them were killed. Emiko . . . Emiko wasn't dead. And Warren . . . not real."

Theo lifted Kaori to her feet, wrapping an arm around her. "Come. Let's get you to a more comfortable spot."

He helped her to the couch, taking a seat next to her. Finally, her tears began to slow, as did the hiccupping as she tried to speak. "Emiko is my cousin."

"Your cousin?" He looked shocked.

"Yes." Her breaths were stuttered. "Tamao, another one of our cousins, set Porter up over three hundred years ago. He deserved what she was going to do to him, but he caught on, and he took her and Emiko in exchange for not destroying our entire lineage."

"And Warren?" he asked.

Kaori explained everything, from why Tamao set Porter up to Emiko impersonating Warren to bring her to Havenwood Falls to take her place with Porter. She included Porter informing them that neither would be able to leave and how he had Kai, which was why Emiko refused to go.

Theo stormed back and forth in the small cabin. "So he and his church are keeping some of your family to experiment on them?"

"Yes. He has Kai there now, threatening him if she doesn't stay . . . if *we* don't stay. And now I don't know what he's doing to them because of me escaping." Tears started falling down her cheeks again.

"Since we don't know what all powers he picked up feeding off her life force, we have to be extra careful. But we have to do something, considering that I don't think you'll just let me get you out of town and safe." He rubbed his temples.

"No, I can't just leave her," she insisted.

He gripped her shoulders gently. "But, Kaori, she pulled you into this mess. Because of her, your heart is broken, displaced, and in serious danger."

She put her hand to his cheek. "She's my cousin. And no matter what horrors came out of all of this, she was just trying to do the right thing."

"Dragging you here by pretending to be a man you would fall in love with just so she can force you to take her place is the right thing?" He let his hands drop.

"No." She lowered her hand as well, entwining her fingers together in her lap. "But if I spent over three hundred years in the *jigoku* . . . sorry . . . hell that she has, I might be ready for someone else to carry the burden, as well." She could see him start to speak, to defend his point, but she held a finger up and stopped him. "I do not agree with her choices, but Emiko has always been a more mischievous kitsune. Seeing her now . . . The life has been drained out of her soul. She is a shell of who she once was. I just want to see her be *her* once again. Abandoning her will not help that. It'll only force her to go further down this path."

He took her hands in his. "You have the kindest soul I've ever met, Kaori."

She turned her hands over, wrapping her fingers around his palms. Her eyes met his, and they stayed like that, looking at each other for a moment. The energy exchange between them was almost palpable. Her eyes fluttered as she leaned in toward him.

Theo watched her, his own body reflexively moving in toward hers. Her breath warmed his lips when then were only inches apart. His fingers touched her hair, running through it and down her neck before coming around and resting on her shoulder.

She shivered in anticipation, letting her eyes close fully. She was so swept away, it took her a moment to realize he wasn't touching her anymore. She looked, and he was across the room, pouring himself a glass of water.

"I didn't mean to overstep," she whispered.

He gulped the water down. "No. It is I who should be apologizing. I shouldn't be taking advantage of your state. I know full well you're fragile right now."

"Fragile?" She furrowed her eyebrows. "I'm not fragile."

The glass clinked as he sat it in the metal basin. His hands planted on the side of the counter, he took in a breath. "You learned so much today that has got to have you shaken. I can't imagine how you're not falling apart right now. And it's wrong of me to burden you any further."

She crossed the room and stood behind him. "But you're not a burden. You've helped me in so many ways. You've been . . ."

"In the wrong." He gripped the edge of the counter harder.

Kaori reached out and touched his shoulder. "Theo—"

He growled. "Warren."

"Warren?" She reeled back. "Warren was a lie. He wasn't real. I told you that."

"But you must be heartbroken. You were so in love and excited to see him." His expression was pinched.

"I am over five hundred years old, Theo. He was a lie, and I won't spend my life dwelling on that. It's hard enough for me to let someone in as it is. I will process my anger for what Emiko has done and, more so, what Porter has done. But I don't shed tears for someone who didn't even exist, beyond that first moment of finding out. Period. I followed Warren because I felt fate calling me. I thought he was it. But sometimes fate isn't what it seems." She touched his shoulder again, letting her fingers brush down his arm before turning and walking away.

Theo let out a low, deep, guttural growl. The sound of wood creaking came from where his hands were pressing into the wood of the counter. He let go, whipped around, and caught up with Kaori in only a few paces. He spun her around and pulled her in. Placing his hands on her cheeks, Theo pressed his lips against hers.

Kaori's arms went up, wrapping around his shoulders, her fingers entwining in his hair. His hands slid down her sides, and gripping her thighs, he lifted her up. Colliding with the wall, he pressed against her. Her fingers slipping up under his shirt, she pushed it up and over his head. Moans escaped their lips, accompanied by growling from Theo as their passion grew.

With one arm holding her up, Theo moved them over to the bed, tossing the dusty comforter off onto the floor. He laid her down softly, pushing the hair out from in front of her face. His muscular frame looming over her, he let his eyes roam over her figure as she lay beneath him. Her hands went up, fingertips tracing lines down his chest.

"Kaori." His breaths were heavy.

"Yes?" She tucked her fingers into his waistband.

He smirked.

Without saying anything more, his hands gripped the collar of her dress and pulled, splitting the fabric down the front. Her exposed body lying there, he took in her every curve. "You are absolutely beautiful."

She giggled. "Thanks. I made her myself."

He chuckled, remembering her abilities. "Well, you did good."

Her giggle turned into a full laugh. "Shut up and kiss me."

THE SUN WAS COMING in through the break in the curtains, warming Kaori's face when she woke. A smile played on her lips as flashes from the night before ran through her head. She yawned, stretching her arms up over her head as she rolled over. A rush of panic ran through her when she saw the other side of the bed empty.

She sat up, pulling the sheet up around her to cover herself. Her dress lay torn on the floor next to the bed. Dropping her feet onto the floor, she stood and made her way to a nearby wardrobe. As quietly as she could, she opened the door and looked through the few articles of clothing inside.

"Crap." She sighed as she pulled out a long-sleeved flannel shirt. "I guess this will have to do."

Kaori tucked the sheet up under her arms to hold on to it as she opened the shirt to put it on. But a gust of wind came in as the door opened, blowing the shirt into her face. Unable to see, Kaori instinctively shifted into her fox form and ran for the open doorway.

"Wait!" a female called out.

Kaori scurried between her feet as fast as she could.

The woman turned, shouting to the running fox that was bolting down the front steps. "I'm Theodore's sister!"

Kaori stopped, turned, and looked at her, sniffing the air and assessing if she'd come alone.

The red-haired woman stepped out onto the porch. "I visit my brother as often as I can, never announced. When I saw a woman's things in the spare room and him not there, I simply came out here to see if he'd locked himself in. Can you imagine my surprise to find him in bed with a woman?"

Her nose working the air still, Kaori stood and watched her as she spoke, slowly approaching the front step.

Lifting the shirt off the floor, the sister held it out. "How about I set this inside, and you can go in to get dressed in private. Let me know once you're human and clothed, and we can start over?" She stepped inside, tossing the flannel onto the arm of the nearby chair before returning to the porch, giving Kaori a wide berth to make it through.

Kaori went in, keeping her eyes on the woman the entire way. Once she was in, the door closed. Kaori paused, still unsure about the entire situation. *What did I do? Did I just walk back inside into a trap? Did I let this strange woman just shut me in here?*

"I understand if you need a moment. Just scratch on the door if you'd rather I open it back up and let you run out into those woods alone. I'd rather you didn't, though. Theo would be furious with me." She walked past the door, casting a small shadow over the light shining through as she did.

Letting out a huff, Kaori shifted back into her human form, tossing the shirt over her head and pulling it down as fast as she could. She took inventory of the items in the small cabin she could use for a weapon, if needed, as well as peeked out the windows to get a feel for the grounds. Once feeling as prepared as she was going to be, she opened the door.

"Hi! I'm Heather, Theo's little sister. You're Kay?" Heather bounded into the doorway with a huge grin on her face.

Kaori jumped back a pace. Eyeing the exuberant woman, she took her hand. "Kay. Yes. Nice to . . . meet you?"

Heather pulled her in for a hug. "Sorry. It's just been ages since my brother has let anyone in. He hadn't even written that he'd met someone. But I suppose there wasn't time, was there? No worries. At least I came for a visit and got to meet you."

"Heather, let her breathe. I already explained she's been through a lot. I wanted you to wait until I came back before you met her." Theo stood in the doorway.

"I know," she playfully whined, "but you were taking *forever*."

Theo kicked his boots on the door jamb, knocking mud off his soles. "I hope she didn't scare you too much." He looked at her, confused. "Umm . . . Kay?"

"Yes?" She blinked.

"Kaori Ishida?" he asked.

"Are you okay?" Kaori stepped back. She froze as she caught a glimpse of herself in the mirror. "Oh no! I . . . I'm so sorry!" She whipped around and put her back to the brother and sister, shifting from the olive skin, jet-black hair, and dark eyes of her Japanese appearance back into the brunette form she'd taken on to be allowed into America.

"Ah!" Heather exclaimed. "I was curious how you hadn't been put back on a boat and sent home."

"I heard about the Immigration Act before I came here. I shifted on my way. I guess being startled brought back old habits."

"Well, either way, you look adorable in my shirt." He put an arm around her and kissed her.

Kaori's cheeks turned red. "I'm sorry. I didn't have anything else to wear.

"Don't be sorry." He kissed her forehead, leaning in. "I may ask you to dress like this when we're alone."

She slapped his chest. "Theo!"

He chuckled. "Heather, Kay. Kay, Heather." He handed Kaori a suitcase. "I went back to the house to check on things and to get you a change of clothes. I'll go back later, once we have a plan, but I feared Heather would get impatient and scare you, so I didn't stay long."

Kaori took the bag. "Thank you. And don't worry about it." She looked at Heather. "I'm just a bit jumpy. I hope I wasn't rude."

Heather giggled. "Not at all. I completely understand." She turned to her brother. "Theo here explained a bit about the situation." She looked back at Kaori. "Looks like I came just in time to help."

"To help?" It was Kaori's turn to look confused.

"Yeah!" Heather made her way over to one of the chairs and plopped down on it. "But I guess I need more details than my brother meeting you by chance to clear up a favor for some scoundrel, and the moment he saw you, he knew he—"

He cut her off. "I knew something was amiss if Porter Patterson was involved."

"Yes." She smirked. "And that you have a cousin here that you thought was dead, and now you may not be safe. I'm curious how it is all connected."

"I'm still trying to figure that all out myself," Kaori replied. "Theo, I'll make something to eat if you want to tell her. You're probably less discombobulated than I am."

He kissed her again. "Sounds good. You may need this, then." He went out to the porch and brought in a sack. "I also brought some provisions. Again, we will get more later."

She took the canvas bag, gave Heather a nod, and crossed the small room into the kitchen portion.

Heather mock-whispered to Theo, "I like her."

He chuckled. "I do, too."

Kaori spent the next hour cleaning up the kitchen and making a light lunch and beverages while Theo filled Heather in on the details of the situation. Heather, being lively and still wound up from her travels, was animated in her responses.

Once Theo finished, she went to where Kaori was standing and gave her a huge hug. "You poor dear! I can't even imagine how you must feel."

Kaori gently pried herself out of the woman's arms. "That's what your brother said, as well."

Heather grabbed the plates of food and headed back to the living room area. "Well, he might know a bit better than I."

"What do you mean?" Kaori tilted her head at the two of them. She brought in a pitcher of lemonade and a stack of cups.

Heather looked to her brother, handing him a plate. "You want to share your story?"

"Not really," he grumbled, taking the dish of food.

Heather shrugged. "My brother was once taken by another who was not who they said they were. And the tangled mess cost him dearly."

Kaori handed out the cups and took her plate, sitting on the sofa next to Theo. "Is that why you were so angry yesterday?"

"I was angry because you were in danger," he explained. "But yes. The fact that I have been hurt by someone posing to be another just to get something from me, the fact that Porter is involved, *and* the fact that you were hurt—I did everything I could to keep my temper in check."

"I'm so sorry to put you in this position." Kaori curled up against his side. "What happened to you, and how did you get out of it all?"

"My brother has never let anyone in easily, not even family," Heather jumped in. "That is, other than me. We've always been thick as thieves. That's why I was surprised when I learned he'd been spending time with someone."

"She was a human in a village we had moved to." Theo put a hand on Kaori's knee. "You age significantly slower than us, but as lycan, we age slower than humans. So, as you have had to do, we've had to move around to not be detected. Heather and I moved there first to scout it out. When I started seeing Karen, the rest of our family was concerned about my association with a human, because I wasn't willing to turn her first. So they stayed back."

He continued, "Karen had no powers or anything, but I was sure she reciprocated my emotions. She had recently moved to the small town shortly after we settled in. And as things progressed, I knew I'd have to reveal my other sides to her . . . my were side in particular."

Heather balled her fists. "That stupid b—"

Theo held a hand up, stopping his sister. "In the end, Karen was part of a group of hunters. They had been tracking us for a while. Their plan was to get actual proof, and they knew that if they got close to one of us emotionally, we would reveal who we are. And the moment I did, she tried to kill me."

"She tried to kill you? Right then?" Kaori gasped.

He squeezed her knee reassuringly. "Yes. With it being the full moon, she also had some of her friends nearby. They rushed our home, bringing guns and torches. Heather was shot in the side."

"Thankfully, Theo got me out of there." Heather's hand went to her side, the recollection of the event plain on her face.

"They burned our home, wagon . . . everything. They took our horses and food. I've always had a separate cabin for transitioning away from my home ever since. That night, all I could do was watch from the woods and keep an eye on Heather until she turned back. I took her to a doctor the next morning, then set out to find them." Theo removed his hand, sitting upright as if slightly uncomfortable. "They couldn't bother us after that, but Heather almost died, we lost everything, and our family banished us."

"Banished you?" Kaori's eyebrows pulled in. "They didn't help?"

"They gave us clothes, food, and a few supplies," Heather replied. "Oh, and a couple horses. But that's it. We've not heard from them since and were instructed not to reach out to anyone."

"We've abided by their wishes ever since." He wrapped his arm around Kaori's shoulders, looking over at his sister with an empathetic expression. "When you explained that you'd learned that your family didn't go after those they claimed left for a life on their own, it hit home. I understood the level of betrayal it must have felt for you, because I felt betrayed by our family. We were young. It was a mistake."

"They should have protected us and taken us back in. But no.

They left us out in the cold. I don't know any other packs that are so cruel to their members." Heather downed her lemonade and went to the kitchen.

"There may be some, but as a rule, no. Packs stick together through just about everything." Theo turned slightly to face Kaori. "Heather and I have been close ever since. No matter how much she tries to move away and be on her own."

Kaori nodded. "That's exactly it. I'd always thought of our family as nurturing and protective. I don't know other kitsune families, though. Emiko was the brave one. She would sneak out and go play with other foxes when we were just kits. Leaving to come to America to see Warren was the most daring thing I've probably done. And I only did it after my *okaasan* told me to follow fate."

"*Okaasan?*" asked Theo.

Kaori blushed. "Yes. Sorry. My mother."

"Your mother encouraged you? That's so sweet!" Heather returned with a full glass of lemonade. "Getting back to the situation you two have gotten yourselves into, what do we do now? Relocate you both and hope they don't come after you again?"

"No," Kaori snipped. "Sorry. It's just, I can't say I wouldn't have turned into the person Emiko is now, if I were in her situation. We need to help her and Kai. Meanwhile, I'll send word to my family about the others."

"I agree. I don't care what our family did to us. If I knew one of them was in danger, I'd want to help." Theo kissed the top of Kaori's head.

Heather let out a sigh. "Fair enough. But how? If this Porter guy is as dangerous as you say he is, and if Emiko went back to working for him to keep Kai alive, then we'd better have a pretty damned good plan before we do anything."

"Again, I agree," Theo exclaimed. "For now, I need to run the perimeter. Once I'm sure all is set here, if you stay with Kaori, Heather, I'll go back to the main house. I need to gather more of Kaori's things and some supplies, and I'll come back with the car."

"If Kaori feels safe enough to stay with me." Heather gave Kaori a smile.

She smiled back. "Yeah. I may not have known my cousin's energy, but I'm pretty sure Theo knows and trusts it's you."

Theo laughed. "Yeah. That's my sister for sure."

"But first"—Kaori set her hand on his knee—"food. You can't get all this done on an empty stomach."

"Oh, I *do* like her." Heather roared with laughter. "Finally, I don't have to keep you in line."

Theo threw a chunk of bread at his sister. "Like you've *ever* been the mature one!"

She threw it back. "You're not exactly the pinnacle of adult behavior, mister!"

Both siblings lifted their plates, threatening to throw them, when Kaori stood. "Stop!"

Both looked up at her. "What?"

"I worked hard on those lunches. Do *not* make me mother the both of you. Now eat." She wagged her finger.

"Yup." Heather lowered her plate back onto her lap. "I like her."

Theo took a bite of his sandwich. "Me too."

THAT NIGHT, none of them had come up with a viable plan. Theo, despite his loner status and tendency to handle his own situations, mentioned the Court. He'd been careful to not get entangled with anything that would put him in front of them or even in a situation that went in front of them. However, at a loss for what to do or how to get Emiko and Kai out of there, he suggested they ask for help. The women quickly shot down the suggestion, not wanting to involve others.

Heather leaned away from her brother. "No. You know how we don't like authorities."

"You don't know who is in his pocket, Theo," Kaori added.

"I've not dealt with them much, but I can't imagine that would be the case here," Theo explained.

But Kaori was adamant. "No. Let's do this on our own. I can't tell my family that I got them killed. I just can't. And bringing in people we don't know is risking that."

Reluctantly, Theo conceded. "For now. I'll admit, I'm not one for running to anyone to handle my situations. I was not raised to have others clean up my messes. But I know the Court here. Not informing them of something like this happening in their town could be viewed as a crime. It's a huge risk. So, like I said, for now. But if this can't be easily handled, we tell them. If for no other reason, we will have backup."

"For now," both women agreed.

Heather's journey there had caught up with her. Kaori was exhausted from several days of events. And Theo, still on edge, was hesitant to take action, knowing his anger was still ruling a good portion of his emotions on the matter. So they all stepped away from the topic.

Once Theo returned from the main house, Kaori changed into her own clothes. They sat down to a dinner that Theo and Heather made, forcing a reluctant Kaori to sit, rest, and read for a bit. Theo stoked the fire as the night's chill settled over the woods. The trio sat, reading, curled up with hot cocoa.

There was a looming sense over the three of them that things were going to get worse before they got better. Despite the relaxing atmosphere and sounds of the crackling fire, occasionally one of them would look up and around at the others before checking the doors and windows. The feeling of being on high alert wound through every fiber of the evening.

Finally, feeling Theo's head droop for the third time, Kaori nudged him gently. "Shall we go to sleep?"

"Huh?" he snorted, only half awake. "Sleep? You should get some sleep. Yes."

Heather quietly giggled from her chair.

"Will you come to bed with me?" Kaori patted his leg.

He adjusted, sitting up a bit higher.

She smiled. "I'd sleep better if you would."

He hesitated another moment. "You do need your sleep."

The couple moved from the sofa to the bed as Heather made her own makeshift bed where they'd been sitting. Theo got up one last time and checked the door and windows, then returned to the bed, curling Kaori up against his chest. She nuzzled in and sighed.

CHAPTER 9

Theo's hold on Kaori went slack as he fell asleep. She opened her eyes and checked on Heather, who was fast asleep and snoring softly on the sofa. Something about them both sleeping put Kaori more at ease. She leaned back into Theo's shoulder and drifted off.

"Kaori? Are you here, Kaori?"

"*Okaasan*?" Kaori's eyes began to focus.

She was back in one of the small Japanese villages. A fog was settled over the small town at the base of a mountain. Nobody was around that she could see.

Kaori's mother stepped out from behind one of the nearby trees. "Kaori!" She rushed over and embraced her daughter. "You've had me so worried!"

She hugged her mother tightly, tears welling up in her eyes. "*Okaasan*, I have so much to tell you."

She pulled Kaori back to look at her. "I expected tears but happy tears. These do not look like happy tears, *watashi no kodomo*. Tell me, what has you so troubled?"

"Emiko." Kaori broke down, sobbing in her mother's arms.

The leaves of the cherry blossom trees around them rustled in the wind, sending petals across the landscape.

Her mother gasped. "Emiko? I have not heard of your cousin in so very long. If you've found her, should that not be a happy thing?"

"No, *Okaasan*. She is in danger. She told me of how Tamao, many years ago, put our family in a terrible situation. Emiko sacrificed herself, becoming this man's prisoner so he didn't send people to kill us all."

"Is she alive?" she asked.

"Yes. But there's more. There's so much more." Kaori's words broke as she spoke them. "Many have died to keep her with him, and some are prisoner, being experimented on. He's sent some to his church. It is possible Tamao may still be there and alive. Oh, *Okaasan*, I don't know what to do. She won't leave, because he has Kai."

"Kai?" Her mother took her by the hands. "As in Kai Saito? From the Saito kitsune family?"

"Yes, *Okaasan*," Kaori confirmed. "And because he's being held by this Porter Patterson, Emiko would not leave when Theodore rescued me."

"Theodore? Rescue? Murders?" She pulled her hands back and held her head. "My mind is spinning." Quickly, she dropped her hands again, gripping Kaori's upper arms. "Kaori, I feel the waking world pulling at me. You *must* get us all of this in a letter. Every detail that you have learned. It is not possible for us to get there to help save Emiko and Kai. You will have to do what you can. But I will push our elders to go retrieve those being kept at the church." The older woman looked around her as if seeing something. "Please be safe. I love you."

Kaori hugged her mother once again as her image was fading out. "I love you, too, *Okaasan*."

EVERYTHING WAS blurry as Kaori struggled to see, her mind

forcing her awake in a panic. She longed to see her mother longer, to get another hug, to get some sort of reassurance that everything was going to be all right. Having that moment with her mother and watching her image dissipate left Kaori with an ache in her chest.

Lifting the comforter off of her, she started to slip out of the bed. She paused, feeling Theo's arm sliding off her side. The cool air seeped in, sending a chill over her skin.

She pulled her feet back under the covers and rolled over, facing him. His hair, slightly curly and disheveled, fanned over his forehead. His breathing was shallow, his breath warm on her as she lay there studying his features.

Kaori pulled his arm back around her, feeling the ache of missing her mother lessen. He stirred, pulling her against him closer. His lips, warm on her forehead, kissed her softly. "*Cadal math mo ghr`adh. Bidh mi gad dh`ion.*"

Kaori pressed her lips to his and curled up against his chest. He wrapped both arms around her.

WHEN THEO and Heather woke the next morning, it was to the smell of ham and eggs frying on the stove. Kaori was busily working in the kitchen, making breakfast. Sleep did not come the rest of the night. She lay in Theo's arms thinking over possibilities for getting Emiko and Kai free. Frustrated and not any further toward a plan than the evening before, she chose to get up and put some energy into something else. The scents of her cooking wafted through the small cabin, rousing the others.

"Good morning!" Heather chimed in her singsong voice.

"Good morning, Heather." Kaori handed her a plate of ham, eggs, and potatoes. "Did you sleep well?"

"Yum!" She took the plate. "I did. Thank you."

Theo made his way across the room, snaking his arms around Kaori's waist. "Good morning, doll."

A smile formed on Kaori's lips that she couldn't fight. "Good morning, Theo."

He kissed her neck. "Not going to ask if I slept well?"

Kaori giggled. "Oh. I *know* you slept well. You spoke in your sleep . . . in your native tongue."

His cheeks turned red. "I apologize. I hope I didn't keep you up."

"No." She turned, holding a plate of food out for him. "Whatever you said, which," she put a hand on his chest, "do *not* ask me to repeat. I don't think I could if I tried, but it sounded sweet, and you said it while being very tender. It was perfect timing, since I couldn't sleep."

Theo stepped around Kaori and dished up a plate for her, motioning for her to have a seat. Joining her on the sofa, he took a bite. "Don't worry. We will think of something."

"I spoke with my mother in a dream last night." Kaori's eyes were cast down, the forlorn look returning to them.

"You spoke with your mother in a dream?" Heather sat forward in her chair. "How?"

Kaori blinked. "I don't know, actually. I was taught that I could at a very young age, before I could even turn human."

"Can all kitsune do it with every other kitsune?" Heather asked.

"I've only ever been able to with my mother." Her eyebrows pulled in. "But I've never tried, and I—" She stopped, her shoulders slumping. "I'm learning that I've never asked many questions. I've simply lived as I was taught and told, never truly being curious. I think seeing loved ones leave our family in search of something more, or so I thought, made me not want to be a curious creature. I was happy in my safe little bubble."

"The world is a harsh and sometimes an evil place," Theo said, setting his plate down and turning toward her. "You've been spared some of that torture by having a supportive and loving family. Would it have been right to wage wars and subject everyone to those evils? Or turn your heads and just live, turning a blind eye to it all? Nobody can say what's right and what's wrong. Don't beat yourself up over the past." He ran a hand through her hair. "We just have to focus on what matters."

She placed her hand on his. "You're right. And in our case, fight for a future. I guess that's my struggle—this whole mess is because of things in the past."

"Kaori." He spoke softly.

She looked down. "I know. So what are we going to do? We need to get Emiko and Kai out of there, but are we going to do something about Porter, or are we going to run and hope he doesn't come after us?"

"Tell me about this life force exchange. If Emiko breaks her bond with him, and you're not there to replace her, does he go back to aging normally? Does he have reserves that'll keep him aging slower for a while?"

"His aging will catch up with him faster than a normal human," Kaori explained. "If he would have lived a mere extra ten or even fifty years, it would just shave time off of him. But in his case, three hundred years would probably catch up with him in only a couple years or maybe months. The longer you're kept alive, the faster it comes back on you."

"Can we just lock him in a room and sever their connection so we can watch him age? Give him a small taste of what he inflicts on others?" Heather was leaned back, picking at her nails.

"No," Theo replied with a brotherly, scolding tone. "Knowing this is happening should be enough. We're *not* stooping to his level."

"Fine," Heather dragged out the word. "Don't have to kill him while saving them."

Theo let out a sigh and leaned over Kaori. "My sister has read too many adventure books. I'm pretty sure she would be a pirate if she could."

"The Dreaded Pirate Scott, being from Scotland and all." She laughed. "My reputation would proceed me. But when I arrived to pillage, they'd be shocked I am a woman." She pulled her shoulders back as if proud of her fantasy.

Theo lifted a shoulder. "See?"

Kaori joined in the laughter. "Actually, it's probably needed right now. If we get too serious, we'll probably just mess it all up. Maybe that's our problem. Maybe we're thinking too much, too seriously. Maybe that's why we're coming up with nothing."

"Maybe." Theo picked his plate back up and started eating. "All right, looking at it like that, we simply need to go in and retrieve Emiko and Kai. Then we decide what to do with Porter."

"Okay, but how do we get in for them?" Kaori's shoulders slumped. "That's my biggest roadblock."

"Take a nap!" Heather blurted out.

"A nap?" Kaori was confused.

"Yes! Both of you," she said. "You two take a nap and see if you can communicate. If so, then turn yourself over to Porter tomorrow."

"Absolutely not!" Theo growled.

"Turn myself over?" Kaori blinked.

"Yes. And once you're back inside his house, you can get a good look of who is there and the layout of the house and grounds. See where he's keeping Emiko and Kai. Find out how many people are standing guard. Then, when you sleep, tell all this to Theo in a dream, and we can come after all of you."

"Like I said, absolutely not." Theo had thrown his arm around Kaori protectively. "It's far too dangerous. Why don't you just reach out to Emiko, Kaori?"

"I don't know if I can. I mean, I'm not sure I can even connect with you. I want to save her. She's family, but I still hold my reservations, and that could affect my connection with her. Plus, what if she talks? Can we trust her? Kai doesn't deserve this fate, no matter what she does." Kaori's eyes were full of worry.

"I agree. It's too risky. You and Theo doing this is the best way we have to find out all we need to know in order to wage an attack." Heather looked to Kaori.

Kaori clasped her hands in her lap and looked down.

"That's too risky? But you don't think sending Kaori in by herself is too risky?" Theo almost roared.

Heather glared back at him. "We can trust her. Can you honestly say we can trust Emiko? Kaori, please," Heather pleaded. "He doesn't want to kill you. He wants to keep you."

Theo's anger was boiling over. "Drop it, Heather."

"I'll do it," Kaori finally responded.

"No!" Theo got up and started pacing.

She joined him, placing her hands on his arms. "She's right. It's the best way to get a look at what we're facing."

"But—"

"I can do this." Kaori looked into his eyes.

He returned her gaze, begging her without words to change her mind. They both stood, locked in a silent argument. Seeing she wasn't backing down, Theo winced. "I don't like it."

"She's not some fragile little girl, brother. She's over five hundred years old. I'm pretty sure she's strong enough to handle this. We are the ones who have to be capable of holding up our end and getting them out of there." Heather took her last bite of ham.

Still looking at Kaori, Theo sighed. "I would never forgive myself if something happened to you."

She rested her forehead against his chest. "Then be sure to find me when you sleep so you can come get me out of there."

Theo hesitated, longing to think of some other way to handle things. He stood, mind frozen, stroking Kaori's hair. Coming up with nothing, he growled, a sound deep from within his chest. "Fine. But I don't have a good feeling about this."

Heather patted his shoulder. "We're not asking that you like it." She took her plate out to the kitchen area and washed it. "You two sleep. Let's see if this crazy plan will even work."

Kaori and Theo went to the bed as Heather finished cleaning up the meal, stoked the fire, then sat on the couch. She picked up a book and started to read aloud. The warm fire, calm atmosphere, and overall exhaustion blanketed the couple as they curled up together. It wasn't long before they both drifted off to sleep.

KAORI FOUND herself in an open field. A gentle breeze blew through the delicate blossoms that would, one day soon, become cherries. Fluffy clouds floated by lazily as birds swooped through the sky, playing out aerial shows.

A fallen tree that appeared to have been down for a long time was covered in moss, tall grasses growing up in patches along its bark. Kaori made her way over to it, sitting down and scanning the area. Her shoulders slumped.

"Theo?" She looked around more.

Not seeing him, she felt defeated. She was at a loss for how else to tackle their situation. Determined not to give up, she took the moment to sit in the serene setting and think over a few more possible plans.

"Kaori?"

She felt a hand on her shoulder and jumped.

"Woah! I didn't mean to scare you."

Theo had his hands up as she spun around and saw him. Not hesitating, she thrust herself into his arms and against his chest. "Oh thank goodness! I didn't think it worked!"

He chuckled. "I didn't think I was going to be able to get to sleep. Forcing sleep was a lot more difficult than I expected."

She looked up, smiling. "Hi."

"Hi." He grinned back. "I have to admit, this is"—he rubbed her shoulders while looking up at the trees—"different. I take it this is what your home country looks like?"

Kaori's eyes shone bright. Her arms were wrapped around his waist and her head on his chest as she looked up at him. "Yes. I hope that's all right. I think I'm just used to the setting for my dreams when I meet my mother."

He kissed the top of her head. "It's more than all right. I get to see where you're from. It's perfect."

A happy sigh escaped Kaori.

After a moment, Theo finally pulled back, guiding her to sit on the log with him. "Okay. So there's no guarantee this will work once you're in there. Which makes it that much more dangerous."

"It worked this time. Why wouldn't it work then?" she asked.

He shook his head. "I have no reason to think it won't, but it's possible. If nothing else, planning to sleep at the same time. A number of factors can break that. So we need a plan for times we will both strive to sleep just so if one of us misses one point, we know it's not an entire day before we try again."

She nodded. "Okay. Makes sense."

"And I need you to not take any chances on your own. I want to be prepared when it's time to move." He put her hands between his own. "We are stronger in numbers."

"True," she agreed.

"No matter what, I'm coming in after you if I haven't reached you after two days," he added.

"Wait—"

He stopped her. "No. Anything could happen in there. Including you being killed. I'm not taking any chances that you're tied up and being starved or worse, and if I waited, you die. No. Out of the question."

"Fine. But you have to trust what I tell you when we *do* meet up in our dreams," she stated.

"Of course." He nodded in agreement.

He took her back in his arms and went over a few things for her to watch out for and things he would need her to relay to him. She leaned into his shoulder, listening and adding in her suggestions as well. The sun set over the horizon of the mountains that shaded the backdrop behind the cherry blossom forest that surrounded them.

"So?" Heather's voice betrayed just how eager she was.

Kaori rubbed her eyes. "Huh? What?"

"Did it work?" She practically bounced.

Theo sat up. "Why did you wake us?"

"Because I wanted to know!" She frowned at her brother. "So?" Heather dragged out the word.

Kaori swung her legs off the side of the bed. "Yes. We were discussing a plan before you interrupted."

Heather waved her hand. "You can discuss that while awake. I'm just glad it worked!"

"Hopefully it will again." Theo spoke cautiously.

"It will." Heather clapped, looking at the couple sitting in front of her.

CHAPTER 10

*W*alking up to the front steps, Kaori wrung her hands. The ornate wood doors loomed in front of her, flanked by landscaped topiaries.

"This is ridiculous, Kaori. You should have just stayed in Japan with your family," she scolded herself.

Three raps on the door, and Kaori took a step back. She crossed her arms over her chest as if there was a chill in the air. But it wasn't the weather that made her cold to the bones. And as she heard someone shuffling on the other side of the door, the chill deepened.

"Hello?" A tall, slender man in a suit greeted her as the door opened.

Kaori gave a slight bow, looking down as she did, then back up. "Kaori Ishida here for Porter Patterson." She offered a smile. "He will know what it is in regard to."

The man took a step aside, opening the door wider. "He is expecting you in the den. Please. After you." He waved an arm for her to enter.

"Of course he is," Kaori replied under her breath as she entered.

Patterson was sitting in an oversized leather chair facing a roaring fireplace, sipping something from a brandy glass. His head twitched slightly when he heard Kaori enter, but he didn't turn. "Come. Sit."

She sighed at the cliché supervillain act he was putting on. "I just want to know that my cousin is safe. And I want to talk about all of these experiments. There's got to be a part of you that *knows* this is wrong."

He didn't reply. Instead, he set his jaw. "I do believe I said to sit."

"This is not a social call, Patterson." She stood her ground.

The man scoffed, his head turning side to side as if she amused him. He placed his hands on the armrests of the chair and lifted himself up. Turning to face Kaori, he looked at her for a long moment, the gaze causing her to grow increasingly more uncomfortable. She felt as if she was under a microscope with how his eyes studied her.

Finally, she broke. "Enough! I want my cousin. And Kai."

The corner of his mouth turned up in an unsettling smirk. "I know what you want. But you see, that's simply not possible. I need her."

"No. You need the life force she and I can provide. We can arrange that. How often does she transfer with you? We can make sure one of us is here to do it. You let us go, release our families and leave us be, and we will keep giving you life. This has gone on long enough! You've had more than the one lifetime you felt you were owed. You've had over a dozen! Enough is enough!"

"Oh Kaori. Sweet, sweet Kaori." He walked forward, closing the gap between them, and placed his hands on her shoulders, leaning in slightly to catch her gaze with his. "But there's so much more I not only need but want."

"You're a—"

He laughed, gripping her shoulders tightly and spinning her around. With a swift movement, he wrapped an arm across the front of her, pulling her in and trapping her against his chest, facing the same way as he was. "Monster? No. That's what your kind is.

I'm an opportunist. I'm a product of my own ability to grasp what is before me. Much like this, actually." He turned his head so he could see the side of her face and placed a kiss on her cheek.

He lifted his free hand and motioned to the guard at the door. Kaori watched, searching for Emiko and Kai to come around the corner, ready to try to break free, grab them, and dart out, if there was a chance for it.

Patterson tilted his head back down slightly, his lips grazing her ear. "You see, I've learned a lot through getting to know various people in your family. Not only about your kind but those you love, the world around us, and even myself. And the one thing I know about myself most is that I will do anything to survive at whatever cost."

Kaori heard shuffling from the hallway. Panic rose in her as his words began to fade to the background, her fear of what she was about to see growing.

"I've done a lot to keep this whole thing up, Kaori," he continued. "And I have no intention of stopping. Which is why I am not making the same mistake I did in not taking precautions when I brought you here the first time."

Kaori's vision narrowed as two more large men came into view, but her brain refused to recognize what else she was seeing for a long moment. Finally, things came into view as one man held a limp Heather in his arms and the other struggled to keep his grip on Theo.

Theo roared, a deep, guttural noise.

Patterson waved a finger at him. "Tsk tsk. You don't want to lose your temper so close to the two women you love. Whatever would you do if you hurt one of them?"

Theo's eyes glowed golden; it was a visual struggle for him to not shift. "You take me for some savage animal. Shall we see which of us would win in a fight?"

Patterson wrinkled his nose and chuckled. "You challenge me as if I don't already have the upper hand. Speaking of . . ." He shifted and wrapped his hand around Kaori's throat, tightening just enough to cause her to cough, choking in through a limited airway. "Shall I just snap her neck? I have two of them."

Theo thrashed against the man who held him, and his features began to distort, his nails growing as his facial features started to elongate. And once he started to grow taller, Patterson nodded to the man who held Heather. With a thud, she hit the floor. He was picking up the large, heavy ashtray off the table nearby and swinging it at Theo's head.

Kaori clawed at Patterson's arms. "No!" She tried to escape his grip and get to the unconscious lycan on the floor. She called out, "Theo!"

Patterson started to lose his grip as the small-framed kitsune worked to get to those on the floor. "Ouch!" He let go, reeling back and inspecting a bleeding gash on his hand. "Her, too, David."

And with that, the ashtray was swung again, and Kaori fell to the floor.

"THEO? THEO!" Kaori searched the space around her. Then it dawned on her. She wasn't in the waking world any longer. She was in a dream state. Despair hit her as tears started streaming down her face. This wasn't her dreamscape. This was a dense forest with tall, oppressive trees, moss-covered logs, half-dead leaves slowly floating to the ground, skittering wildlife, strange animal noises, a bubbling creek. Nothing like the serene landscape of her Japanese homeland.

Her feet carried her as she stumbled over a fallen log, causing her to ram her shoulder into a nearby tree. She wasn't sure if that was part of her actions there or some sort of forced movement from her waking-world self running into something. But her debate on that came to a halt when she looked down at the log she'd tripped over and saw that it wasn't a piece of wood. It was Theo, unconscious, still, unresponsive on the forest floor.

She ran back over to him, skidding slightly as she dropped to her knees, gripping his shirt.

"Theo! Wake up! Please wake up!" She shook him slightly, but he didn't stir. He was limp against the cold, damp landscape and moss beneath them.

Kaori's heart sank.

She looked around but saw nothing and no one. Closing her eyes, she listened. Nothing came to her except one thing that gave her at least a little comfort—the sound of Theo's beating heart. It was slow and faint but there. Taking comfort in that, Kaori grabbed him by the shoulders and dragged him the short way to the nearest tree. She propped herself up against the bark and cradled his head on her lap, holding his hand with her. "Wake up, Theo. I can't do this without you."

Her eyes scanned the area. She wasn't sure what she was looking for, but every bit of her was on high alert.

Unsure how much time had passed, Kaori jumped when she felt his hand twitch.

"Theo?" She ran her hand over his cheek.

His voice came low, rumbling, deep, and his words incoherent at first. His eyes rolled back, and his lids fluttered.

She sat up more, careful to not jostle him too much. "Are you all right? Theo? Can you hear me?"

"Kaori?" He coughed hard enough to cause him to curl up slightly. His lungs calming a bit, he finally lifted himself up on his elbows. "Where are we?"

She looked around again. "I don't know. I think this is your dreamscape."

"Mine?" He coughed a little more, his hand going to his head. "I didn't know I had one. How did we get here?"

She blinked. "I think it's because you were knocked out first, and the moment they came after me, I reached for you mentally."

He chuckled, a hint of pain in it. "Sounds plausible as this situation will ever get . . . still in awe of this whole dream walking thing." He cringed, his head obviously hurting. "So, wait. They came after you, too? Are you hurt? What did they do?"

She put her fingers to the spot on her head the ashtray had collided with, pulling them away to check for blood. They came off clean, and she wondered if they would in the waking world. "I tried to get to you when they knocked you out."

He nodded, a smirk pulling up one corner of his mouth. "All right then . . ."

His eyes shut, pulling in his eyebrows, betraying his pain.

Kaori scrambled to her knees, leaning over him as she helped him lay back against the tree. "No! Theo, I need you to help. Stay awake. Stay with me. I can't do this on my own."

He swallowed hard and adjusted his sitting position. "I'm here."

"Good." She sat back on her feet. "I mean, I need you to wake up, but I need you to wake up and shift."

"You need what?" He became more alert with her alarming proposal.

"Shift," she stated plainly. "You're stronger in wolf form, both wolf forms. So, shift. I wanted to just break Emiko and Kai out of here, but he's never going to let any of us go, let alone her. It's time we finish my family's nightmare. I've been too soft all these years, too easily persuaded to believe what people wanted me to believe . . . too easily persuaded to see the good in the world around me. But I see now, sometimes there's just evil. Patterson is evil. And if I want any of us to survive this, he has to be taken out of the equation."

"Kill him? I'm not a . . . uh . . ." He stammered over his words.

She scrunched her eyes and shook her head. "I don't mean kill him. You're not a murderer. But if he gets hurt as we get out, then so be it. It's time to stop underestimating him."

Theo sat up and faced her. "I don't want *you* getting hurt, though. We need to consider turning him over to the Court."

She moved to kneel in front of him. Placing one hand on his

cheek, she smiled. "Then don't hurt me. I trust you. As far as the Court goes, once we're out of here safely, then the Court can have him. But first we have to get us all out of here." She leaned forward and placed her lips on his.

～

THEO LAY STILL on the concrete floor. His breathing and heart rate were as slow as they had been in the dreamscape. The noises of people shuffling around him seeped into his consciousness as he began to come around.

"Just put that one in there. She's his sister. We'll find a use for her at some point." Patterson's voice resonated through the room. "Is the kitsune secure?"

"Yes, sir." Another man's voice sounded from across the room.

For a few moments, Theo lay there, assessing how many people were in the room and where. He set his jaw and allowed the shift to start as quiet and still as he could be, trying to give himself a head start before they noticed.

"Shit!" the other man exclaimed. "He's awake."

Footsteps rushed toward Theo, and he sprang up, claws bared and already well into the transformation. The guard who had been holding him in the study was only a few steps away, but it wasn't enough time for the man. As he reached out for Theo, Theo's clawed hand came up, fur-covered and far stronger than his human hand, gripping the man by the throat.

Patterson spun around and saw Theo holding the guard. "Huff and puff, little wolf. Your little girlfriend is tucked away in my brick house."

Theo was deep in his feral state, but he caught a glimpse of Emiko and Kai, each secured in small holding cells across the room, unconscious, and Heather, locked in a cage, lying listless on the floor. Then he saw Kaori. Her arms were strapped to a post on the corner. She, too, was unconscious, slumped against the post.

The sight of both of them enraged him. He lunged forward, headed straight for Patterson.

The man brought his fist up, connecting it with Theo's jaw. Theo gripped him by the shoulders and slammed him against the wall behind him. The two clashed for a moment before Patterson lost his grip and slammed back fully.

Theo's clawed fingers dug into Patterson's shoulders, causing him to cry out in pain. "You freak. I have other men in this place. None of you have a prayer of getting out of here alive."

The words washed over Theo in his lycan form. Somewhere deep, they connected with Theo's human brain, but he was more in tune with his savage side that wanted to destroy the man in his grip. This focus faltered only as he heard stirring from where he remembered Kaori sitting unconscious.

The lycan snapped his head to look, seeing her petite form rousing. He was about to turn back to Patterson when something hard collided with the side of his head. Theo stumbled backward a couple steps. It only took a moment before he gathered himself. A low growl welled up from within his chest, and he went for the man, blowing through another slam from the lead pole in Patterson's hand, sending stars through Theo's vision. They scuffled, knocking several items off the nearby table.

KAORI'S VISION WAS BLURRY, but she could see them fighting. Unable to move her hands, she realized they were buckled to a post with a set of thick, leather straps. She pulled at them, but they didn't budge. Any thought to shift in order to escape was far from her mind as she stared, frozen with fear at the scene before her.

The two men fell to the floor with Theo on top, pinning Patterson down. A large hand came up and was about to swipe downward, aimed to connect with the side of Patterson's head when the pinned man pulled a syringe out of a fallen wooden box

COLLEEN NYE

and sunk the needle deep into Theo's side, compressing the plunger fast.

Kaori screamed.

Theo jumped up, the syringe still in his side. Being that he was still in lycan form, his body burned off most of the substance, but he faltered in his footing as some of it rushed through him. His eyes went wide with the understanding that even his heightened metabolism wasn't burning off its full effects.

He looked down at Patterson, who was scrambling on the floor, trying to get up. Then his gaze went to Kaori. Feet awkwardly carrying him over to her, he dropped down, his lycan form slipping away as he slowly started shifting back to his human form. His fingers were clumsy as they wrestled with the straps binding her wrists. Unsuccessful at fully unbinding her, he dropped to the floor.

Kaori called out to him as she worked the straps. "Theo! No!" She was able to finish loosening them enough to free her hands. "What did you give him?" she roared as she stood.

Patterson, out of breath and unable to fully stand, propped himself up against the wall. "A very large dose of what I use to subdue your cousin when she gets out of line. Don't worry there, doll. He's got a system that can take it. He'll have a headache, but he will wake up soon. So let's get you back in those straps. This has gone on long enough."

"I don't think so." Kaori's jaw set.

He laughed. "I just took on a lycan. What do you think you can do to stand up against me?"

"Patterson, this is enough," she warned him.

Another man came rushing into the room at that time, the backup making Porter's face contort into a smirk. "You have no chance against me, let alone against us both."

Her eyes were fixed on him when the other man came at her. The sight of the room around her filled Kaori—Emiko, Kai, and Heather were all locked in cages and Theo was on the floor, unconscious. Patterson was before her, regaining his footing as the other man came closer.

Kaori heard the echo of her mother's voice in her head as they practiced different abilities when Kaori was younger. She wasn't sure it would work, but she raised a hand and allowed it to land on the man's arm as he gripped her. She slowly turned her head and whispered, "Sleep."

To her surprise, with a loud thud, the large man hit the floor.

"What the . . ." Patterson's eyebrows knitted together as he watched his thug go down. And for the first time since she met him, he had fear in his eyes.

She started for him, waving a hand out around her, speaking one word, "Wake." As she did, the others began to stir.

Patterson bent down, shuffling items on the floor around, looking for a weapon. As he gripped a hammer and went to stand, Kaori stepped up to him, placing her hand on his forehead. "You do not deserve this life. You may have been wronged by Tamao, but the exchange you've not only demanded but taken has been far worse."

Patterson's eyes rolled back in his head. His grip on the hammer loosened, and it tumbled to the floor. Lines deepened on his face, and his breath caught.

She continued, not hearing the others coming to around her. "You've caused immeasurable pain. You've taken countless lives. You've done more harm in this world than any amount of good you've done."

A light started to glow around her palm, an essence pulling out from him, swirling around her hand and arm.

"I cannot allow you to continue bringing evil into this world. You must be stopped." She stared into his eyes, which were being drained of their color. "You must be stopped," she repeated.

The lines continued to deepen on Patterson's features. His hair turned white, then a drab gray. And his skin was turning translucent with splotches of darker pigment. His frame become frail.

"Kaori." A hand landed on her arm. Theo's voice penetrated her trance. "You're not a murderer, either."

An inner battle waged in Kaori. Her brows pulled in as her jaw set, her energy pulling harder at Patterson's essence.

"Kaori," Theo pleaded. "You'll have to live with this for the rest of your life."

Her voice cracked as she spoke. "He killed them all. He hurt us beyond repair. He is evil on this earth." A single tear fell down her cheek, her eyes still fixed on the now elderly man in front of her.

Theo wrapped his arms around her. Heather, Kai, and Emiko could be heard as if from a far distance, but she couldn't make out what they were saying. Theo moved into her peripheral vision. "The Court will know what to do with him. They handle supernaturals in this town. It's time to let them choose his fate. Don't take this on your conscience. Trust me."

She blinked a few times, the inner battle still waging, but seeing him, her eyes darted back and forth. The tug on Patterson's essence pulled back some before flickering out. "I . . . I . . ."

Theo ran a hand over her hair. "I know." He kissed her forehead.

The two stood there for a moment before the voices of the others filtered in. Theo held Kaori's shoulders. "Are you all right?"

She looked down at the frail old man on the floor in front of them. "I will be."

Finding a set of keys in Patterson's pockets, Theo refused to speak to him. He simply shook his head before going to each of the cages and opening the doors. Heather embraced her brother for a long moment before joining Emiko and Kai, who were next to Kaori.

They stood over Patterson, looking down on him. He pushed himself up, returning their stare. "What have you done?"

Kaori pursed her lips, her nostrils flaring. "I've ended you."

He looked at his hands and roared. "No!"

Emiko stepped forward, slapping the man across the face. "She might not be able to kill you, but I can, you monster!"

Kai grabbed Emiko by the shoulders. "No. He doesn't deserve that stage in our history. Theo is right. Let the authorities deal with him."

Blood pooled under the thin skin that covered Patterson's cheek, instantly bruising. "It doesn't stop the others from experimenting on those we already have or searching for more of you."

Kaori shook her head. "It's a start."

She closed her eyes, tilting her head up and taking a breath. Her lips parted to say something more, but when her eyes landed on Patterson, she shook her head and abruptly left the room.

Picking up the phone in the parlor, Kaori phoned in the emergency through the operator. Heather helped Emiko and Kai as they secured the unconscious guard and the aged Patterson. Theo made a round through the house, retrieving clothes and making sure there wasn't anyone else being held there.

Finding Kaori in the kitchen, arms folded around herself as she stood at the large picture window that overlooked the grounds, he wrapped his arms around her and pulled her in. "She's free."

Kaori nodded. "It's over."

"Yes." He kissed the top of her head.

"It's over," she repeated.

They stood there with those two words hanging over them.

After a moment, Theo kissed her head once more, a gentle smile playing on his lips. "We're just beginning." He went to the door to let Sheriff Kasun in.

ABOUT THE AUTHOR

Colleen Nye started writing as a teen. Through her school days, she won awards for her poetry and short stories, including a Sarah Endres Award for Young Writers. As an adult, she found that her heart is in the art of writing novels. She is the author of The Unattainable Series (*When in Maui*, *When in Doubt*, *When in Love*) (*When in Maui* was a B&N best seller in 2013), *Immersion* (an award-winning novel), *The Long Summer*, *Letters To Cora*, the Manifest Experiment series (*The Pull* is out as of 2018) and more!

She also has taken part in various anthologies and writing projects such as Writing at the Ledges' second, third, and fourth anthologies (*Seasons of Life*, *Voices from the Ledges*, and *Promptly Speaking*), all five Debut Collective anthologies, and the Lunchtime Anthologies (*Gable Heights*), among others.

When she's not writing, she's working as a freelance book formatter, among other author services, as well as a corporate merchandiser. Colleen is an avid movie collector and online RPGer and loves to dance.

Follow and contact Colleen at:

Facebook - https://www.facebook.com/authorcolleennye

Twitter - @Colleen_Nye - www.Twitter.com/colleen_nye

Instagram - Authorcolleennye - www.Instagram.com/authorcolleennye

ACKNOWLEDGMENTS

The list of people that I would like to thank and acknowledge as having been a part of my journey up to now are included in the acknowledgments and dedications of my other books.

Yet, for this one, I'd also like to include people like Dan, Steve, Jeff, Bob, Scott, Chris, and the many people that helped me learn pen & paper and tabletop games; my old L.A.R.P. gamers. Plus, Malachi, Garrett, Serephia, Edward, Freki, Mary, Craig, Damiyn, Garrix, Sebastian, Ming, Ye-Seul, Mattaku, Kerli, Kym, Tobias, Zane, Trixie, Emi, Dakota, Logan, illy, Joe, Cade, Raymond, Robert, Atreyou, Faust, Arius, Ruin, Ethan, Asryaal, Weaver, Chigan, Fenice, Wulla, Kosho, Sebastian, Freya, Savannah, Amforte, Rhina, Lucious, Hibiki, Aaron, Aker, Finn, the Lindens, and so many others that have made my virtual-world gaming experience educational and entertaining. Not all have stayed around. And some have been lessons learned. Yet some have enriched my life in ways I will always be thankful for and cherish in ways I cannot explain. But all have taught me about virtual worlds and gaming.

And as always, my girls are my rock, my support system, and my cheering squad: the two people I can count on to always tell me what I need to hear when I need to hear it.

WRATH AND RETRIBUTION

BELINDA BORING

~ A Legends of Havenwood Falls Novella ~

Havenwood Falls
Legends

WRATH AND RETRIBUTION

BELINDA BORING

ALSO BY BELINDA BORING

THE MYSTIC WOLVES SERIES

The Mystic Wolves

Forget Me Not

Testing Fate

Forever Changed

Savage Possession

Darkness Unleashed

Last Wolf Standing

Blood Oath

A Very Mystic Christmas (Collection of Christmas Memories)

DAMAGED SOULS SERIES

Bittersweet Melody

Bittersweet Symphony

Enchanted Heart

Loving Liberty

Broken Promises

From My Heart To Yours

HAVENWOOD FALLS TITLES

Nowhere to Hide

Addicted to You (Sequel to Nowhere to Hide)

Blood & Damnation (Legends of Havenwood Falls)

The Collector: Awakening

Short Story Anthology 2018

Wrath & Retribution (Sequel to Blood & Damnation)

To my sister from another mister, Laura Benedict.

Thank you for being such a wonderfully supportive friend and someone to go on adventures with! Don't ever change! Love you!

PROLOGUE

CATRIONA

1879

*T*he brisk night air felt like a rough slap across my face.

After weeks of endless travel, we'd finally come to what I hoped was the end of our grueling journey. Not that our sudden stop would aid my escape. I was in no condition to flee—to gather up my tattered rags of a skirt and run as though the Devil himself was after me.

Days had stopped making sense in my jumbled thoughts. The months had long since blended into one another, and although I'd valiantly tried to keep track in the beginning, the world was merely a haze of places and strange faces.

There was a small part of me that tried to remain brave and strong. It was from there that a voice whispered to not give up hope, because my husband would find me. Marcus St. James. How the mere thought of him had roused my spirits in the beginning.

Now, a more sinister feeling crept around the edges of my mind—delivering the sober truth that no one was going to rescue me, because I wasn't something he treasured. Should Marcus and

Knox indeed find me all the way across the sea, it would be for the sole purpose of satisfying his thirst for vengeance.

No matter how hard I struggled to keep that realization from taking root, the evidence became clearer and clearer as time continued to blur by. He'd once told me I was his property. It was foolish to cling to my heart's hope that he'd grown to care for me.

A brusque female voice broke through my despondent musings. "Is this her?"

I was roughly pulled off the horse, my captor's strong grip wrapped around my arm.

He grunted in response, shoving me hard so I stood within the light's faint halo. "Can you take her?"

My heart skipped a beat. Was this finally the end of the road—an end to the harrowing journey the gypsy had taken me on?

England felt so far away as I slowly looked up and found myself under the intense scrutiny of a dark-haired woman. My gaze quickly darted up and took in my surroundings. Dusk was now upon us, and the night air was filled with the sounds of people heading home for the day. Not this building, however. More light spilled out from the plain glassed windows, seeping out through the lace curtains that hung within.

Piano music unlike any I'd heard before echoed about, matched only by the cheery sounds of chatter and laughter. If I was to wager a guess, my captor had brought me to a saloon or some kind of establishment that catered to drinking and pleasures. We'd stopped at enough along the way for me to recognize the telltale scent of ale and whiskey.

I was definitely a long way from home and the sheltered life I'd been brought up in.

The woman began her slow catlike stalking around me, and suddenly, I felt very, very naked beneath her gaze.

"I have no use for more girls," she tutted as her lips pursed in thought. "Unless you believe she has a talent to please." Without warning, the strange lady grabbed hold of my face, her fingers squeezing my chin until I squirmed in pain. "Do you still have your virtue?"

Part of me wanted to scream . . . wanted to reach out and slap her hard. Once upon a time I would've scratched out her eyes, fought tooth and nail to be free from both of them, but that was then, and this was now. Wisdom was needed—courage—to survive.

I shook my head and looked at my captor, Dimitri. My own personal monster had a name, one he'd boasted in sharing the second he knew we were free from England and his revenge had been successful.

For the briefest of moments, I thought I caught a glimpse of compassion in her eyes. Dimitri was a hulk of a man with a dark piercing stare that caused other men to give him a wide berth. The woman had assumed rightly that he'd taken from my body what he wanted, and that he was far from a gentle lover.

Those were memories I buried deep inside me—far away from the light of day where they wouldn't drive me insane. There were many things I locked away now. The only memory I entertained was Marcus's shout into the night air that he would find me.

I knew that made me a fool, but my stubbornness was the only thing I had left. My pride had been stripped away with each of Dimitri's rough touches.

"She is for my pleasure alone," he responded, slapping me hard on the behind. Gritting my teeth, I forced myself not to cringe or fall to the ground from the force. I still didn't know whether this new woman would become my new jailor or indeed my salvation. I wouldn't show her weakness. I wouldn't show her how completely broken I felt.

"If I take her on, and that is a huge if, Dimitri, I ask that you not manhandle the poor thing." The gypsy male easily towered over her, yet she showed no fear as she pointed her finger, chastising him. Wrapping her arm around my shoulder, she did the unthinkable. For the first time since this whole ordeal begun, someone protected me. "I'll do this because of our family."

And then, as the conversation broke down into a familiar language, my stomach dropped, and my fragile hope was shattered yet again.

Romani.

She wouldn't become my savior or someone I could possibly win over and earn my freedom from. The more I stared at the woman, the easier it was to see the similarities she shared with Dimitri. There was no mistaking that they were kin. The false sense of security that had begun to blossom within me shriveled and died like a neglected rose beneath a cruel sun.

I stared down at the ground and wrapped my arms tightly around myself, hoping to keep the chill from shaking me into pieces. The harder I tried, though, the stronger the quaking became. I was just so tired—exhausted from trying to remain brave. Tears began to flow down my cheeks. They were a luxury I refused to allow myself, but as the sound of their heated conversation broke against me, I lowered my guard and the pain swept in.

Tears for me.

Tears for my future.

Tears for the life that I'd been cruelly ripped from. Never would I complain again about Marcus and his neglect. My heart longed to be back at Smithersby Field—to be standing outside the door to his office where I'd faithfully knocked, hoping to be admitted. I would welcome back that uncertainty a hundred times over if it meant that I could be safe within his home.

"Look, you have made her cry, you oaf," the woman blurted, finally turning her attention back to me. The look of compassion had returned to her face—features I'd only just judged as kind, but now couldn't believe. Even as she gently wiped away my tears with the lace handkerchief she pulled out from the front of her bosom, I steeled my resolve. If she was related to Dimitri, then she couldn't be trusted. She was simply another threat to endure.

Pushing past her, Dimitri grabbed me once more and shook me by the arm.

"You're to stay here until I return." His demand was delivered with enough force not to brook any argument. I already knew that any disobedience would incur his anger.

I nodded quickly and returned my gaze to the floor. Submission pleased him. It always hurt less when I pleased him.

He barked out something else in Romani before swinging his leg up and over his horse. Dimitri was going to leave me here—leave me alone for the first time in a year. Traveling from England, he masqueraded us as a married couple, playing the overly protective husband. There hadn't been more than a few seconds where I wasn't being watched by him, yet now he rode off into the night without a single glance back.

The thought of being here in this strange place alone would've once excited me with all the possibilities for adventures. Now, it sent another round of tremors through my body, weakening my knees to the point I staggered forward and clutched onto my new jailor.

"You are safe for now," the woman whispered as she steadied me back on my feet. She remained quiet until I eventually looked up and found her waiting. Now that Dimitri was gone, I studied her.

Her dark hair was pinned back from her face into a loose bun that had pretty white flowers threaded through the strands. I imagined her the age of my mother, had she survived the pox that had rampaged through our small town when I was still a young child. Her cheeks were reddened, and I couldn't tell if it was from the chilly air kissing her skin or because she was a woman who wore rouge. Unlike mine, her clothing was beautifully stitched, fitting her form perfectly.

"My name is Mrs. Fanny Webster, and this is my home." She gestured back to the building where music still flowed from. That wasn't what confused me, however. She must've been used to people responded to her name because she broke out into laughter. "That is my English name. I adopted a more appropriate one when I arrived in this great country. In my family, what you are called

257

holds certain power, and in the case of the Romani, it often generates fear and hatred."

All I could do was nod in agreement. I'd seen that same emotion consume Marcus—his loathing for gypsies was deep-seated and overshadowed his life. His wrath was at least justified, because of the curse he bore as a result of dealing with them. I'd also seen that same skepticism in the strangers I encountered with Dimitri.

"So," I spoke, my voice soft and scratchy from the lack of use, "you are to be my new owner?"

This earned me another round of laughter, this time louder and heartier than before. "Do you desire that?" She reached to brush aside a strand of hair, and this time I did flinch. I wasn't used to being shown such kindness. "What shall I call you?"

"Catriona," I answered reluctantly.

"Well, Catriona, while you are not free to leave, you are not prisoner here in my home. You will simply stay with me until Dimitri returns." She said it so matter-of-factly, as though the lies that came rolling off her tongue didn't bother her.

"I believe that's the very definition of being owned, Mrs. Webster," I uttered, surprised at my brazenness. I waited, breath held, for the slap that would've followed such a retort to Dimitri, but none came.

"We all have our parts to play," came her response. Hitching up her skirts, she guided me up the back wooden stairs into the building she called her home. One glance inside told me everything I needed to know. This was far from the kind of "home" I was accustomed to, and more like the establishment I'd assumed it to be.

Everywhere I turned were half-dressed women being intimate with gentlemen. Some were leaning in close, engaged in sordid conversations that made them blush. Even more disturbing were the few who had hands up their skirts, their heads tipped back in fake delight.

"He left me here in a whorehouse!" I exclaimed in shock. My

eyes grew as wide as saucers. Soon other sounds filled my ears—a different kind of music than the piano. I started to back away to the door, careful not to touch anything.

"Things are not what they seem, child." I expected Mrs. Webster to be offended by my disgust, but instead she looked quite proud. "You'll learn that quickly here."

I shook my head back and forth. I squeaked out loud as I bumped into a very large, extremely jovial man. His arms shot around me, and he bellowed in excitement over catching me.

"A new girl!" the drunk gentleman called out, his fingers splayed across my waist. It didn't matter that I hadn't bathed in weeks and carried the dirt from the road on my clothing. Judging from the way his tongue lolled out of his mouth and how his lecherous lips then pursed into a kiss, he only had one thing on his mind.

Mrs. Webster stepped into action and slapped away his advances while tugging me toward her. "Patience, Mr. Jefferson. This one is not for you."

Before he could pout or argue his case, she called for someone —a young girl in a deep green dress—to bring him something more to drink.

I followed behind her in silence as we crossed through the room and then up the stairs to the second floor. It wasn't until she'd successfully gotten me through a small door at the end of a very long hall that she spoke.

"While you reside here with me, I will protect you, but make no mistake. The life you were once accustomed to is over. The sooner you welcome your new reality, the easier you will adjust." She rattled off a short list of instructions—where I'd be sleeping, the few meager dresses she'd managed to find for me, and eating arrangements, but it all became a blur again as exhaustion took over.

"Will . . ." I couldn't quite finish my most pressing question. All I could do was stare at the door that led back downstairs.

"We'll discuss that in more depth tomorrow. For now, change

out of those clothes and get cleaned up. Someone will bring you something to eat shortly, and then I suggest you get some sleep."

"But—"

She shook her head. "Tomorrow."

Mrs. Webster left me standing there alone in the center of the room. As I closed my eyes and took in a deep breath, there was only one thought that anchored me, kept me from floating away.

Find me, Marcus. Find me and bring me home.

CHAPTER 1

MARCUS

1879 – EARLY SUMMER – HAVENWOOD FALLS

I was restless.

After almost a year of traveling over ocean and then land, we'd arrived in the mysterious town whose name Lady Hannah had scribbled across the paper she had delivered. During that time, I'd clung to the message like it was a lifeline that somehow connected me to my Catriona.

That was something that had changed—the way I viewed the young woman I'd once considered a hindrance and nuisance. She was far from that now. She was the only creature I would ever scour the earth for, but as much as I'd kept my hope in finding her alive and strong, the past week had drastically attacked it.

Even now, as I stared at the crumpled piece of parchment, looking down at the memorized words written there, I dreaded having to face reality.

There was a good chance she would remain forever lost.

There was an even more convincing possibility that she hadn't survived the treacherous trip across the seas.

"We'll find her," came the optimistic voice from across the

room. "Whether we find her alive or find her grave, we'll discover the truth, Marcus."

So much had changed between me and the young man who had left behind everything to follow me on my most important mission. Once he was simply a means to an end—someone to run my errands and provide me with things I couldn't get for myself.

Phineas Knox was now my brother—blood or not.

Our relationship went beyond his oath to help me break the curse that reduced me to a blood-drinking vampire. He had proven in every way that mattered that he would stand by my side —through thick and thin—and his need for justice ran as deep as my thirst for retribution.

We would find the woman who had secured a place in our hearts. Even if it meant dying in the process.

"The thought of her alone out there with that bastard still makes my blood boil," I answered, letting out a heavy sigh and raking my fingers through my hair. There was no disguising the frustration that had become a permanent part of my voice. Everything irritated me, and because of that, my hunger constantly tugged at me. Knox did his best to help assuage the more beastly parts of my nature, but frankly, it was the least of my worries. "Just give me one minute with the Romani scum and I'll be satisfied."

The sentiment was also a steady topic during our daily conversations. While Knox wasn't as bloodthirsty in his plans for revenge, I knew that once this journey came to an end, the thief wouldn't be identifiable—even to the closest of his kin.

I finally put down the note. Staring at it always left an angry, bitter taste in my mouth and a tight feeling in my chest. Helplessness wasn't an emotion I tolerated, yet that's exactly what I'd been reduced to, and it rankled.

My fist slammed down hard on the desk. "She has to be here." Knox approached, rolling up his sleeve. I shook my head in strong refusal. "No. It's too soon."

Being new to Havenwood Falls, we still hadn't located a fresh blood source, and Knox had decided that he would be my willing donor until something surfaced. We were both extremely cautious not to draw attention to ourselves, ensuring that nothing prevented our moving freely from town to town.

Catriona was our priority.

My bloodlust had to be managed, but even now I pushed down the hunger that gnawed away inside me.

"Just enough to take the edge off, Marcus." And with that, he shoved his bare wrist in my face. "Quit being a stubborn arse and take what you need." When I continued to refuse, Knox finally grabbed me by the shirt and dragged me in front of the bronze-framed mirror hanging on the wall. Whisper Falls Inn had comfortable enough accommodations, and while it paled in comparison to Smithersby Field, it met our needs. "Unless you'd like to take up Madame Luiza's offer and have her bring bottled blood to you. There's also the den. You decide."

I hated being reliant on anyone. It was bad enough that I needed Knox in order to survive and not reveal my vampiric nature. Despite being told that arrangement could be made for me, I was hesitant to become indebted to this town and the citizens living here.

I stared into the mirror and saw more evidence that I needed to drink.

The reflection staring back at me looked like a man dancing precariously along the edge of mania. My long hair was tousled from my constant pulling at it in annoyance, and the sunken expression around my eyes spoke of the countless nights when sleep had evaded me.

"You look like shit," Knox commented. There was no humor in his tone. He knew exactly how dangerous I was when my thirst was left unchecked. We'd had to flee a few towns along the eastern coast of America because I'd foolishly overestimated my own strength. The last thing I wanted was to leave a trail of dead bodies behind us.

I finally nodded, submitting to his common sense. "We need

to find her, Phineas." I repeated my desire again before pressing my lips to the pulse at his wrist. I closed my eyes and pictured her face. "I can't lose her."

My fangs dropped instantly, and with gentle care, I slipped them into his flesh. That first drop of blood hit my tongue like a lightning bolt, zinging power and electricity through my veins. It was the same each and every time I tasted blood. Hunger exploded within my chest, and I fought to keep the temptation to gorge myself in check.

Knox placed his hand at the back of my head when I tried to pull away, resisting the urge to take more. He was another one who often overestimated his limits, making us quite the pair. There was nothing more terrifying than realizing how closely I had brought him to death. I'd made that mistake twice and vowed never to let it happen again.

What I didn't confess out loud was I would've rather drained some stranger in an alley than kill the only man I considered my brother. He was the one who kept me human during this past year.

I wouldn't repay him by being greedy.

My teeth slid back in, and I began my count to ten. Just ten seconds, and that would need to be enough.

There was something intimate between us whenever blood was exchanged. It deepened the love that I had for Knox. It produced a level of gratitude I'd never experienced before.

When I pulled back a second time, he didn't stop me. Instead he simply sat there beside me with his eyes closed, a slight sheen of sweat across his forehead.

"Did I take too much?" I asked, already knowing his response. It was always the same.

He shook his head and raised a shaking hand to his mouth, wiping softly across his lips. A trickle of blood streamed from the two bites at his wrist, and I swiftly took hold of his arm and brushed my tongue across the wounds. Within seconds, any hint of what I'd just done was gone.

"You took what I freely gave, Marcus." I didn't like the quiver in his voice. I hated how weak it made him sound—how weak I'd made him.

"No more, you hear me?" I countered firmly. With each breath I took, I grew stronger as his life force swept through my entire body. I didn't need to peer in the mirror again to know that vibrancy had returned to my features. The guilt that always followed feeding from Knox fueled my need to break this curse.

I didn't want to be the monster anymore.

I didn't want to hurt those I loved.

Knox's eyelids fluttered open, and he gave me a sidelong glance. "This is the safest way, and you know it."

There was a slight hint of red returning to his cheeks, but not enough to stem my worry.

"No more," I repeated. Leaving him to sit by himself, I gathered up a plate of leftovers from last night's meal and brought it to him. "I won't risk you again, Knox, and that's the end of it. Look me in the eyes and tell me that it's not taking a toll on you."

He took the plate from me and slowly broke off a piece of stale bread. Knox took a bite before tossing it back with the rest of his meal. "At least let me find an alternative, Marcus. Please. I need to find more ingredients for your daily elixir as well. Perhaps Havenwood Falls has something available for people like us."

That had definitely been a surprise. Not only had Lady Hannah's message led us far from home, but it had brought us to a small, newly established town where supernatural creatures like me lived amongst humans. From what we'd been able to discover, they lived in relative peace, following the rules that the governing council enforced.

"Don't you think Saundra Beaumont would've told us that when we met with her?" I answered, going over that brief meeting in my mind.

While a man called Roman Bishop had met us and led us into town a week ago, it was a young witch who had approached us the next day and provided an introduction and small tour. There weren't many instructions other than the obvious—don't stand out and don't cause trouble. We in turn shared our intentions and what had brought us to Havenwood Falls. Miss Beaumont had patiently listened to our ordeal and offered some suggestions about searching for Catriona. She was especially intrigued—and seemed none too pleased—that a seer all the way in London had revealed the existence of her secret town.

When we parted ways, it was with the promise that she would ask her own questions and perhaps shed more light on my wife's whereabouts. As a witch, she had access to a coven, and no amount of begging and bribery from me could convince her to allow me to be there when she did.

"Things are done differently here," she'd added before excusing herself.

It wasn't until Knox had convinced me that we needed to play by the rules and not storm the keep, so to speak, that I calmed down and accepted that there were things beyond my control.

I would be nice and polite.

I would nod and smile, if needed.

But my patience was wearing thin.

I needed something—anything—some kind of news to hold on to.

Jumping up, I paced back and forth before striding over to the window to peer out. It was still somewhat early in the morning, and the streets were only now starting to get busy. All I could think of was that someone out there held the information I desperately needed. "Eat more and then go run your errands. I need time to think."

"I'd prefer we go out together," came his reply. Knox sounded stronger, and sure enough, his skin had returned to its usual color. A few more meals beneath his belt and he'd be back to normal.

"I don't need babysitting. Contrary to your false assumptions, I am quite capable of looking after myself." My response came out harsher than I intended. The room fell silent as I felt him measure my words. "Knox," I added curtly, "I won't be coddled."

I saw the exact moment when he relented. With a brisk nod, his gaze returned to his plate as he polished off the remaining food.

"Be careful," Knox answered after swallowing the last mouthful of his meal.

Peeking through the curtains again, I gazed up at the sky. It was another bright, sunny summer day, and my eyes trailed up to where the mountain peaks stood tall and proud. "Perhaps we should go exploring. The gypsy may have her camping out there in the wilderness somewhere. That may be why we haven't found her here in town."

"I'll gather provisions, then."

Suddenly I needed to be out in the fresh air, and not breathing in the staleness of the room. "Good."

With a quick farewell, I closed the door behind me and made my way toward the stairs leading down. In my haste to get out, I bumped into the small human woman responsible for cleaning the rooms.

"Sorry, sir," she exclaimed, ducking her head apologetically. "I didn't see you there."

Steadying her, I offered a smile that said no harm was done. It triggered a thought. "Do you mind if I ask you a question?"

Her stricken expression turned into one that was willing to help. "Of course." Her blue eyes brimmed with eagerness. "How can I assist?"

"If I wanted to find something here in town but I didn't know who best to ask, where would you suggest I go?" When her brow furrowed in concentration, I added more to clarify what I needed. "Is there someone I could talk to that knows things about the town?"

That appeared to make things much easier, as she nodded excitedly. Looking to see if anyone else was nearby, she leaned in and whispered like we were joint conspirators. "I'm not supposed to know what goes on in there, but everyone does, and it's not really a secret. Just don't tell anyone who told you, because I would get a thrashing from my father. Respectable folks don't go there."

Her response intrigued me. "This will be between you and me. You have my word as a gentleman."

That elicited a giggle from her.

"You need to talk to Mrs. Fanny Webster." She said it as if the name should spark some kind of recognition. I'd never heard it before, and my face must've reflected that, because in an even softer whisper the young maid continued. "She runs the whorehouse here in town."

It was my turn to laugh.

Of course. If there was one truth that was universal in this world, it was that loose morals led to looser lips, and many a secret was spilled in such establishments where liquor flowed freely and legs were spread for money.

"Mrs. Fanny Webster," I repeated, making sure I understood her perfectly. I had. "You have done me a great service this morning, Miss." Kissing the back of her hand like she was one of England's finest ladies in the peerage, I bowed deeply and continued on my way.

I was about to visit my first whorehouse.

Perhaps this journey hadn't led to a dead end after all.

CHAPTER 2

*M*rs. Fanny Webster was not what I expected. Standing there on the front porch of her establishment, she gently stroked a black raven, whispering something to the creature before it spread its inky wings and took to the sky.

Dressed in a bold red dress that practically screamed her profession, she was far from the coarse imagery I'd held in my mind. I had assumed I would find someone old and weathered by years dedicated to debauchery and boozing, and instead she was a dark-haired enchantress.

As she extended her hand gracefully to me, I honored the gesture with a soft kiss and smile.

"They tell me if there are answers to be found in Havenwood Falls—secrets to uncover—that you are the lady to talk to." I didn't bother beating around the bush or playing along with the charade of false intentions. I wasn't here to bury myself between the legs of one of her girls.

Unfortunately, she felt she knew better.

"Sooner or later they all come looking for me, Mr. St. James." There was a sultry tone to her voice and in the way she peered at me through her eyelashes. "So, tell me, what kind of pleasure do you seek?" She took her hand back and placed it delicately over her stomach. "Or would you rather I guess? I've been doing this for a while, and I pride myself in knowing what's best for my clients."

Before I could answer, Mrs. Webster placed her finger over my lips, briefly silencing me. With a swish of her skirts, she sashayed around me with a smirk slowly curling the edges of her mouth. "Oh, yes."

"Is this really necessary?" I muttered beneath my breath. That earned me a disappointed glance and head shake. "I've come on business."

"As am I," she cooed in return. "May I call you Marcus?" As she threaded her arm through mine and led me to the stairs, she gazed up at the sky. "I believe it's the perfect weather for a walk about town. You know, to discuss business." There was a slight hint of teasing to the last part of her comment.

I let out a sigh and reluctantly nodded. "Then lead the way, madam." The formality drew out a giggle from her. The irony wasn't lost on me either. "And you may call me whatever you'd like."

I already knew this conversation was going to be exhausting. There were so many pretenses to observe when being social, and it was why I preferred to hide away in my home and let Knox deal with people. He had much more patience than I ever did—even before I was cursed. He seemed to understand what was required, and a part of me wished I'd sent him to come talk with this woman.

I didn't have time for foolishness.

We walked in relative silence. It was interesting to see how other town members treated her, especially those wives who knew where their husbands often spent their time. Dagger-like glares didn't seem to faze her, however. With all the dignity of a queen, she simply tipped her head in greeting and continued on.

"Mrs. Webster," I started, when I couldn't bear the quiet a second longer. In my mind, all I could hear was the ticking of a clock signaling time wasted and lost.

She patted my arm affectionately. "Fanny, Marcus. Please. I want us to become good friends, so let's abandon such politeness."

I'd call her whatever she wanted if it meant she had the information I needed.

"Fine. Fanny."

Her lips slipped into an easy smile. Damn woman.

"My friend and I are here in town searching for someone extremely important to us. Perhaps, with your . . . occupation and talents, you've seen her."

This piqued her interest. "Ahh, so you *have* come to me for a lady. Like I said before, they always do."

The smugness in being correct all but dripped from her words. My tolerance was about to reach its limits.

Counting to ten in my head, I gritted my teeth and faked sincerity. "I'm looking for my wife."

"And you're assuming she's in my employment? I assure you, any of my girls would make a fitting bride for you with the right presentation." All the while, she nodded back and forth with people we passed. She may have run the house of ill repute here in town, but that didn't stop men from calling out her name to bid her good morning.

Something tugged at the back of my mind. This woman was out on display. The swishing of her dress skirts was constantly filling the air, and that was when I realized that I was also being watched and studied.

"Enough!" I said, stopping abruptly. "Let me speak plainly with you, Mrs. Webster."

"Fanny," she corrected just as quickly.

"No. We are not friends. I'm in town for a very specific reason, and once I've found the person I'm looking for, my friends and I will be leaving. Forgive me for being rude, but you either have the answers I need, or you don't." I paused long enough to study her face and recognized the shrewd expression in her eyes. I'd been right. This had all been a show and distraction.

"Continue on then, Mr. St. James, although I warn you,

despite what you might have heard about me, I'm too busy to be caught up in whatever town gossip is circulating. If your wife has come to Havenwood Falls, you might be better off asking the Court whether they've met her."

So, there was definitely more to this woman than I first judged.

"Court?" I tested. It was one of the rules Miss Beaumont had emphasized—that the human citizens here remained oblivious to my supernatural nature.

"Now who's playing games?" Her eyebrow cocked as she placed a hand on her jutted hip. "You were met by one of the founding members upon arrival. Or have I assessed you incorrectly?" She leveled a brazen glare my way, holding my gaze.

I barked out a laugh.

"So, you're one of us?" I asked, hoping my question would lead to her divulging more information.

"Who I am is my business and not open for discussion. My suggestion still stands, however." Gone was the flirtatious tilt of her head, the softness in her touch, and the batting of her eyelashes. Before me stood a bolder woman, one who had suddenly tired of our conversation. "I leave the Court alone, and they return the favor. I'm sure if you approach them with your questions, they'll be happy to assist you." She cast a quick look over her shoulder to where we'd just walked. "Now if you'll excuse me, I have things to attend to."

I didn't think. I simply acted, reaching out with lightning reflexes, and grabbed her arm. "I'm convinced you're the one to help me. I'm looking for my wife. Her name is Catriona, and she would've been traveling with a filthy . . ." I abruptly stopped mid-sentence and corrected myself. "Excuse me, she was last seen with a man of Romani descent."

Rattling off the description I'd repeated countless times over the past year, I kept my gaze trained on her features for the slightest hint of recognition.

Nothing.

But then again, what did I expect from an actress? Everything about this woman was about putting on a performance and pleasing an audience.

She at least had the decency to pretend to think. "Neither of them sounds familiar, Mr. St. James. I'm sorry, but I don't believe I can help you after all." Without drawing attention, she pulled her arm from my grasp before plastering another fake smile on her face. "But should you change your mind and seek some form of nightly pleasure—"

I didn't let her finish. "I won't." Frustration surfaced in my voice finally.

She held up her hand to keep me from interrupting. "As I was saying, I'm sure some kind of arrangement can be made. Now, if you'll excuse me."

With a hasty half curtsy, she backed away and left me standing on the side of the dusty street. I watched her leave, mulling over our conversation.

All I could think was how quickly the discussion had soured. True, I'd played my part in that by letting my impatience get the better of me. The blood that Knox had graciously supplied me had burned through my system and left me feeling somewhat cranky. Images of Catriona calling out in fear, of her begging for me to find her, were constantly pressed to the front of my mind. Even now I could hear her voice as if it were yesterday—the gut-wrenching scream she'd released as the gypsy rode off into the darkness with her.

That's why I couldn't ignore the nagging feeling that Mrs. Webster hadn't been completely honest with me. It wasn't something I could put my finger on, but I'd learned to trust my gut, and it was churning something fierce right now.

"What are you hiding?" I whispered to no one in particular. Finally turning away, I glanced about the street and let out a tired sigh. Lady Hannah's note had been so very specific. Havenwood Falls in Colorado, USA. There were no ifs or buts, no mistaking her meaning.

BELINDA BORING

We'd only been here for a short time, but deep down, the truth shone brightly. I'd expected to find Catriona easily. I had assumed that we would be greeted by someone and then I'd be reunited with my wife promptly.

What I didn't anticipate was more mystery.

"Good morning, Marcus."

A deep voice broke through my thoughts, and I looked up to see Roman Bishop standing up on the sidewalk.

Burying my emotions and pulling down the guarded façade I wore like an expert, I smiled. "Good morning. This is quite the town you have here."

Pride beamed from his blue eyes. "It's home." It was his turn to glance about, and realizing I was alone, he gestured for me to join him. "Where's your companion today? Did you say his name was Mr. Knox?"

I wanted to laugh because if there was one thing I believed about this man, it was that he wasn't someone likely to forget details. I wouldn't be surprised if he knew exactly where Phineas was and what he was doing.

I humored him anyway. "Yes, my friend's name is Phineas, but I've always called him Knox. He's running a few errands at the moment, so I took advantage of the fine weather and took a stroll."

His next comment confirmed that nothing was his beneath his notice. "I saw you talking with Fanny Webster." Interesting. He didn't use formalities when mentioning her. "I trust that you were able to find what you were looking for?"

There was no holding back the chuckle that rose up from my chest. "If you're wondering whether I inquired after one of her girls, then I'm sorry to disappoint you. My questions for Mrs. Webster were strictly business. Someone suggested she might know something about my wife and the Romani who kidnapped her. That she may have seen them passing through."

"And?"

I dragged my fingers through my hair in annoyance. "Another dead end."

Roman rubbed his fingers across his mouth while looking down the street. "I've given your predicament a lot of thought since we last talked. I've asked around to see if anyone matching the description of your Catriona even briefly stopped in town."

It was my turn to repeat his question. "And?"

"I haven't uncovered anything yet, but don't give up hope. A town like this . . . with our particular citizens . . . Everyone holds their own secrets. It might just be that she hasn't arrived yet. Are you sure that's what your note was referring to?"

I'd shown him the seer's message that first night.

"What other answer would I be seeking? I was told I'd find what I'd been searching for here. That Havenwood Falls held the answer." Hunger started to gnaw at my gut, but I ignored it. I refused to go back and drink more from Knox. He'd already sacrificed enough blood. The curse was my problem, and I'd be the one to find a way to slake my thirst.

Roman caught my gaze and held it. "Have you not considered that maybe coming here had nothing to do with finding your wife and everything to do with breaking your curse?"

The simplicity of his question struck me like a sharp punch to the gut.

I hadn't considered it. Well, maybe I'd entertained the thought for a second, but I'd dismissed it instantly. When we'd gone to see Lady Hannah in London, it was for the sole purpose of seeing whether she knew of a cure, but once the attack happened, my priorities and thinking shifted. My need for revenge had been surpassed by my longing to have Catriona back in my arms where she belonged. I felt like an idiot now because maybe, just maybe, I'd come here to America while the gypsy had taken her somewhere else. Perhaps up into Scotland or even across the channel to Europe.

The reality that was a likely possibility robbed my breath.

Could we really have been that wrong?

"Damn," Roman uttered. "You didn't."

I scrambled to contain my emotions.

Each conversation Knox and I had replayed in my mind.

Every witness we'd talked to who gave vague accounts of maybe seeing a couple with a woman who matched Catriona's description tumbled about.

I'd been so sure.

But, again, I couldn't start doubting my gut now. If I began to let uncertainty chip away at my convictions, all would be lost. The hope that I held within my heart still flickered valiantly.

"She's here," I answered firmly. "She's here, and I'll find her."

Roman slapped my shoulder and squeezed the top of my arm. "Then, until you learn otherwise, I'll also ask around and see what I can uncover. While I can't promise anything, it's worth trying."

A need to keep searching flared inside me, making it almost impossible to stand still. "I appreciate your help, Mr. Bishop. I'm staying at Whisper Falls Inn, so if you find anything at all, send a message there."

As I walked away, heading in no particular direction, one thought alone reverberated in my head. No matter how hard I tried to bury it, to silence its insistence to be heard, I couldn't deny the truth.

Doubt had taken root.

More than ever, I needed to find Knox.

But most importantly, my hunger demanded immediate attention.

CHAPTER 3

"*Y*ou're quieter than usual."

I grunted. There weren't any words, and I wasn't someone who spoke just for the sake of it. Knox had found me in a state of panic when he returned to our room. With his arms filled with packages, it took him a few moments to figure out what had reduced me to a state of desperation.

I didn't do well with showing weakness, even when it was in front of someone I considered a brother. Walking about the streets had done nothing but set a steady beat inside my head for doubt to drum along with. By the time I returned to the inn, I was ready to tear down the walls and scream to the heavens.

Despite my adamant refusal, Knox sliced at his wrist once again, this time pouring some of his blood into a glass where he mixed it with some of the herbs he'd purchased. The familiar taste of my elixir hit my tongue, and I suppressed a cringe as I sank into the blessed relief it brought.

My bloodlust was satiated once more, and hopefully, now that I'd ingested Knox's concoction, the beast could be appeased for a little longer.

"Do you want to talk about it?" he asked, stepping over the fallen branch that lay across the faint trail we were following.

Instead of remaining cooped up inside the room, we'd taken the opportunity to go searching in the woods on the outskirts of town, breathing the fresh mountain air in deeply.

I wasn't much of a nature lover, but even I couldn't deny the almost healing influence it had on my psyche. After walking for a steady ten minutes, my raw nerves had finally stopped throbbing, and I could begin to think clearer once more.

"There's nothing to discuss, Phineas," I answered softly. I kept my eyes trained on the green leaves that hung from the trees around me. I could feel his gaze and knew that he was worried. This morning had definitely rattled me. Rehashing it would be the same as shaking a sleeping bear. Some things were better left alone.

It was his turn to grunt.

I was grateful he didn't push the issue.

"So, did you learn anything today while you were finding the ingredients?" I assumed he had, because he'd been very specific about the direction we were heading in. After packing a few provisions and shoving them into his shoulder bag, we'd begun walking.

Plucking a leaf from the nearby branch and bringing it to his nose, Knox inhaled and then nodded. "Apparently the town often has people entering the box canyon or at least close to the crossroad some twenty-five miles away. The man in the general store said that every so often, travelers would camp out here in a group, only coming in for food and other supplies. He remembered seeing a group of men enter the blacksmith to repair the shoes on their horses. They were chased off when it was revealed they couldn't pay and wanted to barter instead."

That same burning fire that sparked inside me each time I heard tales of gypsies blazed inside me again. My fingers curled up into fists, and a new thirst raged in the pit of my stomach. Vengeance. If I had my way, I would wipe each and every one of them from the face of the earth. While Knox and I had destroyed the clan who'd attacked us back in England, that didn't mean the sole survivor didn't have family everywhere. To me, they were like the bugs that hid beneath rocks—lift up a stone and a million more came fleeing out.

There was no doubt in my mind that the Romani bastard had joined up with others and that we were looking for another clan. The thought didn't bother me at all. The depth of my wrath would take time to avenge, and I wouldn't stop until retribution was finally delivered to those who had done nothing but take from me.

"And they were last seen out here?" My gaze swept back and forth. The sun above pierced through the leafy cover, and I shielded my eyes from the glare. "How long ago, Knox?" When he didn't answer immediately, I repeated my question.

Knox shrugged. "Maybe a month ago. He couldn't quite remember. From what I gather, his memory isn't always the best. In fact, I noticed that about a lot of the people I talked with. They'll begin to tell me what they've seen, then things get vague."

Damn town. "I wouldn't be surprised if that's due to the Court keeping their secrets. Can't have the humans asking too many questions and discovering that they're bumping shoulders every day with freaks and monsters."

"I resent that comment, you ass," Knox exclaimed, punching my arm. "I'm not the freak here."

I rolled my eyes. "So, you think you're the monster? You hiding something from me, brother?"

I knew this man like I knew myself, and there was nothing monstrous about him.

"Truth be told, I consider you both freak and monster. You'd be lost without me."

He gave me a look that all but challenged me to contradict him.

"No offense, but you're the one leading this expedition, and I'm pretty sure we're lost, so what does that say about you now?" Our bantering back and forth did a lot to ease the tension I still felt in my body.

Knox suddenly stopped and held his head, shaking it briskly as if to dislodge something. "I don't know . . . I can't remember."

With wide eyes that couldn't hide his twinkle of merriment, he stepped back with his hand pressed against his chest. "Who are you? Where am I?"

"I rest my case. You, Phineas Knox, are a freak, and nothing you can ever say will convince me otherwise." I shoved him hard as he laughed. "Idiot."

"Sorry, I couldn't resist," he joked. It was good to laugh together.

We started walking again, foliage crunching beneath our footsteps. I imagined that during the winter, everything would be buried under a thick layer of snow. The thought sent a pang of homesickness for Smithersby Field through me. For what felt like the millionth time since leaving England, I wished we were on our way home.

Knox pulled out a folded piece of paper from his pocket and studied it again. "From what I could learn, one of the popular places for the clans to stop is in a glen just up ahead. It gives them some privacy and is somewhat close enough for them to go into town and be back before nightfall. That way they're not leaving their womenfolk alone to ward off predators."

A predator like me, I silently mused.

"Did anyone recognize the description of Catriona?" It was the same question I asked every time Knox ran errands. Wherever we were, he spread the word that we were searching for a beloved family member who'd been violently stolen from her husband. We'd received a few leads, but they didn't ever pan out.

I was starting to believe these gypsies were demons or the very Devil himself. Their ability to keep hidden from me was infuriating

"Just the same vagueness. He thought he remembered seeing a beautiful young woman with dark hair, but then the details got fuzzy." I was clearly not the only one frustrated as Knox kicked at the stone, watching it bounce a few times before disappearing into a bush.

"I'll take it," I chimed in. What I didn't add was I used the tidbit of information as a shield against my doubt. If someone thought they saw Catriona here, I would believe it until shown otherwise.

I was changing.

Gone was the arrogant monster persona that I'd enshrouded myself with. As each day passed, I felt that façade break away, and in its place stood a man who felt vulnerable and uncomfortably exposed. It scared me. When that moment arrived, and it came time to exact my revenge and destroy those who had cursed me, I wondered whether I'd have the commitment to follow through.

Would I falter?

Could I do what needed to be done?

Would I unleash the beast that raged and frothed in the depths of my being, or would I buckle beneath the weight of my reemerging humanity?

"Knox?" I asked, keeping my eyes ahead on the path. I was about to do something foolish again. Damn the bloody emotions that begged for a voice.

"Marcus?" he quipped back.

"Have I changed?" Shit, what a loaded question.

I'd taken him by surprise, judging from the way his step briefly faltered. He hadn't expected me to get so personal.

"Can I answer honestly, or is this a trick question where you remind me who the master is?" From the corner of my eye, I could see him staring, trying to judge my mood. I was tempted to tell him if he figured that out, he'd need to let me know as well, because I was clueless.

"I haven't been your master for over a year now, Knox, and you're fully aware of that fact." When he didn't respond, I threw caution to the wind, and looked over at him. Sure enough, he was smiling at me, and I instantly regretted opening my mouth. "Forget I asked."

Stomping off in the lead, I took in a deep breath and silently chided myself for giving in to softness. Who cared if I'd changed or not? When the time came, and it would come, I would do whatever was required. Even if that meant making it rain the blood of my most hated enemies, I wouldn't stop until it was over.

Before Knox could catch up, we were suddenly in a clearing, and a shot of adrenaline pulsed through me, followed closely by one of disappointment.

We'd found the glen Knox had heard about, and it was completely empty. Signs of people being there—abandoned campfires, tree stumps that may have been used as a table surface or makeshift chairs, and caravan tracks still marked the ground, but that was it. As I walked about, kicking at a few forgotten cups and bottles, I let out a shout of pure anger and shook my fist at the sky.

"For once, couldn't luck be on our side?" I dropped to my knees, burying my face in my hands. The endless searching, months of traveling, vague descriptions, and possible leads threatened to break me completely. I was tired of having my hope constantly challenged and attacked.

That was when my rage turned into something deeper. The stronger emotion seethed inside me and ravaged my soul. Catriona was lost. It was time to finally face the truth and accept it.

"Don't give up," Knox said softly behind me. It pained me to hear his own hope dwindling. "As long as there is breath in our bodies, we will search until we find her."

"I can't do this anymore," I countered, and damn it all to hell, but tears began to fill my eyes. I was splitting apart. The man Catriona believed me to be—needed me to be—was dying a slow death here in the empty glen. "I have surely killed her."

That's what hurt the most. Had it not been for my pride and cruelty, Catriona would be safely tucked away in some other man's home. She would never have become mine, a piece of property to exchange because of financial debt. I should've taken her father's estate—anything other than the young girl who dreamed of love and happiness. What had I given her but a life of misery and loneliness? Now, because of my relentless need to avenge wrongdoings, she was most likely dead.

I felt Knox's hand on my shoulder, and instead of shrugging it away, I took comfort in it. I didn't deserve his pity and compassion, but I accepted it anyway. Like the selfish monster I was, I took and took without any thought of the consequence. How long would it be before I ruined Phineas as well?

"Leave me," I demanded. Bitterness coated my tongue. Self-loathing filled my words. "Go and never look back. I will be your destruction. The gypsies were right. I am nothing but blood and damnation to all who cross my path."

A sob rose up and formed a large lump in my throat. There was no swallowing it, and in my mind, I willed myself to choke on it. I silently begged for the ground to open up and consume me. I prayed that God would strike me down and incinerate me to ash. It was what I deserved.

"Yes." That was all Knox said. Just a simple yes.

He knelt beside me, wrapped his arm around my shoulders, and pulled me in. I couldn't remember the last time I'd been embraced—that someone had held me close for no other reason but to offer me solace. The gesture caused the lump in my throat to move, and the sob finally broke free. Only it wasn't mere tears. The sound came out as an agonized howl.

I cried until there was nothing left.

I wept until there were no more tears to shed.

I grieved for the man I'd been and the life that had been denied him.

I said goodbye to the hope that brought me this far only to leave me shattered.

"You asked me if you'd changed, Marcus, and the answer is yes." His voice was soft, barely above a whisper. There was a stillness in the air around us, and I wondered if he spoke that way because he didn't want to disturb the sense of peace that had somehow replaced my cries of despair. "And before you say anything, there's nothing wrong with changing. We all must evolve and become something different, something more, if we're to survive and become whom we're meant to be."

"So I'm meant to be this pathetic creature?" I asked, staring down at the dirt on my hands. I was still on the ground. "Is my only purpose to inflict pain?"

"I can't tell you what your purpose is, brother, but what I will say is that you're far from pathetic. You've been dealt cruel blows throughout your life, and you've tried to rise above it. You've tried to do the best you could with the knowledge you had."

I let out a strangled laugh at the absurdity. "Are you making excuses for the horrible things I've done, Knox? Because if you are, you're a bigger fool than I am. I have reveled in brutality. I have ripped into those I believed my enemies without thought or remorse."

Anger heated my words. I could feel it burn my cheeks as I spat them out.

"I never said you were a saint. You are far from perfect. Yes, you were a monster. You didn't know any better. Yet here you are. You're searching for the woman you once viewed as beneath your attention. You're feeling anguish at the thought of never seeing her again. The Marcus you once were didn't feel guilt or remorse. You've changed for her. Don't give up and throw that away." He let out a ragged breath, licking his dry lips as he stared at me. "I'm proud of the man you are . . . whether you are the monster or the man or both. Hold on to your hope so one day, you can show Catriona who you are and let her love you completely."

In all the many years we'd been together, I'd never heard Knox talk so passionately or earnestly. Gripping my hand tightly, it was as though he was trying to will me into believing that all was not lost. And despite everything that still churned within me, I felt that spark flicker back to life. The flame of my hope was minuscule, but it was there.

I just hoped it would be enough.

Brushing my sleeved arm across my face, I wiped away the remaining tears and dusted off my pants before standing. The glen was still empty, yet I saw it with fresher, clearer eyes.

"Thank you."

"That's what family is for, Marcus. We stand by each other's side as a light and speak the truth whenever necessary." And because it was the person he was, he couldn't resist adding, "It's also the role of a brother to kick the ass of the other when needed."

"What do we do now?" I asked, the storm that had raged inside my chest now calm.

"You tell me why you are here on my land."

And suddenly, we were no longer alone.

CHAPTER 4

I'd heard talk about Indians when we'd first arrived in America, but this was the first time we'd actually come face to face with one. Despite the declarations of their savage attacks against towns and travelers, there was nothing to suggest the man staring at us with a wide smile on his face had any kind of violent intentions.

Still, Knox stepped in front of me as if to offer protection. One thing we both knew with perfect clarity was that looks could be deceiving. I was a prime example of that. People often saw the handsome façade of a gentleman without knowing the true beast I could be.

I was pretty sure we weren't in danger, so Knox's caution was more out of habit than necessity.

Placing my hand on his shoulder, I greeted the stranger with a smile of my own. "We didn't mean to intrude. We were walking along the trail and discovered this break in the trees. I hope we didn't interrupt you."

The Indian held a piece of rope that was attached to a few dead rabbits that he obviously had trapped and killed. With long dark brown hair that was parted down the middle and into two thick braids, he didn't rush forward to attack or even raise his voice in anger.

He gently placed his catch down on one of the tree stumps and brushed his hand along the side of his buckskin leggings. Once he knew his hand was clean, he held it up in greeting, nodding his head. "You are most welcome to walk amongst the forest and mountains." Pointing to where I assumed Havenwood Falls lay, his gesture was filled with surprising warmth. "I am accustomed to sharing this land with those who live within the town. We leave each other in peace, as I hope you both will also do."

That's when I caught the thinly veiled wariness in his black eyes. Gossip was always circulating about Indian tribes rising up and attacking white settlements. I saw the wisdom in him presenting a friendly demeanor, yet not fully trusting that we would act with civility.

"We mean no harm," Knox added, relaxing enough to soften the tension around us. "My name is Knox, and this is Marcus." He returned a wave of hello.

The man came forward, and I noticed the vest he was wearing. He had added his own decoration to it by sewing on beads, leather strips, and eagle feathers.

With his hand now over his chest, the man's face lit up. "My name is Ehzno."

I repeated his name over in my head, liking the way it sounded. "Pleased to meet you."

We stood there quietly, looking and measuring each other up. I knew I was staring, but I couldn't help it. I wanted to memorize everything about him so when we did find Catriona, I could describe our encounter perfectly for her.

"Do you need help finding your way back to the town?" Ehzno finally asked, peering up to the sky. "The woods are not safe at night for those who are unfamiliar with its dangers."

Knox beat me to it. "Then why do you live here? Where are your family?"

We both looked about, and sure enough, there wasn't any sign of others approaching and hiding amongst the trees.

"My father gave me my name when I was born. He tells the story of going on a spirit quest when he learned my mother was pregnant. A bear came to him and whispered my name into his ear. Ehzno means the one who walks alone, so when I became a man, I left my tribe to find where the Great Spirit would lead me." He spread his arms wide and turned about in a slow circle. "For a time, this is where I am needed."

I marveled at how open he was with us—two white men he'd come across alone. His voice was soft and clear . . . inviting even. As each moment passed, I became more and more intrigued.

"You don't get lonely?" It was an honest question. While I thrived living as a recluse on my estate, I still had the companionship of Knox to break the long tediousness of the day. I couldn't imagine being isolated from my family. "Do you miss your kin?"

His face revealed the truth. "There are times I miss my tribe, but I carry them here." He touched his chest over his heart. "And I'm not alone. I commune with the earth and the animals that share these mountains. I have everything I need."

I really was impressed. It didn't happen often, but there was something about this man that touched me deeply. His candor gave me an idea. "Maybe you can help us. We are looking for a woman—my wife. She was taken by someone, and we've come from far away to find her."

As I talked, Ehzno kept nodding, his aged face filled with compassion. "And you want to know if I've seen her here."

I hadn't even needed to finish my request.

"We were told to come to Havenwood Falls to find the answers we seek, but so far, we've uncovered nothing. The man she's with generally camps in woods like this instead of in town. It may just be them two, or perhaps they're now in a group." I stepped forward and waved my hand through the air. "They would camp in an area just like this."

Ehzno's brow furrowed. "I have seen these people. They wear colorful clothing, and at night, they fill the air with music and singing." Scratching his head, he let out a long breath. "This woman . . . describe her for me."

Knox and I both began painting a verbal description of Catriona—explaining even the smallest detail and nuance about her. We also spoke of the bastard gypsy, and it was hard to keep the anger out of my voice.

"You love her very much." His eyes watered slightly. "I wish I could tell you I have seen her, my friends, but the Great Spirit whispers to not give up hope. You will find your lost treasure."

Excitement burst inside my chest, and I looked over to Knox to find he was stunned as well. Less than thirty minutes ago, we were in the pits of despair, and I'd been ready to admit defeat. Now I felt like I could walk on air. This man had given us a much-needed gift.

"Thank God," Knox exhaled, grinning like a fool. It demonstrated how much value and trust we placed in Ehzno's declaration that we so easily accepted it as truth. "You have no idea how much that means for us to hear."

It was the Indian's turned to look surprised. "You believe me so freely?" He glanced between us with his eyebrows arched. "These are strange times indeed."

"You have no idea." I laughed in return. "We've learned to never discredit something at first without giving it some thought. The fact that we're standing here, and not in England, where we're from, is a testament to that. We were told to come, and so we did."

Ehzno chuckled, standing with his arms now crossed against his chest, relaxed. "You are both fools or inspired. I believe you are the latter."

"Oh, trust me. I've often questioned my sanity over the past year." My confession was met with more smiles. "But the world we live in has taught us to entertain even the most improbable."

"And sadly, my own world has taught me the opposite. My people are being scattered and forced to abandon their heritage and way of life. There is great sorrow in this land—a pain that won't fade or stop crying to be avenged."

Now there was a sentiment I understood completely. This conversation continued to amaze me.

A warm breeze rippled through the trees around us and with it, the loud caw of a black bird that perched high on a branch. The sound of it made Ehzno suddenly tense, his head cocking as he quietly listened. Something clouded his features—concern—and his entire demeanor altered.

"I will watch out for your wife and leave word in town should I remember anything. Perhaps the animals will share their stories with me." Backing away, he retrieved his collection of rabbits, leaving Knox and me confused over what had just happened.

"Did we say something to offend you?" I blurted out, needing to understand.

To this, he emphatically shook his head. "No." He then pointed up to the branches where a raven sat, watching us from above. "The woods have eyes—ones that have no business being here. I caution you to take care in your search. Not everyone you meet will be your friend."

His cryptic message reminded me of Lady Hannah, the seer we'd tried to meet in London. As much as I appreciated his warning, part of me wished someone would speak plainly with us and expose those trying to deceive us and withhold information. Like a pirate with his cherished treasure map, for once I wanted to look at the note in my pocket and find a large red cross that said, "Here she is. Come get her."

"We appreciate your help, Ehzno. If we can do anything to return your kindness, you need only ask." Knox's sentiment was reinforced with my murmured agreement. We didn't have much, but this Indian had brought us comfort. We were grateful.

Just as we began returning back to the trail that led away, our new friend called out, waving for us to meet him halfway. In his hand was a leather pouch, and he shoved it into mine before curling my fingers around it. "I was a medicine man for my people. You could say I am a shaman. I believe this will help you with your problem."

Loosening the strings and opening the small sack, I showed its contents to Knox. I had no idea what the plant was, and it seemed he didn't either.

"This is burdock root. My people use it to help with hunger and to purify the blood."

My mouth gaped open. "How did you—?" I couldn't even finish my sentence.

Ehzno simply smiled. "You are not like other men, Marcus. You carry your own burden that weighs your spirit down. Partake of this root, and it will ease your hunger." There was so much knowing in his inflection that I didn't bother questioning him to see if he truly realized what afflicted me. "Should you need more, you'll find it growing beside the waterfall. The water there contains great magic. Go in peace."

And before I could thank him again, Ehzno strode away and disappeared into the trees.

"Shit." Knox's utterance reflected my own. "I've seen some strange things, Marcus. Weird occurrences I couldn't begin to explain, but that . . . that was different."

I bounced the pouch in my hand before giving it over to him. "Do you think it'll help?"

Sniffing the contents, he shrugged. "It's worth a try."

We headed back to town in silence, both of us lost in our own thoughts. Later that night, after he'd brewed the root into a tea, I downed a small cup of it in one mouthful, waiting to see if I felt any effects.

The results were borderline miraculous.

The constant pressure in my gut to feed softened. My thirst for blood didn't feel so overwhelming.

"That must be some water," I exclaimed.

One thing was definitely clear.

There was magic in these mountains.

For the first time in a long time, I was looking forward to tomorrow.

CHAPTER 5

A piercing shriek exploded in the still night air.

Knox had only just fallen asleep when he bolted upright, looking over to where I was sitting by the window. "What the hell was that?"

Instead of answering, I pushed aside the curtains, and to my surprise saw people filing into the streets from their homes and establishments that were still open. I couldn't quite see where the source of screaming had come from, but there was no denying that things were becoming chaotic quickly.

"Something's happened," I finally replied, stating the obvious. "And whatever it is, it sounds like trouble." More and more lanterns were being lit and illuminating the now vacated buildings. At this rate, I was pretty sure that all of Havenwood Falls was awake and seeking answers.

Knox was already getting dressed, pulling on his boots before quickly running his fingers through his tousled hair. "You coming?"

I hadn't moved to join him.

"Is it really any of our business? We don't belong here, Knox, so what kind of help could we possibly offer? If anything, we'd just get in the way, along with every other onlooker." As tempting as it was to join the crowd that I'd seen forming, there was an uneasy feeling in the pit of my stomach. Trouble was brewing, and I wanted no part of it.

"How can we ask for help if we're not willing to extend that same gesture?" He didn't usually show his annoyance over my stubbornness, but tonight he displayed it boldly. "Imagine how differently your life would have been if others had come to your aid that night in the alley?"

I visibly flinched at the sharpness of his tongue. "That was a low blow, Phineas, and you know that." My voice trembled with hurt. "You've been awoken abruptly, so I'm going to blame that on your still being half asleep." Standing up, I walked over to the neglected bed I'd failed to sleep in. There'd been too many thoughts rumbling around in my mind for me to even consider lying down. "You can't go down there alone."

I reluctantly began putting my own shoes on. I was still in my clothes from the day.

"Marcus," he started, contrition entering his voice.

"You're right." I left it at that. The night air was cool, but I didn't bother grabbing my coat. "Let's see what's happening."

Knox reached for my arm as I strode past him toward the door. "I didn't mean to say that, Marcus. I spoke without thinking."

I simply nodded, holding the brass doorknob so he could go into the hallway. Locking the door behind me, I soon discovered we weren't the only ones in the inn to hear the melee and decide to see what the commotion was. The inn's manager, Irina, was standing outside with her hand raised to her eyes like it would somehow help her see better.

"I knew one day that saloon would bring trouble to this town. Drinking and gambling to all hours of the night. Folks stop having common sense the moment the sun goes down. Why they don't all head home to bed is beyond me." She tutted her disapproval, but that instantly changed the moment she saw Knox and me descend the front steps. "Oh, gentlemen. Please forgive the disturbance. Go back up to your room and think no more about this craziness."

Madam Petran tried to shoo us away with her hand. Apparently, she wasn't worried in the slightest.

"I'm guessing screaming like a banshee is a common occurrence here?" I ventured, not quite ready to return inside. Now that I was up, my curiosity had been piqued. Knox had been right. If I wanted the help of others in finding Catriona, I couldn't turn my nose up at a chance to offer my own goodwill.

"Listen to me closely. Haven Saloon caters to all kinds of people in town, and that means a lot of hotheaded men with something to prove." As much as she dismissed the commotion, Irina still cast a look or two over her shoulder.

"We're no strangers to drama. Is it normal for a woman's scream to come from the saloon, however?" That was what kept me in the street. I'd been in enough bars at this time of night to know that if a fight broke out, it would be masculine voices disturbing the peace. Hell, we would've heard gunshots fired into the air.

No, something else was creating this scene.

Knox, in an unusual display of impatience, gently took the lady by the elbow and maneuvered her so she didn't block our path. "We appreciate your concern, but neither of us will be able to sleep until we see for ourselves. By all means, let me help you back inside so you're not out in the night air." Before she could argue, he swiftly led her up the stairs, returning within a few moments. "Okay, let's go."

It didn't take long before Madam Petran's theory was proven wrong. The saloon stood empty as everyone had already rushed out, forming a large group outside a familiar building.

It was Mrs. Fanny Webster's bordello.

I broke into a run.

What I found as we finally reached the crowd made me come to a grinding halt, Knox banging into me shortly after.

"Good God." It was the only thing I could utter.

"Shit." That was becoming one of Knox's favorite words.

The scene unfolding before us was like something out of some macabre story, but that wasn't what hit me like I'd been kicked in the chest by a horse. The sight of Mrs. Webster rocking the body of a dead girl in her arms, blood everywhere, instantly transported me out of Havenwood Falls, and immediately dumped me back in my own personal nightmare.

Even the smell was the same—that cloying, coppery scent that permeated through the air and clung to every breath I inhaled. I could taste it. I was suffocated by it. Shaking my head as if to refuse this as real, I stepped back into Knox.

"No," I whispered, my voice ragged with distress. "Not again. Not again."

My friend didn't move but instead drew his arm around me as he leaned in closer. "Compose yourself, Marcus. This is not the time or place to fall apart."

His counsel broke against me, yet the warning didn't touch my thoughts. All I could see was the lifeless body Fanny was gripping tightly. I remembered that rocking motion. I knew without a shadow of a doubt that I wore that same disbelieving, horrified expression that night as well.

I choked on the emotions bubbling in my throat. Without thinking, I began wiping my hands over and over, as if somehow my fingers were coated with the same red ichor and gore.

Someone shook me sharply—one, two, three times. Then as if out of a daze, I finally registered the alarming sounds that filled the night air. The crowd was rapidly becoming a mob, different sections calling for justice over the death of the girl. I didn't want to look too closely, but judging by the clothes she wore, she'd been one of Fanny's workers.

It felt wrong to call her what she was.

Death had all but stripped away the taint of being a whore.

"If you ask me, that's what you get when you make sinning your business!" came a cry, followed closely by more muffled cries of agreement. It shocked me to hear the life of this woman be so callously dismissed

"Where's the sheriff?" came a voice from just in front of me. "Find the bastard before he murders innocent women!"

There was going to be a lynching if order wasn't established again. As I glanced about nervously, not liking the way the dark energy pressed against me as though at any moment the atmosphere would suffocate me, I caught a glimpse of a man staring at me intently.

"Knox," I murmured beneath my breath. "We're being watched." As carefully as I could, I told him where the gentleman was, and sure enough, Knox saw him as well.

"He's looking at us instead of the body."

I'd thought the exact same thing. "I don't like this."

I saw Knox nod from the corner of my eye.

"I'm beginning to think you were right, Marcus. Perhaps we should've left this up to the locals and not gotten involved." He chewed on his bottom lip nervously, shifting his weight between his two feet.

The tension in the crowd continued to grow more volatile.

"What's the chance of us leaving without having that stranger follow us?" I asked, willing myself not to look his way again. The trouble with that is my focus immediately went back to the blood, and I was blasted with a wave of hunger.

Damn, I cursed. Now was not the time for my bloodlust to flare up.

Knox let out a noticeable sigh of relief. "I guess we don't need to worry, because he's no longer there. That teaches us to be paranoid."

Sure enough, the space where the man had been standing was empty. Being triggered by past memories had set my nerves on edge, and the result had me making assumptions.

"Still," I answered, this time a little louder, "I think we should take our leave now before things get even more out of control." Groups of men had begun to form, and guns were being passed about and loaded. "The humans are restless and needing to avenge one of their own." That stirred up a more obvious question. This time I returned to whispering because I didn't want to be overheard. "Speaking of which, I thought the town was governed by people like us. You'd think they'd be here to contain the mayhem. Keep the peace."

Knox murmured he'd thought the same thing.

Slowly taking my eyes away from the distraught Fanny, careful not to lower my gaze to the body again, I gave one last sweeping inspection of the street and started my retreat. What I needed now more than anything was some of the burdock that Ehzno had given me. With the air coated with freshly spilled blood, I needed additional help.

We only made it a few steps away before the man who'd been watching me blocked our retreat.

"Mr. St. James. Mr. Knox. Follow me." He swept his arm to the side, inviting us to join him.

Knox offered his apologies, politely declining the offer. "Could it wait until tomorrow? We're returning to our room at Whisper Falls Inn."

The expression the stranger wore spoke volumes. He wouldn't accept any kind of refusal from us. "The Court wishes to have a conversation with you both." And as if to hurry us along, he added with a firm voice, "Now."

CHAPTER 6

*T*he man remained silent as he escorted us away from the growing crowd and back through the town's streets. After introducing himself as Elsmed Fairchild, and a member of the Court, he remained tight-lipped, refusing to answer any of the questions I fired at him.

His stony expression and ice-cold eyes added to the whole cloak-and-dagger act he was performing, and I wondered if anyone had ever refused to instantly jump with obedience any time Havenwood Falls' most elite clicked their fingers. Knox and I weren't part of their community. As far as we were concerned, the exact second our mission was completed, we were going to get the hell out of this country and back to the comfort and familiarity of home.

Where others viewed this new land as a place of freedom and opportunity, all it did was remind me how alone and out of place I felt. I enjoyed the anonymity and being able to leave the estate without a hundred tongues wagging with gossip, but not enough to abandon the ease and wealth I'd grown up with.

I knew my place back in Suffolk County—recluse or not.

"Can you at least inform us why we're being summoned?" I asked, trying again to elicit some kind of response. "Does your

Court usually hold these secret sessions in the middle of the night?"

Knox cleared his throat beside me, ever the diplomat. I could almost hear him begging me to stop and not aggravate the situation. I didn't care if my anger spoke against me. As far as I was concerned, neither of us had done anything wrong, and their time would be better spent trying to catch the killer who had struck after dark.

"Are you worried, Mr. St. James?" He sounded calm, bored even, like this was something he did on a regular basis.

"Should I be?" I fired back with enough heat that it caused the man's lips to slightly turn upward. Whatever he was thinking, he kept it to himself. His lack of conversation was infuriating.

"Marcus, please," Knox chided as he grabbed hold of my wrist, making me stop for a second. "We don't know why this meeting has been called, so how about we not jump to conclusions before they provide an explanation. They may be needing our help."

He was the optimist to my pessimist.

Mr. Fairchild made a noise that sounded a lot like a suppressed laugh. "I assure you, we are quite self-sufficient, gentlemen." As we reached a darkened home, he approached the wooden door and opened it quickly. "After you." The wave of his hand did little to soothe my agitation.

I shook my head. "No, after you." Childish or not, there was no way I was walking into an ambush. If he wanted us to meet with the Court, we'd do so following him in. "Please."

He didn't miss a beat. "As you wish."

Knox went in after him, but not before throwing me a pleading look. I knew he was just as concerned as I was, but the man trusted too easily. Experience had taught me time and time again that when people weren't upfront with their intentions, it usually meant there was a hidden agenda.

A thin line of light shone through the crack at the bottom of a door toward the back of the hallway we entered. It was pointless to look about and try to gain my bearings, because whoever owned this building had kept it in shadow. Voices started to reach us, setting my nerves on edge again. I had a bad feeling about this.

"Bring them in, Elsmed," a female voice called out, one I recognized. Sure enough, we found Saundra Beaumont and another man standing close together inside the official-looking room. With chairs and tables arranged neatly inside, it appeared like this was where they conducted their town business.

"Mr. St. James. Mr. Knox," she greeted, striding forward to shake both our hands. "Allow me to introduce Raffaele Augustine to you both. He is from one of Havenwood Falls' founding families and holds a seat on the Court. He'll be joining us for our conversation tonight, along with Mihail Petran, whom you already know from the inn."

I studied the other man, trying to get a feel for who he was, but there was no penetrating his blank expression. He caught my gaze and held it briefly. He was studying me just as openly as I was him.

Needing a break from the intense scrutiny, I nodded my head to Mihail. I didn't know whether it was a comfort or not to see a familiar face amongst the group. Mr. Petran had been the one to approach us at the inn about my need for blood.

Taking a page from Knox's book of manners, I chose to change tactics. "Good evening, Miss Beaumont. You seem to have both me and my friend at a disadvantage. Your fellow Court member forgot an important piece of information when he invited us both to this discussion."

She cast Mr. Fairchild an amused glance. "Is that so?"

He simply shrugged and took one of the chairs at the long wooden table.

"We don't know why we're here," Knox interjected. "We heard the commotion earlier and went to investigate. It was in the crowd that he ordered us to follow."

Like a hostess at a fancy soiree, Miss Beaumont directed us to each take a seat, and it became crystal clear that this wasn't merely a talk, but an interrogation. The three of them sat behind one

301

table, and Knox and I behind the other. It left me with the impression that we were appearing before a judge in court.

I didn't hesitate in bringing my observation up.

"Are we being accused of something?" I asked as I perched on the edge of my seat. This wasn't some casual meeting at all, and I wouldn't allow them to lull me into believing this was anything but friendly.

"Do you have a guilty conscience, Mr. St. James?" Mr. Augustine questioned, watching me closely. He was a handsome man, yet there wasn't a smile or glimpse of affability in his features. If anything, I saw suspicion and annoyance in his clear eyes.

Before I could speak, Knox once again put his hand on my arm. He did that a lot, especially when he wanted me to exercise caution. Now was not the time for my sarcasm and temper to take center stage.

"We're only confused over the nature of this meeting. We would've gladly come in the morning and answered whatever questions you might have." Knox offered them all an open smile that seemed to break the tension I'd created. "We have nothing to hide. I feel we've been honest about why we're here in Havenwood Falls and our intentions."

Mr. Fairchild leaned forward and rested his elbows on the table. "You are a vampire, Mr. St. James." Statement.

I nodded, taking a breath before answering. "A cursed blood drinker, and again, call me Marcus. Surely we can forgo formalities this late at night." I hoped that reminder would be enough to show him that he hadn't believed us suspicious enough to decline our request to stay at the inn. I tried to relax. "I let Mr. Bishop know that when he met us at the edge of the town's limits. I then repeated that information to you, Saundra, the next day."

She acknowledged the truth with a bob of her head. "You were completely upfront, Marcus, which we appreciate. Hopefully you'll extend that same consideration tonight. As you saw outside, a crime has been committed, and a young woman has lost her life. You can see why we're puzzled."

Her response surprised me. "Actually, I can't. I thought that it would be obvious."

Raffaele cut through the confusion. "Where are you getting your blood? We know that the Petrans have told you where you can go within Havenwood Falls to feed your thirst. We also know you haven't used the blood den's services either."

Was that what this was about? My drinking habits?

Knox raised his hand. "While we've been here in town, Marcus has fed on me. We were told where to find a reliable source, but have declined it for the moment. Back home, I was the one who arranged it and created an elixir for him that helped ease his bloodlust, so Marcus decided to continue using me." He glanced my way, his forehead crinkled. He didn't add anything about the argument we'd had about using the town's supply and how I was loathe to rely on strangers for nourishment. "Again, we've been upfront about it."

The sinking feeling in my gut that had surfaced once we entered the room strengthened into a growing fear. "What are you blaming me for?" And that's when it hit me. With my mouth gaped, I finally sat back in my chair, stunned. "You think I was the one who killed that young woman." Another statement.

"That's insane!" Knox exclaimed. "You can ask Irina of Whisper Falls Inn. We've been in our room all night. We even took our meal upstairs because we were wanting an early evening. Madame Luiza will confirm that."

I looked sharply to Mihail, hoping that he'd speak up in our defense. While I hadn't seen him as frequently at the inn, surely he would be kept abreast of what his guests were doing. He seemed to sense my concern and leaned in toward Saundra, whispering in her ear.

Saundra nodded and glanced down at the parchment she had in front of her. From where we were sitting, it didn't seem to have a lot of writing on it—just a few notes she jotted down with her feathered fountain pen now. "We'll be calling on Irina tomorrow morning to check your alibi, but for now, we'd like you to answer the questions we have."

I could see her lips moving, but the only thing I heard was the pounding of my heart in my ears. This was beginning to feel like history repeating itself. Why was I always in a place where something heinous had happened? More importantly, why did it seem I was always the first one to point a finger at? Those gypsy women had refused to listen to my pleas of innocence that night in the alley. No matter what I said, or how much I wanted them to understand, all they saw was the man who had murdered their kin.

Was the same thing happening here, all these thousands of miles away? Would I be declared guilty, despite knowing that I was blameless of all fault?

"Not again," I murmured to Knox. "Whatever I say won't matter."

"And why's that, Marcus?" Saundra asked. My gaze didn't rest on her; however, it was firmly squared on the man whose piercing eyes had already judged me as guilty. "Are you saying Knox is wrong? Were you not in your room tonight?"

My mouth instantly dried. "We were, but . . ." I hated that I had to say that word. "After my friend had retired for the evening and fallen asleep, I slipped downstairs for some fresh air."

The incredulous look on Knox's face hurt. While I knew he would always back me up and that his loyalty was with me, I'd surprised him with this confession.

"Where did you go?" Elsmed demanded.

"Good God," Knox whispered softly beneath his breath.

Closing my eyes, I willed myself to stay calm. "I merely sat on the inn's front steps and watched the stars appear in the sky." It was the truth, as flimsy as it might appear to the others. "I give you my word, that was all that happened. I was feeling somewhat stifled in the room, and my thoughts were troubling me. Instead of waking Knox, I took a few moments of respite outside. Once I felt better, I rejoined him in our room. He found me there when he awoke to the screaming."

My admission hung dangerously in the air—as though the balance could tip either way. I knew how it sounded, and if they truly wanted to blame me for the murder, this could very well give them the proof they needed. They were strangers to me. They owed me no allegiance. All I could do was trust that my word was enough, or that someone else would come forward with the criminal's real identity.

"I still find it hard to believe that someone of your nature could be satisfied with such a limited blood supply. I've known many kinds of vampires, and having only just met you, there's no denying the fact that Mr. Knox is beginning to look somewhat depleted." Relief coursed through me that Raffaele didn't instantly point his finger in accusation and declare me guilty.

He was trying to understand. I could work with that. There was still a chance of convincing them I wasn't their villain. All this time of playing the monster, and now that one had been released in Havenwood Falls, I was desperate not to be viewed that way.

"I'm quite comfortable with the arrangement I have," I answered, not caring that it was a lie. I'd already resigned myself to using the blood den once this fiasco was over, but I didn't want to let them know they were right.

There was no reading Saundra's expression. "So your conversation with Mrs. Webster wasn't about making arrangements to feed while you were here in Havenwood Falls?" She held her pen poised over the paper, waiting for my answer.

I didn't bother hiding my confusion. "What does she have to do with this?"

The three of them glanced at each other, bewildered. The more this meeting continued, the more it felt like vital pieces of information were missing. "She owns the town's blood den."

I shook my head. "No. She's a human who runs the whorehouse. I was told to approach her and see if she'd heard anything about my missing wife and her kidnapper. While I trust that you and your Court were upfront with what you knew, I also know with her clients and business, Fanny Webster might've heard a different kind of gossip."

The spark of understanding I saw sweeping across all of their faces caused me to exhale in relief. A missing puzzle piece had just been revealed.

"She provides both blood and other pleasures to the town members here, Marcus. The assumption was made when you were sighted talking with her that you were making plans to visit later that day."

The atmosphere in the room lightened some more. The air didn't feel as suffocating and oppressive as before.

"Surely Roman Bishop told you about our conversation, then?" When they didn't acknowledge it, I continued. What a mess. "He approached me afterward, and I explained why I'd been seen with her. He'd assumed differently, however, that I was after the other pursuits with her girls."

I looked at each of them, hoping to see that they believed me. I had nothing to hide. With our search for Catriona still going, I wouldn't do anything to jeopardize our finding her. My days of leaving a trail of bodies in my wake were behind me.

Saundra scribbled down something before addressing me again. "We haven't spoken to Roman yet, but I'm sure he'll corroborate your story."

Her comment brushed against my patience and temper. "It is no story. I give you my word that I'm telling you the truth."

"While I'm sure you feel that way, Marcus," Raffaele interjected, his gaze fixed on me, "I hope you can understand why we can't blindly believe you without sufficient evidence. We have a responsibility to the citizens of this town. We must ensure that justice is served."

Hurried footsteps interrupted the proceedings, and before another word was spoken, Roman entered the room. Dark storm clouds thundered in his expression. Whatever news he brought, there was no denying that it didn't bode well.

"Good, you have him. I suggest we end the investigation and arrest Mr. St. James for murder."

I exploded into action, pushing myself from the table and standing up tall. "On what grounds?"

Saundra also stood, and on hearing the latecomer's accusation, thoroughly chastised him for the interruption. "I hope you have a good excuse why you're here, Roman, and not your father. This meeting is for Court members only. Do you need yet another reminder that you weren't invited?"

The stoic man didn't even flinch, his blue eyes boldly holding her gaze. "I have necessary information the Court needs to hear."

Elsmed spoke up again. "And what, pray tell, is that?"

"That Marcus St. James is guilty of the murders." Roman didn't even appear frazzled or repentant over interrupting the discussion. Instead he stood tall, his tanned features strong and unflinching.

Elsmed let out a sigh as he shook his head. "He has an alibi, Roman. One that I'm positive Irina or Luiza can testify to."

Roman continued to stand his ground. He wore a smug expression that told me he was about to deliver a brutal blow to my innocence.

"Then perhaps he can explain why another dead body drained of blood was just found in his room."

CHAPTER 7

*D*amn.

I staggered back in horror, not wanting to accept the revelation that had just been leveled at me. I refused to be blamed for yet another person's death. I couldn't relive the trauma from the past.

"No!" Knox yelled, standing up to join me. While the accusation hadn't involved him, the fact we shared the room at the inn also implicated him in the crime. "I don't know exactly what is happening here, but one thing I know for sure is you're looking at the wrong person. Marcus is innocent."

Roman wasn't having any of his excuses. "Of course you would believe that. How much does he pay you to keep his secrets?"

The anger being directed our way was practically palpable.

I knew tempers would be high tonight with everything that had transpired, but this new development had rendered me speechless. The more I opened my mouth to try to provide some kind of answer, the more I resembled a fish out of water. I couldn't speak what I didn't know, and once again words failed me.

"I don't doubt that something sinister is happening here in your town, but I assure you, again, that we are not involved in it. Please. Why would we jeopardize any help you might offer in finding our family member by going on a killing spree? Yes, Marcus is a blood drinker—a vampire as you call him—but he has been one for decades. He is not this sloppy or reckless. You have to believe me." Knox cast me a sidelong glance, his eyes begging me to speak up in defense of myself. "Believe us."

Roman shook his head. As far as he was concerned, the case was closed, and the mystery was solved. The other four had remained silent during the last few moments, and if their expressions were anything to go by, the only one who looked even the slightest bit skeptical was Saundra.

Elsmed was the next to speak. "We will do no such thing, Mr. Knox. We welcomed you into Havenwood Falls and gave you the benefit of the doubt when you promised that neither of you would bring trouble with you. You gave your word that you would honor and obey the rules of this town. You have been found guilty. You have broken your oath."

It was then that I finally found my voice. "A body in our room does not equal guilt, sir."

Roman actually laughed out loud, the sound of it bitter and full of scorn. "Here in America, that most certainly proves your culpability. Before coming here, I questioned others like yourself, and found each had a solid alibi."

Knox's voice was filled with incredulous disbelief. That and his eyebrows were all but raised into his hairline. "Marcus has one as well. Me. I was with him."

Elsmed cleared his throat, drawing our attention back to him. "While you may not have been the one to drain both bodies of blood, you are guilty by association. I agree with Roman. We have found the ones responsible for this despicable lack of control and crime."

Suddenly I felt like the walls were closing in on me. Any hope of convincing this group that we had nothing to do with the deaths had evaporated the second Roman Bishop had entered the room.

"Knox," I uttered, his name coming out like I was being

strangled. "Catriona." Yet another obstacle had been placed in front of us, stopping our investigation from continuing.

He nodded in frustration. "How can we prove our innocence?"

"You assume that you can?" Raffaele asked, a look of amazement returning to his face. "I would think the evidence is pretty damning."

"True, but one thing I know is that given time, the truth will always surface." He said it so matter-of-factly. His optimism was showing again, and I didn't have the heart to correct him. I'd faced this same thing before, and once a person had judged you as guilty, the matter was closed in their minds.

As much as I hated to say it, our time in Havenwood Falls had come to an end. It also signaled the conclusion of our search for my wife.

"Allow us to leave, then," I suggested, knowing it was a fool's hope, but I had to try. My need to find Catriona was still a priority, even over clearing my name. If I allowed this Court to detain me and exact false justice for these deaths, I would never be able to see her safe again. "We will leave town and never return."

It was obviously the wrong thing to say.

Saundra's eyes widened. "You will be going nowhere but a jail cell until we figure out what to do with you. You will be sentenced and then punished accordingly."

I wanted to argue.

I wanted to rush forward and flee.

I wanted to attack before they did so.

Instead Knox let out a sigh and nodded. "Very well. We'll surrender ourselves into your custody and trust that the truth will be revealed. Once that happens, we'll discuss the consequences of this meeting."

Roman's back straightened. "What does that mean exactly —consequences?"

There was no sign of weakness or hesitation in Knox's response. "It means you've falsely accused both me and Marcus and that will need to be addressed. The slandering of our reputations and honor can't be ignored."

Roman's jaw tightened significantly, his teeth clenched together, and Raffaele looked as though he was ready to explode into an angry rant.

Thankfully, cooler heads interceded.

Saundra was the next to speak up. "I agree, Mr. Knox. Yet, for the time being, I appreciate your cooperation while we take a moment to regroup and look at all the evidence. I've written down your testimonies, and will personally validate your alibis. Until then, you will need to come peacefully down to the jail cell."

We were all standing now, and before anyone could lay hands on both Knox and me, I held my hands up in surrender. "Fine. We'll comply with your wishes. I have to believe that truth is on our side."

Both Saundra and Mihail walked us down to where they housed their prisoners. For a makeshift prison, it looked comfortable enough, with two bed cots, a table with a basin on it, and a bucket for waste.

"It's just for the night," Knox murmured as we walked inside, the door slamming behind us. Mihail quickly turned the key, locking us in. "We've slept in worse since arriving in this godforsaken country."

We had, but unlike now, we'd still had the freedom to come and go as we pleased.

"Until tomorrow, gentlemen. Try to get some sleep."

The suggestion was practically laughable, but I didn't smile. There was nothing funny about this predicament.

Sitting down on one of the beds, I stared down at my hands, suddenly exhausted beyond anything I'd ever felt before. With the predictability of a well-tuned clock, my hunger reared its ugly head. Once again, I wished that I'd never been cursed, that I'd never walked into that alley with the gypsy girl that caught my eye.

Knox dropped down into the space beside me and offered me

his wrist. He never failed to show how observant he was and how well he knew the signs of my encroaching thirst.

"No."

"Drink."

"No."

I could actually hear his teeth grind together in annoyance. "Quit being stubborn, Marcus. It's not going to help our case if you neglect yourself. You need to remain level-headed and in control."

The only thing I wanted right now was to escape reality, even if it was just for a moment.

"No." Getting up, I crossed the small cell to the second cot and lay down—my back to him.

The springs creaked beneath his own weight as silence descended upon us. It wasn't like him to give up so easily, but that just proved how much he really knew me. It wouldn't matter how long I refused him, because eventually, I'd reach for him and his wrist, and take what I needed.

"Try to rest then, Marcus. Something tells me tomorrow won't be any easier."

I grunted in response. When had my life ever been easy?

As I closed my eyes and willed myself to sleep, I took solace in the images that surfaced.

Catriona.

My beautiful, precious Catriona.

CHAPTER 8

The first rays of the new day shone through the high window of our cell. I didn't need to ask if Knox was awake. He'd been unable to fall asleep as well, but instead of talking, we'd simply lain there consumed by our own thoughts.

Over and over, I tried to understand what had happened and how we'd become embroiled in the town's drama. I analyzed my conversation with Fanny Webster, Roman Bishop, with each and every person I'd met since arriving. While I knew I wasn't always the most approachable of people, I couldn't pinpoint the exact moment where my behavior could prove my guilt.

As for Knox, it was absurd that he could be responsible either. He held himself to a higher standard than I did. Yes, he'd been required to perform all manner of duties for me as his master, but his conscience was just as clear as mine.

"I can hear you thinking from over here, Marcus," my brother chimed softly. "I know you view the world with skepticism, but I need you to trust me with this. I refuse to let this stop us from finding her."

I let out a short chuckle. "And how are you going to do that? We're not exactly in a position of power here. We're completely at the mercy of this town and the Court. If they deem us guilty, we're as good as dead."

That was the other thing that kept rattling around in my brain all night. There was no way they were going to let us go. It didn't matter that we were supernatural. Regardless of our nature, murder was usually punished with death. Execution wasn't just a human response to violence.

"Then we'll escape."

Just once, I wished I could view the world through his less jaded eyes. "Have you tried getting out of this cell?"

I knew he hadn't, but what we hadn't acknowledged was the flicker of magic that emanated from the metal bars that surrounded us. Even if we couldn't feel the magic that buzzed and crackled quietly, we were dealing with witches. They would've taken precautions. We were stuck in here until they came to let us out.

"If you want to wallow in self-pity, Marcus, then by all means find the negative in everything. You can apologize for your lack of faith in me when I find a way out for us." He didn't say it with malice or condemnation. Just with that same resigned tone he used whenever I dragged my feet and didn't instantly join his belief. "I haven't let you down once since meeting you."

Shame filled me. He was right. I might be looking at the situation with my usual bleakness, but I'd forgotten that I wasn't alone in this. Phineas Knox had always stood by my side, and he wouldn't give up without a fight.

The old me—the one that had been ruthless and unbending— wouldn't have either.

It was time to resurrect him—me.

"Then we will face whatever comes today together."

I could hear the smile in his voice. "To the death."

His enthusiastic response had the desired effect. I laughed. "Always so bloody cheery."

There was a bang of a door above us, closely followed by another one opening.

"Someone needs to be." We both fell silent as we heard someone approaching.

It was Roman Bishop who appeared with a key in his hand, an annoyed expression on his face. "Against my recommendation, you two are being brought before the Court again. Just know, one wrong move from either of you, and I won't hesitate. You'll regret the day you ever entered this town."

We didn't reply or ask any of the questions I knew we both had. Instead we retraced our steps from last night and found ourselves back in that room with the chairs and tables.

"Mr. St. James. Mr. Knox." Raffaele addressed us first, and we quickly took our seats again. "We've asked Elsmed to join us again."

I looked at him, wondering what he could possibly say or do that could change our circumstances, especially considering he'd remained quiet throughout most of last night's meeting.

He cleared his throat and looked down at his own set of papers. They were filled with all manner of notes, and another sinking sensation filled me. A black leather pouch lay beside his hand, piquing my curiosity.

"I'm sure you're aware how serious the charges against you are, gentlemen," Elsmed began. He held a no-nonsense tone that matched his demeanor. "I've been up all night going over the evidence we've gathered so far and read the notes Saundra has provided. I have valuable gifts that are needed in this case." He held my gaze, not blinking until I did. "As a fae, I have a talent in knowing when magic has been misused and of reading minds. If you are guilty, I will uncover it." He paused long enough to let those words sink in with full force. If he thought to intimidate me, he'd miscalculated, because I'd zeroed in on the one word that gave me hope.

If.

Elsmed hadn't said when or even that we were.

He'd said if, and the implication was intoxicating.

I nodded with a newfound sense of confidence. "And what

have you learned so far?" I asked, careful not to appear overly enthusiastic. "I trust you were able to find the truth in our alibis?" I sat up straight in my seat, my hands folded neatly in front of me on top of the table.

He nodded. "I spoke with both Irina and Luiza Petran earlier, and they assure me that not only were you both in your rooms, but Luiza noticed you slipping outside to briefly sit on the front steps. She had been tempted to come out and join you. You've both made an impression on the inn's cook, with your search for your wife. She was very insistent that once this was all cleared up, the Court needed to step up its efforts in helping you."

The gesture touched me deeply. I hadn't spoken for very long to the lady, only a few exchanged pleasantries as I came and went from the inn. Her compassion was definitely the result of Knox. He must've had conversations with her that I'd missed.

"What about the body found in their room?" Roman asked, glaring at me. "While we can't prove that Marcus killed one of Fanny's girls, no one else had access to their accommodations."

I wasn't upset that he brought it up. If truth be told, I was curious about it too.

"The likelihood that we're dealing with two different crimes with the same method of killing is unlikely, Roman. I'm convinced that whoever it is, they're responsible for all of them," Elsmed interjected.

All of them.

I wasn't the only one that noticed her choice of terms.

"What do you mean by *all*, Elsmed?" Saundra asked urgently. "Were there more we don't know about?"

All I could think was thank God we'd agreed to be locked up for the night. If there had been more deaths, it would be easier to prove our innocence, because we'd been in the custody of the Court.

"There were three other bodies found." The gasp that echoed in the room was loud. The fae had just delivered a devastating blow, and it had sent the Court members reeling.

"Who?" Raffaele asked, his face bleached white from shock.

Elsmed's voice lowered out of respect for the newly departed. "Two more of Fanny's girls, and a human boy." This time the new revelation that blasted through the room included Knox and me. A child. Whoever this person was, the one responsible was truly a monster. Only someone truly evil could ever harm a child. I'd never felt so horrified as I did in that moment.

"Where was he found?" Saundra's body had slumped with the new revelation. Supernatural or human, it didn't matter. This death was the hardest to swallow and accept.

"Up in the glen the gypsies like to use whenever they pass through."

I couldn't help it. I gasped so loud it reverberated in my ears—overwhelming the thoughts now exploding in my head.

"What?" Elsmed pressed, seeing my distress. "What do you know, Mr. St. James?"

All I could do was shake my head as I looked to Knox.

The glen. We had just been there. Right when I thought I could see a light at the end of this nightmare, we were thrown back into chaos.

"Do you think it's him?" I asked Knox, ignoring the others and the way their stares seemed to bore into me. "This can't be a coincidence. Is he here?"

If he was, that could only mean one thing. So was Catriona.

Knox's gaze narrowed as I watched him scramble for an answer. We'd searched everywhere we could think of. We'd talked with people around town. Yet, was there a chance we'd missed or overlooked something—a sign that she'd been here all along?

"I don't know what to think."

Saundra tapped her knuckles on top of the table, drawing our attention back to the room. "Explain yourself. Who are you talking about?"

It was Knox who answered. I was thankful, because I didn't think I could trust myself to speak. All I could focus on was that that bastard had been here all along—evading us.

"We were in that glen yesterday." I knew what it looked like, that by admitting it we added yet another check in the guilty column. There was too much on the line now. We needed to prove our innocence so we could be released. Our search had to be intensified.

When no one spoke up, Knox murmured thank you and continued his explanation. "We were following a lead but came up empty-handed. The clearing was empty." He added extra emphasis on that last word. "Had we found a body there, we would have immediately returned to town and reported it."

"Unless you were the one to kill the poor child," Raffaele retorted. He didn't look like he was convinced about our story.

Finally, Knox replied with equal force and impatience. He'd reached his limit with the continuous accusations. There was only so far he could be pushed before he snapped and dropped all pretense of politeness. "Do you honestly believe we would be this sloppy? I have been with Marcus for decades. I have served him faithfully, which includes finding him blood and cleaning up whatever mess resulted from him losing control. If this was him, don't you think I would've taken the necessary precautions to hide our crime? Honestly. Ask yourself that. Why would I leave bodies out to be found that would implicate him?"

No one said a word. They couldn't. Knox's impassioned speech was filled with undeniable truth. Had I been newly turned, perhaps they could've argued against his logic, but I wasn't.

"You're right," Saundra said, followed quickly by Elsmed who nodded in agreement. Raffaele was somewhat reluctant to show he accepted what he'd heard. Roman flat out shook his head, refusing to even entertain that we'd been wrongly accused.

"That is one of the reasons I am slow to condemn you both," Elsmed confessed. He stood from his chair and, rubbing his hand across his face, revealing his own tiredness, began to pace back and forth. "Can you explain the look of guilt on your face last night when you arrived at the scene outside Mrs. Webster's establishment? You didn't react like someone shocked. I watched you."

It was time to share my secret.

"Because it brought back painful memories." I took a deep breath and committed to retelling my past shame. "I told you that I had been cursed to become a blood drinker by a gypsy clan when I was a young man. What I didn't share was that it was because they'd found me holding the dead, blood-covered body of their kin."

I didn't lower my gaze as I continued relaying the details of that night. I spoke of the horror I felt waking up and finding Primrose, the woman I had snuck into the alleyway with, dead. No matter how hard I had tried to explain my presence there, they had allowed their grief and anger to consume them. It wasn't until I finished my account that I broke eye contact with the Court members.

"So my reaction wasn't one of guilt at being confronted with my recent crimes, but at being taken back to my past . . . memories that continue to haunt me. I did not kill these people. I didn't kill Primrose either." I stared back at Elsmed. "I don't know what I need to do to convince you of my innocence, but if you're going to condemn me because of my past, then do so. I only ask that you not punish Knox. All he has ever done is show loyalty to me. He doesn't deserve whatever consequences I face now."

I could feel Elsmed studying me—weighing what I'd shared with whatever he'd written down on his papers. "I could invade your mind to reveal the truth. I could place you under enchantment that would force you to confess any indiscretion you've done while here. I have methods that would rip what we need out of your mind . . . out of your soul." There was clearly a threat in there.

Without blinking, I nodded. "Then I submit to these spells. Do what you will. I have nothing more to hide."

He tapped his fingers on the table top, peering to each side at the others. They seemed to be waiting to see what his judgment would be. I wondered if it rankled against Roman's better instincts not to be the one with the final say in matters.

"I was visited at dawn by someone I trust implicitly. It was his testimony on your behalf that assured me that you're not the killer we're looking for. Even though what you just shared is concerning, it's not enough to sway my recommendation that you be released."

"Do you mind if we ask whom you talked with?" Knox had straightened in his chair, leaning forward with interest.

Instead of answering us directly, Elsmed turned to the other court members. "You'll agree that this man's word holds a lot of weight." When their faces clouded over with renewed confusion, he finally offered up the mystery person's name. "Ehzno came down from the mountain to share what he believed with me."

Our new friend was the one who had spoken up in my defense.

"The shaman," Saundra whispered, and I could immediately see the change that came over her. Whatever her dealings had been with the Indian, it was enough to remove any doubt casting a shadow in her mind. "Are you sure?"

"Yes. We need to be searching for someone else. In fact, I'd like to talk more with Mr. St. James to see if perhaps these murders are connected to them being here. There's a reason why the killer has targeted these two, or at least used places they've been to dump the bodies."

Freedom was within sight. "Whatever you need, we're both at your disposal."

Elsmed nodded before picking up the leather pouch and handing it over to Saundra.

Miss Beaumont untied the strings and emptied the contents in her hand. "It's with that recommendation that we apologize for whatever inconvenience this has caused you and release you with one condition." Uncurling her fingers to reveal what lay in her palm, Saundra spoke on behalf of the other members. "While you remain in Havenwood Falls, you're to wear these amulets. They've been spelled with protective wardings. Should you have somehow managed to fool us, and you are indeed guilty, these will expose you."

I didn't wait for her to bring them over to where we sat. "If that will give you peace of mind, then we'll wear them."

I'd carry whatever trinket they required if it meant we could leave.

"Then this meeting is concluded. Tread carefully, gentlemen." It was one last warning meant to remind both Knox and me that they'd still be watching us.

More than ever I wanted to leave and head back to England, but not without Catriona. Tucking the amulet beneath my shirt, I took one look at Knox. We were in total agreement.

There was no more time to waste.

If the gypsy was indeed here, his days were numbered.

CHAPTER 9

"*Y*ou're not going to like what I'm about to say."

After returning to the inn and having Madame Luiza show us our new room, Knox and I both took a few moments to catch our breath and come up with a new plan of action. As much as we needed to rest, we agreed that there would be plenty of time to relax once we knew the gypsy wasn't behind last night's reign of terror. Even as we hurried through the streets earlier, the town members were still rattled and up in arms, calling for justice on behalf of the dead.

"When you put it that way, Knox, I probably won't." I chuckled softly and took another long drink from the glass of blood he'd prepared. I resented having to take more from him, especially when he was already weakened. What I wanted more than anything was for him to agree to remain in the room and regain his strength before renewing our search. "You might as well spit it out, then. I might just surprise you."

We were definitely in better spirits. Freedom had that effect on a person.

"You're going to need more blood than I can provide." When I rolled my eyes at him, he smirked and waved me off. "That wasn't the part I meant. You do remember what they said, right? That they have a blood den here in town."

He was right. I didn't like where this was going. It wasn't that I didn't agree with him. It was plain to see the toll multiple feedings were taking on Knox, his coloring slow to return now. I just couldn't quite shake the feeling that it was like hiring a prostitute. It was funny where I chose to draw the line when it came to being a blood drinker. In the beginning, I had no problem going out and taking whatever I needed—from whomever I saw.

Place that source in a brothel, and suddenly it offended my sensibilities.

I mulled over his comment before answering. I hated the thought, but if it was the only way to keep the suspicion off me and the Court from detaining us again, I would swallow my pride and do it.

I slapped my hands on my knees before standing up. If this was what it took, I might as well grab the bull by the horns and take care of it now. "Fine. I'll go, but while I'm gone, you need to eat and try to rest. We both need to be at our best. You're just going to slow me down if you're passing out like a swooning woman."

His only reply was a rude gesture. I deserved it.

One thing I had to admit about Havenwood Falls was that it was beautifully situated with the majestic mountains as a backdrop. There was a crispness to the air as I stepped outside and took an appreciative look about. I could see why the Court wanted to protect the town and safeguard it from danger. I would do everything in my power to shield the citizens from corruption too, if this was mine. No matter which way you gazed, the view was truly breathtaking.

It didn't take me long to find myself once again at the bordello, and unlike before, I wasn't met outside by the owner. She'd kept me from entering the last time, inviting me to join her on a walk, so as I entered the main room now, it took me a few seconds to adjust from the brightness of the day.

Tables were set up throughout, with most of them being used by the girls and their clients. Whiskey was flowing from the long wooden bar along one side of the room—glasses lined up while a worker poured shots for thirsty patrons. The acrid smell of tobacco filled the air. Someone played at the piano that tinkled out a tune. The atmosphere was lively . . . jovial even, for how early it was.

I scanned the merry crowd for Fanny and found her perched on the lap of a large man whose hand rested precariously high on her thigh. I half expected her to slap him or in the very least move his roaming fingers lower, but instead, she tipped back her head and laughed at whatever he whispered in her ear. Judging by the rosiness in the man's cheeks and empty glasses on the table, he'd definitely had his fill of liquor and was now hoping for a little entertainment.

I hated that I needed to be here. Witnessing everyone's frivolity simply reminded me that I couldn't afford such luxuries. There was no way I could lower my guard to this extent—not that it posed any kind of temptation.

Stepping farther into the room, I began to draw attention from those I passed. Murmurs and stares told me everything I needed to know—word had spread that I'd been under suspicion —and it didn't take long before Fanny looked up to see what had caused the disturbance.

She blanched, her face registering shock before making her excuses to the gentleman. His arms wrapped around her waist, pulling her back down into his lap again. A drunken, slobbery kiss quickly followed, and I wasn't the only one who shuddered. Fanny untangled herself from his grasp and hurried toward me, rearranging her clothes before she reached me.

"Mr. St. James," she greeted, finally composed. "What a surprise. I didn't expect to see you here today." Her gaze rose to the ceiling, and for a split second, I caught a glimpse of apprehension. Maybe she thought I'd come back to kill one of the remaining girls in her employment.

"I wanted to offer my condolences," I began, raising my voice so she could hear me over the noise and chatter. "Is there somewhere we can talk? Perhaps in a quieter room?" I glanced around to the other doors that led to somewhere else in the building. "Unless they're occupied?"

She licked her lips and smoothed down the side of her hair. There really wasn't a reason to do so, because not a strand was out of place. "Umm." She was nervous.

I should've known that this would be the response. While you would never guess that this had been a crime scene last night because it was business as usual now, with no signs of people mourning, I had been the only suspect. Even though I'd been released, there was a good chance this woman didn't agree with the Court's decision.

"I haven't come to make trouble, Mrs. Webster. I understand that this is a tough time for you and your"—I searched for an appropriate word—"workers, but it won't take but a minute."

For a woman who showed nothing but unruffled composure, Fanny fidgeted before my eyes until she nodded. "If you're hoping to take advantage of one of my girls, I'm afraid I can only disappoint you. They've heard that you were believed the killer, and although you were deemed innocent, the news has left them shaken."

This was why I preferred Knox taking care of my needs. It was less complicated than having to navigate society.

"I understand. I'm not here as a client. Well, I am, but it's not what you think. Saundra Beaumont informed me that you also provide—" I stopped long enough to look about and make sure we weren't being overheard. There were still a few pair of eyes watching us keenly, so I leaned forward so I could keep the next part private. "That you also run a blood den here."

She signaled for the man behind the bar to bring us both drinks. I didn't usually drink whiskey, but I knew better than to refuse the gesture. While I took a small sip, the amber liquid burning a path down into my stomach, Fanny downed hers in one gulp.

Liquid courage.

"I do," she finally answered after licking her lips and placing her glass on the table by us. "Will you be needing that service?"

She shuffled slowly on her feet, and I took a step back so there could remain an appropriate amount of space between us. It felt like a dance, and before too long, I found we'd moved closer to the door leading outside.

"Will that be a problem?" Something was off. Something more than just a little anxiety over last night. "They led me to believe that you could help me."

A ray of sunlight fell between us with dust and dirt particles floating in the air. Just as I was about to repeat my question, she smiled. Perhaps the alcohol had taken the needed effect, because I started to see the woman I'd talked with yesterday—that same self-assurance and flirtatious demeanor.

"Sorry, you'll have to forgive my manners. As you can imagine, I have a lot on my mind at the moment." She brushed her fingers over her brow, stirring sympathy within me. "I haven't slept a wink, and it's beginning to take a toll."

All I could do was nod. I understood that sentiment perfectly. "Then I won't keep you. I don't know how long I'll be remaining here in Havenwood Falls, but until then, I need a reliable blood source. I'm willing to pay whatever price you set." Money. It opened so many doors and softened whatever resistance I encountered.

This was no different. "Would you be opposed to having one of my girls visit you at the inn?"

Her request surprised me. "Is there a reason why I couldn't meet her here in one of your rooms?" I didn't know how I felt about inviting the stranger into the room where we slept. "I'm not sure how the Petrans would feel having one of your girls there at the inn."

I could see she saw the sense in my observation, but that didn't deter her. "While I'd usually agree with you, after last night . . . I just think it would be better if we made alternative arrangements. Your presence here has already stirred my clients up."

Annoyance tightened my chest, and it was on the tip of my tongue to remind her that despite what the town's gossips said, I wasn't the one responsible for the recent deaths. I was tempted to thank her for her time and continue feeding from Knox, but that wasn't feasible anymore. I needed Fanny Webster. I needed to swallow my pride and be grateful for her willingness to help.

I surrendered. "If that's what you require, then I'll be happy to meet in my room at the inn." Beggars couldn't be choosers, and there was no other option available. Not if I didn't want to be accused again.

"Very well, then. Are you requiring the service now, or at a later time?" She took another step toward me, forcing me to retreat again. "I'm sure I could have someone ready within the hour."

I couldn't shake the feeling that she was eager to get rid of me. The feeling was mutual. I was tired of the constant stares. "This evening will be fine. Would you like me to pay now or do I give the money to the girl?"

"I'll set up an account for you, and we can discuss payment after your first visit." Glancing over her shoulder to the now impatient gentleman she'd been entertaining, Fanny offered me a fake smile. "Enjoy your day, Mr. St. James. Claire will arrive to your room tonight after sunset."

Knowing that I'd been dismissed, I thanked her for her time and escaped back into the street. The whole situation had been the polar opposite of our first meeting. I could only assume that I'd lost whatever appeal she'd seen in the beginning, and now I had as much charm as a leper.

It didn't bother me.

Other than blood, I had no use for her or her bordello.

"Thank God that's over," I murmured and stepping down into

the street, I threw the building one last glance before putting the conversation behind me. That was when something caught my attention from the corner of my eye. It wasn't the movement from one of the top windows, the way the curtains had parted slightly as though a breeze had made the fabric dance.

No, it was the face that peered down—eyes wide, mouth open, hands frantically pounding against the glass window.

I stood there—transfixed, barely able to comprehend what I was seeing. For a second, I wondered if my mind was playing a trick on me, or perhaps I'd just witnessed a ghost. All it took was a few seconds before the truth came crashing down.

I wasn't hallucinating.

Storming back up the steps, I entered the brothel, and instead of trying to catch Fanny's attention again, I raced up the stairs that led to a second floor. I didn't stop as her workers screamed for help and angry clients swore at having their time disrupted. Somewhere in the back of my mind, I could hear people calling for Fanny, and my name being hollered.

I knew what I'd seen, and no one was going to keep me from confirming it.

I pushed each closed door open until I found one that was locked.

"Hello?" I pounded against the frame, hoping that whoever occupied the room would answer. The brass handle jiggled, but that was all. I was left with no other choice but to raise my foot and kick the damn thing down.

"Stand back!" I yelled through the door, and without hesitation, thrust my heel against the door. It flew open, the frame splintering from the force.

I stood there stunned, my chest heaving from exertion.

All this time.

She'd been here.

Catriona.

"Marcus?" she cried, tears streaming down her cheeks. "Is that really you? Am I dreaming?"

I couldn't speak. My mouth opened yet nothing came out. Instead I spread my arms as she came rushing toward me. Even feeling her body pressed against me, all I could do was soak in the fact that it was truly my beautiful wife.

My very *pregnant* wife.

I had found her.

CHAPTER 10

"*I* must ask you to leave, Mr. St. James." Fanny had the audacity to act as though I were the one trespassing. Behind her, the man serving drinks at the bar stood with a rifle aimed directly at me. "The sheriff has already been summoned."

Fury unlike anything I'd ever felt almost consumed me. This woman—she'd known I was searching for my wife, and all this time had been keeping her locked up in a whorehouse. Shielding Catriona with my body, I kept my eyes on the two in front of me.

"Are you okay?" I asked, hating the way we were being reunited.

"Take me home, please." Her voice broke my heart. I could hear the tears in her plea. When Catriona touched my back, I wanted to whip around and take her back into my arms, never to let her go. "I just want to go home."

"I will, sweetheart," I promised, trying hard to keep my tone soft with her. Who knew what kind of treatment she'd experienced from this woman, let alone the bastard who took her. From the quick look I'd been able to have, she looked well enough, despite being very, very pregnant. I shuddered to think how that had transpired—what kind of liberties were taken with her. "I'm taking you now."

"I'm afraid I can't let you take her, Marcus," came the smug reply from Fanny. "And if you take one more step toward me, I'll have my man here shoot you. It's not as if anyone will mourn your death, and frankly, I'm getting good at blaming you for my crimes."

"So that was your handiwork last night?" I accused, not doubting her bragging for a second. "Let me commend you for your performance. You're quite the actress. No one suspected that you were the one killing your own girls."

Fanny shrugged, her confidence bordering on arrogance. If she truly thought she was safe from the wrath that was steadily eroding any common sense I held, she was mistaken. The man could shoot me as many times as he wanted. I wouldn't stop coming until I'd squeezed the very breath from her lungs.

"Dimitri expected me to get rid of you. I do what I'm told."

Dimitri.

The Romani scum.

"You need to run." My voice was cold and low, filled with unflinching menace. When she didn't budge, I started walking forward. The rifle exploded, but the fool missed. I didn't have to turn around to know that the bullet had become lodged in the wall behind me. Catriona was safe. I would never let her get hurt again.

As Fanny's hired help struggled to reload, I sprang into action, cocking my fist back before throwing it with the full force of my might. Bones crunched beneath the contact, and I reveled in the satisfaction of seeing him drop to the ground like a stone. If she'd expected me to cower at the sight of him, Fanny had been sadly mistaken. The man could've resembled Goliath from the Bible, and I still would've charged in with everything I had.

Her smugness immediately dissolved, and instead of a conceited smirk, Fanny dropped to her knees, begging for mercy. "Please, I didn't know she was your wife. Dimitri threatened to destroy everything I've worked so hard to build for myself here. All I had to do was keep her hidden until he returned for the baby."

I refused to listen. Instead, I kicked out at her, roaring in anger. "Get up! You will answer for your deceit."

When she held her hands up in front of her, I swiped them aside and breached the space between us. I couldn't think straight. All I could see was the face of someone who had deliberately kept me from my wife.

My fingers curled around her slender throat, squeezing just enough to make her panic. I wasn't someone who thought I could ever raise a hand against a woman, but retribution was needed. This bitch knew how to find her co-conspirator, and he was the one I wanted to vent my fury on.

"Please," she gurgled, her face turning a bright red. Tears streamed down over her cheeks. Gone was the enchantress. Fanny was now reduced to a sobbing, pathetic charlatan. "I'll do anything you want. Just please don't hurt me."

"You deserve to be hurt," I thundered. My body trembled from the adrenaline coursing through my veins. It finally made sense why she didn't want me returning here to feed. We had gone for the walk yesterday, not because she wanted to enjoy the fresh air, but because Catriona had been sequestered upstairs. "You deserve to feel how I do . . . what it means to have everything ripped away until you think you'll surely go mad."

All the while, my wife stood behind me, watching. She didn't say a word, not even to calm me down and keep me from killing her captor. It was a testament to what she'd had to endure, that the one who had boldly defied me to protect the prisoner in my dungeon last year had nothing to say now.

My fingers tightened a little more around Fanny's throat, bruising her pale skin. I could hear a commotion down in the main room and knew that the cavalry had arrived to save the poor Mrs. Webster from the madman.

If I was going to do anything, now was the time. If I waited any longer, my chance to exact revenge would be gone.

Leaning in close until she could feel the warmth of my breath on her face, I held her gaze until all she could see was me. "Where is he? Tell me now and you'll live."

"I don't know," she spluttered, panic filling her eyes.

I gripped harder. "Wrong answer. Try again."

Loud footsteps pounded on the floor outside the room. Help was almost here.

"He'll kill me."

I banged her hard against the wall, frustrated with her obstinacy. "I will kill you. It's me you should be afraid of."

Someone came flying into the room, and seeing the chance disappear, I reluctantly let Fanny go, not bothering to catch her as she fell to the carpeted floor.

"Mr. St. James! What is the meaning of this?" It was Mihail Petran who stood beyond the doorway, his gaze sweeping over the room like he couldn't believe he'd caught me in the very act. Whatever he'd been told, I knew my towering over a weeping woman, while another stood terrified behind me, didn't look good or in my favor.

I held my hands up in surrender and backed away from Fanny. I could already see the mottled coloring from where my hand had been at her throat. She was heaving dramatically now that she had an audience, clutching her chest in desperation.

"Thank goodness you're here, Mr. Petran," she prattled, knowing the focus was solely on her. "He came here in such a rage and refused to listen. I was terrified for my life!" Accepting Mihail's extended hand, she stumbled into him, forcing the man to wrap his arms around her. "Please, help me."

The look Mihail leveled at me was brutal.

"Explain yourself," he demanded.

Before I could defend myself, Catriona came forward, her hand curved around her stomach protectively. "If I could, I'd like to answer that, sir."

Fanny sniffled against his chest. "Pay no heed to her. She's simpleminded and easily manipulated. That's why her husband has asked me to care for her. She's prone to fits and fantasies." Finally breaking away from Mihail, Fanny attempted to cross the room to Catriona.

She didn't make it more than a step before I growled low at her —a reminder not to challenge my patience. Now I'd found Catriona, no one would ever come between us again.

Mihail nodded as he grasped hold of Fanny. Kindness now filled his features. He believed Fanny that he was talking with someone who was more child than adult.

"I'm sure you've had quite a shock, Miss," he said gently. His mannerisms were as though he was approaching a small deer that he didn't want to spook. "If you could just come with me." He extended his hand to her. "I'll see that you are returned safely to your husband."

If he thought Catriona was quiet because she was weak and submissive, he was mistaken. Shaking her head, she cleared her throat. Her answer came out loud and crystal clear. "Marcus is my husband. If I go anywhere, it will be with him."

There was so much strength in her words. Whatever shock she had felt, it was quickly being replaced with the same spark and fire that had melted my heart back in England.

She slipped her hand into mine, and the sensation made me want to shout with joy. I had found her. The message from Lady Hannah had been right. Every sacrifice we'd made, every decision that brought us here to Havenwood Falls, had been worth it.

My hope had been rewarded.

Mihail's brow furrowed, and holding Fanny at arm's length now, he looked between us both. "Is this young woman correct? Is Marcus her husband?" She refused to answer him. Even when he threatened to bring her before the Court. "Sooner or later, you're going to have to tell the truth, Mrs. Webster. We've often looked the other way with regard to what happens in this building because you agreed to also host a blood den. If you want to continue to keep the arrangement, you're going to need to explain yourself."

Something had changed within her. While Mihail had

addressed Catriona, Fanny had obviously decided what her best course of action was. The smugness had returned. She peered down her nose at the Court member with a haughtiness that bordered on stupid. There was no way she could believe this would end well for her.

"I have only one thing to say." She turned to me, and I wanted to wipe the demented smirk from her face. "Enjoy her while you can. When Dimitri returns—and he's on his way—he will take the child and kill you all. I curse you to never have a day's peace as long as you walk this earth." And with that, she spat at me, uttering a few words in Romani.

"I'll need you to also come with me, Marcus. Bring the young lady with you." Tugging on Fanny again, he held on to her. Catriona was still holding my hand, and as we started following them out, I kissed the back of her hand.

"I can't believe you're really here," she uttered. The light was returning to her eyes, and all I wanted to do was take her back to Knox so he could celebrate with us. "That you found me."

"We haven't stopped looking for you since he rode off with you on that horse." I helped her down the stairs and through the room that had been cleared of patrons. The only people left inside the bordello were the girls who worked for Fanny. Wisely, they kept their distance.

We'd managed to take a few steps into the street before I heard my name being called. Knox came running toward me. Somehow, he'd heard that I'd been involved in something at the brothel and had come to help. I recognized the precise moment when he realized who I was holding hands with.

"How?" he exclaimed as he came to a screeching halt, his gaze darting back and forth in disbelief. "Catriona?"

She dropped my hand and threw her arms around his neck. "Knox!"

He looked at me over her shoulder, a million questions reflected in his face. "How is this even possible? Was she here this whole time?" That's when her condition finally registered. Releasing her, he stared at her stomach. "Marcus?"

I nodded. "We have a lot to discuss, but first the Court is going to want to talk with us." All I could think was as soon as the truth was revealed, we could get the hell out of this town.

My family was back together.

The realization that our search was finally over still hadn't sunk in.

But pulling her into me again, wrapping my arm around her waist . . . that was a start.

I was never going to let her go.

CHAPTER 11

*I*n the end, the Court found Fanny guilty. Locked up in the same cell Knox and I had previously occupied, she was charged with being an accomplice to kidnapping, but most importantly, she was found guilty of murder.

Once the Court apologized again for their mistake, we were free to go. It was like music to my ears, because I couldn't wait to return to the inn, pack up our belongings, and leave immediately. Havenwood Falls would hopefully become a distant memory, and for as long as I lived, I never wanted to step foot in this town again.

Catriona and Knox agreed as well.

We were all eager to put this behind us.

The only problem was that Dimitri was still out there, and Fanny's final words still rang loudly in my mind. He would come for my wife again. Not just her, but the baby she carried. I tried not to think about the fact that he had defiled Catriona, sullying her spirit and body with his filth. There was no mistaking the love that she felt for the babe growing inside her, the longing that filled her voice whenever she mentioned the child.

I didn't have the heart to remind her who the father was. She was painfully aware of that truth. Instead, I vowed to protect her and the infant. I would step forward and be the man she needed me to be. They would want for nothing, and we'd be the family she'd always desired.

"Are you sure you're okay with this, Marcus?" She bit her lip nervously, peeking at me from the corner of her eyes. Every time I'd tried to talk with her and see what was on her mind, she brushed my concern off as her being tired. We seemed to tiptoe around each other while Knox was out settling the accounts and finding us a way to travel safely with her.

"Is that why you've been lost in your thoughts?" I paused amid folding my clothes, dropping them into my open trunk. If she was finally ready to talk about what she'd experienced, I would listen for as long as it took. "What can I say that will show you how I feel?"

This was all my fault. I'd sowed the seeds of doubt when we were first married, nurturing a sea of insecurity concerning where we stood with each other. Of course, she worried that I would feel indifferent still. I wouldn't be surprised if she saw my being here to search for her as merely me retrieving my property.

Self-loathing cut deep like a knife. I would never forgive myself for acting so badly.

"You haven't touched me since we returned to this room. Do I disgust you now that we're alone and away from onlookers?" Catriona stared down at her stomach and ill-fitting clothes. She couldn't see how incredibly beautiful she was to me—what a miracle she was in my mind.

Tears welled in her eyes, threatening to spill over and stain her cheeks.

I blamed myself for them as well.

"Catriona," I started, choking around the emotions that suddenly rose up. "I have so much to explain . . . so many things to make amends for. Please." I reached for her now, hoping that I could convey what I felt through my touch. Careful not to overwhelm her, I took her hand and held it to my chest. "The thought of never finding you again has haunted me this past year."

When she didn't look at me, I tipped her chin up with my finger. Shame filled her gorgeous green eyes now. "I know how you see me, Marcus. I understand the relationship we have, and that all we can ever be is friends. I accepted that back in England." As she tried to place some distance between us, I shook my head, and held her in place.

"Would you believe me if I told you I've realized how much of a fool I was then? That I didn't truly appreciate you and what you meant to me until after you were taken?" I needed her to hear the words I was saying—to feel the way my heart was reflected in each sentiment.

More than anything, I hoped I hadn't damaged what might have been between us, what I hoped could be, because I'd been too afraid to let her close enough to see me—the monster and the man.

"You're not making any sense," she cried, and I could feel her starting to pull away again.

Had I hurt her beyond forgiveness?

Did my following her across the world to bring her home mean nothing compared to my neglect of the past?

"I love you, Catriona," I blurted out, desperate enough to lay myself completely bare before her.

I could see she was struggling to accept what I was saying. Her gaze kept dropping to my mouth as if she expected it to reveal my true intentions. I wasn't lying, though. The second I'd walked into that room at the whorehouse and found her standing there, I'd known it. Love had struck like a blessed revelation, the emotion enmeshed in my soul. For the first time I wasn't afraid to speak my heart.

And now, I felt like I would burst if I kept it trapped inside a second longer. It strengthened me—filling me with a light and peace I hadn't known was possible. This beautiful woman had rocked my world and helped rebuild me into someone much more than I expected.

She'd shown me redemption was within my reach.

"You don't have to say that, Marcus. It's enough that we can still be friends and that I have a home with you and Knox." It was her turn to be stubborn now. I almost burst out laughing at the irony. So many nights she'd stood outside my study, poised to knock on the door. Starved for affection, for any scrap of decency, she'd risked looking like a fool by approaching me.

Now it was my turn to wear my heart on my sleeve and beg. It was my turn to be vulnerable and take the chance of being denied.

Words weren't reaching her.

No matter how hard I tried to find a way to make her understand, she was too guarded to hear what I was saying—to realize that I wanted it all with her. Everything. I didn't care what had happened or what the future would bring, as long as I could stand by her side and face it together.

Cupping her face between my hands, I used my thumb to brush gently across her cheekbone, marveling again that this was real. This wasn't one of many fantasies I'd had, imagining what our reunion would be like. She was flesh and blood, here before me, looking up at me as though I was a mystery she was trying to decipher.

"I love you, Catriona St. James. I am yours completely, if you'll have me. I can't change my actions from the past. All I can do is promise to never make you feel less than the extraordinary woman you are. I want to be your husband, not just your friend. I want to take you in my arms, and never, ever let you go."

I lowered my mouth to hers, our lips barely touching. I could feel the hitch in her breath, the anticipation of what I was going to do next. It was my turn to be uncertain. What if she pushed me away? What if the damage had been done, if the trauma of the past year had scarred her forever, and convinced her she'd rather be alone?

A million thoughts raced through my mind, but only one stuck. Only one was deemed important enough to act on. With one last brush of my thumb across her warm skin, I pressed my mouth over hers.

I kissed her with all the tenderness I could muster.

I pulled her against me and cradled her body with my arms as though she was the most precious gift I had.

My heart thundered in my chest—the sensation loud enough that I was positive she could hear it. Time seemed to stand still as I waited to see how she would respond. Would she melt into my embrace, signaling that she returned my affection, or would she shove me away, offended by my audacity?

I took courage that she'd allowed me to caress her face. She had wanted me once before. This experience had taught me a powerful truth. There was always hope—even if it was the tiniest of flames. If it flickered in the slightest, it could be rekindled into a burning fire.

"This has to be another dream," she whispered, her eyes still closed.

"Trust me, sweetheart. We're awake. This is real." Feathering my lips gently over hers, I ached to deepen our kiss. "Will you have me?"

Her lids opened, and I finally saw the spitfire young woman who had stood in my office that first day, the one who had eagerly returned the kiss I had stolen.

"You came." Just two small words, but they shifted my world —our world—realigning us. She knew this wasn't some illusion and that I meant everything I'd said. "You came."

Catriona gripped the front of my shirt tightly and pulled my mouth back to hers. Any hesitancy evaporated the instant her tongue touched mine. She poured everything into the way her lips moved like she was finally able to take what she wanted—what had been denied her. Her hand wound around my neck, and I felt her rise up on her tiptoes. She wanted to get closer—echoing the need that was swirling inside me.

There was something sweet about the way she tasted, the way she didn't once try to break the seal of our mouths, the way she kept drawing me into her like she was afraid to end the magic between us.

Kissing her stripped away everything that haunted me, that tried to twist me into a bitter version of myself. I knew how cliché that sounded—that a mere taste of a woman could be so transformative—but there was no denying the change that was unfolding. It wasn't that I was becoming a better man. More like I had finally realized exactly what I stood to lose if I didn't abandon my foolishness.

Someone coughed behind me, and I faintly registered that the door to our room had opened. I didn't want to stop, though. I didn't care how indecent this might appear to whoever had joined us. This kiss had been a long time coming—had taken many tears and fears overcome in order to claim it.

"Hello?"

It was Knox who rudely tried to interrupt us, and I made a mental note to throttle him once we were alone. Trying to tune him out didn't work, however. Not because I couldn't but because he wasn't the only one who'd entered our room.

"Do you think we should maybe wait downstairs for them to finish?" The woman's voice sounded like she was pleased to find Catriona and me in such an embrace. "It seems like a shame to interrupt such a . . . passionate reunion." I could almost picture Madame Luiza blushing, her cheeks flushing a pretty pink.

"They have plenty of time to continue this later, I assure you," Knox countered, clearing his throat again. "In fact, I'll probably spend the journey home being incredibly nauseated from them celebrating."

Catriona burst into laughter, the sound like music to my ears. I would never tire of hearing it.

"Sorry to embarrass you, Knox. We'll try to keep your sensibilities in mind, okay?" She was teasing him. One glance at Knox, and I could practically hear his joy from across the room. We were both grateful that we'd managed to find her, despite the odds.

"Forgive me, Madame Luiza. It just feels so good to be with my wife again." I didn't bother hiding my pride and happiness.

"I'm glad we're able to speak with you before we leave. I wanted to thank you for the kindness you've shown Knox and me while we've been here. It's meant a lot."

Knox looked at me like I'd suddenly sprouted two heads. Usually it was him who shared his appreciation on behalf of us both. He'd just have to get used to it.

Madame Luiza came forward and took my hand in hers. "I was telling this young man that I wish you would stay a little while longer, at least until the baby arrives. The roads aren't always safe to travel on, and I'd hate for you all to get into trouble with no one to come and help." She turned to Catriona, grabbing her hand as well. "I would sleep easier knowing that no more harm comes to you, dear one. The roads can be treacherous at any time of the year. Perhaps waiting until you've all had a chance to recuperate from this ordeal would be better." Looking around the room, she searched for an ally. I didn't like the idea of refusing her, but I was eager to get going.

"I don't mean to offend you, but the sooner we can get home, the sooner we can put all of this behind us. You understand, don't you?" I asked, hoping that she could see why it was so important we didn't linger. I didn't mention that we still had to deal with Dimitri and the threat he still posed to Catriona and the baby. I couldn't shake the feeling that there was no time to waste.

She slowly nodded her head, but not before I caught the look of disappointment. She'd enjoyed the time we'd spent here in the inn. She liked knowing that she could draw Knox into a conversation or that he couldn't get enough of her cooking. I'd heard him more than once threaten to whisk her away back to England because he couldn't bear going back to the food prepared at the estate. If it meant he was happy, I'd even contemplate offering her a job at Smithersby Field. She'd never leave her family here in Havenwood Falls, but a compliment was a compliment, and she positively radiated with pride whenever Knox moaned over each mouthful.

"You must do what's best for your family, Marcus. Family

always comes first. You're a good man to remember that." Tapping my cheek affectionately, she stepped back and wiped her hands on the apron she wore. "Just know you'll all be missed."

"Marcus," Catriona interrupted before letting out a gasp of pain. In horror I watched her double over instinctively to protect her stomach. "Something's not right. Something—" Her words were cut off as she screamed out, clutching frantically for my arm to keep her upright.

"Is it the baby?" Madame Luiza asked as she pushed past me. Guiding Catriona over to the bed, she helped my wife sit on the edge. Sweat was already beading along her brow, her eyes scrunched closed as another wave of pain crashed over her.

Catriona nodded quickly. Panting, she looked to me for help, but I stood there totally clueless about what to do next. Even Knox seemed at a loss for words.

"Go," Madame Luiza shooed, waving us away. "Fetch my sister-in-law Irina. Tell her we have a baby to deliver. Quick!" Knox and I hurried out from the room.

"You go, Knox," I said, stopping before I reached the top of the stairway. "I can't leave Catriona alone. Not again. Go get whatever the women need. I'll stay right here and make sure they're not interrupted."

He didn't argue. Instead, he pulled me in for a quick hug before running down the stairs on his new errand.

Our travel plans were put on temporary hold.

There would be no leaving for home just yet.

Glancing up at the ceiling, I offered up a prayer to whomever might be listening.

Keep her safe.

Please.

Don't rip her from me now that I've finally found everything I've ever wanted.

CHAPTER 12

I'd been banished to sit outside on the front steps. Apparently, my constant pacing outside our room was distracting and agitating Catriona further. Not that I was allowed to go inside and talk to her myself or see with my own two eyes that she was okay. At one point I'd pressed my ear up against the door, hoping to hear something that could alleviate my worry. Each time a contraction struck, I could hear Catriona scream out in pain. It was torture not to rush inside.

"Leave her to us, Marcus. She's in good hands." I had no doubt Madame Luiza meant to put me at ease, but nothing seemed to calm the rampant thoughts tumbling in my mind. All I could imagine was the worst. It was then that she stuck her head back through the door and ordered me away for the good of the baby.

Knox hadn't been any help either. He took one look at the furrowed brow and tried to get me to come with him to the waterfall Ehzno had talked about. He wanted to harvest as much of the burdock root as he could for our trip home. Now that we'd be traveling with a baby, we wanted to make sure that my hunger never raged out of control. This child hadn't even entered the world and already was the most important priority of our small family.

We joked back and forth about whether the babe would be a girl or a boy. Despite what I'd once thought—that I could only ever be satisfied by having an heir—all I could focus on and hope was that the child be healthy. I would love the child regardless of how conceived. I would claim my place as parent with a full heart and strive to be the father the child deserved.

A loud squawk of a nearby bird drew my attention from its perch on a branch in front of the inn. An unsettling sensation washed over me. It was a raven. Heaven help me, but it looked exactly like the same creature Knox and I had seen up in the glen the other day. Ehzno's words echoed in my mind—that we were being watched and there was an ill wind blowing in the air.

I didn't fully understand all of the Indian's customs and beliefs, but I didn't forget his expression as he hurried away. I also remembered that Fanny had been whispering to a bird before our first meeting.

This raven had made its presence known, and I couldn't shake the feeling that maybe there was something else at play. I wasn't one to give in to paranoia, but my instinct nagged that I couldn't lower my guard. Something was coming for my family. Perhaps this fowl was being used as a way to spy from a distance without drawing suspicion.

"Shoo," I called out, flapping my hand at the bird. It cocked its head to the side as though it was studying me as hard I was watching it. Looking around for something to throw at it, I stood up instead and rushed toward it. The raven took to the sky, only to settle back on the windowsill outside the room Catriona was in.

Fear sent me running.

I didn't care how I looked as I burst in and surprised everyone. Excusing my interruption, I tried not to notice how exhausted Catriona looked, how drenched with sweat she was, as she reclined against the pillows propped behind her.

"What's the meaning of this, Mr. St. James?" Irina asked, clearly alarmed that I hadn't warned them before entering. "You can't just rush in here. We need to keep everything calm for your wife. Any stress she experiences can hurt the baby."

I glanced outside to see the raven peering in. I did the only thing I could—I slammed the curtains closed, effectively shutting the blasted creature out.

"My apologies, ladies." I stopped briefly beside the bed and leaned in to kiss Catriona's cheek. "Do you need anything, sweetheart?" Now I was here, I was reluctant to return to my stoop outside.

She forced a smile on her face, even though pain filled her eyes. "I'm okay, Marcus. You don't need to stay with me. The baby and I are fine."

Luiza saw that as her opportunity to move me along. "You can see for yourself that things are progressing. I promise you, I'll fetch you as soon as the infant arrives. Until then, you'll just be under foot and worry your poor wife."

With every step I took toward the door, I felt a weight pulling me back. I didn't care that other men chose not to welcome their child into the world and stay. I'd already missed so much, and I still worried that if Dimitri were to show up, I would be too far away to protect her.

I was abruptly pushed the rest of the way out the door, turning only to have it slammed in my face. Maybe I should've gone with Knox instead of obsessively staring up at the window. Anything had to be better than impatiently waiting.

"How much longer, Madame Luiza?" I called through the wooden door.

"At least a few hours, maybe more." Came her response.

Hours.

I wasn't going to survive this.

Thankfully I wouldn't be pacing the front porch alone, because it wasn't long before Knox came rushing back, his face bursting with excitement. The bag that he'd taken with him to gather the needed root was nowhere to be seen. Whatever was happening had caused him to leave it behind.

"You need to come now." He didn't wait for me to answer. He all but dragged me down the stairs and back in the direction he'd come. As much as I wanted to share in his news, I dug in my heels, bringing his effort to a grinding halt.

"I'm going nowhere, Knox. Not while Catriona needs me." I couldn't believe he'd forgotten why I'd stayed behind. Even now he was trying to get me to move.

"You don't understand. I found it. Lady Hannah was right. The answer to all your problems is here in Havenwood Falls. Ehzno, bless the Indian's heart, showed us where to find it. Hurry up!" he exclaimed fervently. "There's no time to waste."

He wasn't making any sense. We'd both agreed that the seer's message had been referring to Catriona and where the gypsy had taken her. Seeing that prophecy come true, the case was closed in my mind.

"You're not listening. I can't go anywhere right now." I resorted to pointing up to the window where the raven still sat. "Especially not while that blasted thing stays. Recognize anything?" I gestured again, hoping that he would calm down long enough to see it wasn't safe to go on some errand with him.

"Is that the same one?" Finally, Knox was beginning to see reason. Dropping my arm, he sauntered closer, peering up to the ledge. "Do you suspect magic?"

I nodded. "Call me crazy, but I think the gypsy has somehow spelled that raven to spy for him. What better way to keep track of Catriona and the baby while remaining hidden? All he'd need to do is watch, and when he sees the time is right, return. He's probably feeling desperate now Fanny is locked up and no longer doing his bidding."

I'd given it a lot of thought, and the more I did, the stronger the possibility that I was right grew.

Knox bent down, grabbed a rock, and threw it at the bird. "I think this is a case where it's better to kill the messenger."

When the stone missed its target, the raven let out a loud

screech and retreated to a different tree away from the inn's property. It wouldn't remain gone forever, but for the next few moments, it couldn't watch for any news.

"How is she?" His question revealed how nervous he was. "Has anyone come down to let you know how things are?"

I started laughing. "I'm pretty confident if I knock on that door one more time, Madame Luiza will begin throwing rocks at me too."

That got a reaction out of him. "Being a nuisance, huh?" Knox chuckled, casting another look up to our room. "Maybe I should go up and ask? I haven't worn out my welcome yet. I should be safe."

I shrugged my shoulders. "I wouldn't risk it. Those two mean business up there. Nothing short of the inn burning to the ground will make those women relent. It's what's best for Catriona and the baby. That's the only reason why I didn't force myself in there to stay."

There was no way I'd jeopardize the birth.

Knox chewed on the inside of his cheek. He had something on his mind, but knowing I wouldn't leave my wife alone obviously posed a problem.

"What is it?" I asked, my curiosity finally piqued. "Tell me what's got you so excited, and once I know everything's okay, I'll go with you to see whatever it is. Deal?"

I was so sure that nothing he said could convince me otherwise, I almost dropped to the ground when he told me his good news—information that saw me abandoning my post and running after him.

Knox. My wonderful Phineas had somehow managed the impossible.

He'd found a cure for my curse.

Within the hour, if all went well, I would be able to welcome my child into the world.

As a man.

A *human* man.

My time as a blood drinker was finally going to come to an end.

CHAPTER 13

I could hear the rushing sound of the waterfall long before we stepped out from among the trees. An involuntary gasp escaped my lips. Even though I'd been told that this place held strong elemental magic, it did nothing to prepare me for the breathtaking sight before me.

The bold colors instantly dazzled me, and the scents that wafted throughout the air were as intoxicating as the blood I craved.

"Have you ever seen such perfection?" Knox whispered, and I couldn't tell whether he was also caught up in the scenery, or if his remark was directed to the woman who stood quietly at the water's edge.

With the sun still high in the sky, her figure all but glowed as it emanated a softness that revealed she wasn't human. Her golden hair fell down below her waist, and while there wasn't a breeze to be felt, strands that looked like fine-spun silk danced about around her.

The mystery woman wore a delicate cream dress that rivaled the beauty of her fair skin. Whoever she was, the crown of blue and white flowers that were laced together on top of her head

BELINDA BORING

paled in comparison, and I hadn't even seen her face yet. With her back to us, all I could imagine was this was truly an enchantress.

More importantly, this was the bestower of a great gift—the one to give me back my life.

"Who is she, Knox?" I asked, unable to tear my gaze around her.

"She's Unseelie," he murmured, awe filling each breath he exhaled. "She appeared while I was here picking burdock root. One minute I was alone, and the next I could hear the tinkling of her voice."

Fae.

There was no telling the true intention of this woman, but one glance at Knox, and I could see he was besotted by her. He believed she was the answer to our prayers, so for him, I would humor the meeting.

"You've returned to me, Phineas." A warm, delicious wave skirted over my skin as her voice was carried over the breeze. "Are you ready to strike our agreement?"

When she finally turned about, it was evident why she held such power over my friend. If I hadn't prepared myself—if Catriona didn't already own my heart—I would've walked through fire for this creature. Beautiful wasn't even the right word to describe her. Ethereal, exquisite—there was nothing in the human language that came close.

He nodded, and stepping to the side, introduced me to her. "Yralli, may I present my kin, Marcus St. James. It's for him that I ask a favor of you. It is his curse that I humbly beg you remove."

Her gaze turned to me, and the effect felt like a piercing blow to my soul. Whatever magic she was performing, the moment her eyes narrowed to study me, I felt everything strip away—who I was, my fears and insecurities, my hopes and dreams. Nothing was left untouched by her scrutiny, and while I knew it would be disastrous to offend her, it was hard not to resent the invasion.

"Your friend thinks very highly of you, Marcus St. James. It is not often I meet with a human who ignores his own wants and desires and places another before himself. He tells me you suffer from a gypsy curse, that you are damned to be a blood drinker for the rest of your days." Her slender fingers trailed along the tops of the tall grass that grew by the water. The long-stemmed flowers that appeared to grow almost instantly beside her bowed their heads in reverence. Nature seemed to worship the fae. If she actually healed me, I would bend at the knee as well.

"I've been fortunate enough to know such a man as Knox," I answered honestly. "There've been times I wondered whether I deserved such loyalty. Especially now, in your presence."

My response pleased her. "Do you understand what has passed between him and me?"

The sun's rays encompassed her as she came closer. Even though I could see the tips of her feet beneath her long flowing dress, it wouldn't have surprised me if she was floating on air. Each movement she made was filled with an otherworldly grace and elegance. It was impossible not to feel overwhelmed watching her —to feel unbelievably unclean.

"I will explain it to him afterwards," Knox interjected, and for the first time since approaching the waterfall, he looked at me. I couldn't quite recognize the emotion that filled his gaze, but before I could question him, he continued speaking. "Before him now, as my witness, I agree to your terms, Yralli, freely and without coercion."

"What terms?" I pressed, suddenly worried that whatever price she required to perform the healing would be too high, and one I would never ask him to give. "Knox. Please, what have you done?"

"Do you trust me?" was his response.

I didn't need to think. Nodding, I searched his features for some kind of hint. "With my life. You know that. You are the one I trust most above all else." I turned to face him completely. "Now please explain."

I didn't care what he'd promised this creature. This was my life that would change, and it was up to me to strike the deal if I didn't like his answer.

"She's agreed to make you human again."

Yralli spoke up now. She was within arm's reach now, and the magic emanating from her caused the air to ripple around us. It almost felt too stifling and oppressive to breathe.

"I will do this for you, for Phineas, on the condition that for the rest of your natural life, you spill no more blood. You will become human again and forgo your thirst for vengeance. Your enemies will continue to walk the earth. They will not be killed by your hand."

The agreement seemed simple enough, but I couldn't quite shake the stories that I'd heard—of hidden agendas and fae trickery. If something appeared too good to be true, it often was.

"And you believe this?" I asked, questioning Knox. "You accept her words at face value?"

An earnestness filled his features as he placed his hand on my shoulder. "With my whole heart. I know what you're thinking, Marcus, that she can't be trusted, but I wouldn't make this decision lightly. The seer told us we would find what we were seeking in Havenwood Falls, and it didn't just mean Catriona. One of the few portals that connect this world with Faerie is beyond these waterfalls. It's part of what gives this town, this land such power."

I gripped his hand and squeezed it. I knew he was being sincere, but I couldn't let him risk himself on my behalf. "But her intentions?"

There was a touch of coldness in Yralli's tone. "Do you question my honor, blood drinker?" Her using that title with me was a stark reminder that the future of my curse was hanging in the balance and relied heavily on the outcome of this conversation. "Tell me, how have you fared in finding those who cursed you? Do you know the true nature of these beings and how they are able to hide in the shadows, evading you?"

Her words confused me. "True nature? They are mere humans —gypsies who practice limited magic."

Her laughter teased my ears. "There is nothing simple and limited about the power they yield. I can see their magic woven in the very fibers of your being. I see the truth of their enchantment. You will not be freed from your curse so easily, Marcus St. James. Mark my warning. Finding them will only bring your ruination and despair. Are you willing to lose all you hold dear because your pride dictates it?"

She had seen through my hesitation. This fae had peered into my mind and seen my fear of her.

"And all you ask of me is that I not shed any more blood?" I repeated part of the deal to her, hoping that if there was some kind of deceit, the truth would be revealed.

"Yes. This is how you will make amends for the deaths you are responsible for. A balance must be returned to nature. Her cries and tears demand it."

It couldn't be that simple, but I found myself beginning to believe her.

"And you think this is our only option, Knox?" I asked. He was the one who took on the responsibility of finding a cure through his alchemy. He had sworn to never leave my side until he'd restored my humanity, and it was hard to ignore the hope I felt radiating off him. The feeling went beyond him being enraptured by her beauty.

"I have searched the world, studying until my head has throbbed. I have experimented with elements until exhausting every shred of knowledge I've obtained, but only found failure. Catriona is right now giving birth to a child—a baby that will become yours. Can you not see how plausible this solution is and how perfectly this encounter is timed?"

His conviction pierced my skepticism, and my mind wandered back to the inn, where my wife was ready to deliver either a son or a daughter. What kind of father would I be if there was always a threat of losing control of my bloodlust? What if something happened and I did the unforgivable?

That truth, more than anything, left me with the only choice I could accept.

"Then I graciously accept your gift, Yralli," I said, her name rolling off my tongue like a melody. "And I swear on my restored life that I will never spill the blood of others again."

As the words left my body, I could almost see the magic touch them, making my oath visible to the eye in a glittery silver script. I had just made a deal with a dark fae.

I could only hope that I hadn't just invited more trouble into my life.

CHAPTER 14

"*I*t is done."

One moment I was standing, bracing myself to feel the magic rushing through my veins, and the next I dropped to my knees, screaming. The pain that I'd experienced when the curse was first cast was nothing compared to the agony that torched my insides, incinerating everything it touched. Over and over, I clawed the ground around me, desperate to escape the pain.

My vision clouded to where there was nothing but darkness. Blinded and sobbing, I curled myself up into the fetal position and prayed that I would survive this. All I could do was picture Catriona in my mind—her beautiful smile, the way her eyes lit up whenever something pleased her. I was doing this for her—for our new child—and most of all, for me.

This was my chance to right the wrong done to me. It was a fresh start for someone who yearned for normalcy. I didn't care what I was giving up. I'd had my fill of fury and revenge. All it had done was bring bitterness and isolation to my life. The curse had cast me into shadow and blood. I was ready to say goodbye to damnation forever.

I couldn't stop screaming as fae magic ravaged my soul. Somewhere in the back of my mind, I knew Knox was watching.

Did he view this as the freedom that I did? Was he also ready to be released from the oath he'd sworn to me?

Each thought crashed and burned around me. Nothing else mattered. All there was—all I could feel—was this moment. This blistering moment.

My body began convulsing, slamming hard to the ground as wave after wave left me shaking. Gasping for breath, I dug my nails into the dirt, anything that would help me find some way to control the process. Everything hurt. My muscles twisted and contorted like they had a mind of their own.

Then with one last, drawn out scream, I finally saw the light at the end of the tunnel. The pain began to ebb and gradually diminish. Sweat dripped from my body. Fast trickles of salty water ran across my face, clinging to the tip of my nose before spilling onto the ground.

With ragged breath, weakened, I grunted. The spell was completed, and I was beyond exhausted. If it wasn't for the fact that Catriona was waiting for me to return, I would have feebly found the strength to cover myself with dirt, burying myself. Death had felt so close.

"Marcus," came Knox's voice through the muddied fog that surrounded me. "My God, talk to me." He gently laid one of his hands over my arm, and I buckled beneath his touch. Everything felt tender and sore.

I'd grown so accustomed to being a vampire—to the benefits that came from existing on blood and the power it gave me. Each second that passed proved one thing.

I was human again.

I was mortal, and the fading pain was proof.

"I'm fine," I eventually stammered. My body felt strange, and panic fluttered when I couldn't quite move my limbs properly. It was as if there was still a disconnect between my body and brain. "I think."

My lashes flickered open, the light causing a throb to explode behind my eyes. Once they adjusted, I stared straight up into my friend's worried face. His blond hair hung straight down like a curtain. "I thought she was going to kill you! Was that what it was like when you were cursed?"

Licking my dry lips, trying to swallow to alleviate my sore throat, I shook my head. "This . . . this was much worse." And it was. The only difference was that I'd blacked out before. This time I'd been disturbingly aware of everything. "But it worked."

And that made it worth it.

Cradling my head in his lap, Knox was hesitant to move me. "No more bloodlust?"

I reached out within myself for the sensations I'd lived with for way too many years. Nothing. No beast. No ravaging need to gorge myself on blood.

"I'm human." A burst of laughter erupted from me. Despite the agony, there was a new emotion that surfaced.

Joy.

I was finally free. I could let go of the monster and find myself again.

Gradually, Knox helped me to my feet, and I slowly began moving my body. It really was intoxicating to not have that urge and need to feed constantly pulling my focus.

"Thank you," I exclaimed, and I threw my arms around him in an embrace. "You said you wouldn't rest until you found a way, and you did it. Thank you, brother."

He pounded my back with his hand affectionately. "No, we did it."

A soft twittering sound came from behind me, a reminder that we weren't alone in our celebration. Staggering around, I grinned so hard I was surprised it didn't crack my face.

"I am in your debt, Yralli," I declared, grateful for her magic. I still didn't quite understand why she would grant such a wish where the only requirement was a promise. She gained nothing directly from helping me. Yet, there she stood in benevolence, her hands gracefully grasped before her.

"As long as you honor your word, Marcus St. James, no debt is required from you. I have received what I yearn for." And her gaze drifted over to Knox.

Something passed between them—unspoken words—and seeing the way Knox's face paled triggered a spark of anxiety.

What had he done? What was I missing?

"Marcus," he began, his own smile dwindling beneath his now unsure expression. "There's something I must tell you."

I glanced back and forth, not liking where this might lead. A shimmering portal appeared beside the water, and with it came a sinking sensation.

"No," I muttered, reaching for him. "Whatever it is, I don't want to hear it. We need to return to town and see whether Catriona has given birth. She'll be eager to see us." When he wouldn't budge and instead, bit his bottom lip, I threw my focus toward the fae.

"Whatever he's done, the agreement was between you and me. The bargain was to free me from the curse. Nothing else was mentioned."

Yralli simply stood there, the sun encasing her in a glowing light.

"No!" I repeated to Knox. "No."

"I owed you a life debt, Marcus. I saw an opportunity and took it. Whatever the sacrifice. Remember?" I could see he was trying to make me understand, but I refused to acknowledge the nagging feeling that wouldn't leave me be.

"Think of Catriona," I said, leading him away from the water and portal. With each step, my heart pounded inside my chest. All I could feel was an impending sense of doom. "She needs you, brother. The baby will need you." The words choked in my throat. "I need you."

The sadness in his smile broke my heart. "You're a family now. What more could you possibly want for?" Gripping my hand, Knox loosened my hold and took a step back toward Yralli. "I am only as strong as my word. You once said that, and I've used it as a marker for how I conduct myself."

"No," I countered. "All I have been is a monster. Stay. Let me show the man you and Catriona have inspired me to be. Brother. Do not leave."

That was what the thoughts screaming in my head were telling me—the truth that I was desperate to deny and prove false. The deal I'd made with the fae was but a pittance in comparison to the secret oath Knox had made.

A life for a life.

I begged him to tell me I was wrong. "Please." Never had I sounded so needy and devastated. "Knox."

All he could do was shake his head. Sorrow filled his eyes. All while the fae witnessed the rift she'd caused between us.

Just as I was ready to unleash my anger toward her, a crack of branches from nearby footsteps drew my attention. Knox turned about to see what was causing the interruption.

"You!" he thundered, the change in his voice as different as night and day. Gone was the heartfelt need for me to accept this was his decision. In its place, a look of wrath descended, and he curled his hands into fists.

"I thank you for conveniently being together and away from prying eyes." A dark-haired man stood smirking at us, and it only took a few moments to realize who he was.

Dark hair.

European descendant.

A knowing look when his gaze fell on me.

This was the bastard who had stolen Catriona from under our noses that night of the attack. It had been dark when he'd ridden off with her, but I would've recognized that face anywhere.

He'd come back for her.

He'd returned to face our retribution.

"You're a fool if you think you're leaving this place alive," I growled, my perfectly honed anger rising inside me. "Prepare to meet your maker."

He strode closer with all the swagger of someone who felt no fear. "I could say the same for you both. Imagine my surprise when I arrived in Havenwood Falls and found you both had left my Catriona unprotected." The way he emphasized *my* made my skin crawl. "My pet brought news that she's about to give birth. Such a pity you will never see them again."

The raven. I suspected there'd been something about that bird, and now we knew. All this time it had been watching us.

I didn't answer. I was done with talking about it, and the merry little dance Dimitri was doing in bragging about his intentions. I'd dreamt of this day, when I'd come face to face with the gypsy who'd taken my wife. He had a lot to atone for, and there was no way I'd allow him to continue breathing now we were together.

Rushing forward, I cocked back my fist and slammed it into his head. He'd seen me coming and had tried to meet me halfway. I didn't care that his own blows connected. All I could think—feel—was that I could finally get retribution on behalf of Catriona.

We fell to the ground and rolled about, each one trying to get the upper hand. At one stage I had him pinned, my hands wrapped firmly around his neck, but with one painful strike, Dimitri broke my stronghold. He twisted his body out from under me and stood to his feet.

"It will take much more than a slight tussle to kill me, Marcus." He spat to the side and wiped his mouth with the back of his hand. He quickly looked to where Knox was and gestured for him to approach. "I thought you vowed to be the one to end my life, Englishman."

Both Knox and I began stalking around the gypsy like he was our prey and we were superior predators. We didn't rush in or do anything hasty. We were united in one purpose. If we were ever to have a moment's peace and keep Catriona and the baby safe, we would need to end this fight here.

"Cowards!" he screeched, as an angry red vein throbbed at his temple. Dirt smudged his jaw, and his coat sleeve revealed a tear. "Perhaps you need to hear how I defiled your wife, Marcus. How I had her beneath me, screaming for help . . . screaming for you to rescue her."

I couldn't stand to hear another word. With murderous intent, I lunged at Dimitri, clawing at him with a savagery even my time as a vampire hadn't produced. All I could think was this man—this animal—needed to be destroyed.

In the back of my mind, I could hear Knox yelling for me to stop. Hands grabbed me and attempted to pull me off the gypsy, but I couldn't be reasoned with. Dimitri had found my weakness, the one thing that could've unraveled my self-control and rendered me a beast again.

Catriona.

Image after image of her tear-stained face, beseeching me to stop her assailant from raping her, appeared before my eyes. I could hear my name reverberating in my ears—the anguish and utter desolation that filled her voice. I had failed her so completely. How would she ever forgive me, let alone let me back into her heart?

"Monster!" I slammed my fist into his face. "She was innocent. Innocent," I repeated. With each word I cursed him like the braggart he was. There would be no redemption for him. No mercy shown, either.

"Your oath!" Knox said, finally gaining enough leverage to pull me away. "Or have you forgotten so quickly?"

Shocked to find that I had, I turned quickly to where Yralli was still standing. She'd done nothing to lift her hand and help. Instead, she watched on in veiled boredom.

I couldn't give full rein to my anger.

I wouldn't be able to have the satisfaction of ripping this brute into pieces.

No blood could be spilled. Not by my hand. Not from me.

By accepting my humanity and enjoying the first moments in what felt like a lifetime as a man, I had also ensured that Dimitri couldn't die from my efforts.

With a heaving chest, my breath ragged from overexertion, I cursed with disappointment.

"Grant me another favor," I demanded from the silent fae. "You must be aware of what this man is to me and how he has harmed my family. Grant me an exception, and I will give you whatever you want." I couldn't stop pacing from the adrenaline that pulsed thickly through my veins.

When she didn't respond, I looked to Knox. "You have a rapport with this creature. Strike another bargain. Do whatever is necessary so that this fiend's threat is extinguished."

Dimitri started laughing. The sound was filled with derision. He was seeing a chance to escape the death sentence he deserved. "Only a fool would strike an accord with the fae. Intervening is beneath such cold and callous beings. Face me and accept that once the life has drained from your eyes, I will take your wife and my child. I will bury you alongside your naïve friend."

He slipped out of his coat, and quickly rolling up his sleeves, the gypsy began toward us again.

I weighed my options.

If I drew blood and killed him, I would also return to being a blood drinker. The existence I'd had to endure would come crashing back, and in all honesty, take away any chance of being cured. I knew the odds of finding the clan responsible. I'd spent so much time hunting them that I'd ignored the fact that they also held the power to remain hidden.

Was my humanity truly worth my thirst for revenge?

Knox didn't wait for me to act. He had made his own decision and, with his fingers curled around a gold bladed knife, slashed at Dimitri—the razor-sharp edge slicing across his throat. Blood began to gush from the wound, and no amount of pressure from the gypsy's hand could stem the reality that it was a fatal blow.

Blood gurgled up through his throat and out of his mouth. With wide, dark eyes, Dimitri staggered forward only to fall heavily to his knees.

I stared at Knox, noting the spray of blood that had struck his face. In that moment, I remembered the young boy he'd been when I found him in London and witnessed the man he'd become. A muscle in his jaw twitched from his clenched teeth, and as Dimitri took his last breath and slumped to the side, Knox released his death grip on the knife.

"It is done," he uttered, not realizing he'd just said the same thing as Yralli had. "It is over."

I looked down at the knife. Intricate scrollwork was etched alongside the top of the blade, and the hilt was made from deer antler. I'd never seen the weapon before, but when it twinkled out of existence, I knew exactly where it had come from.

A slight nod from Yralli confirmed my suspicion. She'd stepped in to help Knox and end the attack. While she hadn't granted me the right to avenge my wife, the fae had given aid nevertheless.

"Phineas," she spoke, "you must say your goodbyes."

I shook my head. Not now. Not just yet. There was so much to say and do before that. All I needed was a chance to find a way to break his promise. I refused to allow this to be our last moment together.

My mind was made up. "Remove my humanity," I ordered. "Take it from me and give me back the blood lust. The price is too high. He is mine. You cannot have him."

Moving to stand in front of Knox, I held my arms out to the side, blocking him from her.

Her gaze narrowed so dramatically that I felt an icy cold breeze blast me. She waved her hand through the air, and as pain gripped me once more, her thundering voice filled the air. "Vow breaker."

A tremor coursed through me, and then to my horror, a familiar sensation flowed into me, filling the deepest recesses of my soul.

"Nooooo!" I cried in agony, clutching my sides as I desperately tried to escape the onslaught. Hunger like nothing I'd ever experienced flared, and all I could focus on was my thirst for blood. I wanted to bathe in it, drown in the simplicity and power.

My body contorted so under the demand to feed that I worried my limbs would shatter beneath the unrelenting pressure.

"Yralli!" Knox cried, rushing toward her. "He's broken no vow! Why have you done this?" He reached for her, only for the fae to disappear a second before he could touch her. She reappeared beside Dimitri and pointed down to his lifeless body.

"Blood has been shed. Our agreement has been nullified."

With what little strength I had, I crawled my way to the body, desperate to see if what she was saying was true. I hadn't been the one to wield the knife. I had punched him, strangled him, but as far as I had seen—no blood had been spilt. At least not by my hand.

I tugged on the gypsy, moving his body and limbs about to study him closer. Everywhere I looked, I found bruises and red welts, but no blood.

It wasn't until Knox joined me and flipped the body onto his back, that the truth proved undeniable. There was the faintest of scratches along the dead man's hairline. It had yielded the tiniest speck of blood. If I hadn't peered so close, I would've easily assumed it was dirt.

Yralli was right.

I had without intention broken my vow.

My humanity was stripped away.

I was a blood drinker once more.

CHAPTER 15

I hadn't known what hope felt like until I stood there, having watched it evaporate before me. In the blink of an eye, my world had brightened, only to be reduced to shadows again.

It wasn't fair.

The bitterness that coated my tongue and filled my mouth was hard to swallow. All I could do was pray that this had all been some brutal nightmare—a twisted dream.

"Knox," I uttered. "Tell me this isn't happening."

He looked equally distraught. "In order to strike the deal, I had to offer her what she wanted. Even though her agreement with you is broken, ours still holds."

I looked over to the fae, who wisely remained silent. The portal had reappeared, shimmering and glittering behind her.

"How long?" I asked, staring at the opening that would lead to another world—one where I couldn't follow. "Please tell me you didn't blindly accept her terms. You provided yourself a way out?"

Here was a man who I knew could negotiate himself out of even the strangest of situations. There was a reason why I trusted him with not only my estate's affairs, but also my own. I couldn't imagine him locking himself into an ironclad contract without some kind of loophole.

He gave me a look as if my doubting him was offensive. "Ten years. I promised her my companionship for a decade, and once that time is over, I'm free to return. She's agreed to arrange safe passage back to Havenwood Falls."

Ten years. I could handle that. This wasn't a forever goodbye. While I still felt like I'd been tricked to accept the bargain, it wasn't as though Knox was about to completely disappear into Faerie.

I nodded my head and let out a sigh of relief. "I'll miss you, brother."

He pulled me against him and clapped his hand over my back. "Try not to get into trouble while I'm gone." He squeezed me tightly. I did the same. I knew that once he let go, he would need to leave. "I won't stop looking. Even though I won't be here, perhaps there's an answer to your curse in Faerie."

Even now he was thinking of me instead of himself.

"Forget about my curse, Knox. I've lived with it for this long. Perhaps it's time to accept that this is who I am and embrace it." Tears stung my eyes. He blinked back his own.

His voice broke as he struggled to get out the words. "Brothers. Always. I still owe you a life debt. I will never stop searching."

Our embrace ended, our eyes locking in silent communication. Promises were exchanged. Encouragement and love were shown. We'd been through so much. This wouldn't be the end of a friendship that had been forged in strength and loyalty.

"I'll tell my child about you. Catriona and I will be waiting here for you."

"You'd better." He chuckled, already backing away. Right before he breached the portal, Knox turned to wave. "Until then."

And then he was gone. I'd blinked, hoping to call out one more time, but the shimmering flickered before fading away to nothing. I was left there alone—a dead body on the ground, and the splash of the waterfall filling the air.

I don't know how long I remained there, staring at the spot I'd last seen Knox. The threat to Catriona had also been taken care of, leaving me with only one thing to do.

I was about to become a father.

Blood drinker or not, I owed this child only the best version of myself.

And that's what I would do.

I had faced the blood and embraced damnation.

Wrath had all but consumed me as I focused solely on my need for retribution.

But as I walked slowly back to town and was greeted with the joyous news that Catriona had delivered a healthy baby girl, I knew that those things could never be allowed into my heart again.

Not now.

Not ever.

Hope and love. Those would be the virtues I clung to.

For Catriona.

For Knox.

For me.

I was Marcus St. James, and in the wake of loss and heartbreak, I would rise.

EPILOGUE

KNOX

*T*ime moved slowly here. Painstakingly slow.

Once Yralli had taken me through the portal, the beauty that had held me mesmerized quickly evolved into something less enchanting and intoxicating.

I was her captive for the next ten years, but what she'd failed to confess—what I had failed to ask—was that here in Faerie, time almost stood still, while the world I left behind marched forward at a steady pace.

I knew returning to the spot where my life changed was foolish and nothing but pure torture. Yralli mocked the sentiment, her once tinkling voice now filled with derision and scorn. She'd wanted me simply for the sake of claiming me, and where I thought I might've had some freedom, I was nothing more than a pet to her.

A possession.

A toy to pleasure and satisfy her every whim and desire.

A week had passed since I followed her and said goodbye to Marcus. The illusion she'd magically created to lure me had already begun to wear thin, but I refused to show her that I could see her for what she truly was.

It was why I always came back here. It drew me like a siren

370

and reminded me why I'd made the deal and what I was fighting for. Marcus had deserved a shot at true happiness. He needed to know that he didn't have to be the monster he believed himself to be.

They came every week to the waterfall. With a basket of food and blanket in hand, the family I missed made the slow walk through the woods to the place that held so many memories.

It was there that I learned that Catriona had given birth to a beautiful daughter. The sound of her name still echoed in my ears from the moment Marcus had said it.

Esther.

It meant star.

There was no denying that this bundle of joy had shone a light into their lives, giving Marcus something to hold on to, a reason to let go of his darkness.

My arms longed to breach the barrier that kept us apart and gather Esther up. I wanted to witness her first smile and celebrate as she spoke her first words. I would miss all of that—milestones that cemented their little family together.

I wondered whether I would find myself at home in their presence once my time was over and I could return to their world. How changed would I be? Would they even be alive when the ten years were over?

"Should I be jealous?" came her voice from over my shoulder. "Do you regret the sacrifice of love you made?" Yralli had revealed her own weakness whenever she found me here, waiting for my family to show up. Human emotions intrigued her, and for some reason, she wanted to understand.

"I stand by my choice," I answered. In my mind, I'd exchanged one master for another. "There's nothing I wouldn't do for my brother." Those words rang as true as the day I'd made the bargain.

"Even if it means you must always watch from a distance?" She crept closer, as if hoping she could somehow see what I did. "Does this not make you lonely?"

I shook my head, not quite sure how I could explain my

reasoning. "It helps me stay connected. Seeing them happy and together reminds me to never give up hope." A smile curled the ends of my lips as Esther played with her father's fingers. I would never grow tired of seeing my dear friend soften around his daughter—the way everything seemed to melt away whenever he looked at her. She was the miracle. She was why I knew I'd had to give whatever Yralli asked for.

Esther needed Marcus and vice versa.

"Come," the woman said. The command came with the same musical tone, but it also held the warning that her patience was growing thin. There was only so much she would tolerate before the fae would reveal her darker nature. That was a side of her I hoped never to see directed my way.

Her treatment of the other human she held captive was enough to give me nightmares every time I closed my eyes.

With one last longing glance, I offered up a silent prayer of protection over Marcus and his family.

Don't forget me, I whispered, as I reluctantly followed Yralli back to the palace.

I was bound to a princess of the Unseelie Court.

God give me the strength to survive it.

We hope you enjoyed this story in the Legends of Havenwood Falls series featuring a variety of supernatural creatures. The series is a collaborative effort by multiple authors.

Other Havenwood Falls books by Belinda:
Nowhere to Hide
Addicted to You
The Collector: Awakening
Blood and Damnation
Havenwood Falls Anthology 2018

Books in the historical Legends of Havenwood Falls series:

Lost in Time by Tish Thawer
Dawn of the Witch Hunters by Morgan Wylie
Redemption's End by Eric R. Asher
Trapped Within a Wish by Brynn Myers
Blood and Damnation by Belinda Boring
Fated Beginnings by E.J. Fechenda
Emeline by Katie M. John
Released From a Curse by Brynn Myers
A Pack of Lies by Kallie Ross
Kiss the Ashes by Desiree Lafawn
Hidden Truths by Colleen Nye
Wrath and Retribution by Belinda Boring
Changing Fate by Char Webster
Rise of the Witch Hunters by Morgan Wylie
The Drowning Bride by Seven Jane

Also try the signature New Adult/Adult series, Havenwood Falls, and the YA series, Havenwood Falls High
Stay up to date at www.HavenwoodFalls.com

Subscribe to our reader group and receive free stories and more!

ABOUT THE AUTHOR

International and #1 multi-genre bestselling Author Belinda Boring is known to many readers as the Queen of Swoon and also the Queen of Cliffhangers. Her Mystic Wolves series has topped many charts along with receiving several awards and nominations such as Paranormal Book of the Year, Best Debut Book, as well as being in the Top 3 Best Rated on Amazon. With additional titles like *Bittersweet Melody*, *Bittersweet Symphony*, *Enchanted Hearts*, *Loving Liberty* and *Broken Promises*, it's easy to see why readers are captivated by this swoon worthy author! You can also find Belinda writing alongside the incredible authors of the Havenwood Falls world. To date, she's published within their main Havenwood Falls line, as well as sharing the past tales of characters within the Legends of Havenwood Falls.

A homesick Aussie living amongst the cactus and mountains of Arizona, Belinda Boring is a self-proclaimed addict of romance and all things swoon worthy. It wasn't long before she began writing, pouring her imagination and creativity into the stories she dreams. Whether urban fantasy, paranormal romance, or romance in general, Belinda strives to share great plots with heart and characters that you can't help but connect with. Of course, she wouldn't be Belinda without adding heroes she hopes will curl your toes. Surrounded by a supportive cast of family, friends, two adorable Chiweenies, and the man she gives her heart and soul to, Belinda is living the good life. Happy reading!

YOU CAN FIND BELINDA ON SOCIAL MEDIA:

Official Website: http://www.belindaboringauthor.com/
Facebook: www.facebook.com/BelindaBoringAuthor
Twitter: https://twitter.com/BelindaBoring
Instagram: www.instagram.com/BelindaBoring
BookBub: www.bookbub.com/profile/belindaboring
Amazon Profile: https://www.amazon.com/Belinda-Boring/e/B005C1IRFC/

Subscribe to her newsletter: http://bit.ly/2UPQ81f

ACKNOWLEDGMENTS

"Gratitude unlocks the fullness of life. It turns what we have into enough, and more. It turns denial into acceptance, chaos to order, confusion to clarity. It can turn a meal into a feast, a house into a home, a stranger into a friend."

– Melody Beattie

Whenever I finish a story, I'm reminded just how fortunate I am for the supportive people in my life. I'm grateful that I can pursue my dreams and give voice to my imagination because I know I don't have to do it alone. From a loving husband, to close family and friends, to the group of incredible authors and gracious readers . . . I'm lifted up and inspired by their acts of kindness and encouraging words. While writing can often be a solitary task, if you look closely, you can see their tendrils of faith and loyalty that add fuel to the author's dream. I love my tribe. I love each of the hearts and minds that stand with me throughout each book. I'd be lost without them. I am better because of them. Thank you from the bottom of my heart. I hope I continue to make you all proud.

"It's not where you are in life, it's who you have by your side that matters."

– Unknown

Bels xoxo

AN EXCERPT

Changing Fate (**A Legends of Havenwood Falls Novella) by Char Webster**

From this *USA Today* Bestselling Author - For a vila warrior, love only comes with death.

During World War I, vila warrior Jerina Ventus's life irrevocably changed when she saved a wounded soldier's life and helped him return to his hometown in Colorado. Twenty-five years later, she's restless and longing for another adventure beyond her forest. Little does she know, her sister Kosa will deliver the opportunity to her.

Thane Beltaine grew up hearing stories about the beautiful and fierce immortal warrior who saved his father's life. When Jerina's sister Kosa shows up in his hometown on the arm of a wicked mage, Thane volunteers to find Jerina and bring her back. He never expected to meet the woman who was more legend than real and definitely didn't think they would clash about every little thing.

Jerina's temper and patience are tested as they travel to Colorado to rescue her sister, who at first seems reluctant to be saved. She needs to outsmart the mage and find a way to release Kosa from his control, and she needs Thane's help to do this.

Reluctantly, they work together to save Kosa, and an unexpected love begins to grow. But vila are cursed to never find true love—if they do, he will quickly die a gruesome death.

CHANGING FATE

BY CHAR WEBSTER

Obnoxious laughter followed Jerina's ungraceful and rapid descent to the ground from the thick branch she had been perched upon. With a wave of her hands, gusts of wind pushed up against her free fall, slowing her plummet to a slight drop and landing her lightly on her feet.

Her sister, Kosa, was still cackling like a hyena when Jerina stalked over to her. Scooping up a handful of snow, she dumped it on Kosa's blond head in retribution for the snow blast her sister sent to knock her out of the tree. The icy shower coated her soft leather handmade jacket.

Kosa shook the snow from her long straight hair. "I've never caught you unaware! You should have seen your face when you fell."

Jerina growled at Kosa. "You should be patrolling, not messing around!"

The sisters faced each other with the same graceful height, same lithe build, and same long blond hair. Even though there were a few years separating them, they could nearly pass for twins.

"My shift is finished. You would know that if you hadn't been pouting in that tree!" Kosa prepared herself for Jerina to attack. This was a fight that had been brewing for years.

Jerina swung out with her fist, but Kosa ducked out of the way while thrusting her leg out to trip her sister.

The girls ended up in a tangle of long arms and legs as they rolled across the forest floor, kicking up snow and leaves in their fury. They ignored the fierce growl that continued to gain in volume but were pulled apart when sharp teeth sank into the soft leather of Jerina's left boot.

"Damn it, Rela! If you tear my boots, I'm going to send you off to the next country!" Jerina yelled at the regal mountain lion that was still growling and showing lethal fangs. Rela was not intimidated in the least by her outburst. The mountain lion shook her head while still grasping Jerina's brown suede boot, making sure the girls knew she wasn't going to let go until they stopped fighting.

Jerina raised her hands, and wind started to whip through the trees, blowing the mountain lion's fur, but she stood firm. Sighing dramatically, Jerina released Kosa and fell back onto the forest floor, breathing heavily.

Rela dropped the boot with what sounded like a snort, but she stood close to the sisters, making sure they didn't continue to brawl.

Kosa ruffled the velvety tan fur of their good friend. "You could have waited a little longer before interrupting us."

Jerina glared at her sister. "Why are you picking a fight today, Kos?"

"You have not been yourself for years, not since you returned from your trip, but lately it's become far more severe. What is the matter?" Kosa wasn't the only one to notice the change in Jerina. Their mother had begun to ask questions, and that was never good.

Rela's head was leaning over Jerina's shoulder as she sat up, so she pushed it out of the way. It sounded like Rela was laughing at her. She was about to reply that nothing was wrong but decided to speak the truth. "I find myself restless."

"You've always been content here in our forest." Kosa was the one who would seek adventure whenever possible.

Rela settled down on some soft moss, not minding the patches of snow, and closed her eyes, ignoring them since they had stopped fighting.

"I love it, but . . ."

"You need something more," Kosa finished for her.

"Yes!" Jerina whipped her hands up, creating a cyclone of leaves, sticks, snow, and wind around the three of them. "I feel as if I should be doing something, but I do not know what."

"We could venture into town and find some humans to have fun with." Kosa had been sneaking off to town whenever she could, but she didn't want her sister to know how often.

Jerina narrowed her gaze. "What have you done?"

"We are not speaking about me. We are discussing your melancholy mood." Kosa was not going to let Jerina intimidate her.

"You know we cannot become attached to humans."

Kosa rolled her eyes. "We cannot get involved with anyone." Kosa spread her hands out wide, and the cyclone stopped. Everything rained down to the ground in a flurry of debris. "No one is around to hear us. You don't need to draw unwanted attention to this area."

"Kosa, I've seen the little gifts that are left for you."

Kosa's eyes grew round, but she smoothed her shock away and tried to act casual. "I have happened upon a few trinkets. They don't mean anything. They could have been left for anyone."

Jerina raised an eyebrow. "Who is he?"

Kosa had no idea how the conversation shifted to Jerina interrogating her. "I don't have any idea what you're talking about."

"Kos."

"Maybe you should go back and visit Tannor."

"Your attempt at diverting the conversation will not work. Tell me about him." Jerina didn't like the dreamy look in her sister's eyes. She also didn't want to talk about Tannor and her trip across the world. She felt drawn to Colorado but not romantically. She had developed a friendship with Tannor, and that was it. No deeper feelings were involved. Tannor loved his wife more than anything, and Jerina had helped him get back to her when he had been seriously injured.

"There is nothing to say." Kosa began to bounce in place, something she did when she was nervous and not being entirely truthful. She forced herself to stop and face Jerina. "I'd rather talk about you and why you have become insufferable lately."

Jerina thrust her hands toward her sister, and hurricane force winds blasted Kosa back several feet before Kosa diverted the gust upward. Jerina's glare would have scared some of the warrior trainees.

"Do not trifle with me." She stopped the wind when Rela roared.

Kosa cracked her neck back and forth. "You have been horrid to everyone, and you have been drifting off alone whenever you're not on duty."

Jerina sank down onto a fallen tree trunk. Her first reaction was to argue, but her sister's tone stopped her. "You should not exaggerate."

"Mother has noticed." Kosa had told their mother that some of the newer trainees had been goofing off instead of working hard, and that was the reason for Jerina's moodiness. It had only been half of the truth, but it had satisfied her.

Jerina pulled a stick from the log and picked at its bark. "I've been feeling a pull toward Colorado. I do not know why it's so strong after all these years."

Kosa sat down next to Jerina.

"I've been longing to travel." She knew it was the wrong thing to say as soon as it came out of her mouth.

"Tell me about the gifts and the man." Jerina narrowed her eyes at Kosa.

Kosa growled silently, cursing her big mouth. "You cannot let anyone know about this."

"Tell me at once." Jerina knew that a man had been leaving little things for her sister, but those gifts had become more frequent and more elaborate.

Kosa took a deep breath. It was time to explain everything to Jerina. Out of all the vila warriors, her sister was the only one who went out into the world and returned. Others had left, but only to find tragedy and heartache. Men were the downfall of the vila.

"I've been watching the humans in town. They fascinate me."

Jerina inhaled quickly. "Were you seen?"

"Not at first, but then I found a note pinned to the tree I take shelter behind."

"What did it say?" Jerina stood and began to pace the small clearing, scanning the area for anyone who might be listening to their conversation.

Kosa sighed wistfully. "It said, 'I thought only angels had the power to stop a man's heart.'"

Jerina rolled her eyes. "He was trying to charm you with pretty words."

"It was sweet." Kosa sighed again. "The next day, a white camellia was tied to the tree with another note. This one said, 'My destiny is in your hands.'"

"That sounds ominous." Jerina was starting to get worried. Something didn't feel right.

Purchase *Changing Fate* where books are sold.